KANE AND ABEL

JEFFREY ARCHER, whose novels and short stories include *Not a Penny More, Not a Penny Less*, *First Among Equals* and *A Twist in the Tale*, has topped the bestseller lists around the world, with sales of over 210 million copies.

Paths of Glory, his most recent novel, was a global number one bestseller and remained on the *Sunday Times* bestseller list for ten weeks.

The author is married with two children, and lives in London and Cambridge.

www.jeffreyarcher.com

ALSO BY JEFFREY ARCHER

NOVELS

Not a Penny More, Not a Penny Less

Shall We Tell the President?   The Prodigal Daughter

First Among Equals   A Matter of Honour

As the Crow Flies   Honour Among Thieves

The Fourth Estate   The Eleventh Commandment

Sons of Fortune   False Impression

The Gospel According to Judas
(with the assistance of Professor Francis J. Moloney)

A Prisoner of Birth   Paths of Glory

SHORT STORIES

A Quiver Full of Arrows   A Twist in the Tale

Twelve Red Herrings   The Collected Short Stories

To Cut a Long Story Short   Cat O' Nine Tails

PLAYS

Beyond Reasonable Doubt   Exclusive   The Accused

PRISON DIARIES

Volume One – Belmarsh: Hell

Volume Two – Wayland: Purgatory

Volume Three – North Sea Camp: Heaven

SCREENPLAYS

Mallory: Walking Off the Map   False Impression

JEFFREY ARCHER

KANE AND ABEL

PAN BOOKS

First published 1979 by Hodder & Stoughton Ltd

This revised edition published 2009 by Pan Books
an imprint of Pan Macmillan Ltd
Pan Macmillan, 20 New Wharf Road, London N1 9RR
Basingstoke and Oxford
Associated companies throughout the world
www.panmacmillan.com

ISBN 978-0-330-50968-8

3 5 7 9 8 6 4 2

A CIP catalogue record for this book is available from
the British Library.

Typeset by SetSystems Ltd, Saffron Walden, Essex
Printed in the UK by CPI Mackays, Chatham ME5 8TD

Visit www.panmacmillan.com to read more about all our books
and to buy them. You will also find features, author interviews and
news of any author events, and you can sign up for e-newsletters
so that you're always first to hear about our new releases.

Kane and Abel

Publishing History

Copyright © 1979 by Jeffrey Archer
First published in hardback on September 1, 1979
in Great Britain by Hodder & Stoughton Limited

Coronet edition, September 1980
Second impression, October 1980
Third impression, October 1980
Fourth impression, February 1981
Fifth impression, February 1981
Sixth impression, March 1981
Seventh impression, April 1981
Eighth impression, May 1981
Ninth impression, July 1981
Tenth impression, September 1981
Eleventh impression, September 1981
Twelfth impression, October 1981
Thirteenth impression, January 1982
Fourteenth impression, April 1982
Fifteenth impression, July 1982
Sixteenth impression, August 1982
Seventeenth impression, September 1982
Eighteenth impression, December 1982
Nineteenth impression, March 1983
Twentieth impression, April 1983
Twenty-first impression, August 1983
Twenty-second impression, October 1983
Twenty-third impression, December 1983
Twenty-fourth impression, April 1984
Twenty-fifth impression, June 1984
Twenty-sixth impression, July 1984
Twenty-seventh impression, October 1984
Twenty-eighth impression, January 1985
Twenty ninth impression, May 1985
Thirtieth impression, July 1985
Thirty-first impression, 1985
Thirty-second impression, 1985
Thirty-third impression, 1986
Thirty-fourth impression, 1986
Thirty-fifth impression, June 1987
Thirty-sixth impression, March 1988
Thirty-seventh impression, 1988
Thirty-eighth impression, March 1989
Thirty-ninth impression, July 1989
Fortieth impression, November 1989
Forty-first impression, July 1990

Forty-second impression, October 1990
Forty-third impression, January 1991
Forty-fourth impression, March 1991
Forty-fifth impression, May 1991
Forty-sixth impression, September 1991
Forty-seventh impression, November 1991
Chancellor Press edition, March 1992
Forty-ninth impression, July 1992
HarperCollins edition, February 1993
Fifty-first impression, April 1993
Fifty-second impression, July 1993
Fifty-third impression, November 1993
Fifty-fourth impression, May 1994
Fifty-fifth impression, January 1996
Fifty-sixth impression, September 1996
Fifty-seventh impression, January 1997
Fifty-eighth impression, April 1997
Fifty-ninth impression, September 1997
Sixtieth impression, March 1998
Sixty-first impression, January 1999
Sixty-second impression, April 2000
Sixty-third impression, March 2001
Sixty-fourth impression, September 2002
Sixty-fifth impression, January 2003
Sixty-sixth impression, April 2003
Sixty-seventh impression, September 2003
Sixty-eighth impression, December 2003
Pan Macmillan edition, February 2004
Seventieth impression, August 2004
Seventy-first impression, November 2004
Seventy-second impression, March 2005
Seventy-third impression, October 2005
Seventy-fourth impression, February 2006
Seventy-fifth impression, September 2006
Seventy-sixth impression, January 2007
Seventy-seventh impression, June 2007
Seventy-eighth impression, October 2007
Seventy-ninth impression, January 2008
Eightieth impression, April 2008
Eighty-first impression, July 2008
Eighty-second impression, October 2008

The thirtieth anniversary edition is the eighty-third impression, October 16, 2009

Kane and Abel **has also been published in 37 languages and 97 countries**

To Michael and Jane

PART ONE

1906–1923

1

April 18, 1906, Slonim, Poland

SHE ONLY stopped screaming when she died. It was then that he started to scream.

The young boy who was hunting rabbits in the forest was not sure whether it was the woman's last cry or the child's first that alerted his youthful ears. He turned, sensing possible danger, his eyes searching for an animal that was obviously in pain. But he had never known an animal to scream in quite that way before. He edged towards the noise cautiously; the scream had now turned to a whine, but it still did not sound like any animal he knew. He hoped it would be small enough to kill; at least that would make a change from rabbit for dinner.

He moved stealthily towards the river, where the strange noise came from, darting from tree to tree, feeling the protection of the bark against his shoulder blades, something to touch. Never stay in the open, his father had taught him. When he reached the edge of the forest he had a clear line of vision all the way down the valley to the river, and even then it took him some time to realize that the strange cry emanated from no ordinary animal. He crept towards the whining, even though he was now out in the open.

Then he saw the woman, her dress above her waist, her bare legs splayed. He had never seen a woman like that before. He ran quickly to her side and stared down at her belly, too frightened to touch. Lying between the woman's legs was a small, pink animal, covered in blood and attached to her by something that looked like rope. The young hunter dropped his freshly caught rabbits and fell to his knees beside the little creature.

He gazed at it for a long, stunned moment, then turned his eyes to the woman. He immediately regretted the decision. She was already blue with cold; her tired young face looked middle-aged to the boy. He did not need to be told that she was dead. He picked up the slippery little body that lay on the grass between her legs. Had you asked him why, and no one ever did, he would have told you that the tiny fingernails clawing at the crumpled face had worried him.

The mother and child were bound together by the slimy rope. The boy had watched the birth of a lamb a few days earlier and he tried to remember. Yes, that's what the shepherd had done. But dare he, with a child? The whining suddenly stopped, and he sensed that a decision was now urgent. He unsheathed his knife, the one he skinned rabbits with, wiped it on his sleeve and, hesitating only for a moment, cut the rope close to the child's body. Blood flowed freely from the severed ends. Then what had the shepherd done when the lamb was born? He had tied a knot to stop the blood. Of course, of course. The boy pulled some long grass out of the earth beside him and hastily tied a crude knot in the cord. Then he took the child in his arms. It started to cry again. He rose slowly from his knees, leaving behind him three dead rabbits and a dead woman who had given birth to this child. Before finally turning his back on the mother, he put her legs together and pulled her dress down over her knees. It seemed the right thing to do.

'Holy God,' he said aloud, the thing he always said when he had done something very good or very bad. He wasn't yet sure which this was.

The young hunter ran towards the cottage where his mother would be cooking supper, waiting only for his rabbits; everything else would be prepared. She would be wondering how many he'd caught today; with a family of eight to feed, she needed at least three. Sometimes he managed a duck, a goose or even a pheasant that had strayed from the Baron's estate, on which his father worked. Tonight he had caught a different animal.

When he reached the cottage, he didn't dare let go of his prize, even with one hand, so he kicked at the door with his bare foot until his mother opened it. Silently, he held up the child to her. She made no immediate move to take the creature from him but stood, one hand covering her mouth, gazing at the wretched sight.

'Holy God,' she said, and crossed herself. The boy looked up at her face for some sign of pleasure or anger, to find her eyes shining with a tenderness he had never seen before. He knew then that the thing he had done must be good.

'It's a little boy,' said his mother, taking the child into her arms. 'Where did you find him?'

'Down by the river, Matka,' he said.

'And the mother?'

'Dead.'

She crossed herself again.

'Quickly, run and tell your father what has happened. He will find Urszula Wojnak on the estate, and you must take them both to the mother. Then be sure they come back here.'

The boy rubbed his hands on his trousers, happy enough not to have dropped the slippery creature, and ran off in search of his father.

The mother closed the door with her shoulder and called out for Florentyna, her eldest child, to put the pot on the fire. She sat down on a wooden stool, unbuttoned her bodice and pushed a tired nipple to the little puckered mouth. Sophia, her youngest daughter, only six months old, would have to go without her supper tonight. Come to think of it, so would the whole family.

'And to what purpose?' the woman said out loud, tucking her shawl around the child. 'Poor little mite will be dead by morning.'

She did not repeat that sentiment to Urszula Wojnak when she arrived a couple of hours later. The elderly midwife washed the little body and tended to the twisted umbilical stump. The woman's husband stood silently by the open fire, observing the scene.

5

'A guest in the house brings God into the house,' declared the woman, quoting the old Polish proverb.

Her husband spat. 'To the cholera with him. We have enough children of our own.'

The woman pretended not to hear him as she stroked the sparse dark hairs on the baby's head.

'What shall we call him?' she asked.

Her husband shrugged. 'What does it matter? Let him go to his grave nameless.'

2

THE DOCTOR picked up the newborn baby by the ankles and slapped its bottom. The baby started to cry.

In Boston, Massachusetts, there is a hospital that caters mainly for those who suffer from the diseases of the rich, and on selected occasions allows itself to deliver the new rich. The mothers rarely scream, and they certainly don't give birth fully dressed.

A young man was pacing up and down outside the delivery room; inside, two obstetricians and the family doctor were in attendance. This father did not believe in taking risks with his firstborn. The obstetricians would be paid a large fee to stand by and witness events. One of them, who wore evening clothes under his long white coat, was late for a dinner party, but he could not afford to absent himself from this particular birth. The three had earlier drawn straws to decide who should deliver the child, and Dr MacKenzie, the family doctor, had won. A sound, reliable man, the father thought, as he paced up and down the corridor.

Not that he had any reason to be anxious. Roberts had driven the young man's wife to the hospital in their hansom carriage earlier that morning, which the doctor had calculated was the twenty-eighth day of her ninth month. Anne had gone into labour soon after breakfast, and he had been assured that the birth would not take place until his bank had closed for the day. The father was a disciplined man and saw no reason why the arrival of a child should interrupt his well-ordered life. Nevertheless, he continued to pace. Nurses and doctors hurried past him, lowering their voices as they approached him and raising them again only when they were out of his earshot. He didn't notice, because everybody always treated him this way. Most of the hospital staff had never seen him in person, but all of them knew who he was. When his son was born – it never occurred to him, even for a moment, that the child might be a girl – he would build the new children's wing the hospital so badly needed. His grandfather had already built a library and his father a school for the local community.

The expectant father tried to read the evening paper, looking over the words but not taking in their meaning. He was nervous, even anxious. It would never do for them (he looked upon almost everyone as 'them') to know how important it was that his firstborn be a boy, a boy who would one day take his place as president and chairman of the bank. He turned to the sports pages of the *Evening Transcript*. The Boston Red Sox had beaten the New York Highlanders – other people would be celebrating. Then he saw the headline on the front page: the worst earthquake in the history of America. Devastation in San Francisco, at least four hundred people dead – other people would be mourning. He hated that. It would take away from the birth of his son. People would remember that something else had happened on this day.

He turned to the financial pages and checked the stock market: it had fallen a few points; that damned earthquake had taken nearly $100,000 off the value of his holdings at the bank, but as his personal fortune remained comfortably over $16 million, it was going to take more than an earthquake in California to register on his Richter scale. After all, he could now live off the interest on his interest, so the $16 million capital would remain intact, ready for his son, still unborn. He continued to pace while pretending to read the *Transcript*.

The obstetrician in evening dress pushed through the swing doors of the delivery room to report the news. He felt he had to do something to justify his large fee and he was the most suitably dressed for the announcement. The two men stared at each other for a moment. The doctor also felt a little nervous, but he wasn't going to show it in front of the father.

'Congratulations, sir, you have a son. A fine-looking little boy.'

What silly remarks people make when a baby is born, was the father's first thought; how could he be anything but little? Then the news dawned on him – a son. He thought about thanking a God he didn't believe in. The obstetrician ventured a question to break the silence.

'Have you decided what to call him?'

The father answered without hesitation: 'William Lowell Kane.'

3

Long after the excitement of the baby's arrival had passed and the rest of the family had gone to bed, the mother remained awake, holding the child in her arms. Helena Koskiewicz believed in life, and she had borne nine children to prove it. Although she had lost three in infancy, she had not let any of them go easily.

At thirty-five, she knew that her once lusty Jasio would give her no more sons or daughters. God had offered her this one; surely he must be destined to live. Helena's was a simple faith, which was good, for destiny would never allow her anything but a simple life. Although she was only in her thirties, meagre food and hard work caused her to look much older. She was grey and thin, and not once in her life had she worn new clothes. It never occurred to her to complain about her lot, but the lines on her face made her look more like a grandmother than a mother.

Although she squeezed her breasts hard, leaving dull red marks around the nipples, only little drops of milk squirted out. At thirty-five, halfway through life's contract, we all have some useful piece of expertise to pass on, and Helena Koskiewicz's was now at a premium.

'Matka's littlest one,' she whispered tenderly to the child, and drew the milky teat across its pursed mouth. The eyelids opened as he tried to suck. Finally the mother sank unwillingly into a deep sleep.

Jasio Koskiewicz, a heavily built, dull man with a luxurious moustache, his only gesture of self-assertion in an otherwise servile existence, discovered his wife and the baby asleep in the rocking chair when he rose at five. He hadn't noticed her absence from their bed that night. He stared down at the bastard who had, thank God, at least stopped wailing. Was it dead? He didn't care. Let the woman worry about life and death: the most important thing for him was to be on the Baron's estate by first light. He took a few long swallows of goat's milk and wiped his moustache on his sleeve. He finally grabbed a hunk of bread with one hand and his traps with the other before slipping noiselessly out of the cottage, for fear of waking the child and starting it wailing again. He strode off towards the forest, giving no more thought to the little intruder other than to assume that he had seen him for the last time.

Florentyna was next to enter the kitchen, just before the old clock, which for many years had kept its own time, chimed six times. It was no more than a vague assistance to those who wished to know if it was the hour to rise or go to bed. Among her daily duties was the preparation of breakfast, a minor task involving the simple division of a skin of goat's milk and a lump of rye bread among a family of eight. Nevertheless, it required the Wisdom of Solomon to carry it out so that no one grumbled about another's portion.

Florentyna struck those who saw her for the first time as a pretty, frail, shabby little thing. Although for the past two years she'd had only one dress to wear, those who could separate their opinion of the child from that of her surroundings understood why Jasio had fallen in love with her mother. Florentyna's long fair hair shone and her hazel eyes sparkled in defiance of her birth and upbringing.

She tiptoed up to the rocking chair and stared down at her mother and the little boy, whom she had adored at first sight. She had never in her eight years owned a doll. In truth, she had seen one only once, when the family had been invited to a celebration of the feast of St Nicholas at the Baron's castle. Even then she had not actually touched the beautiful object, but now she felt an inexplicable urge to hold this baby in her arms. She bent down and eased the child away from her mother, and staring down into its blue eyes – such blue eyes – she began to hum. The change of temperature from the warmth of the mother's breast to the cold of the little girl's hands made the baby start to cry. This woke the mother, whose only reaction was to feel guilty for having fallen asleep.

'Holy God, he's still alive, Florcia,' she said. 'You must prepare breakfast for the boys while I try to feed him again.'

Florentyna reluctantly handed the baby back to her mother and watched as she once again pumped her aching breasts. The little girl was mesmerized.

'Be about your work, Florcia,' chided her mother. 'The rest of the family must eat as well.'

Florentyna reluctantly obeyed when her four brothers began to appear from the loft where they all slept. They kissed their mother's hands in greeting and stared at the intruder in awe. All they knew was that this one had not come from Matka's stomach. Florentyna was too excited to eat her breakfast that morning, so the boys divided her portion among themselves without a second thought, leaving their mother's share on the table. No one noticed that she hadn't eaten anything since the baby's arrival.

Helena Koskiewicz was pleased that her children had learned early in life to fend for themselves. They could feed the animals, milk the goats and tend the vegetable garden without any help or prodding.

When Jasio returned home in the evening, Helena had not prepared supper for him. Florentyna had taken the three rabbits Franck, her brother the hunter, had caught the previous day, and started to skin them. Florentyna was proud to be in charge of the evening meal, a responsibility she was entrusted with only when her mother was unwell, and Helena rarely allowed herself that luxury. Their father had brought home six mushrooms and three potatoes: tonight would be a veritable feast.

After supper, Jasio Koskiewicz sat in his chair by the fire and studied the child properly for the first time. Holding him under the armpits, his splayed fingers supporting the helpless head, he cast a trapper's eye over the infant. Wrinkled and toothless, the face was redeemed only by the fine, blue, unfocused eyes. As the man directed his gaze towards the thin body, something attracted his attention. He scowled and rubbed the delicate chest with his thumbs.

'Have you noticed this, woman?' he said, prodding the baby's chest. 'The little bastard only has one nipple.'

His wife frowned as she rubbed the skin with her thumb, as though the action would somehow miraculously cause the missing nipple to appear. Her husband was right: the minute and colourless left nipple was there, but where its mirror image should have appeared on the right-hand side, the skin was completely smooth.

The woman's superstitious tendencies were immediately aroused. 'He has been given to us by God,' she exclaimed. 'See His mark upon him.'

The man thrust the child angrily at her. 'You're a fool, woman. The child was given to its mother by a man with bad blood.' He spat into the fire, the more forcefully to express his opinion of the child's parentage. 'Anyway, I wouldn't bet a potato on the little bastard surviving another night.'

Jasio Koskiewicz cared even less than a potato whether or not the child survived. He was not by nature a callous man, but the boy was not his, and one more mouth to feed would only add to his problems. But it was not for him to question the Almighty, and with no more thought of the child, he fell into a deep sleep.

◄○►

As the days came and went, even Jasio Koskiewicz began to believe that the child might survive, and had he been a betting man, would have lost a potato. His eldest son Franck, the hunter, made the child a cot out of some wood he had collected from the Baron's forest. Florentyna cut little pieces off her old dresses and sewed them together into multi-coloured baby clothes. They would have called him Harlequin if they had known what the word meant. In truth, naming him caused more disagreement in the household than anything had for months, only the father had no opinion to offer. Finally, they agreed on Wladek.

The following Sunday, in the chapel on the Baron's great

estate, the child was christened Wladek Koskiewicz, the mother thanked God for sparing his life, and the father resigned himself to having another mouth to feed.

That evening there followed a small feast to celebrate the christening, augmented by the gift of a goose from the Baron's estate. They all ate heartily.

From that day on, Florentyna learned to divide by nine.

4

ANNE KANE had slept peacefully through the night. After a light breakfast, her son William was brought to her private room in the arms of a nurse. She couldn't wait to hold him again.

'Good morning, Mrs Kane,' the white-uniformed nurse said briskly, 'it's time to give baby his breakfast.'

Anne sat up, painfully aware of her swollen breasts. The nurse guided the two novices through the procedure. Anne, aware that to appear embarrassed would be considered unmaternal, gazed fixedly into William's blue eyes, bluer even than his father's. She smiled contentedly. At twenty-one, she was not aware of needing anything. Born a Cabot, she had married into a branch of the Lowell family, and had now delivered a son to carry on the tradition summarized so succinctly in the card sent to her by Millie Preston, her old school friend:

> *And this is good old Boston,*
> *The home of the bean and the cod,*
> *Where the Lowells talk only to the Cabots,*
> *And the Cabots talk only to God.*

Anne spent half an hour talking to William, but obtained little response. Matron then whisked him off in the same efficient manner by which he had arrived. Anne nobly resisted the fruit and candy that had come from friends and well wishers, as she was determined to get back into all her dresses in time for the summer season, and resume her rightful place in the pages of the fashionable magazines. Had not the Prince de Garonne declared her to be the only beautiful object in Boston? Her long golden hair, fine delicate features and slim figure had excited admiration in cities she had never even visited. Anne checked in the mirror, and was pleased with what she saw: people would hardly believe that she was the mother of a bouncing boy. Thank God it's a boy, she thought, understanding for the first time how Anne Boleyn must have felt.

She enjoyed a light lunch before preparing herself for the visitors who would appear at regular intervals throughout the afternoon. Those who visited her during the first few days would either be family, or from the very best families in Boston; others would be told she was not yet ready to receive them. But as Boston was the one city in America where everyone knew their place to the finest degree, there were unlikely to be any unexpected intruders.

The room she occupied could easily have taken another five beds had it not been filled with flowers. A casual passerby might have been forgiven for mistaking it for a minor horticultural show, if it were not for the presence of the young mother sitting upright in the bed. Anne switched on the electric light, still a novelty in Boston; her husband had waited for the Cabots to have them fitted, which Boston then considered to be an oracular sign that electromagnetic induction was socially acceptable.

Anne's first visitor was her mother-in-law, Mrs Thomas Lowell Kane, the head of the family following the premature death of her husband. In elegant late middle-age, Mrs Kane had perfected the technique of sweeping into a room to her own total satisfaction, and to its occupants' undoubted discomfiture. She wore a long silk dress which made it impossible to view her ankles; the only man who had seen them was now dead. She had always been slim. In her opinion – often stated – an overweight woman meant bad food and inferior breeding. She was now the oldest Lowell alive; the oldest Kane, too, come to that. She therefore expected, and was expected, to be the first to arrive on any significant occasion. After all, had it not been she who had arranged the first meeting between Anne and Richard?

Love was of little consequence to Mrs Kane. Wealth, position and prestige she understood. Love was all very well, but it rarely proved to be a lasting commodity; the other three undoubtedly were.

She kissed her daughter-in-law approvingly on the forehead. Anne touched a button on the wall, and a quiet buzz could be heard. The noise took Mrs Kane by surprise as she was yet to be convinced that electricity would ever catch on. The nurse reappeared carrying the son and heir. Mrs Kane inspected him, sniffed her approval and then waved the nurse away.

'Well done, Anne,' she said, as if her daughter-in-law had won a minor rosette at a regatta. 'All of us are so very proud of you.'

Anne's own mother, Mrs Edward Cabot, arrived a few minutes later. She differed from Mrs Kane so little in her appearance that those who observed them from afar tended to get the two ladies muddled up. But to do Mrs Cabot justice, she took considerably more interest in her grandson and her daughter than Mrs Kane had. The inspection moved on to the flowers.

'How kind of the Jacksons to remember,' murmured Mrs Cabot, who would have been shocked if they hadn't.

Mrs Kane made a more cursory inspection. Her eyes skimmed over the delicate blooms before settling on the donors' cards. She whispered the soothing names to herself: Adamses, Lawrences, Lodges, Higginsons. Neither grandmother commented on the names they didn't recognize; they were both past the age of wanting to learn of anything or anyone new. They left together, well pleased: an heir had been born, and appeared on first sight to be quite satisfactory. They both considered that their final family obligation had been carried out, albeit vicariously, and that they themselves might now progress to the role of chorus.

They were both wrong.

Anne and Richard's close friends and relations appeared throughout the afternoon bearing gifts and good wishes, the former of gold or silver, the latter in clipped Brahmin accents. By the time the last well-wisher departed, following the close of business, Anne was exhausted. Richard seemed a little less stiff than usual. He had drunk a glass of champagne at lunch for the first time in his life – old Amos Kerbes had insisted, and with the whole Somerset Club looking on, he could hardly have objected. In his long black frock coat and pinstripe trousers he stood fully six feet one, and his dark hair, parted in the centre, gleamed in the light of the large electric bulb. Few would have guessed his age correctly. Youth had never been that important to him; some wags even suggested that he had been born middle-aged. It didn't worry him: substance and reputation were the only things that mattered. Once again William Lowell Kane was called for and inspected, as if his father was checking a balance sheet at the end of a banking day. All seemed to be in order. The boy had two legs, two arms, ten fingers, ten toes. Richard could see nothing that might later embarrass him, so William was sent away.

'I wired the headmaster of St Paul's yesterday evening,' he informed his wife. 'William has been registered for September 1918.'

Anne didn't comment; Richard had obviously begun planning William's future long before he had been born.

'Well, my dear, I hope you're fully recovered,' he said, having only spent the first three days of his life in a hospital.

'Yes – no – I think so,' his wife responded timidly, suppressing any emotion she thought might displease him. He kissed her gently on the cheek and left without another word. Roberts drove him back to the Red House, their family home on Louisburg Square. With a new baby plus his nurse to add to the existing staff, there would now be nine mouths to feed. Richard did not give the matter a second thought.

—◦—

William Lowell Kane received the church's blessing at the Protestant Episcopal Cathedral of St Paul's, in the presence of everyone in Boston who mattered, and a few who didn't. Bishop William Lawrence officiated, while J. P. Morgan and A. J. Lloyd, bankers of impeccable standing, stood alongside Anne's school friend Millie Preston as the chosen godparents. His Grace sprinkled the holy water on William's head, and uttered the words, 'William Lowell Kane.' The boy didn't murmur. He was already learning to accept the Brahmin approach to life. Anne thanked God for the safe birth of her son, while Richard bowed his head – he regarded the Almighty as little more than an external bookkeeper whose function was to record the births and deaths of the Kane family. Still, he thought, perhaps he had better be certain, and have a second boy – like the British royal family, he would then have an heir and a spare. He smiled at his wife, well pleased with her.

5

WLADEK KOSKIEWICZ grew slowly. It soon became apparent to his foster mother that the boy's health would always be a problem. He caught all the illnesses and diseases that growing children normally catch, and many that most don't. He then passed them on indiscriminately to the rest of the family.

Helena treated Wladek like one of her own, and vigorously defended him whenever Jasio began to blame the devil, rather than God, for the child's presence in their tiny cottage. Florentyna also took care of Wladek as if he were her own child. She had loved him from the first moment she set eyes on him, with an intensity that grew from a fear that because no one would ever want to marry her, the penniless daughter of a trapper, she would therefore be childless. Wladek was her child.

The eldest brother, Franck, who had found Wladek on the riverbank, treated him like a plaything. He would never admit that he was fond of the frail infant, as his father had told him children were a woman's concern. In any case, next January he would be leaving school to start work on the Baron's estate. The three younger brothers, Stefan, Josef and Jan, showed little interest in Wladek, while the remaining member of the family, Sophia, only six months his senior, was happy enough just to cuddle him. What Helena had not been prepared for was a character and a mind so unlike those of her own children.

No one could fail to notice the physical or intellectual differences. The Koskiewicz children were all tall, heavily set, with red hair and, except for Florentyna, grey eyes. Wladek was short and stocky, with dark hair and intense blue eyes. The Koskiewiczes had no interest in education, and left the village school as soon as age or necessity demanded. Wladek, on the other hand, though he was late to crawl, could speak at eighteen months, read before his third birthday – but was still unable to dress himself – and write coherent sentences at five – but continued to wet his bed. He became the despair of his father and the pride of his mother. His first four years on this earth were memorable mainly because of how many attempts he made through illness to depart from it; he would have succeeded in doing so had it not been for the sustained efforts of Helena and Florentyna. He would run around the little wooden cottage barefoot, usually dressed in his harlequin outfit, a yard or so behind his mother. When Florentyna returned from school he would transfer his allegiance, never leaving her side until she put him to bed. In her division of the food Florentyna often sacrificed half of her own share to Wladek or, if he was sick, the entire portion. Wladek wore the clothes she made for him, sang the songs she taught him and shared with her the few toys and presents she possessed.

Because Florentyna was away at school for most of the day, Wladek wanted to go with her. As soon as he was allowed to, he walked the eighteen-*wiorsta* path through the woods of moss-covered birches and cypresses to the little school in Slonim, holding firmly on to her hand until they reached its gates.

Unlike his brothers, Wladek enjoyed school from the first bell; for him, it was an escape from the tiny cottage that had until then been his whole world. School also made him painfully aware that the Russians occupied his homeland. He learned that his native Polish was only to be spoken in the privacy of the cottage, and that at school Russian would be the mother tongue. He sensed in the other children a fierce pride in their oppressed language and culture, and he too came to share that same pride.

To his surprise, Wladek found that he was not belittled by Mr Kotowski, the schoolteacher, the way he was at home by his father. Although still the youngest, as he was at home, it was not long before he rose above his classmates in everything other than height. His tiny stature misled his contemporaries into underestimating him: children so often assume biggest is best. By the age of five Wladek was top of his class in every subject except woodwork.

At night, back at the little wooden cottage, while the other children tended the violets that bloomed so fragrantly in their springtime garden, picked berries, chopped wood, hunted rabbits or made clothes, Wladek read and read, until he was reading the unopened books of his eldest brother and then those of his elder sister. It began to dawn slowly on Helena that she had taken on more than she had bargained for when Franck had brought home the little animal in place of three rabbits. Already Wladek was asking questions she could not answer. She knew it wouldn't be long before she couldn't cope with him, and she didn't know what to do about it. But she had an unquestionable belief in destiny, so was not surprised when the decision was taken out of her hands.

The first major turning point in Wladek's life came one evening in the autumn of 1911. The family had finished their usual supper of beetroot soup and rabbit. Jasio was snoring by the fire and Helena was sewing while the other children were all playing. Wladek was sitting at the feet of his mother, reading, when above the noise of Stefan and Josef squabbling over the possession of some newly painted pine-cones, they heard a loud knock on the door. They all fell silent. A knock was always a surprise to the Koskiewicz family, for visitors at the little cottage were almost unknown.

The whole family looked towards the door apprehensively. As if it had not occurred, they waited for the knock to come a second time. It did – a little louder than the first. Jasio rose sleepily from his chair, walked across to the door and opened it cautiously. When they saw who was standing there, they all leapt up and bowed their heads except Wladek, who stared up at the broad-shouldered, handsome, aristocratic figure draped in his heavy bearskin coat, whose presence had instantly brought fear into the father's eyes. But the visitor's cordial smile removed any anxiety, and Jasio quickly stood aside to allow Baron Rosnovski to enter his home. Nobody spoke. The Baron had never visited the cottage before, so they did not know what to do next.

Wladek put down his book, rose, walked up to the stranger and thrust out his hand before his father could stop him.

'Good evening, sir.'

The Baron shook his hand, and they stared into each other's eyes. When the Baron released him, Wladek's eyes came to rest on a magnificent silver band around his wrist, with an inscription on it that he couldn't quite make out.

'You must be Wladek.'

'Yes, sir,' replied the boy, seemingly unsurprised to find that the Baron knew his name.

'It is about you that I have come to see your father,' said the Baron.

Jasio signified by a wave of his arm that the other children should leave him alone with his master, so two of them curtsied, four bowed, and all six retreated silently up into the loft. Wladek remained, as no one suggested he should join the other children.

'Koskiewicz,' began the Baron, still standing, as no one had offered him a seat, firstly because they were too frightened, and secondly because they assumed he was there to issue a reprimand. 'I have come to ask a favour.'

'Anything, sir, anything,' said the father, wondering what he could possibly give the Baron that he did not already have a hundred-fold.

The Baron continued. 'My son, Leon, is now six years of age, and is being taught privately at the castle by two tutors, one from Poland, the other from Germany. They tell me he is a bright child but lacks competition, as he has only himself to beat. Mr Kotowski at the village school tells me that Wladek is the only boy there who is capable of providing such competition. I have come to ask you if you would permit your son to leave the village school and join Leon and his tutors at the castle.'

Before Wladek's eyes there appeared a wondrous vision of books, and teachers far wiser than Mr Kotowski. He glanced towards his mother. She was gazing at the Baron, her face filled with a mixture of wonder and sorrow. His father turned to her, and the moment of silent communication between them seemed an eternity to the child.

The trapper gruffly addressed the Baron's feet. 'We would be honoured, sir.'

The Baron turned his attention to Helena.

'The Blessed Virgin forbids that I should ever stand in my child's way,' she said softly, 'though she alone knows how much I will miss him.'

'Be assured, Madam Koskiewicz, that your son can return home whenever he wishes.'

'Yes, sir. I expect he will do so, at first.' She was about to add some plea but thought better of it.

The Baron smiled. 'Good. It's settled then. Please bring him to the castle tomorrow morning by seven o'clock. During the school term he will live with us, and at Christmas he can return to you.'

Wladek burst into tears.

'Quiet, boy,' said the trapper.

'I will not leave you,' Wladek said, turning to face his mother, although in truth he wanted to go.

'Quiet, boy,' repeated the trapper, this time a little louder.

'Why not?' asked the Baron, with compassion in his voice.

'I will never leave Florcia – never.'

'Florcia?' queried the Baron.

'My eldest daughter, sir,' interjected the trapper. 'Don't concern yourself with her, sir. The boy will do as he is told.'

No one spoke. The Baron remained silent for a moment, while Wladek continued to cry controlled tears. 'How old is the girl?' he finally asked.

'Fourteen,' replied the trapper.

'Could she work in the kitchens?' asked the Baron, relieved to see that Helena Koskiewicz did not look as if she was going to burst into tears as well.

'Oh, yes, Baron,' she replied. 'Florcia can cook, and she can sew and she can . . .'

'Good, good, then she can come as well. I shall expect them both tomorrow morning at seven.'

The Baron walked to the door, looked back at the boy and smiled. This time Wladek returned the smile. He had struck his first bargain, and allowed his mother to cling to him after the Baron had left. He heard her whisper, 'Ah, Matka's littlest one, what will become of you now?'

Wladek couldn't wait to find out.

—◆—

Helena packed for Wladek and Florentyna before going to bed that night, not that it would have taken long to pack the entire family's possessions. At six the following morning the rest of the family stood by the door and watched them depart for the castle, each holding a paper parcel under one arm. Florentyna, tall and graceful, kept turning to look at them, crying and waving; but Wladek, short and ungainly, never once looked back. Florentyna held firmly on to his hand for the entire journey. Their roles had been reversed: from that day on, she would depend on him.

They were clearly expected by the magnificent manservant in an embroidered suit of green livery covered in golden buttons who answered their timid knock on the great oak door. Both of them had often gazed in admiration at the grey uniforms of the soldiers who guarded the nearby Russian–Polish border, but they had never seen anything so resplendent as this giant towering above them, who they thought must be of overwhelming importance. There was a thick rug in the hall, and Wladek stared at the green-and-red pattern, amazed by its beauty, wondering if he should take off his shoes, and was surprised that when he walked across it, his footsteps made no sound.

The dazzling being conducted them to their bedrooms in the west wing. Separate rooms – how would they ever get to sleep? At least there was a connecting door, so they need never be too far apart, and in fact for many nights they slept together in the same bed.

Once they had unpacked, Florentyna was taken off to the kitchen and Wladek to a playroom in the south wing of the castle where he was introduced to the Baron's son. Leon Rosnovski was tall for his age, a good-looking boy who was so charming and welcoming that Wladek abandoned his prepared pugnacious attitude within moments of meeting him. Wladek quickly discovered that Leon was a lonely child, with no one to play with except his *niania*, the devoted Lithuanian woman who had breast-fed him and attended to his every need since the premature death of his mother. The sturdy boy who had come out of the forest promised companionship. And at least in one matter they were considered equals.

Leon immediately offered to show Wladek around the castle – every room of which was bigger than the entire cottage. The adventure took the rest of the morning, and Wladek was astounded by the sheer size of the castle, the richness of its furniture and fabrics – and those carpets were in every room. Wladek admitted only to being agreeably impressed. The main part of the building, Leon told him, was early Gothic, as if Wladek was sure to know what *Gothic* meant. He nodded. Next, Leon took his new friend down a stone staircase into the immense cellars, with row upon row of wine bottles covered in dust and cobwebs. But Wladek's favourite room was the vast dining hall, with its massive pillared vaulting, flagged floor and the largest table he'd ever seen. He stared at the stuffed heads mounted on the walls. Leon told him they were bison, bear, elk, boar and wolverine that his father had shot over the years. Above the fireplace was the Baron's coat of arms. The Rosnovski family motto read: 'Fortune favours the brave.'

At twelve, a gong sounded and lunch was served by liveried servants. Wladek ate very little as he watched Leon carefully, trying to memorize which instruments he used in the bewildering array of silver cutlery. After lunch he met his two tutors, who did not welcome him as Leon had done. That evening he climbed up onto the largest bed he had ever seen, and told Florentyna about his adventures. Her disbelieving eyes never once left his face, nor did she even close her mouth, agape with wonder, especially when she heard about the knives and forks.

Lessons began at seven sharp the next morning, before breakfast, and continued throughout the day, with only short breaks for meals. To begin with, Leon was clearly ahead of his new classmate, but Wladek wrestled manfully with his books, and as the weeks passed the gap began to narrow. The two boys' friendship and rivalry developed at the same pace. The tutors found it hard to treat their two pupils – one the son of a baron, the other the illegitimate son of God knows who – as equals, although they reluctantly conceded to the Baron that he had made the right academic choice. Their uncompromising attitude never worried Wladek, because Leon always treated him as an equal.

The Baron let it be known that he was pleased with the progress the boys were making, and he would often reward Wladek with clothes and toys. Wladek's initial distant and detached admiration for the Baron quickly developed into respect.

When the time came for Wladek to return to the little cottage in the forest for Christmas he was distressed at having to leave Leon. Despite his initial happiness at seeing his mother, the three short months he'd spent in the Baron's castle had introduced him to a far more exciting world. He would have rather been a servant at the castle than master at the cottage.

As the holiday dragged on, Wladek felt himself stifled by the little cottage with its one room and overcrowded loft, and dissatisfied by the food dished out in such meagre amounts and eaten with bare hands: no one divided things up into nine portions at the castle. After a few days Wladek longed to return and be with Leon and the Baron. Every afternoon he would walk the six *wiorsta* to the castle and sit and stare at the great walls that surrounded an estate he would not consider entering without permission. Florentyna, who had lived only among the kitchen servants, adjusted more easily to the return to her former simple life, and could not understand that the cottage would never again be home for Wladek.

Jasio was not sure how to treat the six-year-old boy, who was now so well dressed and well spoken, and talked of matters that the father did not begin to understand; nor did he want to. And worse, Wladek seemed to do nothing but waste the entire day reading. Whatever would become of him, the trapper wondered, if he could not swing an axe or trap a rabbit. How could he ever hope to earn an honest living? He too prayed that the holiday would pass quickly.

Helena was proud of Wladek, and at first refused to admit

even to herself that a wedge had been driven between him and the rest of the children. But it was not long before it could not be avoided. Playing at soldiers one evening, both Stefan and Franck, generals of opposing armies, refused to have Wladek in their ranks.

'Why must I always be left out?' cried Wladek. 'I want to join in the battle.'

'Because you are no longer one of us,' declared Stefan. 'And in any case, you're not really our brother.'

There was a long silence before Franck added, 'Father never wanted you in the first place; only Matka allowed you to stay.'

Wladek looked around the circle of children, searching for Florentyna. 'What does Stefan mean, I am not your brother?' he demanded.

Thus Wladek came to learn the manner of his birth, and to understand why he had always felt different from his brothers and sisters. He was secretly pleased to discover that, untouched by the meanness of the trapper's blood, he came from unknown stock, containing with it the germ of spirit that would make all things possible.

Once the unhappy holiday finally came to an end, Wladek returned to the castle before first light, a reluctant Florentyna following a few paces behind. Leon welcomed him back with open arms; for him, as isolated by the wealth of his father as Wladek was by the poverty of the trapper, it had also been a Christmas with little to celebrate. From that moment the two boys became the closest of friends, and were inseparable.

When the summer holidays came, Leon begged his father to allow Wladek to remain at the castle. The Baron agreed, for he too had grown attached to the trapper's son. Wladek was overjoyed. He would return to the wooden cottage again only once in his life.

6

WILLIAM KANE grew quickly, and was considered an adorable child by all who came in contact with him; in the early years of his life these were generally besotted relatives or doting servants.

The top floor of the Kanes' eighteenth-century house in Louisburg Square had been converted into nursery quarters, crammed with toys. A bedroom and a sitting room had been set aside for the newly acquired nurse. The nursery was far enough away from Richard Kane for him to be unaware of problems such as teething, wet diapers and any irregular and undisciplined cries for more food. First smile, first tooth, first step and first word were all recorded in a family book by William's mother, along with the progress of his height and weight. Anne was surprised to find that these statistics differed very little from those of any other child with whom she came into contact on Beacon Hill.

The nurse, an import from England, brought the boy up on a regimen that would have gladdened the heart of a Prussian cavalry officer. William's father would visit him each evening at six o'clock. As he refused to address the child in baby language, he ended up not speaking to him at all; the two merely stared blankly at each other. Sometimes William would grip his father's index finger, the one with which balance sheets were checked, and Richard would allow himself a smile.

By the end of the first year his routine was slightly modified, and the boy would be brought downstairs to see his father. Richard would sit in his high-backed, maroon leather chair, watching his firstborn weave his way on all fours between the legs

College of the Ouachitas

of the furniture, reappearing when least expected, which led Richard to observe that he would undoubtedly become a politician. William took his first steps at thirteen months while clinging to the tails of his father's topcoat. His first word was *Dada*, which pleased everyone, including Grandmother Kane and Grandmother Cabot, who made regular inspections. They did not actually push the perambulator in which William was accompanied around Boston, but they did deign to walk a pace behind the nurse on her Thursday-afternoon outings, glaring at infants with a less disciplined routine. While other children fed the ducks in the public parks, William succeeded in charming the swans by the lake of Mr Jack Gardner's magnificent Venetian Palace.

After two years had passed, the grandmothers intimated by hint and innuendo that it was high time for another progeny, a sibling for William. Anne obliged them by becoming pregnant, but found herself feeling off-colour as she entered her fourth month. When Anne miscarried after sixteen weeks, Dr MacKenzie did not allow her to become self-indulgent. In his notes he wrote: 'pre-eclampsia?', and told her, 'Mrs Kane, the reason you have not been feeling well is that your blood pressure has been too high, and would probably have become even higher as your pregnancy progressed. I fear doctors haven't found the cure for high blood pressure yet; in fact, we know very little about the problem, other than that it's a dangerous condition, particularly for a pregnant woman.'

Anne held back her tears as she considered the implications of a future without more children.

'Surely it wouldn't recur if I were to become pregnant again?' she asked, phrasing her question to dispose the doctor to a favourable reply.

'Frankly I would be very surprised if it didn't, Mrs Kane. I am sorry to have to say this, but I would strongly advise you against having another child.'

'But I don't mind feeling off-colour for a few months if it means . . .'

'I am not talking about feeling off-colour, Mrs Kane. I am talking about not taking unnecessary risks with your life.'

It was a terrible blow for Anne and also for Richard, who had assumed he would sire a large enough family to ensure that the Kane name survived for ever. Now that responsibility had been passed on to William.

◄○►

Richard, after six years on the board, had taken over as president of the Kane and Cabot Bank and Trust Company. The bank, which dominated the corner of State Street, was a bastion of architectural and fiscal solidity and had branches in New York, London and San Francisco. The San Francisco branch had presented Richard with a problem on the day of William's birth when, along with the Crocker National Bank, Wells Fargo and the California Bank, it collapsed to the ground, not financially but literally, during the great earthquake of 1906. Richard, by nature a cautious man, was comprehensively insured with Lloyd's of London. Gentlemen all, they had paid up to the penny, enabling Richard to keep his fortune intact. Nevertheless, Richard spent an uncomfortable year jolting back and forth across America on four-day train journeys between Boston and San Francisco in order to supervise the rebuilding. He opened the new office in Union Square in October 1907, just in time to turn his attention to problems springing up on the Eastern Seaboard. There was a minor run on the New York banks: many of the smaller establishments were unable to cope with unexpectedly large withdrawals, and in some cases had to close their doors. J. P. Morgan, the legendary chairman of the establishment bearing his name, invited Richard to join a consortium to work together during the crisis. Richard agreed. The courageous stand paid off, and life began to return to normal, but not before Richard had had a few sleepless nights.

William, on the other hand, slept soundly, unaware of the significance of earthquakes or collapsing banks; after all, there were swans to be fed, and endless trips to and from Milton, Brookline and Beverley so that he could be shown off to his adoring relatives.

◄○►

In October of the following year Richard Kane acquired a new toy in return for a cautious investment in a man called Henry Ford, who was claiming that he could manufacture a motor vehicle for the people. The bank entertained Mr Ford to luncheon, and Richard was persuaded to purchase a Model T for the princely sum of $825. Ford assured him that if the bank would back him, the cost could eventually fall to $350, and everyone would want to buy his cars, ensuring a large profit for his backers. Richard did back him: it was the first time he had placed good money with someone who hoped his product would halve in price.

Richard was initially apprehensive that his motor vehicle, sombrely black though it was, might not be regarded as a sufficiently serious mode of transport for the president and chairman of a leading bank, but he was reassured by the admiring glances from the sidewalks that the machine attracted. At ten miles an hour it was noisier than a horse, but it did have the virtue of leaving no mess in the middle of Mount Vernon Street. His only quarrel with Mr Ford was that he would not listen to his suggestion that the Model T be made available in a variety of colours. Ford insisted that every car should be black, in order to keep the price down. Anne, more sensitive than her husband to the approbation of polite society, refused to travel in the back seat until the Cabots had acquired a car themselves.

William, however, adored the 'automobile', as the press described it, and immediately assumed that it had been bought to replace his redundant and un-mechanized pram. He also preferred the chauffeur – with his goggles and peaked cap – to his nurse. Grandmother Kane and Grandmother Cabot said they would never travel in such an infernal contraption, and they never did, although many years later Grandmother Kane was driven to her funeral in a motor car, but was not informed of that fact.

-<o>-

During the next two years, the bank grew in strength and size, as did William.

Americans were once again investing for expansion, and large sums of money found their way to Kane and Cabot's, to be reinvested in such projects as the expanding Lowell leather factory in Lowell, Massachusetts. Richard watched the growth of both his bank and his son with unbridled satisfaction.

On William's fifth birthday, he took the child out of women's hands and engaged a Mr Munro, at $450 per annum, to be his private tutor. Richard personally selected Munro from a list of eight applicants who had earlier been screened by his private secretary. His single purpose was to ensure that William would be ready to enter St Paul's by the age of twelve. William immediately took to his tutor, whom he thought to be very old and very clever. He was, in fact, twenty-three and the possessor of a second-class honours degree in English from the University of Edinburgh.

William quickly learned to read and write, but he saved his real enthusiasm for numbers. His sole complaint was that, of the six daily lessons, only one was devoted to arithmetic. He was quick to point out to his father that one-sixth of the working day might not be enough time for someone who would one day be the president and chairman of a bank.

To compensate for his tutor's lack of foresight, William dogged the footsteps of any accessible relatives, with demands for sums to be calculated in his head. Grandmother Cabot, who had never been persuaded that the division of an integer by four would necessarily produce the same answer as its multiplication by one quarter found herself quickly outclassed by her grandson; however, Grandmother Kane, who was far more learned than she would admit, grappled manfully with vulgar fractions, compound interest and the division of eight cakes between nine children.

'Grandmother,' said William kindly but firmly when she had failed to find the answer to his latest conundrum, 'you could give me a slide rule, and then I won't need to bother you again.'

Grandmother Kane was astonished by her grandson's precocity, but she bought him a slide rule just the same, wondering if he really knew how to use it.

Meanwhile, Richard's problems began to gravitate further eastward. When the chairman of the London branch died of a heart attack at his desk, Richard found himself required in Lombard Street. He suggested to Anne that she and William accompany him, feeling that the journey would add to the child's education. After all, he could visit all the places Mr Munro had taught him about. Anne, who had never been to Europe, was excited by the prospect, and filled three steamer trunks with elegant and expensive new clothes in which to confront the Old World. William considered it unfair that she would not allow him to take that equally essential aid to travel, his bicycle.

The Kanes travelled to New York by train to join the *Aquitania* on her voyage to Southampton. Anne was appalled by the sight of the immigrant street traders hawking their wares on the sidewalks. William, on the other hand, was struck by the size of New York; he had, until that moment, imagined that his father's bank was the biggest building in America, if not the world. He wanted to buy a pink-and-yellow ice cream from a man with a little cart on wheels, but his father would not hear of it; in any case, he never carried small change.

William adored the great liner the moment he saw it, and quickly made friends with the white-bearded captain, who shared with him all the secrets of the Cunard Line's prima donna. Not long after the ship had left America, Richard and Anne, who had been placed at the captain's table, felt it necessary to apologize for the amount of the crew's time their son was occupying.

'Not at all,' replied the skipper. 'William and I are already good friends. I only wish I could answer all his questions about time, speed and distance. I have to be coached every night by the first engineer in the hope of first anticipating and then surviving the following day.'

When the *Aquitania* sailed into Southampton after a ten-day crossing, William was reluctant to leave her, and tears would have been unavoidable had it not been for the magnificent sight of a Rolls-Royce Silver Ghost parked at the quayside, complete with chauffeur, ready to whisk them off to London. Richard decided on the spur of the moment that he would have the car transported back to New York at the end of the trip, a decision more out of character than any he would make during the rest of his life. He informed Anne that he wanted to show it to Henry Ford. Henry Ford never saw it.

The family always stayed at the Savoy Hotel in the Strand when they were in London, which was conveniently situated for Richard's office in the City. During a dinner overlooking the River Thames, Richard learned first-hand from his new chairman, Sir David Seymour, a former diplomat, how the London branch was faring. Not that he would ever have described London as a 'branch' of Kane and Cabot while he was on this side of the Atlantic.

Richard was able to conduct a discreet conversation with Sir David, while his wife was preoccupied with learning from Lavinia Seymour how they should best occupy their time while in town. Anne was delighted to learn that Lavinia also had a son, who couldn't wait to meet his first American.

The following morning Lavinia reappeared at the Savoy, accompanied by Stuart Seymour. After they had shaken hands, Stuart asked William, 'Are you a cowboy?'

'Only if you're a redcoat,' William immediately replied. The two six-year-old boys shook hands a second time.

That day, William, Stuart, Anne and Lady Seymour visited the Tower of London, and watched the Changing of the Guard at Buckingham Palace. William told Stuart that he thought everything was 'swell', except for Stuart's accent, which he found difficult to understand.

'Why don't you talk like us?' he demanded, and was surprised to be informed by his mother that the question should more properly be put the other way around, as 'they' had come first.

William enjoyed watching the soldiers in their bright red uniforms with large, shiny brass buttons who stood guard outside Buckingham Palace. He tried to talk to them, but they just stared past him into space and never seemed to blink.

'Can we take one home?' he asked his mother.

'No, darling, they have to stay in London and guard the King.'

'But he's got so many of them. Can't I have just one? He'd look just swell outside our house in Louisburg Square.'

—<o>—

As a 'special treat' – Anne's words – Richard allowed himself an afternoon off to take William, Stuart and Anne to the West End to see a traditional English pantomime called *Jack and the Beanstalk*, which was playing at the Hippodrome. William loved Jack, although he was puzzled that he had long legs and wore stockings. Despite this he wanted to cut down every tree he laid his eyes on, imagining them all to be sheltering a wicked giant. After the curtain had come down they had tea at Fortnum and Mason in Piccadilly, and Anne allowed William two cream buns and something Stuart called a doughnut. After that, William had to be escorted to the tea room at Fortnum's daily to consume another 'dough bun', as he described them.

The time in London passed by all too quickly for William and his mother, but Richard, satisfied that all was well in Lombard Street, and pleased with his newly appointed chairman, was already making plans to return to America. Cables were arriving daily from Boston, which made him anxious to be back in his own boardroom. When one such missive informed him that 2,500 workers at a cotton mill in Lawrence, Massachusetts, in which his bank had a heavy investment, had gone out on strike, he changed his booking for the return voyage.

William was also looking forward to getting back to Boston so that he could tell Mr Munro all the amazing experiences he'd had in England, as well as being reunited with his two grandmothers. He felt sure that they could never have done anything as exciting as visiting a real live theatre with members of the general public. Anne was also happy to be returning home, although she had enjoyed the trip almost as much as William, for her clothes and beauty had been much admired by the normally undemonstrative English.

As a final treat the day before they were due to sail, Lavinia Seymour invited William and Anne to a tea party at her home in Eaton Square. While Anne and Lavinia discussed the latest

London fashions, William learned about cricket from Stuart, and tried to explain baseball to his new best friend. The party, however, broke up early when Stuart began to feel sick. William, in sympathy, announced that he too was feeling ill so he and Anne returned to the Savoy earlier than they had planned. Anne was not greatly put out, as this gave her a little more time to supervise the packing of the large steamer trunks filled with all her new acquisitions, although she was convinced William was only putting on an act to please Stuart. But when she put him to bed that night, Anne found that he was running a slight temperature. She remarked on it to Richard over dinner.

'Probably just the excitement at the thought of returning home,' he offered, sounding unconcerned.

'I hope so,' replied Anne. 'I don't want him to be sick on the voyage.'

'He'll be fine by tomorrow,' Richard tried to reassure her.

But when Anne went to wake William the next morning, she found him covered in little red spots and running a temperature of 103. The hotel doctor diagnosed measles, and was politely insistent that the boy was on no account to undertake a sea voyage, not only for his own sake, but for that of the other passengers.

Richard was unable to countenance any further delay, and decided to sail as planned. Reluctantly, Anne agreed that she and William would remain in London until the ship returned in three weeks' time. William begged his father to let him accompany him, but Richard was adamant, and hired a nurse to look after William until he was fully recovered. Anne travelled down to Southampton with Richard in the new Rolls-Royce to see him off.

'I shall be lonely in London without you, Richard,' she ventured diffidently when they parted, risking his disapproval of any suggestion of sentimentality.

'Well, my dear, I dare say I shall be somewhat lonely in Boston without you,' he said, his mind on 2,500 striking mill-workers.

Anne returned to London on the train, wondering how she would occupy herself for the next three weeks.

William had a better night, and in the morning the spots looked a little less ferocious. However, the doctor and nurse were unanimous in their insistence that he should remain in bed. Anne passed much of the next four days writing long letters to the family. On the fifth day, William rose early and crept into his mother's room. He climbed into bed next to her, and his cold hands immediately woke her. She was relieved to see that he appeared to be fully recovered, and rang to order breakfast in bed for both of them, an indulgence William's father would never have countenanced.

A few minutes later, there was a quiet knock on the door, and a man in gold-and-red livery entered with a large silver tray: eggs, bacon, tomato, toast and marmalade – a veritable feast. While William looked at the food ravenously, as if he could not remember when he had last eaten, Anne glanced casually at the morning paper. Richard always read *The Times* when he was in London, and the hotel management continued to deliver it.

'Oh, look,' said William, staring at the photograph on an inside page, 'a picture of Daddy's ship. What's a ca-la-mity, Mommy?'

7

WHEN WLADEK and Leon had finished their work in the classroom, they would spend their spare time before supper playing games. Their favourite was *chow anego*, a sort of hide-and-seek, and because the castle had seventy-two rooms, any chance of repetition was very slight. Wladek's favourite hiding place was in the dungeons, where the only light came through a small grille set high in the wall and one needed a candle to find one's way around. Wladek was not sure what purpose the dungeons served, and none of the servants ever made mention of them, since they had never been occupied for as long as anybody could remember.

The River Shchara, which bordered the estate, became an extension to their playground. In spring they fished, in summer they swam, and in winter they would pull on their wooden skates and chase each other across the ice, while Florentyna sat on the bank anxiously warning them where the surface was thin. Wladek never heeded her advice, and was always the first to fall in.

Leon grew tall and strong; he could run fast, swim well and didn't seem to tire and was never ill. Wladek knew he couldn't hope to match his friend at any sport, even if they were equals in the classroom. Worse, what Leon called his belly button was almost unnoticeable, while Wladek's was stumpy and ugly, and protruded from the middle of his plump little body. Wladek spent long hours in the privacy of his room studying himself in a mirror, wondering why he had only one nipple when all the boys he had ever come across had the two that symmetry seemed to require.

Sometimes as he lay awake at night he would finger his naked chest and tears of self-pity would flood onto the pillow. He prayed that when he woke in the morning, a second nipple would have grown. His prayers were not answered.

Wladek put time aside each night to do physical exercises. He did not allow anyone to witness these exertions, even Florentyna. Through sheer determination he learned to hold himself so he appeared taller. He built up his arms with press-ups, and hung by the tips of his fingers from a beam in the bedroom in the hope that it would stretch him. But Leon continued to grow ever taller, and Wladek was forced to accept that he would always be a foot shorter than the Baron's son, and that nothing, *nothing* was ever going to produce the missing nipple. Leon, who adored Wladek uncritically, never commented on any difference between them.

Baron Rosnovski had also become increasingly fond of the fierce, dark-haired trapper's child who had replaced the younger brother Leon had lost when the Baroness died in childbirth.

—◇—

Once Leon had celebrated his eighth birthday, the two boys began to dine with the Baron in the great stone-walled hall each evening. Flickering candles cast ominous shadows from the stuffed animal heads on the walls. Servants came and went noiselessly with great silver trays and golden plates bearing geese, hams, crayfish, fruit and sometimes the *mazureks* that had become Wladek's particular favourite. Once the table had been cleared, the Baron would dismiss the servants and regale the boys with stories from Polish history, allowing them a sip of Danzig vodka, in which tiny gold leaves sparkled in the candlelight. Wladek begged as often as he dared to be told once again the story of Tadeusz Kosciuszko.

'A great patriot and hero,' the Baron would respond. 'The very symbol of our struggle for independence, trained in France . . .'

'. . . whose people we admire and love just as we have learned to hate the Russians and Austrians,' volunteered Wladek, whose pleasure in the tale was enhanced by his word-perfect memory of it.

'Who is telling this story, Wladek?' The Baron laughed. '. . . and then after Kosciuszko fought alongside George Washington in America for liberty and democracy, in 1792 he returned to his native land to lead the Poles in battle at Dubienka. When our wretched king, Stanislaw Augustus, deserted his people to join the Russians, Kosciuszko came back to the homeland he loved, to throw off the yoke of Tsardom. He won the battle of where, Leon?'

'Raclawice, Papa,' replied Leon. 'And then he marched on to liberate Warsaw.'

'Good, my child. But alas, the Russians mustered a great force at Maciejowice where he was finally defeated and taken prisoner. My great-great-great-grandfather fought with Kosciuszko on that day, and later alongside Dabrowski's legions for the mighty Napoleon Bonaparte.'

'For his service to Poland he was created the Baron Rosnovski, a title your family will ever bear in remembrance of those glorious days,' said Wladek.

'Yes. And in God's chosen time,' said the Baron, 'that title will pass to my son, when he will become Baron Leon Rosnovski.'

―◦―

At Christmas the peasants on the estate would bring their families to the castle for the celebration of the Blessed Vigil. On Christmas Eve they fasted, the children staring out of the windows for the first star, which was the sign the feast might begin.

Once everybody had taken their seats, the Baron would say grace in his deep baritone: '*Benedicte nobis, Domine Deus, et hic donis quae ex liberalitate tua sumpturi sumus.*' Wladek felt embarrassed by the huge presence of Jasio Koskiewicz, who tucked in to every one of the thirteen courses, from the *barszcz* soup through to the cakes and plums, and would surely, as in previous years, be sick in the forest on the way home.

After the feast Wladek enjoyed distributing gifts from a

Christmas tree, laden with candles and fruit, to the awestruck peasant children – a doll for Sophia, a forest knife for Josef, a new dress for Florentyna – the first gift Wladek had ever requested of the Baron.

'Is it true,' asked Josef of his mother when he received a gift from Wladek, 'that he is not our brother, Matka?'

'No,' she replied, 'but he will always be my son.'

—◦—

As the years passed, Leon grew even taller, Wladek grew stronger, and both boys became wiser. But then, in July 1914, without warning or explanation, the German tutor left the castle without even bidding them farewell. They never thought to connect his departure with the recent assassination in Sarajevo of the Archduke Franz Ferdinand by a student anarchist, an event described to them by their other tutor in solemn tones. The Baron became withdrawn, but no explanation was forthcoming. The younger servants, the children's favourites, began to disappear one by one; and still neither boy could work out why.

—◦—

One morning in August 1915, a time of warm, hazy days, the Baron set off on the long journey to Warsaw to put, as he described it, his affairs in order. He was absent for three and a half weeks, twenty-five days that Wladek marked off on a calendar in his bedroom each evening. On the day he was due to return, the two boys travelled to the Slonim railway station to await the weekly train with its three carriages, so they could greet him on his arrival. Wladek was surprised and alarmed to see that the Baron looked weary and broken, and although he wanted to ask him many questions, the three of them returned to the castle in silence.

During the following week the Baron was to be found conducting long, intense conversations with the head servant that were broken off whenever Leon or Wladek entered the room, making them uneasy, in case they were somehow the unwitting cause of his distress. Wladek even feared that the Baron might send him back to the trapper's cottage – always aware he was a guest in the Baron's home.

One evening the Baron called for the two boys to join him in the great hall. They crept in, fearful of this break in his usual routine. The brief conversation would remain in Wladek's memory for the rest of his life.

'My dear children,' began the Baron in a low, faltering tone, 'the warmongers of Germany and the Austro-Hungarian Empire are at the throat of Warsaw once again, and will soon be at our gates.'

Wladek recalled a phrase spat out by the Polish tutor after his German colleague had left without explanation. 'Does that mean that the hour of the submerged peoples of Europe is at last upon us?' he asked.

The Baron regarded Wladek's innocent face tenderly. 'Our national spirit has not been broken in one hundred and fifty years of oppression,' he replied. 'It may be that the fate of Poland is in the balance, but we are powerless to influence history. We are at the mercy of the three mighty empires that surround us, and therefore must await our fate.'

'We are both strong, so we will fight,' said Leon.

'We have swords and shields,' added Wladek. 'We are not afraid of Germans or Russians.'

'My boys, your weapons are made of wood, and you have only played at war. This battle will not be between children. We must find a more quiet place to live until history has decided our fate. We must leave as soon as possible. I only pray that this is not the end of your childhood.'

Leon and Wladek were mystified by the Baron's words. War sounded to them like another exciting adventure, which they would be sure to miss if they left the castle.

The servants took several days to pack the Baron's possessions, and Wladek and Leon were informed that they would be departing for the family's small summer house to the north of Grodno the following Monday. The two boys continued, often unsupervised, with their work and play, because no one in the castle seemed willing to answer their myriad questions.

On Saturdays, lessons only took place in the morning. They were translating Adam Mickiewicz's *Pan Tadeusz* into Latin when they heard the guns. At first they thought the familiar sound was no more than a trapper out shooting on the estate, so they returned to the Bard of Czarnotas. A second volley of shots, much closer, made them look up, and then they heard screams coming from downstairs. The two boys stared at each other in bewilderment, but still they were not afraid, because they had never experienced anything in their short lives to make them fearful. The tutor fled, leaving them alone, and as he closed the door, there followed another shot, this time in the corridor outside their classroom. Now terrified, the two boys hid under their desks, not knowing what to do.

Suddenly the door crashed open, and a man no older than their tutor, in a grey uniform and steel helmet, holding a rifle, stood towering over them. Leon clung to Wladek, while Wladek stared at the intruder. The soldier shouted at them in German, demanding to know who they were, but neither boy replied, even though both had mastered the language as well as their mother tongue. Another soldier appeared, grabbed the two boys by the necks like chickens and pulled them out into the corridor. They were dragged past the dead body of their tutor, down the stone steps at the front of the castle and into the garden, where they found Florentyna screaming hysterically. Row upon row of dead bodies, mostly servants, were being laid on the grass. Leon could not bear to look, and buried his head in Wladek's shoulder. Wladek was mesmerized by the sight of one of the bodies, a large man with a luxuriant moustache. It was the trapper. Wladek felt nothing. Florentyna continued to scream.

'Is Papa there?' asked Leon. 'Is Papa there?'

Wladek scanned the line of bodies once again. He thanked God that there was no sign of the Baron, and was about to tell Leon the good news when a soldier appeared by their side.

'*Wer hat gesprochen?*' he demanded fiercely.

'*Ich,*' said Wladek defiantly.

The soldier raised his rifle and brought the butt crashing down into Wladek's stomach. His legs buckled, and he dropped to his knees. Where was the Baron? What was happening? Why were they being treated like this in their own home?

Leon quickly jumped on top of Wladek, trying to protect him from the second blow that the soldier was aiming at Wladek's head, but as the butt of the rifle came crashing down, its full force caught the back of Leon's neck.

Both boys lay motionless, Wladek because he was dazed by the blow and the weight of Leon's body on top of him, and Leon because he was dead.

Wladek could hear another soldier berating their tormentor for striking them. They tried to pick Leon up, but Wladek clung to him. It took both of the soldiers to prise his friend's body away and dump it unceremoniously alongside the others, face down on the grass. Wladek's eyes did not leave the motionless body of his only friend until he was marched back inside the castle and, with a handful of dazed survivors, led to the dungeons.

Nobody spoke, for fear of joining the line of bodies on the grass, until the dungeon doors were bolted and the last words of the soldiers had faded into the distance. Then Wladek murmured, 'Holy God,' for there in a corner, slumped against the wall, was the Baron, staring into space, alive and uninjured only because the Germans needed him to take charge of the prisoners.

Wladek crawled across to him, while the servants sat as far away from their master as possible. The two gazed at each other as they had on the first day they met. Wladek put his hand out once again, and the Baron took it. He told him what had happened to Leon. Tears coursed down the Baron's proud face. Neither spoke. Both of them had lost the person they had loved most in the world.

8

WHEN ANNE KANE first read the report of the sinking of the *Titanic* in *The Times*, she simply refused to believe it. Her husband must still be alive.

After she'd read the article a third time, she burst into uncontrollable tears, something William had never witnessed in the past, and wasn't quite sure how to handle.

Before he could ask what had caused this uncharacteristic outburst, his mother smothered him in her arms and clung tightly to him. How could she tell him that they had both lost the person they most loved in the world?

—◦—

Sir David Seymour arrived at the Savoy a few minutes later, accompanied by his wife. They waited in the lounge while the widow put on the only dark clothes she had with her. William dressed himself, still not certain what a calamity was. Anne asked Sir David to explain the full implications of the tragedy to her son.

When he was told that the great liner had hit an iceberg and sunk, all William said was, 'I wanted to be on the ship with Daddy, but they wouldn't let me go.' He didn't cry, because he refused to believe that anything could kill his father. He would surely be among the survivors.

In Sir David's long career as a politician, diplomat and now chairman of Kane and Cabot, London, he had never seen such self-containment in one so young. 'Presence is bestowed on very few,' he was heard to remark some years later. 'It was bestowed on Richard Kane, and was passed on to his only son.'

On Thursday of that week William turned six, but he didn't open any of his presents.

The names of the survivors, listed in *The Times* every morning, were checked and double-checked by Anne. Richard Lowell Kane was still missing at sea, presumed drowned. But it was to be another week before William abandoned hope of his father's survival. On the fifteenth day, William cried.

Anne found it painful to board the *Aquitania*, but William seemed strangely eager to put to sea. Hour after hour he would sit on the observation deck, scanning the dark grey water of the ocean.

'Tomorrow I will find him,' he promised his mother again and again, at first confidently but later in a voice that barely disguised his own disbelief.

'William, no one can survive for three weeks in the North Atlantic.'

'Not even my father?'

'Not even your father.'

◄◦►

When Anne and William arrived back in Boston, both grandmothers were awaiting them at the Red House, mindful of the duty that had been thrust upon them. Anne passively accepted their proprietary role. Life had little purpose left for her other than William, whose destiny his grandmothers now seemed determined to control. William was polite but uncooperative. During the day he sat silently through his lessons with Mr Munro, and at night he held his mother's hand, but neither spoke.

'What he needs is to be with other children,' declared Grandmother Cabot. Grandmother Kane agreed. The following day they dismissed Mr Munro and the nurse and sent William to Sayre Academy, in the hope that an introduction to the real world, and the constant company of other children, might bring him back to his old self.

Richard had left the bulk of his estate to William, to remain in trust until his twenty-first birthday. There was a codicil attached to the will. Richard expected his son to become president and chairman of Kane and Cabot on merit. It was the only part of his father's testament that inspired William, for the rest was no more than his birthright. Anne received a capital sum of $500,000 and an income for life of $100,000 a year after taxes, which would cease only if she remarried. She also inherited the house on Beacon Hill, the summer mansion on the North Shore, a summer house in the Hamptons and a small island off Cape Cod, all of which were to pass to William on her death. Both grandmothers received $250,000, and letters leaving them in no doubt about their responsibilities should Richard die before them. The trust was to be administered by the bank, with William's godparents acting as co-trustees. The income was to be reinvested each year in conservative enterprises.

It was a full year before the grandmothers came out of mourning, and although Anne was still only twenty-eight, she looked older than her years.

The grandmothers, unlike Anne, concealed their grief from William until he finally reproached them.

'Don't you miss my father?' he demanded, gazing at Grandmother Kane, his blue eyes bringing back memories of her son.

'Yes, child. But he would not have wished us to sit around feeling sorry for ourselves.'

'But I want us to always remember him – always,' said William, his voice cracking.

'William, I am going to speak to you for the first time as though you were quite grown up. We will always keep his memory hallowed between us, and you shall play your own part by living up to what your father would have expected of you. You are now the head of the family and heir to his estate. You must therefore prepare yourself, through diligence and hard work, to be fit for such a responsibility, in the same spirit in which your father carried out his duties.'

William didn't respond, but he immediately began acting upon his grandmother's advice. He learned to live with his sorrow without ever complaining, and from that moment on he threw

himself steadfastly into his work at school, satisfied only if Grandmother Kane seemed impressed. At no subject did he fail to
excel, and in mathematics he was not only top of his class, but
far ahead of his years. Anything his father had achieved, he was
determined to better. He grew even closer to his mother, and
became suspicious of anyone who was not family, so that he was
often thought of by his contemporaries as a solitary child, a loner
and, unfairly, a snob.

The grandmothers decided on William's eighth birthday that
the time had come for the boy to learn the value of money. With
this in mind, they allocated him one dollar a week as pocket
money, but insisted that he keep an inventory accounting for
every cent he spent. Grandmother Kane presented him with a
green leather-bound ledger, at a cost of 95 cents, which she
deducted from his first week's allowance. From then on the
grandmothers divided the dollar up every Saturday morning.
William could invest 50 cents, spend 20 cents, give 10 cents to
charity and keep 20 cents in reserve. At the end of each quarter
they would inspect the ledger and his written report on any
unusual transactions.

After the first three months had passed, William was well
prepared to account for himself. He had given $1.30 to the
recently founded Boy Scouts of America, and invested $5.55,
which he had asked Grandmother Kane to deposit in a savings
account at the bank of his godfather, J. P. Morgan. He had spent
$2.60 on a bicycle, and had kept $1.60 in reserve. The ledger was
a source of great satisfaction to the grandmothers, even if they
weren't certain about the bicycle: there was no doubt William was
the son of Richard Kane.

—◦—

At school, William made few friends, partly because he was shy
of mixing with anyone other than Cabots, Lowells or children
from families wealthier than his own. This restricted his choice
somewhat, so he became a rather broody child, which worried his
mother. She did not approve of the ledger or the investment
programme, and would have preferred William to lead a more

normal existence: to have lots of young friends rather than a couple of elderly advisors; to get himself dirty and bruised, not always remaining neat and spotless; to collect toads and turtles rather than stocks and company reports – in short, to be like any other little boy. But she never had the courage to voice her misgivings to the grandmothers, and in any case, they were not interested in any other little boy.

–◄◊►–

On his ninth birthday William presented the ledger to his grandmothers for their annual inspection. The green leather book showed a saving during the past year of more than twenty-five dollars. He was particularly proud to point out to the grandmothers an entry marked 'B6', showing that he had taken his money out of J. P. Morgan's bank immediately on hearing of the death of the great financier, because he had noted that stock in his father's bank had fallen in value after the death had been announced. William had reinvested the same amount three months later, making a healthy profit.

The grandmothers were suitably impressed, and allowed William to trade in his old bicycle and purchase a new one. At his request Grandmother Kane invested his remaining capital in the Standard Oil Company of New Jersey. The price of oil, William asserted, could only rise now that Mr Ford had sold over a million model Ts. He kept the ledger meticulously up to date until his twenty-first birthday. Had the grandmothers still been alive then, they would have been proud of the final entry in the right-hand column marked ASSETS.

–◄◊►–

In September 1915, following a relaxed summer holiday at the family house in the Hamptons, William returned to Sayre Academy. Once he was back at school, he began to look for competition among pupils older than himself. Whatever he took up, he was never satisfied until he excelled at it, and beating his contemporaries provided him with few challenges. He began to realize that most people from backgrounds as privileged as his lacked any real incentive to compete, and that fiercer rivalry was to be found from boys who had not been born with his advantages. He even wondered if it was an advantage to be disadvantaged.

In 1915 a craze for collecting matchbox labels hit Sayre Academy. William observed this frenzy for several days but did not join in. Within a fortnight, common labels were changing hands for a dime, while rarer examples commanded as much as fifty cents. William considered the situation for another week, and although he had no interest in being a collector, he decided this was the moment to become a dealer.

On the following Saturday he visited Leavitt and Pierce, one of the largest tobacconist's in Boston, and spent the afternoon taking down the names and addresses of major matchbox manufacturers throughout the world, making a special note of those from nations that were not at war. He invested five dollars in notepaper, envelopes and stamps, and wrote to the chairman or president of every company he had listed. His letter was simple and to the point, despite having been redrafted several times.

> *Mr Chairman,*
> *I am a dedicated collector of matchbox labels, but I cannot afford to buy all the boxes. My pocket money is only one dollar a week, but I enclose a three-cent stamp for postage to prove that I am serious about my hobby. I am sorry to bother you personally, but yours was the only name I could find to write to.*
> *Your friend,*
> *William Kane (aged 9)*
> *P.S. Yours are one of my favourites.*

Within two weeks, William had had a 55 per cent rate of reply, which yielded seventy-eight different labels. Nearly all his correspondents also returned the three-cent stamp, as he had anticipated they would.

William immediately opened a label market at school, always checking what he could sell on even before he had made a purchase or swoop. He noticed that some boys had no interest in the rarity of the matchbox labels, only in their appearance, and for them he offered several examples in order to obtain rare trophies for the more discerning collectors. After a further two weeks of buying and selling he sensed that the market had reached its peak, and that if he was not careful, with the Christmas holidays fast approaching, he might end up with surplus stock. With much trumpeted advance publicity in the form of a printed handbill which cost him a half-cent a sheet – placed on every boy's desk – William announced that he would be holding an auction of his matchbox labels, all 211 of them. The auction took place in the school washroom during the lunch hour, and was better attended than most school hockey games.

After the hammer had come down for the final time, William had grossed $56.32, a net profit of $51.32 on his original investment. He put $25 on deposit with the bank at 2.5 per cent interest, bought himself a camera for $10, gave $5 to the Young Men's Christian Association, which had broadened its activities to helping immigrants who were flooding to America from war-torn Europe, bought his mother a bunch of flowers and put the remaining $7 into his cash account. The market in matchbox labels collapsed a few days before term ended. William had got out at the top of the market. The grandmothers nodded sagely when they were informed of the details: it was not dissimilar to the way their husbands had made their fortunes in the panic of 1873.

During the holidays, William could not resist finding out if it was possible to obtain a better return on his capital than the 2.5 per cent yielded on his savings account. For the next three months he invested – again through Grandmother Kane – in stocks recommended by *The Wall Street Journal*. During that time he lost more than half the money he had made on the matchbox labels. He never again relied solely on the expertise of *The Wall Street Journal*. If its correspondents were so well informed, why did they need to work for a newspaper? he concluded.

Annoyed with his loss of almost $30, William decided that it must be recouped during the summer holidays. After he'd worked out which parties and other functions his mother would expect him to attend, he found he was left with only fourteen free days, just enough time to embark upon a new venture. He sold all his remaining *Wall Street Journal* recommended shares, which only netted him $12. With this money he bought a flat piece of wood, a set of pram wheels, axles and a piece of rope, at a cost, after some bargaining, of $5. He then put on a flat cloth cap and an old suit he had outgrown and went off to the central railroad station. William stood outside the exit, looking hungry and tired. He informed selected travellers that the main hotels in Boston were near the station, and there was no need for them to waste their money on a taxi or one of the surviving hansom carriages, as he could transport their luggage on his moving board for 20 per cent of what they charged; he added that the walk would also do them good. Working for six hours a day, he found he could pocket roughly $4.

Five days before the new school term was due to begin, William had made back all his original losses and chalked up a further $9 profit. Then he hit a problem. The taxi drivers were starting to get annoyed with him. He assured them that he would retire, aged ten, if each one of them gave him 50 cents to cover the cost of his homemade dolly. They agreed, and he made a further $8.50. On the way home to Beacon Hill he sold the dolly to a school friend for $2, promising him he would not return to his old beat at the station. The friend quickly discovered that the taxi drivers were lying in wait for him; moreover, it didn't help that it rained for the rest of the week. On the day he returned to school, William put his money back on deposit in the bank, at 2.5 per cent.

Over the following year he watched his savings rise steadily. President Wilson's declaration of war with Germany in April 1917 didn't concern William. Nothing and no one could ever defeat America, he assured his mother. He even invested $10 in Liberty Bonds to back his judgement.

◦

By William's eleventh birthday the credit column of his ledger was showing a profit of $412. He had given his mother a fountain pen for her birthday, and brooches from a local jewellery shop to his two grandmothers. The fountain pen was a Parker, and the jewellery arrived at his grandmothers' homes in Shreve, Crump and Low boxes, which he had found by searching the dustbins behind the famous store. He hadn't wanted to mislead his grandmothers, but he had already learned from his matchbox-label experience that good packaging enhances a product.

The grandmothers noted the missing Shreve, Crump and Low hallmark, but still wore their brooches with considerable pride. They had long ago decided that William was more than ready to proceed to St Paul's School in Concord, New Hampshire, the following September. For good measure he rewarded them with the top mathematics scholarship, unnecessarily saving the family some $300 a year. He accepted the scholarship but the grandmothers returned the grant for the benefit of 'a less fortunate child'.

Anne hated the thought of William going away to boarding school, but the grandmothers insisted and, more important, she knew it was what Richard had wanted. She sewed on William's name tapes, marked his boots, checked his clothes and finally packed his trunk, refusing any help from the servants. When the time came for him to leave, she asked him how much pocket money he would need for the term ahead.

'None, thank you, Mama,' he replied without further comment.

William kissed his mother on the cheek and marched off down the path wearing his first pair of long trousers, his hair cut short, and carrying a small suitcase. He climbed into the car and Roberts drove him off. He didn't look back. His mother waved and waved, and later cried. William wanted to cry, but he knew his father would not have approved.

-<o>-

The first thing that struck William Kane as strange about his new prep school was that the other boys didn't seem to know who he was. The looks of admiration, the silent acknowledgement of his position, were not apparent. One boy even asked his name and, worse, showed no reaction when told. Some even called him 'Bill', which he corrected with the explanation that no one had ever referred to his father as 'Dick'.

William's new castle was a small room with wooden book-shelves, two tables, two chairs, two beds and a comfortably shabby leather settee. One chair, table and bed were occupied by a boy from New York called Matthew Lester, whose father was chair-man of Lester and Company, another old family bank.

William quickly became used to the school routine: up at seven-thirty, wash, and breakfast in the main dining room with the rest of the school – 220 boys munching their way through porridge, eggs and bacon. After breakfast, chapel, three 45-minute classes before lunch and two after, followed by a music lesson, which William detested because he couldn't sing a note in tune, and he had no desire to learn to play any musical instrument. He ended up at the back on the triangle. Football in the fall, hockey and racquetball in the winter, rowing and tennis in the spring left him with little free time. As a mathematics scholar, he had tutorials in the subject three times a week with his housemaster, Mr G. Raglan, Esq., known to the boys as Rags, because of his scruffy appearance.

During his first year William proved to be well worthy of his scholarship, always among the top few boys in almost every subject, and in a class of his own at mathematics. Only his new friend Matthew Lester was any real competition, and that was almost certainly because they shared a room. William also acquired a reputation as a bit of a financial expert. Although his first investment in the stock market had proved unsuccessful, he did not abandon his belief that to make a significant amount of money, sizeable capital gains on the market were essential. He kept a wary eye on *The Wall Street Journal* and company reports, and started to experiment with a ghost portfolio of investments. He recorded every one of his imaginary purchases and sales, the good and the not-so-good, in a newly acquired, different-coloured ledger. He compared his performance at the end of each month against the rest of the market. He did not bother with the leading stocks, concentrating instead on more obscure companies, some of which only traded over the counter, so that it was impossible to buy more than a few shares at any one time. William looked for four things from his investments: a low multiple of earnings, a high growth rate, strong asset backing and a favourable trading forecast. He found few shares that fulfilled all these rigorous criteria, but when he did, they almost invariably showed him a profit.

The moment he had proved that he was regularly beating the Dow Jones Index with his ghost investment programme, William decided to invest real money: his own money. He started with $100, and during the following year never stopped refining his system. He would always back his profits and cut his losses. Once a stock had doubled in price he would sell half of his holding, trading the stock he still held as a bonus. Some of his early finds, such as Eastman Kodak and Standard Oil, went on to become national leaders. He also backed Sears, a mail-order company, convinced it was a trend that was going to catch on.

By the end of his first year he was advising several of the masters, and even some of the parents.

William Kane was happy at school.

9

WLADEK WAS the only person still alive who knew his way around the dungeons. During those carefree days of hide-and-seek with Leon he had spent many happy hours hidden in the small stone rooms, safe in the knowledge that he could return to the castle whenever it suited him.

There were four dungeons in all. Two of them were at ground level. The smaller of these two was dimly lit by a thin glimmer of sunlight through a grille set high in the stone wall. Down five steps were two more stone rooms that were in perpetual darkness with little air. Wladek led the Baron to the small upper dungeon, where he immediately slumped in a corner, staring silently and fixedly into space; the boy appointed Florentyna to look after him.

As Wladek was the only person who dared to stay in the same room as the Baron, the remaining twenty-four servants never questioned his authority. Thus, at the age of nine, he took on the day-to-day responsibility for his fellow prisoners. The new occupants of the dungeons, reduced to miserable stupefaction by incarceration, appeared to find nothing strange in a situation that had put a young boy in control of their lives. In the dungeons Wladek became their master. He split the servants into three groups of eight, trying to keep families together wherever possible. He moved them regularly in a shift system: eight hours in the upper dungeon for light, air, food and exercise, eight hours working in the castle for their captors, and eight hours given over to sleep in one of the lower dungeons.

No one except the Baron and Florentyna could be quite sure

when Wladek slept, as he was always there at the end of every shift to supervise the servants as they moved on. Food was distributed every twelve hours. The guards would hand over a skin of goat's milk, black bread, millet and occasionally some nuts, all of which Wladek would divide into twenty-eight portions, giving two portions to the Baron without ever letting him know.

Once Wladek had the new shift organized, he would return to the Baron in the smaller dungeon. To begin with he expected guidance from him, but the fixed gaze of his master was as implacable and comfortless as were the cold eyes of the constant succession of German guards. The Baron had not spoken from the moment he had been made captive in his own castle. His beard had grown long and matted, and his burly frame was beginning to decline into frailty. The once proud look had been replaced with one of resignation. Wladek could scarcely remember his soft-baritone voice, and accustomed himself to the thought that he would never hear it again. After a while he fell in with what appeared to be the Baron's unspoken wishes, and always remained silent in his presence.

While he had lived in the castle before the arrival of the German soldiers, Wladek had so much to occupy him that he never had time to think about the previous day. Now he was unable to recall even the previous hour, because nothing ever changed. Hopeless minutes turned into hours, hours into days, days into months. Only the changing of the servants' shifts, and the arrival of food, darkness or light, indicated the passing of the time, while the shortening of the days, and the appearance of ice on the dungeon walls, heralded the changing season. During the long nights Wladek became aware of the stench of death that permeated even the farthest corners of the dungeons, only slightly alleviated by the morning sunshine, a cool breeze or the most blessed relief of all, the sound of falling rain.

At the end of a day of unremitting storms, Wladek and Florentyna took advantage of the rain and washed themselves in a puddle of water that had formed in the cracks on the stone floor. Neither of them noticed that the Baron's eyes flickered when Wladek removed his tattered shirt and splashed the cold water onto his body. Without warning, the Baron spoke.

'Wladek,' – the word was barely audible – 'I cannot see you clearly.' His voice was cracking. 'Come to me, child.'

After so long a silence, Wladek was taken by surprise by the Baron's voice and feared it preceded the madness that already held two of the older servants in its grip.

'Come to me, child,' the Baron repeated.

Wladek obeyed fearfully, and stood before the Baron, who narrowed his enfeebled eyes in a gesture of intense concentration. He groped towards the boy and ran a finger over Wladek's chest, before peering up at him.

'Wladek, can you explain this deformity?'

'No, sir,' replied Wladek, embarrassed. 'It has been with me since birth. My father told me that it was the mark of the devil upon me.'

'Stupid man. But then, he was not your father,' the Baron said softly, and relapsed into silence. Wladek remained standing in front of him, not moving a muscle. When the Baron finally spoke again, his voice was firmer. 'Sit down, boy.'

As he did so, Wladek noticed once again the heavy band of silver, now hanging loosely around the Baron's wrist. A shaft of light made the magnificent engraving of the Rosnovski coat of arms glitter in the darkness of the dungeon.

'I do not know how long the Germans intend to keep us locked up here,' continued the Baron. 'I thought at first this war would be over in a matter of weeks. I was wrong, and we must now consider the possibility that it will continue for a very long time. With that thought in mind, we must use our time more constructively, as I know my life is nearing an end.'

'No, no,' Wladek began to protest, but the Baron continued as if he had not heard him.

'Yours, my child, has yet to begin. I will therefore undertake the continuation of your education.'

The Baron did not speak again that day. It was as if he was considering the full implications of his pronouncement. But during the following weeks Wladek found that he had gained a new tutor. As they had neither reading nor writing materials, his lessons consisted of repeating everything the Baron said. He learned great tracts from the poems of Adam Mickiewicz and Jan Kochanowski, as well as long passages from *The Aeneid*. In that austere classroom Wladek learned geography and mathematics, and added to his command of languages – Russian, German, French and English. But as before, his happiest moments were the history lessons. The story of his nation through a hundred years of partition, the disappointed hopes for a united Poland, the anguish of his countrymen at Napoleon's crushing defeat by the Russians in 1812. He learned the brave tales of happier times, when King Jan Casimir had dedicated Poland to the Blessed Virgin after repulsing the Swedes at Czestochowa, and how the mighty Prince Radziwill, scholar, landowner and lover of hunting, had held court in his castle near Warsaw.

Wladek's final lesson each day was on the family history of the Rosnovskis. Again and again he was told – never tiring of the tale – how the Baron's illustrious ancestor who had served in 1794 under General Dabrowski and then in 1809 under Napoleon himself had been rewarded by the Emperor with vast tracts of land and a baronetcy. He learned that the Baron's grandfather had sat on the Council of Warsaw, and his father had played his own part in the building of a new Poland. Once again time passed quickly, despite the horrendous surroundings of his new classroom.

The Baron continued to tutor him despite his progressively failing sight and hearing. Each day Wladek had to sit closer to him.

The guards at the entrance to the dungeon were changed every four hours, and conversation between them and the prisoners was *strengstenst verboten*. Nevertheless, in snatches and fragments Wladek learned of the progress of the war, of the actions of Hindenburg and Ludendorff, of the November revolution in Russia and her withdrawal from hostilities after the Treaty of Brest-Litovsk.

Wladek began to believe that the only way to escape from the dungeons was death. He wondered if he was equipping himself with knowledge that would be useless as he would never again know freedom.

Florentyna Wladek's sister, mother and closest friend – engaged herself in an unending struggle to keep the Baron's cell clean. Occasionally the guards would provide her with a bucket of sand or straw with which to cover the soiled floor, and the stench would be a little less oppressive for a few days. Vermin scuttled around in the darkness for any dropped scraps of bread or potato, bringing with them disease and a reason not to sleep. The sour smell of stale human and animal urine and excrement assaulted their nostrils, regularly causing Wladek to be sick. He longed to be clean again, and would spend hours gazing out of the little slit in the wall, recalling the steaming tubs of hot water and the rough, perfumed soap with which the *niania* had, so short a distance away but so long ago, removed the dirt of a day's fun, with many a *tut-tut* for his and Leon's muddy knees or dirty fingernails.

–◦–

By the spring of 1918, only fifteen of the twenty-seven captives were still alive. The Baron was still treated by everyone as the master, while Wladek was acknowledged as his steward. Wladek felt saddest for his beloved Florentyna, now twenty. She had long since despaired of life. Wladek never admitted in her presence to giving up hope, but although he was only twelve, he too was beginning to wonder if there was any future outside the dungeons.

One evening, in early autumn, Florentyna came to Wladek's side in the larger upper dungeon.

'The Baron is calling for you.'

Wladek rose quickly, leaving the allocation of the food to a trusted servant, and went to join the old man. The Baron was in severe pain, and Wladek saw with terrible clarity how illness had eroded whole areas of his flesh, leaving the green mottled skin covering a now skeletal face. The Baron requested water, and Florentyna rescued some from the half-full mug of rain water that hung from a stick outside the grille in the wall. When the Baron had finished drinking, he spoke slowly and with considerable difficulty.

'You have seen so many people die, Wladek, that one more should make little difference to you. I confess that I no longer fear escaping this world.'

'No, no, it can't be!' cried Wladek, clinging to the old man for the first time in his life. 'Don't give up, Baron. I overheard the guards saying that the war is coming to an end. We will soon be released.'

'They have been saying that for months, Wladek. In any case, I have no desire to live in the new world they are creating.' He paused as the boy began sobbing for the first time in their three years of imprisonment, then said, 'Call for my steward and first footman.'

Wladek obeyed immediately, not knowing why they were required.

The two servants, awakened from sleep, came and stood silently in front of the Baron, waiting for him to speak. They still wore their embroidered uniforms, but there was no longer any sign that they had once boasted the proud Rosnovski colours of green and gold.

'Are they there, Wladek?' asked the Baron.

'Yes, sir. Can you not see them?' Wladek realized for the first time that the Baron was blind.

'Bring them forward so that I might touch them.'

Wladek brought the two men to him, and the Baron touched their faces.

'Sit down, both of you. Can you hear me, Ludwik, Alfons?'

'Yes, sir,' they replied.

'My name is Baron Rosnovski.'

'We know, sir,' the steward responded innocently.

'Do not interrupt me,' said the Baron. 'I am about to die.'

Death had become so commonplace in the dungeon that the two men made no protest.

'I am unable to make a new will, as I have no paper, quill or ink. Therefore I make my testament in your presence, and you can act as my two witnesses, as recognized by the ancient law of Poland. Do you understand what I am telling you?'

'Yes, sir,' the two men replied in unison.

'My firstborn son, Leon, is dead' – the Baron paused – 'and so I leave my entire estate and possessions to the boy known as Wladek Koskiewicz.'

Wladek had not heard his surname for many years, and did not immediately comprehend the significance of the Baron's words.

'As proof of my resolve,' the Baron continued, 'I give him the family band.'

The old man slowly raised his right arm, removed the silver band from his wrist and held it out to a speechless Wladek. He clasped the boy firmly to him. 'My son and heir,' he declared as he placed the silver band over his wrist.

Wladek lay in the arms of the Baron all night until he could no longer hear his heart beating and his arms grew cold and stiffened around him. In the morning the Baron's body was removed by the guards, who allowed Wladek to leave the dungeon and bury him by the side of his son, Leon, in the family churchyard. As the body was lowered into its shallow grave, dug by Wladek's bare hands, the Baron's tattered silk shirt fell open. Wladek stared at the dead man's chest. He had only one nipple.

–◦–

On a mild, dry day, late in the autumn of 1918, the prisoners heard several volleys of shots and the sound of a brief struggle. Wladek was sure that the Polish army had come to rescue them, and that he would be able to lay claim to his inheritance. When the German guards deserted their post at the entrance of the dungeons, the rest of the inmates remained huddled in terrified silence in the lower rooms. Wladek stood alone in the doorway, twisting the silver band around his wrist, waiting for their liberators to release him so he could claim what was rightfully his.

Eventually the men who had defeated the enemy appeared and spoke to Wladek in the coarse Slavic tongue which he had learned from his school days to detest even more than German.

The new conquerors seemed to be unaware that this twelve-year-old boy was the master of the land they were trespassing on. They did not speak his tongue. Their orders were clear and not to be questioned: kill anyone who does not accept the Brest-Litovsk agreement, which seceded this region of Poland to the Russians, and send the rest to Camp 201 in Siberia. The Germans had retreated, with only token resistance, behind their new border, while Wladek and his followers waited, ignorant of their impending fate.

After two more nights, Wladek resigned himself to believing that they would be left in the dungeons for the rest of their lives. The new guards did not speak to him, and he began to think that German purgatory had simply been replaced by Russian hell.

On the third day, Russian soldiers stormed the dungeons and dragged fourteen emaciated, filthy bodies out onto the grass in front of the castle. Two of the servants collapsed in the bright light of the midday sun. Wladek had to shield his eyes as they stood in silence and waited for the soldiers' next move. Would it be a bullet, or freedom?

The guards made them strip, and ordered them down to the river to wash. Wladek hid the silver band in his clothes before walking down to the water's edge, his legs feeling weak long before he reached the river. He jumped in, gasping for breath at the sudden coldness of the water, although it felt glorious on his caked, leathery skin. The rest of the prisoners joined him, trying to remove three years of dirt and squalor.

While Wladek was washing, he noticed that the soldiers were laughing and pointing at Florentyna. None of the other women seemed to arouse the same degree of interest. One of the Russians, a large, misshapen oaf, grabbed Florentyna by the arm as she passed him on her way back up the riverbank. He threw her to the ground and quickly pulled down his trousers. Wladek stared in disbelief at the man's swollen, erect penis. He jumped out of the water and ran towards the soldier, who now had Florentyna pinned to the ground. Wladek charged into the soldier's stomach with his head and pummelled him with his fists. The startled man let go of Florentyna, but a second soldier grabbed Wladek, threw him to the ground and jabbed a knee firmly in the middle of his back. The commotion attracted the attention of the other soldiers and they strolled across to watch. Wladek's captor was now laughing, a loud belly laugh with no humour in it.

'Enter the great protector,' said one.

'Come to defend his nation's honour,' said another.

'Let's at least allow him a ringside view,' added the one who was holding him on the ground.

More laughter punctuated the remarks that Wladek couldn't always understand. He watched the naked soldier advance slowly towards Florentyna, who was speechless with fear. Wladek tried desperately to free himself, but he was helpless. The naked man fell clumsily on top of Florentyna and started mauling her. When he slapped her, she tried to fight and turn away; finally he lunged into her. She let out a scream such as Wladek had never heard before. The other soldiers continued talking and laughing among themselves, some not even watching.

'Goddamn virgin,' said the soldier as he withdrew his blood-covered penis.

They all laughed.

'Then you've made it a little easier for me,' said another man.

More laughter. As Florentyna stared into Wladek's eyes, he began to retch. The soldier holding onto him showed little interest, other than to be sure that none of the boy's vomit ended up on his uniform or his shiny boots. The first soldier, his penis still covered in blood, ran down to the river, yelling in triumph as he hit the water. The second man began unbuckling his belt, while another held Florentyna down. The second guard took a little longer over his pleasure, and seemed to gain considerable satisfaction from hitting Florentyna before he finally entered her. She screamed again, but not quite so loud as before.

'Come on, Vladi, you've had long enough.'

The man came out of her and joined his companion at arms in the river. Wladek forced himself to look at Florentyna. She was bruised, and bleeding between the legs. The soldier holding him spoke again.

'Come and take care of the little bastard, Boris. It's my turn.'

The first soldier took hold of Wladek. Again he tried to hit out, but it only made the soldiers laugh even more.

'Now we know the full might of the Polish army.'

The unbearable laughter continued as yet another guard took his turn with Florentyna, who now lay indifferent to his charms.

'I think she's beginning to enjoy it,' he said once he'd finished. A fourth soldier advanced on Florentyna. When he reached her, he turned her over and forced her legs as wide apart as possible, his large hands moving rapidly over her frail body. The scream when he entered her turned into a groan. Wladek counted as sixteen soldiers raped his sister. When the last one was done, he swore and shouted, 'I think I've made love to a dead woman.' This caused them to laugh even louder.

When Wladek's guard finally released him, he ran to Florentyna's side while the soldiers lay on the grass drinking wine and vodka plundered from the Baron's cellar, and devouring bread and meat from the kitchens.

With the help of two of the servants, Wladek carried Florentyna to the edge of the river, and wept as he tried to wash away the blood and dirt. He covered her with his jacket, held her in his arms and kissed her gently on the mouth, the first woman he had ever kissed. As the tears ran down his face onto her bruised body, he felt her go limp. He wept again as he carried her dead body back up the bank. The soldiers fell silent as they watched him walk towards the chapel. He laid her down on the grass beside the Baron's grave and once again started digging with his bare hands. The sinking sun cast a long shadow over the grave by the time he had buried her. He made a little cross with two sticks, and placed it at the head of her grave. He then collapsed on the ground and immediately fell asleep, not caring if he ever woke again.

10

ANNE KANE had become lonely with William away at St Paul's, and a family circle consisting only of the two grandmothers, now approaching old age.

Once she'd passed her thirtieth birthday, Anne began to notice that she no longer made men's heads turn. She decided to pick up the threads severed by Richard's death with some of her old friends. Millie Preston, William's godmother, whom she had known all her life, began inviting her to dinner parties and the theatre, always including an extra man, in the hope of finding a new partner for Anne. Millie's choices were almost always inappropriate, and Anne used to laugh openly at her attempts at matchmaking, until one day, in January 1919, just after William had returned to school for the winter term, she was invited to yet another dinner for four. Millie confessed she had never met her other guest, Henry Osborne, but she thought he had been at Harvard at the same time as her husband John.

'Actually,' confessed Millie over the phone, 'John doesn't know much about him, darling, except that he is rather good looking.'

Henry Osborne was sitting by the fire when Anne walked into the drawing room. He immediately rose to allow Millie to introduce them. A shade over six feet, with dark, almost black eyes, and wavy black hair, he was slim and athletic-looking. Anne felt a quick flash of pleasure that she was paired for the evening with this energetic and handsome man, while Millie had to content herself with a husband who was fading into paunchy middle-age by comparison with his dashing college contemporary. Henry

67

Osborne's arm was in a sling, which almost covered his Harvard tie.

'A war wound?' Anne asked sympathetically.

'No, a skiing accident; trying to go a little too fast on the slopes of Vermont,' he said, laughing.

It was one of those dinners, lately so rare for Anne, at which the time slipped by happily. Henry answered all her inquisitive questions. After leaving Harvard he had worked for a real estate management firm in Chicago, his hometown, but when war was declared he couldn't resist joining up and having a go at the Germans. He had a fund of self-mocking stories about Europe and the life he had led as a young lieutenant, preserving the honour of America on the Marne. Millie and John had not seen Anne laugh so much since Richard's death, and they smiled knowingly at each other when Henry asked if he might drive her home.

'What are you going to do now that you've returned to a land fit for heroes?' she asked as he eased his Stutz out onto Charles Street.

'Haven't really decided,' he replied. 'Luckily, I have a little money of my own, so I don't need to rush into anything. I might even open my own real estate firm right here. I've always felt at home in Boston since my days at Harvard.'

'You won't be returning to Chicago, then?'

'No, there's nothing to lure me back. My parents are both dead, and I'm an only child, so I can start afresh anywhere I choose. Where do I turn?'

'Oh, first on the right,' said Anne. 'It's the red house on the corner.'

Henry parked the car and accompanied Anne to the front door. He said good night, and was gone almost before she had time to thank him for the lift home. She watched his car glide slowly back down Beacon Hill, knowing that she wanted to see him again.

She was delighted, though not entirely surprised, when he telephoned her the following morning.

'Boston Symphony Orchestra, Mozart, conducted by their flamboyant new maestro, next Monday – can I persuade you?'

Anne was a little taken aback when she realized how much she was looking forward to the concert. It seemed so long since an attractive man had courted her.

Henry arrived at the Red House a few minutes after the appointed hour. They shook hands rather formally, before she offered him a scotch highball. Had he noticed that she remembered what he drank?

'It must be pleasant to live on Louisburg Square. You're a lucky girl.'

'Yes, I suppose I am – I've never really given it much thought. I was born and raised on Commonwealth Avenue. If anything, I find this rather cramped.'

'I might buy a house on the Hill myself if I do decide to settle in Boston.'

'They don't come on the market that often,' said Anne, 'but you may be lucky. Hadn't we better be going? I hate being late for a concert and having to tread on other people's toes in the dark.'

Henry glanced at his watch. 'Yes, I agree – wouldn't do to miss the conductor's entrance. But you don't have to worry about anyone's feet except mine. We're on the aisle.'

After the concert, it felt quite natural for Henry to take her arm as they left the theatre and walked to the Grand. The only other person who had done that since Richard's death had been William, and that took considerable persuasion, because he considered it sissy. Once again the hours slipped by for Anne: was it the beautiful music, the excellent food, or simply Henry's company? This time he made her laugh with his stories of Harvard, and cry with his recollections of the war. Although she was well aware that he looked younger than his years, he had done so much with his life that she felt deliciously youthful and inexperienced in his company. She told him about her husband's death, and shed a few tears. He took her hand when she spoke of her son with glowing pride and affection. He said he had always wanted a son. Although he scarcely mentioned Chicago or his own home life, Anne felt sure he must miss his family. When he took her back to Louisburg Square that night, he stayed for a quick drink and kissed her gently on the cheek before he left. Anne went over the evening minute by minute, hoping he had enjoyed himself as much as she had.

They went to the theatre on Tuesday, visited Anne's summer mansion on the North Shore on Wednesday, drove deep into the snow-covered Massachusetts countryside on Thursday, shopped for antiques on Friday and made love on Saturday. After Sunday, they were rarely apart. Millie Preston was 'absolutely delighted' that her matchmaking had finally proved so successful, and went around Boston telling everyone she had been responsible for bringing the two of them together.

The announcement of her engagement that summer came as no surprise to anyone, except William. He had disliked Henry Osborne intensely from the moment that Anne, with a well-founded sense of misgiving, introduced them to each other. Their first conversation took the form of questions, with Henry trying to prove he wanted to be a friend, and monosyllabic replies from William, showing he didn't. And he didn't change his mind. Anne ascribed her son's resentment to an understandable feeling of jealousy: William had been the centre of her life since Richard's death. Moreover, it was perfectly proper that, in William's estimation, no one could possibly take the place of his father. Anne tried to convince Henry that, given time, William would come round to accepting him.

Anne Kane became Mrs Henry Osborne in October of that year. She took her vows at St Paul's Episcopal Cathedral, just as the golden and red leaves were beginning to fall, a little over nine months after she and Henry had first met. William feigned illness in order to avoid the ceremony, and remained at school. The grandmothers did attend, but were unable to hide their disapproval of Anne remarrying, particularly someone who appeared to be so much younger than her.

'It can only end in tears,' predicted Grandmother Kane.

The newlyweds sailed for Greece the following day, and did

not return to the Red House on the Hill until the second week of December, just in time to welcome William home for the Christmas holidays. William was horrified to discover that the house had been redecorated, leaving almost no trace of his father. Over Christmas, his attitude to his new stepfather showed no sign of softening, despite the present – or as William saw it, the bribe – of a new bicycle. Henry accepted this rebuff with surly resignation. It saddened Anne that her wonderful new husband made so little effort to win her son's affection.

William no longer felt at ease in his own home, and as Henry didn't seem to have a job to go to, the boy would often disappear for long periods during the day. Whenever Anne asked where he was going, she received no satisfactory explanation: it certainly wasn't to either grandmother, as both of them were also complaining of not seeing him. When the holidays came to an end, William was only too happy to return to St Paul's, and Henry was not sad to see him leave.

Anne, however, was beginning to feel anxious about both of the men in her life.

11

'UP, BOY! Up, boy!'

One of the soldiers was digging his rifle butt into Wladek's ribs. He sat up with a start, glanced at the freshly dug graves of his sister and the Baron, before he turned to face the soldier.

'I will live to kill you,' he said in Polish. 'This is my home, and you have trespassed on my land.'

The soldier spat on Wladek and pushed him towards the front of the castle, where the surviving servants were waiting in line. Wladek was shocked by the sight of them, painfully unaware of what was about to happen to him. He was made to kneel on the ground and bow his head. He felt a blunt razor scrape across his head as his thick black hair fell to the grass. With ten bloody strokes, like the shearing of a sheep, the job was completed. Head shaven, he was ordered to put on his new uniform, a grey *rubashka* shirt and trousers. Wladek managed to keep the silver band hidden in his clenched fist as he was roughly pushed back into the ranks of the prisoners.

As they stood there – numbers, now, not names – waiting apprehensively for what would happen next, Wladek became conscious of a strange noise in the distance. The great iron gates opened, and through them came a machine like nothing Wladek had ever seen before. It was a large vehicle, but it was not drawn by horses or oxen. All the prisoners stared in disbelief at the moving object. It came to a halt, and the soldiers dragged the reluctant prisoners to it and made them climb aboard. Then the horseless wagon turned a circle, moved back down the path and out through the iron gates. Nobody dared to speak. Wladek sat at the rear of the truck and stared back at the castle, until he could no longer see his inheritance.

The horseless wagon somehow drove itself through the village of Slonim. Wladek would have thought more about how the vehicle worked if he had not been even more worried about where it was taking them. He recognized the road from his school days, but his memory had been dulled by the years in the dungeons, and he could no longer recall where it led. After a few miles the truck came to a halt and they were all pushed out at the local railway station. Wladek had seen it only once before in his life, when he and Leon had gone there to welcome the Baron home from his trip to Warsaw. The guard had saluted them when they walked into the ticket office. This time no one was saluting.

The prisoners were ordered to sit on the platform, and were given goat's milk, cabbage soup and black bread. Of the original twenty-five servants who had been imprisoned in the dungeons, twelve survived: ten men and two women. Wladek took charge, dividing the portions carefully among them. He assumed that they must be waiting for a train, but night fell and they slept below the stars. Paradise compared to the dungeons. Wladek thanked God that the weather was mild.

They spent the next day waiting for a train that never came, followed by another sleepless night, colder than the previous one. Morning came, and still they waited. Finally an engine puffed into the station. Soldiers disembarked, speaking their hateful tongue, but it departed without Wladek's pitiful army. They spent yet another night on the platform.

Wladek lay awake considering how he might escape, but during the night one of his twelve charges made a run for it across the track and was shot down by a guard even before he had reached the far platform. It was the Baron's steward, Ludwik – one of the witnesses to the Baron's will, and Wladek's heritage. His body was left on the track as a warning to anyone else who might try something similar.

On the evening of the third day another train chugged into the station, a great steam locomotive hauling passenger cars and open freight carriages with the word *Cattle* painted on the sides, their floors covered with straw. Several of the carriages were already full of prisoners, but from where, Wladek didn't know. He and his small group were thrown into one of them to begin their journey – but to where? After a wait of several more hours the train started to move out of the station, in a direction that Wladek judged from the setting sun to be eastward.

Armed guards were sitting cross-legged on the roofs of the passenger cars. Throughout the interminable journey an occasional flurry of shots from above resulted in another body being thrown onto the track, making clear the futility of any thought of escape.

When the train stopped at Minsk, they were given their first proper meal – black bread, water, nuts and millet – but then the journey continued. Sometimes they went for three days without seeing another station. Many of the reluctant travellers died of thirst or starvation and were hurled overboard from the moving train, allowing a little more space for those who remained. When the train did come to a halt, they would often wait for a couple of days to allow another train going west the use of the track. These trains that delayed their progress were invariably full of soldiers and Wladek quickly worked out that troop trains had priority over all other transport.

Escape was always uppermost in Wladek's mind, but two things prevented him from taking the risk. First, there was nothing but miles of wilderness on either side of the track; and second, those who had survived the dungeons depended on him. He may have been the youngest, but it was he who organized their food and drink, and tried to sustain their will to live. He was the only one who still believed in the future.

As each day passed and they were taken further east, the temperature grew colder, often falling to 30 degrees below zero. They would lie up against one another in a line on the carriage floor, each body keeping the next one warm. Wladek would recite *The Aeneid* to himself while he tried to snatch some sleep. It was impossible even to turn over unless everyone agreed, so periodically Wladek would slap the side of the carriage, and they would all roll over and face the other way. One night one of the women did not move. Wladek informed the guard, and four of them picked up the body and threw it out of the moving train. The guards then pumped bullets into her to make sure she was not feigning death in an attempt to escape.

Two hundred miles beyond Minsk, they arrived in the town of Smolensk, where they were given warm cabbage soup and black bread. A bunch of new prisoners, who appeared to speak the same tongue as the guards, were thrown into their carriage. Their leader was considerably older than Wladek. Wladek and his eleven remaining companions, ten men and one woman, were immediately suspicious of the new arrivals, so they divided the carriage in half, with the two groups keeping to themselves.

One night, while Wladek lay awake staring at the stars, trying to keep warm, he saw the leader of the Smolenskis crawling towards the last man in his own line. The Smolenski had a short length of rope in his hand, which he slipped round the neck of Alfons, the Baron's first footman, who was sleeping. Wladek knew that if he moved too quickly, the young lad would hear him and escape back to the protection of his comrades. He inched along on his belly down the line of Polish bodies. Eyes stared at him as he passed, but nobody spoke. When he reached the end of the line, he leapt on the aggressor, waking everyone in the carriage. Each faction shrank back, with the exception of Alfons, who lay motionless in front of them.

The Smolenski leader was taller and more agile than Wladek, but that made little difference while the two were scrapping on the floor. The struggle lasted for several minutes, which attracted the attention of the guards, who laughed and made bets on the outcome. One guard, bored by the lack of blood, threw a bayonet into the middle of the carriage. Both boys scrambled for the shining blade, with the Smolenski grabbing it first. His band cheered as he thrust it into the side of Wladek's leg, pulled the blood-covered blade back out and lunged again. This time the bayonet lodged firmly in the wooden floor of the jolting carriage, next to Wladek's ear. As the Smolenski boy tried to wrench it free, Wladek kicked him in the crotch with every ounce of energy he could muster, and his adversary fell back, letting go of the bayonet. Wladek grabbed it, jumped on top of the Smolenski, and thrust the blade into his mouth. The boy gave out a shriek of agony that awoke the entire train. Wladek pulled the blade out, twisting it as he did so, and thrust again and again, long after the Smolenski had ceased to move. Finally Wladek knelt over him, breathing heavily, picked up the body and threw it out of the carriage. He heard the thud as it hit the bank, followed by the shots the guards pointlessly pumped into it.

Wladek limped towards Alfons and fell onto his knees, suddenly aware of a cold, aching pain in his leg. He shook the lifeless body: his second witness was dead. Who would now believe that he was the chosen heir to the Baron's estate? Was there any reason left to live? He picked up the bayonet with both hands and pressed the blade against his stomach. Immediately a guard jumped down into the carriage and wrested the weapon from him.

'Oh, no you don't,' he grunted. 'We need the lively ones like you for the camps. You can't expect us to do all the work.'

Wladek buried his head in his hands. He had lost his inheritance, in exchange for a dozen penniless Smolenskis.

—◦—

The whole carriage was Wladek's domain, and he now had twenty prisoners to care for. He split them up so that a Pole would always sleep next to a Smolenski, which he hoped would reduce the likelihood of any further warfare between the rival gangs.

He spent a considerable part of each day learning the Smolenskis' strange tongue. He did not realize for several days that it was Russian, so greatly did it differ from the classical language taught to him by the Baron. But then the real significance of this discovery dawned on him when he worked out where the train was heading.

During the day, Wladek took on two Smolenskis at a time to tutor him, and as soon as they grew tired, he would select another two, and so on until they were all exhausted. It was not long before he was able to converse fluently with his new dependants.

Some of them he discovered were Russian soldiers, taken prisoner after repatriation for the crime of having been captured by the Germans. The rest consisted of White Russians – farmers, miners, labourers – all bitterly hostile to the Revolution.

The train jolted on past terrain more barren than Wladek had ever seen before, and through towns of which he had never heard – Omsk, Novosibirsk, Krasnoyarsk: the names rang ominously in his ears. Finally, after two months and more than three thousand miles, they reached Irkutsk, where the track came to an end.

All the prisoners were hustled off the train, fed and issued with grey uniforms with numbers on the back, felt boots, jackets and heavy coats. Although fights broke out for the warmest garments, even the most sought-after provided little protection from the wind and snow.

Horseless wagons like the one that had borne Wladek away from his castle appeared and long chains were thrown out by the guards. The prisoners were then cuffed by one hand, fifty to each chain. They marched behind the trucks, while the guards rode on the back. After twelve hours they were allowed a two-hour rest so the dead and dying could be unchained before the living set off again.

After three days, Wladek thought he would die of cold and exhaustion, but once they were clear of populated areas they travelled only during the day and rested by night. A mobile field kitchen run by prisoners from the camp supplied turnip soup that became colder, and bread that became staler, as each day passed. Wladek learned from these prisoners that conditions at the camp were even worse, hence their volunteering for the field kitchen.

For the first week they were never unshackled from their chains, but later, when there could be no thought of escape, they were released at night to sleep, digging holes in the snow to keep warm. Sometimes on good days they found a forest in which to bed down: luxury began to take strange forms. On and on they marched, past vast lakes and across frozen rivers, ever northward, in the teeth of viciously cold winds and over deeper drifts of snow. Wladek's wounded leg gave him a constant dull pain, soon surpassed by the agony of his frostbitten toes, fingers and ears.

The old and the sick were dying. The lucky ones, quietly as they slept. The unlucky ones, unable to keep up the pace, were uncuffed from the chains and cast off to die alone. Wladek lost all sense of time, and was conscious only of the tug of the chain, not knowing when he dug his hole in the snow at night whether he would wake the next morning. Those who didn't had dug their own graves.

After a trek of nine hundred miles, the survivors were met by Ostyaks, nomads of the steppes, in reindeer-drawn sleds. The prisoners were chained to the sleds and marched on. When a blizzard forced them to halt for the best part of two days, Wladek seized the opportunity to try to communicate with the young Ostyak to whose sled he was chained. He discovered that the Ostyaks hated the Russians of the south and west, who treated them almost as badly as they treated their captives. The Ostyaks were not unsympathetic to the sad prisoners with no future, the 'unfortunate ones', as they called them.

12

THE FUTURE was also worrying Anne. The first few months of her marriage had been happy, marred only by her anxiety over William's increasing dislike of her husband, and Henry's seeming inability to find a job. Henry was a little touchy on the subject, explaining that he was still disoriented by the war, and wasn't willing to rush into something he might later regret. She found this hard to understand, and finally the matter caused their first row.

'I can't understand, Henry, why you haven't set up that real estate business you seemed so keen on before we were married.'

'The time isn't quite right, my darling. The realty market isn't looking promising at the moment.'

'You've been saying that for nearly a year. I wonder if it will ever be promising enough.'

'Sure it will. Truth is, I need a little more capital. Now, if you'd allow me to borrow some of your money, I could get myself started.'

'That's not possible, Henry. You know the terms of Richard's will. My allowance was stopped the day we married, and I only have the capital left.'

'A little of that would be more than enough. And don't forget that precious boy of yours has over twenty million in his family trust.'

'You are not to know a ha'penny of William's trust,' Anne said.

'Oh, come on, Anne, give me a chance to be your husband. Don't make me feel like a guest in my own home.'

'What's happened to your money, Henry? You always led me to believe you had enough to start your own business.'

'You've always known I wasn't in Richard's league financially, and there was a time, Anne, when you said it didn't matter: "I'd marry you, Henry, if you were penniless,"' he mocked.

Anne burst into tears, and Henry tried to console her. She spent the rest of the evening in his arms, neither of them referring to the subject again. She managed to convince herself she was being unfair, and lacking understanding. She had more money than she could ever possibly need. Shouldn't she entrust a little of it to the man to whom she was so willing to entrust the rest of her life?

The next morning, she agreed to let Henry have $100,000 to set up his own real estate business in Boston. Within a month he had rented a smart new office in a fashionable part of town, appointed a staff of six and started work. Soon he was mixing with influential city politicians and established real estate men of Boston. They drank with him in their clubs and talked of the boom in farmland. They told him of investments that couldn't lose, and joined him at the race-track. They put him up for expensive country clubs where he would meet future clients. It wasn't long before Anne's $100,000 had disappeared.

—◇—

When William celebrated his fifteenth birthday, he was in his third year at St Paul's, sixth in his class overall, and top in mathematics. He had also become a rising figure in the Debating Society, if not on the sports field.

He wrote to his mother once a week, reporting his progress, always addressing his letters to Mrs Richard Kane, refusing to acknowledge that Henry Osborne even existed. Anne wasn't sure whether she should talk to him about it, and she was careful to hide the envelopes from Henry. She continued to hope that in time William would come around to liking her husband, but as the months passed it became clear that such a hope was un-realistic. William hated Henry Osborne, and nursed his hatred passionately, although he wasn't sure what he could actually do about it. He was grateful that Osborne never accompanied her when his mother visited him at school; he could not have tolerated having the other boys see his mother with that man. It was bad enough that he had to live with him in Boston.

In one letter William asked if he could spend the summer holidays with his friend Matthew Lester, first at a summer camp in Vermont, then with the Lester family in New York. The request came as a painful blow to Anne, but she took the easy way out and gave her permission. Henry seemed quite happy to go along with her decision.

For the first time since his mother's marriage, William was looking forward to the holidays.

◄○►

The Lesters' Packard chauffeured William and Matthew noiselessly to the summer camp in Vermont. On the journey, Matthew casually asked William what he intended to do when the time came for him to leave St Paul's.

'When I leave, I will be the top student of our year, class president, and will have won the Hamilton Memorial Mathematics Scholarship to Harvard,' replied William without hesitation.

'Why is all that so important?' Matthew asked innocently.

'My father achieved all three.'

'When you've finished battling with your father, I'll introduce you to mine.'

William smiled.

The two boys had a lively and enjoyable six weeks in Vermont, playing every game, from chess to football. When camp finally broke up, they packed and boarded a train for New York to spend the last month of the holiday with the Lester family.

They were greeted at the door by a butler, who addressed Matthew as 'Sir', and by a twelve-year-old girl covered in freckles who called him 'Fatty'. It made William laugh, because his friend was so slim, while it was she who was overweight. The girl smiled, revealing teeth almost totally hidden behind braces.

'You'd never believe Susan was my sister, would you?' said Matthew disdainfully.

'No, I wouldn't,' said William, smiling at Susan. 'She's so much better looking than you.'

Susan adored William from that moment on.

William adored Matthew's father the moment they met; he reminded him in so many ways of his own father, and he begged Mr Lester to let him visit the great bank of which he was chairman. Charles Lester thought carefully about the request. No child had ever entered the orderly precincts of 17 Broad Street before, not even his own son. He compromised, as bankers often do, and showed the boy around the Wall Street building on a Sunday afternoon.

William was fascinated by the large offices on so many floors, the vaults, the foreign exchange dealing room, the boardroom, but most of all the chairman's office. The Lester bank's activities were considerably more wide-ranging than Kane and Cabot's, and William knew from his own small personal investment account, which provided him with a copy of the annual general report, that Lester's had a far larger capital base than Kane and Cabot. He remained silent as they were driven back to the Lesters' home.

'Well, William, did you enjoy looking around?' Charles Lester asked eventually.

'Oh yes, sir,' replied William. 'I certainly did.' He paused for a moment before adding, 'But I feel I should warn you, sir, that it's my intention to be chairman of your bank one day.'

Charles Lester smiled. He told his dinner guests that night about young William Kane's visit to Lester and Company, and the fact that he was after his job. His guests laughed. But William had not meant the remark as a joke.

—◇—

Anne was shocked when Henry asked her for another loan.

'It's as safe as houses,' he assured her. 'Ask Alan Lloyd. As chairman of the bank, he can only have your best interests at heart.'

'But two hundred and fifty thousand?' Anne queried.

'A once in a lifetime opportunity, my darling. Look upon it as an investment that will double within a couple of years.'

After another, prolonged row, with several mentions of Richard and William thrown in, Anne gave in once again, and life returned to normal. When she next checked her investment portfolio with the bank, she found her capital was now only $150,000. However, Henry seemed to be seeing all the right people, and kept repeating that he was about to sign an 'impossible to lose' deal. She considered discussing the situation with Alan Lloyd at Kane and Cabot, but decided against it; after all, it would have meant questioning her husband's judgement. And surely Henry would never have made the suggestion in the first place if he hadn't been sure the loan would meet with Alan's approval.

Anne had started seeing Dr MacKenzie again to find out if there was any possibility of her having another baby, but he still advised against it. After the high blood pressure that had caused her earlier miscarriage, he did not consider thirty-six a sensible age for Anne to start thinking about being a mother again. Anne raised the idea with the grandmothers, but they agreed wholeheartedly with the views of the good doctor. Neither of them cared for Henry much, and they cared even less for the thought of an Osborne offspring making claims on the Kane family estate after they departed this world. Anne resigned herself to being the mother of only one child, but Henry became very vocal about what he described as her betrayal, telling her that if Richard were still alive, she would have tried again. How different the two men were, she thought, and she was unable to explain why she loved them both. She tried to soothe Henry, praying that his business projects would work out and keep him fully occupied, while at the same time replenishing her dwindling coffers. He had certainly taken to working very late at the office.

13

NINE DAYS later, in the half-light of an early Arctic winter night, Wladek and his band reached Camp 201. Wladek would never have believed he could be glad to see such a place: row upon row of wooden huts in the midst of a stark, barren wilderness. The huts, like the prisoners, were numbered. Wladek's hut was number 33. There was a small black stove in the middle of the room, and along the walls were tiered wooden bunks on which rested hard straw mattresses with one thin blanket each. Few of the prisoners managed to sleep that first night, as they had become accustomed to sleeping in the snow. The groans and cries that came from Hut 33 were often louder than the howls of the wolves outside.

Long before the sun rose the next morning, they were roused by the sound of a hammer against an iron triangle. There was thick frost on the insides of the windows, and Wladek thought he must surely die of the cold. Breakfast in a freezing communal hall lasted for ten minutes, and consisted of a bowl of lukewarm gruel with pieces of rotten fish and the suggestion of a cabbage leaf floating in it. The newcomers spat the fish bones out onto the table, while the more seasoned prisoners devoured the bones and even ate the fishes' eyes.

After breakfast, the new prisoners' heads were once again roughly shaved, and then they were allocated tasks. Wladek became a wood chopper. He was taken several miles through the featureless steppes to a forest where he was ordered to cut down ten trees each day. The guard would leave him and his little group of six alone with their food ration, tasteless yellow magara porridge and bread. They had no fear that the prisoners would attempt to escape, as it was more than a thousand miles to the nearest town – even if they knew in which direction to head.

At the end of the day the guard would return and count the number of trees they had felled: if they failed to reach the required number, their food ration would be reduced the following day. But by the time the guard arrived at seven in the evening it was already dark, and he could not always be sure how many new trees they had cut down. Wladek taught the others in his team to spend the last part of the afternoon clearing the snow off two or three trunks they had cut down on the previous day and line them up with those they had chopped that day. The plan always worked, and Wladek's group never lost a day's food. Sometimes they managed to return to the camp with a small piece of wood, tied to the inside of a leg, to put in the stove at night. Caution was required, as there was always a risk they would be searched as they entered the camp, often having to remove one or both boots while they stood in the frozen snow. If they were caught with anything on their person, the punishment was three days without food.

As the weeks went by, Wladek's leg became stiff and painful. He longed for the days when the temperature dropped to 40 below zero, and outside work was called off, even though the lost day would have to be made up on the following Sunday, when they were normally allowed to lie on their bunks all day.

One evening when Wladek had been hauling logs across the waste, his leg began to throb unmercifully. When he looked at the scar he found that it had become red and inflamed. He showed it to a guard, who ordered him to report to the camp doctor before first light in the morning. Wladek sat up all night with his leg almost touching the stove, but the heat was so feeble it didn't ease the pain.

The next morning Wladek rose an hour earlier than usual. If he didn't see the doctor before work was due to start, he would have to wait until the next day. Wladek couldn't face another day of such excruciating pain. He reported to the doctor, giving his name and number. The doctor turned out to be a sympathetic old man, bald-headed, with a pronounced stoop – Wladek thought he looked even older than the Baron had in his final days. He inspected Wladek's leg without speaking.

'Will the wound heal, Doctor?' asked Wladek.

'You speak Russian?'

'Yes, sir.'

'No need to call me sir. My name is Dubien. I'm a prisoner just like you.' Wladek looked surprised. 'Although you will always limp, young man,' he continued, 'your leg will be good again. But good for what? A life of chopping wood in this God forsaken place?'

'No, Doctor. I intend to escape and get back to Poland,' said Wladek.

The doctor looked sharply at him. 'Keep your voice down, stupid boy . . . You must know by now that escape is impossible. I have been here for fifteen years, and not a day has gone by when I haven't dreamed of escaping. There is no way; no one has ever escaped and survived, and even to talk of it means ten days in the punishment cell, where they feed you every third day, and there's no stove. If you come out of that place alive, you wish you were dead.'

'I will escape. I will, I will,' said Wladek, staring at the old man.

The doctor looked into Wladek's eyes. 'My friend, never mention the word again, or they may kill you. Go back to work, keep your leg well covered, and report to me again tomorrow morning.'

Wladek returned to the forest, but the pain was so intense he could do little work. The next morning, the doctor examined his leg more carefully.

'Worse, if anything,' he said. 'How old are you, boy?'

'What year is it, Dr Dubien?' asked Wladek.

'1919.'

'Then I'm thirteen. How old are you, Doctor?'

The man seemed surprised by the question. 'Thirty-eight,' he said quietly.

'God help me,' said Wladek.

'You will look like this when you have been a prisoner for fifteen years, my boy,' the doctor said matter-of-factly.

'Why are you here at all?' said Wladek. 'Why haven't they let you go after all this time?'

'Let the one doctor they have here go?' He laughed. 'I was taken prisoner in Moscow in 1904, soon after I had qualified as a doctor in Paris. I was working in the French embassy at the time, and they said I was a spy and locked me up. After the Revolution, they sent me, without trial, to this hellhole. Even the French have forgotten that I exist. In any case, no one would believe there is such a place as this. Nobody has ever completed a sentence at Camp 201, so I will die here, like everyone else, and it can't be too soon.'

'No, you mustn't give up hope, Doctor.'

'Hope? I gave up hope for myself a long time ago. Perhaps I shall not give up for you. But always remember never to mention that word to anyone; there are prisoners here who will trade in loose tongues for nothing more than an extra piece of bread or a thicker blanket. Now, Wladek, I am going to put you on kitchen duty for a month, but you must continue to report to me every morning. It is the only chance you have of not losing that leg, and I would not relish being the man who has to cut it off. We don't exactly have the latest surgical instruments here,' he added, glancing at a large carving knife hanging on the wall. Wladek shuddered.

Dr Dubien wrote Wladek's name on a slip of paper, and the following morning he reported to the kitchens, where he washed plates in freezing water and helped to prepare what passed as food. He found it a welcome change from chopping logs all day: extra fish soup, thick black bread with shredded nettles, and the chance to remain inside and keep warm. On one occasion the cook even shared half an egg with him, although neither of them could be sure what fowl had laid it. Wladek's leg took some time to mend, and left him with a pronounced limp. There was little Dr Dubien could do for him in the absence of any real medical supplies, except to keep a watchful eye on his progress.

As the days passed, the doctor and Wladek became friends.

They would converse in a different language each morning, but Dubien most enjoyed speaking in French, his native tongue; something he hadn't done for fifteen years.

'In seven days' time, Wladek, you will have to return to forest duty; the guards will inspect your leg and I will not be able to keep you in the kitchen any longer. So listen carefully, for I have been working on a plan for your escape.'

'Together, Doctor,' said Wladek. 'Together.'

'No, only you. I am too old for such a long journey, and although I have dreamed of escape, I would only hold you up. It will be enough for me to know that someone has achieved it, and you are the first person I've met here who has convinced me that he just might succeed.'

Wladek listened in silence as the doctor outlined his plan.

'I have, over the last fifteen years, saved two hundred roubles – you don't get paid overtime when you work for the Russians.' Wladek tried to laugh at the camp's oldest joke. 'I keep the money hidden in a medicine bottle, four 50-rouble notes. When the time comes for you to leave, I will have fastened the money into your clothes.'

'What clothes?' asked Wladek.

'I have a suit, a shirt and a cap. I traded them with a guard in exchange for medicine some twelve years ago, when I still believed that one day I might escape. Not exactly the latest fashion, but they will serve your purpose.'

Fifteen years to scrape together two hundred roubles, a shirt, a suit and a cap, and the doctor was willing to sacrifice his bounty to Wladek in a moment. Never in his life had Wladek experienced such an act of selflessness.

'Next Thursday will be your one chance,' the doctor continued. 'New prisoners are due to arrive by train at Irkutsk, and the guards always take four men from the kitchen to organize the food trucks for the new arrivals. I have already arranged with Stanislav, the senior cook' – he laughed at the word – 'that in exchange for some drugs you will find yourself on the kitchen truck. It was not difficult. No one ever wants to make the trip there and back – but you will only be going one way.'

Wladek was still listening intently.

'When you reach the station, wait until the train arrives. Once the new prisoners are all on the platform, cross the line and get onto the train going to Moscow, which cannot leave until the prisoners' train comes in, as there is only one track. You must pray that with hundreds of new prisoners milling around, the guards will not notice your absence. From then on you'll be on your own. If they spot you escaping, they will shoot you without a second thought. There is only one more thing I can do to help. Fifteen years ago, when I was on that train, I drew a map from memory of the route from Moscow to Turkey. It may no longer be totally accurate so be sure to check that the Russians haven't taken over Turkey as well. God knows what they have been up to recently. They may even control France, for all I know.'

The doctor walked over to the drug cabinet and took out a large bottle that looked as if it was full of a brown substance. He unscrewed the top and removed an old piece of parchment. The black ink had faded over the years. It was marked *October 1904*, and showed a route from the camp to Moscow, from Moscow to Odessa, and from Odessa to Turkey: 1,500 miles to freedom.

'Report to me every morning this week, and we will go over the plan again and again. If you fail, it must not be from lack of preparation.'

◄○►

Wladek stayed awake each night, gazing out of the window at the wolves' moon. He rehearsed what he would do in any situation, preparing himself for every eventuality.

Each day he would go over the plan with the doctor. On the evening before the train was due to arrive, the doctor folded the map into six, and placed it with the four 50-rouble notes in an envelope which he pinned into a sleeve of the suit. Wladek put on the shirt and suit. He had become so thin that the clothes hung on him as if on a coat hanger. As he slipped his uniform over them, the doctor's eye caught the Baron's silver band, which Wladek had always kept above his elbow for fear the guards might spot it and steal it.

'What's that?' he asked. 'It's quite magnificent.'

'A gift from my father,' said Wladek. 'May I give it to you, to show my appreciation?' He slipped it off and handed it to the doctor.

The doctor stared at the silver band for several moments, then bowed his head. 'Never,' he said. 'This can only belong to one person.'

He handed the band back to Wladek and shook him warmly by the hand.

'Good luck, Wladek. I hope we never meet again.'

They embraced, and Wladek departed for what he prayed was his last night in Hut 33. He was unable to sleep that night for fear that one of the other prisoners would notice the suit under his prison clothes and report him to a guard. When the hammer beat on the triangle the next morning, he was the first to report to the kitchen. The senior prisoner pushed him forward when the guards came to select the four members of the truck detail. Wladek was by far the youngest.

'Why this one?' demanded a guard, pointing to Wladek.

Wladek froze. The doctor's plan was going to fail even before they had left the compound, and there wouldn't be another batch of prisoners coming to the camp for at least three months. By then he would no longer be working in the kitchen.

'He's an excellent cook,' said Stanislav. 'He was trained in the castle of a baron. Only the best for the guards.'

'Good,' said the guard, his greed overcoming his suspicion. 'Get moving, then.'

The four prisoners ran to the truck, and the convoy set off. The journey was slow and arduous, but at least Wladek was not walking this time. And as it was summer, it was almost one degree above freezing.

—◦—

It was sixteen days before the convoy arrived at Irkutsk. The train for Moscow was already standing in the station. It had been there for several hours, but was unable to begin its journey until the train bringing the new prisoners had arrived. Wladek sat on the edge of the platform with the three others from the field kitchen. Dulled by their experiences, none of them showed any interest in anything around them. But he was intent on every movement, as he studied the train on the other side of the platform. There were several open doors and Wladek carefully selected the one he would enter when his moment came.

'Are you going to try to escape?' the chief cook asked suddenly.

Wladek began to sweat. He said nothing. Stanislav stared at him. 'You are.' Still Wladek said nothing. The old cook continued to stare at the thirteen-year-old boy; then after a long pause, he smiled. 'Good luck. I'll make sure they don't realize you're missing for as long as I can.'

Stanislav touched his arm, and pointed. Wladek caught sight of the prisoners' train in the distance, slowly inching its way towards them. He tensed in anticipation, his heart pounding, his eyes following the movement of every soldier. At last the incoming train shunted to a halt, and he watched as hundreds of exhausted, anonymous prisoners piled out onto the platform. When the station was a chaos of people and the guards were fully occupied, Wladek ducked under the prisoners' train, ran across the track and jumped aboard the one bound for Moscow. No one showed any interest as he slipped into a lavatory at the end of the carriage. He locked himself in, waited and prayed, expecting someone to knock on the door at any moment. It seemed a lifetime before the train began to move out of the station. It was, in fact, forty-seven minutes.

'At last, at last,' he said out loud. He looked through the little window of the lavatory and watched the station growing smaller and smaller in the distance. A mass of new prisoners were being hitched up to the chains for the journey to Camp 201, the guards laughing as they fastened their cuffs. How many would reach the camp alive? How many would be fed to the wolves? How long would it be before they missed him?

Wladek sat in the lavatory for several more minutes, terrified to move, not knowing what to do next. Suddenly there was a banging on the door. Wladek thought quickly – the guard? The ticket collector? A soldier? – a succession of images flashed through his mind, each one more frightening than the last. The banging persisted.

'Get on with it,' said a deep, coarse voice.

Wladek had little choice. If it was a soldier, there was no way out – a dwarf could not have squeezed through the tiny window. If it wasn't a soldier, he would only draw attention to himself by staying in the lavatory. He stripped off his prison clothes, made them into a small bundle and threw them out of the window. Then he took the soft cap from the pocket of his suit and covered his shaved head, before opening the door. An agitated man pushed in, pulling down his trousers even before Wladek had left.

Once in the corridor, Wladek felt isolated and terrifyingly conspicuous in his out-of-date suit, an apple placed among a pile of oranges. He went in search of another unoccupied lavatory. When he found one, he locked himself in and took one of the 50-rouble notes from the envelope pinned inside his sleeve. He returned to the corridor, looked for the most crowded carriage he could find and pushed himself into a corner. Some men in the middle of the car were playing pitch-and-toss for a few roubles. Wladek had often beaten Leon when they had played the game in the castle, and he would have liked to join in, but he feared it would draw attention to himself. As the game went on, however, Wladek noticed that one of the gamblers was winning consistently, even when the odds were stacked against him. He watched the man more carefully and soon realized that he was cheating.

One of the gamblers, who had lost a considerable amount of money, cursed and left the game when his money ran out. Wladek could feel the warmth of the man's thick sheepskin coat as he sat down beside him.

'The luck wasn't with you,' said Wladek.

'Ah, it's not luck,' the gambler said. 'Most days I could beat that lot of peasants, but I've run out of money.'

'Do you want to sell your coat?'

The gambler stared at Wladek.

'You couldn't afford it, boy.' Wladek could tell from the man's voice that he hoped he could. 'I wouldn't take less than seventy-five roubles.'

'I'll give you forty,' said Wladek.

'Sixty,' said the gambler.

'Fifty,' said Wladek.

'No. Sixty is the least I'd let it go for; it cost over a hundred.'

'That must have been a long time ago,' said Wladek. He didn't want to risk taking more money from the envelope inside his sleeve, as that would draw attention to himself. He touched the collar of the coat and said, with considerable disdain, 'You paid too much for it, my friend. Fifty roubles, not a kopeck more.' Wladek rose as if to leave.

'Wait, wait,' said the gambler. 'All right, I'll let you have it for fifty.'

Wladek took the grimy red 50-rouble note out of his pocket and exchanged it for the coat. It was far too big for him, nearly touching the ground, but it was exactly what he needed to cover his ill-fitting and conspicuous suit. For a few moments he watched the gambler, back in the game, once again losing. He had learned two lessons: never gamble when the odds are tipped against you; and always be ready to walk away from a deal once you have reached your limit.

Wladek left the carriage, feeling a little safer, protected by his new-old coat, and began to examine the layout of the train. The carriages seemed to be in two classes, general ones in which passengers stood, or sat on wooden benches, and special ones with upholstered seats. All the carriages were packed except one of the special ones, in which, inexplicably, there sat a solitary woman. She was middle-aged and dressed more smartly than most of the other passengers. She wore a dark blue dress, and a scarf was drawn over her head. As he stood watching her hesitantly, she smiled at him, giving him the confidence to enter the compartment.

'May I sit down?'

'Please do,' said the woman, looking at him carefully.

Wladek did not speak again, but when he could he studied

the woman and her belongings. She had a sallow skin covered with tired lines, was a little overweight – the little one could be on Russian food. Her short black hair and brown eyes suggested she might have once been attractive. There were two large cloth bags on the overhead rack, and a small valise by her side. Despite the danger of his position, Wladek was suddenly aware of feeling desperately tired. He was just wondering if he dared to sleep, when the woman spoke.

'Where are you travelling?'

The question took him by surprise. 'Moscow.'

'So am I,' she said.

Wladek was already regretting the information he had given, meagre though it was. 'Don't talk to anyone,' the doctor had warned him. 'Remember, trust nobody. Everyone in Russia is a spy.'

To Wladek's relief the woman asked no more questions. But just as he began to regain his confidence, the ticket collector appeared. Wladek started to sweat, despite a temperature of minus 5 degrees. The collector took the woman's ticket, clipped it, gave it back to her then turned to Wladek.

'Ticket, comrade,' he said in a slow monotone.

Wladek started fumbling helplessly around in his coat pocket.

'He's my son,' said the woman firmly.

The ticket collector looked back at her, once more at Wladek, then bowed to the woman and left without another word.

Wladek stared at her. 'Thank you,' he stammered, not knowing what else to say.

'I saw you crawl from under the prisoners' train,' the woman remarked quietly. Wladek felt sick. 'But don't worry, I won't give you away. I have a young cousin in one of those evil camps, and all of us fear that one day we might end up there.' She looked at Wladek for some time before asking, 'What do you have on under the coat?'

Wladek weighed the relative merits of dashing out of the carriage or unfastening his coat. If he dashed out, there was nowhere on the train where he could hide. He unfastened his coat.

'Not as bad as I feared,' she said. 'What did you do with your prison uniform?'

'Threw it out of the window.'

'Let's hope they don't come across it before we reach Moscow.' Wladek said nothing. 'Do you have anywhere to stay in Moscow?'

He thought again about the doctor's advice to trust nobody, but he had to trust her.

'I have nowhere to go.'

'Then you can stay with me until you find somewhere. My husband is the stationmaster in Moscow, and this carriage is for government officials only,' she explained. 'If you ever make that mistake again, you will be taking the next train back to Irkutsk.'

Wladek swallowed. 'Should I leave now?'

'No, not now the ticket collector has seen you. You will be safe with me for the time being. Do you have any identity papers?'

'No. What are they?'

'Since the Revolution every Russian citizen must carry identity papers to show who he is, where he lives and where he works; otherwise he ends up in jail until he can produce them. And as he can never produce them in jail, he stays there forever,' she added matter-of-factly. 'You will have to stay close to me once we reach Moscow. And be sure you don't open your mouth.'

'You are being very kind to me,' Wladek said suspiciously.

'Now the Tsar is dead, no one is safe. I am lucky to be married to the right man. But there is not a citizen in Russia, including government officials, who does not live in constant fear of arrest and the camps. What is your name?'

'Wladek.'

'Good. Now sleep, Wladek, because you look exhausted, and the journey is long and you are not safe yet.'

Wladek slept.

14

It was on a Monday in October, the weekend after they had celebrated their second wedding anniversary, that Anne started receiving the letters from an unsigned 'friend', informing her that Henry had been seen escorting other women around Boston, and one lady in particular, whom the writer didn't care to name.

To begin with, Anne burned the letters, and although they worried her, she never mentioned them to Henry, praying that each would be the last. She couldn't even summon up the courage to raise the matter with him when he asked her to part with her last $150,000.

'I'm going to lose the whole deal if I don't have that money right away, Anne.'

'But it's all I have, Henry. If I give you any more money, I'll be left with nothing.'

'This house alone must be worth over two hundred thousand. You could mortgage it tomorrow.'

'The house belongs to William.'

'William, William, William. It's always William who gets in the way of my success,' shouted Henry as he stormed out of the room.

He returned home after midnight, contrite, and told her he would rather she kept her money and he went under. At least that way they would still have each other. Anne was comforted by his words, and later they made love. She signed a cheque for $150,000 the next morning, trying to forget that it would leave her penniless until Henry pulled off his deal of a lifetime. She couldn't help wondering if it was more than a coincidence that he had asked for the exact amount that remained of her inheritance.

The following month Anne missed her period.

Dr MacKenzie was anxious, but tried not to show it; the grandmothers were horrified, and did; Henry was delighted and assured Anne it was the most wonderful thing that had happened to him in his whole life. He even agreed to build the new children's wing for the hospital, which Richard had planned before he died.

When William received the news by letter from his mother, he sat alone in his study all evening, not even telling Matthew what was preoccupying him. The following Friday, having been granted special permission by his housemaster, Rags Raglan, he boarded the train to Boston and, on arrival, withdrew one hundred dollars from his savings account. He then proceeded to the law offices of Cohen and Yablons on Jefferson Street. Mr Thomas Cohen, the senior partner, a tall, angular man with dark jowls and lips that never seemed to smile, couldn't hide his surprise when William was ushered into his office.

'I have never been retained by a sixteen-year-old client before,' Mr Cohen began. 'It will be quite a novelty for me' – he hesitated – 'Mr Kane. Especially as your father was not exactly – how shall I put it? – known for his sympathy for my faith.'

'My father,' replied William, 'was a great admirer of the achievements of the Hebrew race, and had considerable respect for your firm when you acted on behalf of his rivals. I heard him and Mr Lloyd mention your name with high regard on several occasions. That's why I have chosen you, Mr Cohen, not you me.'

Mr Cohen quickly put aside the matter of William's age. 'Indeed, indeed. I feel sure we can make an exception for the son of Richard Kane. Now, what can we do for you?'

'I need to discover the answer to three questions, Mr Cohen. One, I want to know whether, if my mother, Mrs Henry Osborne, were to give birth to a son or daughter, that child would have any legal rights to the Kane family trust. Two, do I have any legal obligations to Mr Henry Osborne simply because he is married to my mother? And three, at what age can I insist that Mr Henry Osborne leave my house on Louisburg Square?'

Mr Cohen's pen sped furiously across the yellow pad in front of him, spattering little blue spots on an already ink-stained blotting pad.

William placed his one hundred dollars on the desk. The lawyer was taken aback, but picked the bills up and counted them.

'Use the money prudently, Mr Cohen. I will be in need of a good lawyer when I leave Harvard and join my father's bank.'

'You have already been offered a place at Harvard, Mr Kane? My congratulations. I am rather hoping my son will also be admitted.'

'No, I have not,' said William, 'but it's only a matter of time.' He paused. 'I will return in one week, Mr Cohen. If I ever hear a word on this subject from anyone other than yourself, you may consider our relationship at an end. Good day, sir.'

Mr Cohen would have also said good day – if he had been able to splutter the words out before William closed the door behind him.

◄◦►

William returned to the offices of Cohen and Yablons seven days later.

'Ah, Mr Kane,' said Cohen, 'how nice to see you again. Would you care for some coffee?'

'No, thank you.'

'A Coca-Cola perhaps?'

William's face remained impassive.

'To business, to business,' said Mr Cohen, slightly embarrassed. 'We have made some enquiries on your behalf, Mr Kane, with the help of a very reputable firm of private investigators. I think I can safely say we have the answers you require. You asked if Mr Osborne's offspring by your mother, were there to be any, would have a claim on the Kane estate, in particular on the trust left to you by your father. No, is the simple answer, but of course

Mrs Osborne can leave any part of the five hundred thousand dollars bequeathed to her by your father to whomsoever she pleases. However, it may interest you to know, Mr Kane, that your mother has withdrawn the entire contents of her private account at Kane and Cabot during the past eighteen months, although we have been unable to trace how the money has been spent. It is possible she might have decided to deposit it in another bank.'

William looked shocked, the first sign of any lack of self-control that Cohen had observed.

'There would be no reason for her to do that,' William said. 'The money can only have gone to one person.'

The lawyer remained silent, expecting to find out who, but William checked himself and added nothing. Mr Cohen continued, 'The answer to your second question is that you have no personal or legal obligations to Mr Henry Osborne. Under the terms of your father's will, your mother is a trustee of his estate along with a Mr Alan Lloyd and a Mrs Millie Preston, your surviving godparents, until you come of age at twenty-one.'

William's face showed no expression at all. Cohen had already learned that meant he should continue.

'And thirdly, Mr Kane, you can never remove Mr Osborne from Beacon Hill as long as he remains married to your mother and continues to reside with her. The property comes into your possession by right on her death, but not before. If he is still alive at that time, you could require him to leave.' Cohen looked up from the file in front of him. 'I hope that covers all your questions, Mr Kane.'

'Thank you, Mr Cohen,' said William. 'I am obliged for your efficiency and discretion in this matter. Perhaps you could let me know your professional charges?'

'One hundred dollars doesn't quite cover the firm's work, Mr Kane, but we believe in your future, and—'

'I do not wish to be beholden to anyone, Mr Cohen. You must treat me as someone with whom you might never deal again. With that in mind, how much do I owe you?'

Cohen considered the matter for a moment. 'In those circumstances, we would have charged you two hundred and twenty dollars, Mr Kane.'

William took six $20 bills from his inside pocket and handed them over to Cohen. This time, the lawyer did not count them.

'I'm grateful to you for your assistance, Mr Cohen. I feel sure we'll meet again. Good day, sir.'

'Good day, Mr Kane.' He hesitated. 'May I be permitted to say that I never had the privilege of meeting your father but, having dealt with his son, I only wish that I had.'

William smiled for the first time. 'Thank you, Mr Cohen.'

15

WHEN WLADEK WOKE, it was already dark outside. He blinked at his protectress, who smiled at him. He returned her smile, praying that she could be trusted not to tell the police who he was – or had she already done so? She produced some food from one of her bundles, and Wladek devoured a jam sandwich, the tastiest meal he'd eaten in over four years. When they reached the next station, nearly all the passengers got off, some of them to return to their homes and others simply to stretch their stiff limbs, but most to seek what little refreshment was available.

The woman rose from her seat. 'Follow me,' she said.

Wladek stood up and followed her onto the platform. Was he about to be turned in? She put out her hand, and he took it as any child accompanying his mother would do. She walked towards a women's lavatory. Wladek hesitated, but she insisted, and once they were inside she told him to take off his clothes. While he undressed she turned on the tap, which reluctantly yielded a trickle of cold brown water. She cursed but to Wladek it was a vast improvement on the camp supply. She bathed him with a wet rag, wincing when she saw the vicious wound on his leg. Wladek didn't make a sound, despite the pain that came with each touch, gentle as she tried to be.

'When we get you home, I'll make a better job of those wounds,' she said. 'This will have to do for now.'

Then she saw the silver band. She studied the inscription and looked carefully at Wladek. 'Who did you steal it from?' she asked.

Wladek was indignant. 'I didn't steal it. My father gave it to me on the day he died.'

A different look came into her eyes. Was it fear or respect? She bowed her head. 'Be careful, Wladek. Some men would kill for such a valuable prize.'

He nodded, and started to dress quickly. They returned to their carriage. When the train started to lurch forward, Wladek was glad to feel the wheels clattering underneath him once again.

The train took another twelve and a half days to reach Moscow. Whenever a new ticket collector appeared, Wladek and the woman went through the same routine: he unconvincingly trying to look innocent and young, she a convincing mother. The ticket collectors always bowed respectfully to her, making Wladek think that stationmasters must be very important people in Russia.

By the time they had completed the nine-hundred-mile journey, Wladek had put his trust completely in the woman. It was early afternoon when the train came to its final halt. Despite everything Wladek had been through, he was once again fearful of the unknown. He had never visited a big city, let alone the capital of all the Russias. Wladek had never seen so many people rushing in every direction. The woman sensed his apprehension.

'Follow me, do not speak and do not take off your cap.'

Wladek took her bags down from the rack, pulled his cap over his head – now covered in black stubble – and followed her out onto the platform. A throng of people were waiting to pass through the tiny barrier, creating a hold-up because everyone had to show their identification papers to the guard. As they approached the barrier, Wladek could hear his heart beating like a drum, but the guard only glanced at the woman's documents.

'Comrade,' he said, and saluted. He looked at Wladek.

'My son,' she explained.

'Of course, comrade.' He saluted again.

Wladek had arrived in Moscow.

◄◦►

Despite the trust he had placed in his newfound companion, Wladek's first instinct was to run, but he knew that 150 roubles

were not enough to survive on, so he decided to bide his time –
he could run any time. A horse and cart were waiting for them on
the station forecourt, and they took the woman and her adopted
son to his new home. The stationmaster was not there when they
arrived, so the woman set about making up the spare bed for
Wladek. Then she heated some water on a stove, poured it into a
large tin tub and told him to get in. It was the first bath he had
had in years. She heated some more water and reintroduced him
to soap, scrubbing his back. Before long, the water began to
change colour and after twenty minutes it was black. But Wladek
knew it would take several more baths before he could remove
the years of ingrained dirt. Once he was dry, the woman put some
ointment on his arms and legs and bandaged those parts of his
body that looked particularly sore. She stared at his one nipple.
He dressed quickly, then joined her in the kitchen. She had
already prepared a bowl of hot soup and added some beans.
Wladek ate hungrily. Neither of them spoke. When he had
finished the meal, she suggested that it might be wise for him to
go to bed and rest.

'I don't want my husband to see you before I've told him how
you ended up here,' she explained. 'Would you like to stay with
us, Wladek, if my husband agrees?'

'Yes, please,' he said simply.

'Then off you go to bed,' she said.

Wladek climbed the stairs, praying that the woman's husband
would allow him to live with them. He undressed slowly and got
into bed. He was too clean, the sheets were too crisp, the mattress
too soft. He threw the pillow onto the floor, but he was so tired
that he slept despite the comfort of the bed. It was already dark
outside when he was awakened by the sound of raised voices. He
couldn't tell how long he had been asleep. He crept to the door,
eased it open and listened to the conversation taking place in the
kitchen below.

'You stupid woman,' Wladek heard a shrill voice say. 'Don't
you understand what would have happened if you'd been caught?
You would have been sent to the camps, and I would have lost
my job.'

'But if you had seen him, Piotr. He was like a hunted animal.'

'So you decided to turn us into hunted animals,' he replied. 'Has anyone else seen him?'

'No,' said the woman, 'I don't think so.'

'Thank God for that. He must leave immediately, before anyone discovers he's been here – it's our only hope.'

'But where can he go, Piotr? He has no one. And I have always wanted a son.'

'I don't care what you want, or where he goes. He is not our responsibility. We must be rid of him, and quickly.'

'But Piotr, I think he is royal. I think his father was a baron. He wears a silver band around his wrist, and on it are the words—'

'That only makes it worse. You know what our new leaders have decreed. No nobility, no privileges. We would not even be sent to the camp – the authorities would just shoot us.'

'We have always wanted a son, Piotr. Can we not take this one risk in our lives?'

'In your life, perhaps, but not in mine. I say he must go, and go now.'

Wladek did not need to hear any more. The only way he could help his benefactress was to disappear without trace into the night. He dressed quickly, and stared at the bed, hoping it would not be another four years before he slept so soundly again. He was unlatching the window when the door was flung open and the stationmaster marched into the room. He was a tiny man, no taller than Wladek, with a large stomach and a bald head except for a few grey strands of hair vainly combed across his scalp. He wore rimless spectacles, which had produced little red semicircles under each eye. He stared at Wladek. Wladek stared back.

'Come downstairs,' the man commanded.

Wladek followed him reluctantly to the kitchen. The woman was sitting at the table, sobbing.

'Now listen, boy,' the man said.

'His name is Wladek,' the woman interjected.

'Now listen, boy,' the man repeated. 'You are trouble, and I want you out of here and as far away as possible. I'll tell you what I'm willing to do to help you.'

Wladek gazed at him, aware that he would only be willing to help himself.

'I am going to supply you with a train ticket. Where do you want to go?'

'Odessa,' said Wladek, ignorant of where it was or how much it would cost, knowing only that it was the next city on the doctor's map to freedom.

'Odessa, the mother of crime – an appropriate destination,' sneered the stationmaster. 'You'll be among your own kind there.'

'Let him stay with us, Piotr. I will take care of him, I will—'

'No, never. I would rather pay the bastard to go.'

'But how can he hope to get past the authorities?' the woman pleaded.

'I will issue him with a ticket and a working pass for Odessa.' The man turned to Wladek. 'Once you are on that train, boy, if I ever see or hear of you again in Moscow, I'll have you arrested on sight and thrown into the nearest jail. You'll be back in that prison camp as fast as the train can get you there – if they don't shoot you first.'

The man glanced at the clock on the mantelpiece: five past eleven. He turned to his wife. 'There's a train that leaves for Odessa at midnight. I'll take him to the station and put him on it myself. Have you any baggage, boy?'

Wladek was about to say no, when the woman said, 'Yes, I'll go and fetch it.'

She was gone for some time. Wladek and the stationmaster glared at each other with mutual contempt. The clock struck once in her absence, but still neither spoke. The stationmaster's eyes never left Wladek. When she returned, she was carrying a large brown paper parcel tied with string. Wladek stared at it and was about to protest, but as their eyes met, he saw such fear in hers that he only just managed the words, 'Thank you.'

'Eat this before you leave,' she said, thrusting her bowl of cold soup towards him.

He obeyed, and although his shrunken stomach was now full, he gulped down the soup as quickly as possible, not wanting to cause her any more trouble.

'Animal,' the man muttered.

Wladek looked at him, hatred in his eyes. He felt pity for the woman, bound to such a man for life. A prison of her own.

'Come, boy, it's time for you to leave,' the stationmaster said. 'We don't want you to miss your train, do we?'

Wladek followed him out of the kitchen. He hesitated as he passed the woman, briefly touching her hand.

The stationmaster and the refugee crept through the streets of Moscow, keeping to the shadows, until they reached the station. The stationmaster obtained a one-way ticket to Odessa and gave the little red slip of paper to Wladek.

'My pass?' Wladek said defiantly.

From his inside pocket the man drew out an official-looking form, signed it hurriedly and reluctantly handed it over. His eyes kept looking all around him for any possible danger. Wladek had seen eyes like that many times during the past four years: the eyes of a coward.

'Never let me see, or hear, of you again,' the stationmaster said: the voice of a bully.

Wladek was about to say something, but the stationmaster had already disappeared into the shadows of the night, where he belonged.

Wladek looked at the eyes of the people who hurried past him. The same eyes, the same fear; was anyone in the world free? He gathered the brown paper parcel under his arm, adjusted his cap and walked towards the barrier. The guard glanced at his ticket and ushered him through without comment. He climbed on board the train. Although he would never see her again in his life, he would always remember the kindness of the woman, the stationmaster's wife, Comrade . . . he didn't even know her name.

16

PREPARING FOR the baby kept Anne fully occupied; she found herself tiring easily, and had to rest a great deal. Whenever she asked Henry how business was going, he always had some plausible answer to reassure her that all was well, without supplying any actual details.

Then the anonymous letters started to appear again. This time they gave more details – the names of the women involved, and the places they had been seen with Henry. Anne burned them before she could commit the names or the places to memory. She didn't believe her husband could be unfaithful while she was carrying his child. Someone was jealous, or holding a grudge against Henry. They had to be lying.

But the letters kept coming, sometimes with new names. Anne continued to destroy them, but they were beginning to prey on her mind. She wanted to discuss them with someone, but couldn't think of anybody in whom she could confide. The grandmothers would have been appalled, and were in any case already prejudiced against Henry. Alan Lloyd at the bank could not be expected to understand, as he had never married, and William was far too young. No one seemed suitable. Anne considered consulting a psychiatrist after listening to a lecture given by Sigmund Freud when he visited Boston, but she decided that she would never consider discussing a family problem with a complete stranger.

The matter finally came to a head in a way that Anne could not have anticipated. One Monday morning she received three letters: the usual one from William addressed to Mrs Richard Kane, asking if he could once again spend the summer vacation with his friend Matthew Lester; an anonymous letter alleging that Henry was having an affair with, with . . . Millie Preston; and one from Alan Lloyd, asking if she would be kind enough to telephone and make an appointment to see him at the bank.

Anne sat down heavily, feeling breathless and queasy, and forced herself to reread all three letters. William's stung her by its detachment. She hated knowing that he preferred to spend his summer with his friend rather than at home. The anonymous letter claiming that Henry was having an affair with her closest friend was impossible to ignore. Anne couldn't help remembering that it had been Millie who had introduced her to Henry in the first place, and that she was William's godmother. The third, from Alan Lloyd, filled her with even more apprehension. The only other letter she had ever received from him was one of condolence on the death of Richard. What did he wish to offer his condolences about this time?

She called the bank. The operator put her straight through.

'Alan, you wanted to see me?'

'Yes, my dear. I'd like to have a chat if you can spare the time.'

'Is it bad news?' asked Anne.

'Not exactly, but I'd rather not say anything over the phone.' He tried to reassure her. 'There's nothing for you to worry about. Are you free for lunch, by any chance?'

'Yes, I am.'

'Well, let's meet at the Grand at one o'clock. I look forward to seeing you then, my dear.'

One o'clock, only three hours away. Her mind switched from Alan to William, and then to Henry, but finally settled on Millie Preston. Could it be true? She decided to take a long bath and to put on a new dress. It didn't help. She felt, and was beginning to look, bloated. Her ankles and calves, which had always been so elegant and slim, were becoming shapeless. It was a little frightening to imagine how much worse things might become before the baby was born. Anne sighed as she looked at herself in the mirror, and did the best she could to appear attractive and confident.

◄○►

'You look very smart, Anne. If I weren't an old bachelor, I'd flirt with you shamelessly,' said the silver-haired banker, greeting her with a kiss on both cheeks as though he were a French general. He guided her to his usual table.

It was an unspoken tradition at the Grand Hotel in Boston that the table in the corner was always reserved for the chairman of Kane and Cabot if he was not lunching at the bank, but this was the first time Anne had sat there. Waiters fluttered around them like eager starlings, seeming to know exactly when to disappear and reappear without interrupting their conversation.

'So when's the baby due, Anne?'

'Oh, not for another three months.'

'No complications, I hope.'

'Well,' admitted Anne, 'the doctor examines me once a week and pulls a long face about my blood pressure, but I'm not too worried.'

'I'm so glad, my dear,' he said, and touched her hand gently, as an uncle might. 'You do look rather tired – I hope you're not overdoing things.'

Anne didn't respond.

Alan Lloyd barely raised his head, and a waiter materialized at his side.

'My dear, I want to seek some advice from you,' Alan said after they had ordered. Anne was well aware of Alan Lloyd's gift for diplomacy. He hadn't asked her to lunch in order to seek her advice. There was no doubt in her mind that he wanted to dispense it – kindly.

'Do you have any idea how Henry's real estate projects are going?'

'No, I don't,' admitted Anne. 'I never involve myself with his business activities. You'll recall I didn't with Richard's either. Why? Is there any cause for concern?'

'No, no, none of which we at the bank are aware. On the

contrary, we know Henry is bidding for a large city contract to build the new hospital complex. I was only asking because he has applied to the bank for a loan of five hundred thousand dollars.'

Anne was speechless.

'I see that comes as a surprise,' he said. 'Now, we know from your stock holding that you have a little under twenty thousand dollars in reserve, and are running a small overdraft of seventeen thousand dollars on your personal account.'

Anne dropped her soup spoon. She had not realized that she was overdrawn. Alan could see her distress.

'That's not what this lunch is about, Anne,' he said quickly. 'The bank is quite happy to advance money on the personal account for the rest of your life. William is making over a million dollars a year on the interest from his trust, so your overdraft is hardly significant; nor indeed is the five hundred thousand Henry is requesting, if it were to receive your backing as William's legal guardian.'

'I didn't realize I had any authority over William's trust money,' said Anne.

'You don't on the capital sum, but legally the interest earned from it can be invested in any project thought to benefit him, and is under the guardianship of you and his godparents, myself and Millie Preston, until he turns twenty-one. Now, as chairman of William's trust I can put up that five hundred thousand with your approval. Millie has already informed me that she would be quite happy to grant her approval.'

'Millie has given her approval?'

'Yes. Hasn't she mentioned it to you?'

Anne did not reply immediately.

'What is *your* opinion?' she asked, avoiding the question.

'Well, I haven't seen Henry's accounts, because he only registered the company eighteen months ago and he doesn't bank with us, so I have no idea what expenditure is over income for the current year, and what return he is predicting for 1923. I do know he has made an application for the new hospital contract, and rumour has it the bid is being taken seriously.'

'Did you realize that over the past eighteen months I've given

Henry five hundred thousand dollars of my own money?' said Anne.

'My chief teller informs me whenever a large amount of cash is withdrawn from any account. I had no idea what you were using the money for, and frankly it was none of my business, Anne. That money was left to you by Richard, and is yours to spend as you see fit. In the case of the interest from the family trust, that is a different matter. If you did decide to withdraw five hundred thousand dollars to invest in Henry's firm, the bank would need to inspect his books, because the money would be considered as another investment in William's portfolio. Richard did not give the trustees the authority to make loans, only to invest on William's behalf. I have already explained the situation to Henry. If we were to go ahead and make this loan, the trustees would have to be convinced that it was a sound investment.

'William, of course, is always kept up to date on what we are doing with his trust income, as we saw no reason not to comply with his request that he receive a quarterly investment statement from the bank, in the same way as all the trustees do. No doubt he will have his own views on this particular investment, which he will be fully aware of after he receives the next quarterly report. It may amuse you to know that since his sixteenth birthday, he has been sending me his own opinions on every investment we make. To begin with, I looked on them with the passing interest of a benevolent guardian. Of late, I have been studying them with considerable respect. By the time William takes his place on the board of Kane and Cabot, this bank may well turn out to be too small for him.'

'I've never been asked for advice about William's trust before,' Anne said forlornly.

'Indeed you haven't, although the bank sends you reports on the first day of every quarter, and it has always been in your power as a trustee to query any of the investments we make on William's behalf.' He took a slip of paper from an inside pocket and said no more until the sommelier had finished pouring a second glass of wine. Once the man was out of earshot, Alan continued.

'William currently has a little over twenty-one million dollars invested with the bank at four and a half per cent. We reinvest the interest for him each quarter in stocks and bonds. We have never in the past invested in a private company. It may surprise you to learn, Anne, that we now carry out this reinvestment on a fifty-fifty basis: fifty per cent on the bank's advice, and fifty per cent following the suggestions put forward by William himself. At the moment we are still ahead of him, much to the satisfaction of Mr Simmons, our investment director, to whom William has promised a Rolls-Royce should he beat the boy's own returns by more than ten per cent in any calendar year.'

'But where would William get the money to buy a Rolls-Royce? He's not allowed to touch the money in his trust until he turns twenty-one.'

'I don't know the answer to that, Anne. But I'm certain he wouldn't have made the commitment if he could not honour it. Have you by any chance seen his famous ledger lately?'

'The one given to him by his grandmothers?'

Alan Lloyd nodded.

'No, I haven't seen it since he went away to St Paul's. I didn't realize it still existed.'

'It still exists,' said the banker with a chuckle, 'and I would give a month's wages to know what the credit column now stands at. I suppose you are aware that he now banks with Lester's in New York, and not with us? They don't take on private accounts under ten thousand dollars. I'm also fairly sure they wouldn't make an exception even for the son of Richard Kane.'

'The son of Richard Kane,' said Anne thoughtfully.

'I'm sorry, I didn't mean to sound rude, Anne.'

'No, no, there's no doubt he's the son of Richard Kane. Do you know he has never asked me for a penny of pocket money since his twelfth birthday?' She paused. 'I think I should warn you, Alan, that he won't take kindly to being told you're thinking of investing five hundred thousand dollars of his trust fund in Henry's company.'

'They don't get on well?' asked Alan, his eyebrows rising.

'I'm afraid not,' said Anne.

'I'm sorry to hear that. It would certainly make the transaction more complicated if William made it clear that he was opposed to it. Although he has no authority over the trust until he is twenty-one, we've discovered through sources of our own that he is not above going to an independent lawyer to find out his legal position.'

'Good heavens,' said Anne, 'you can't be serious.'

'Oh, yes, I'm quite serious. But there's nothing for you to worry about. To be frank, we at the bank were rather impressed, and once we realized who the enquiry was coming from, we released information we would normally have kept to ourselves. For some private reason William obviously didn't want to approach us directly.'

'Good heavens,' repeated Anne. 'What will he be like when he's thirty?'

'That will depend,' said Alan, 'on whether he is lucky enough to fall in love with someone as lovely as his mother. That was always Richard's strength.'

'You are an old flatterer, Alan. Can we leave the matter of the five hundred thousand until I've had a chance to discuss it with Henry?'

'Of course we can, my dear. As I told you, I am here only to seek your advice.'

Alan ordered coffee, and took Anne's hand gently in his. 'And do remember to take care of yourself, Anne. Your health is far more important than the fate of a few thousand dollars.'

—◦—

When Anne returned home she started to worry about the other two letters she had received that morning. At least she was now certain of one thing after Alan Lloyd's revelations about her son: it might be prudent to give in gracefully and let William spend the forthcoming vacation with Matthew Lester.

The possibility that Henry and Millie were having an affair raised a problem to which she was unable to obtain any such a simple a solution. She sat in the maroon leather chair, Richard's favourite, looking out through the bay window onto a beautiful bed of red and white roses. She was lost in thought, seeing nothing. Anne always took some time to come to a decision, but once she had, she seldom changed her mind.

Henry came home earlier than usual that evening, and she couldn't help wondering why. She soon found out.

'I hear you had lunch with Alan Lloyd today,' he said as he entered the room.

'Who told you that, Henry?'

'I have spies everywhere,' he said, laughing.

'Yes, Alan invited me to lunch. He wanted to know how I felt about allowing the bank to invest five hundred thousand dollars of William's trust money in your company.'

'What did you say?' asked Henry, trying not to sound anxious.

'I told him I would need to discuss the matter with you. But why in heaven's name didn't you let me know you'd approached the bank, Henry? I felt such a fool hearing about it from Alan for the first time.'

'I didn't think you took any interest in business, my dear. I only found out by sheer accident that you, Alan Lloyd and Millie Preston are all trustees, and that each of you has a vote on how William's money should be invested.'

'How did you find that out,' asked Anne, 'when I wasn't aware of it myself?'

'You never read the small print, my darling. As a matter of fact, I didn't myself until recently. Quite by chance, Millie told me the details of the trust. Not only is she William's godmother, it seems she is also a trustee. Now, let's see if we can turn the position to our advantage and make William even more money. Millie says she'll back me if you agree.'

The mere sound of Millie's name made Anne feel uneasy.

'I don't think we ought to touch William's money,' she said. 'I've never looked upon the trust as having anything to do with me. I'd be much happier to leave well alone and let the bank continue to reinvest the interest as it's done in the past.'

'Why be satisfied with the bank's investment programme when I'm on to such a winner with this city hospital contract? Surely Alan was able to confirm that?'

'I'm not altogether certain how he felt. He was his usual discreet self, though he did say the contract would be an excellent one to win, and that you had a good chance of being awarded it.'

'Exactly.'

'But he added that he'd need to see your books before he came to any firm conclusion, and he also wondered what had happened to my five hundred thousand dollars.'

'Our five hundred thousand, my darling, is doing very well, as you'll soon discover. I'll send the books around to Alan tomorrow morning so he can inspect them for himself. I can assure you, he'll be impressed.'

'I hope so, Henry, for both our sakes,' said Anne. 'Let's wait and see what his opinion is – you know how much I've always trusted Alan.'

'But not me,' said Henry.

'Oh, no, Henry, I didn't mean—'

'I was only teasing. I assume you trust your own husband.'

'I would hope so,' she said eventually. 'I've never had to worry about money before, and it's all too much to cope with right now. The baby makes me feel so tired and depressed.'

Henry's manner changed quickly to one of concern. 'I know, my darling, and I don't want you ever to have to bother your head with business matters – I can always handle that side of things. Look, why don't you go to bed early, and I'll bring you some supper on a tray? That will give me a chance to go back to the office and pick up the files I need to send to Alan in the morning.'

Anne agreed, but once Henry had left she made no attempt to sleep, tired as she was, but sat up in bed reading. She knew it would take Henry about fifteen minutes to reach his office, so she waited twenty and then dialled his private line. The ringing tone continued for almost a minute.

Anne tried a second time twenty minutes later; still no one answered. She kept calling every twenty minutes, but no one came on the line. Henry's remark about trust began to echo loudly in her head.

When he eventually returned home a few minutes after midnight, he looked surprised to find Anne still awake.

'You shouldn't have stayed up for me.'

He gave her a warm kiss. Anne thought she could smell perfume – or was she becoming overly suspicious?

'I had to stay on a little longer than I expected – at first I couldn't find all the papers Alan will need. Damn silly secretary filed some of them under the wrong headings.'

'It must be lonely sitting there in the office all on your own in the middle of the night,' said Anne.

'Oh, it's not that bad if you have a worthwhile job to do,' said Henry as he climbed into bed and took Anne in his arms. 'At least there's one thing to be said for it: you can get a lot more done when the phone isn't continually interrupting you.'

–◦–

Henry left for work straight after breakfast the following morning – not that Anne was sure where he went any longer. She turned the pages of a section of the *Boston Globe* she had never consulted before. There were several advertisements offering the services she required. She selected one almost at random, picked up the phone and made an appointment to see a Mr Ricardo at midday.

Anne was shocked by the dinginess of the streets and the forlorn state of the buildings. She had never previously visited the southern district of the city, and in normal circumstances she could have gone through her entire life without even knowing such places existed.

A small wooden staircase littered with matches, cigarette butts and other rubbish created its own paper chase to a door with a frosted window on which the name GLEN RICARDO appeared in large black letters, and underneath:

PRIVATE DETECTIVE
(*Registered in the commonwealth of Massachusetts*)

Anne knocked softly.

'Come right in, the door's open,' shouted a deep whiskey voice.

Anne entered. The man seated behind the desk, his legs stretched over its surface, glanced up. His cigar stub nearly fell out of his mouth when he caught sight of Anne. It was the first time a woman wearing a mink coat had ever walked into his office.

'Good morning,' he said, rising quickly. 'I'm Glen Ricardo.' He leaned across the desk and offered a nicotine-stained hand to Anne. She took it, glad to be wearing gloves. 'Do you have an appointment?' Ricardo asked, not that he cared whether she did or not. He was always available for a consultation with a mink coat.

'Yes, I do.'

'Ah, then you must be Mrs Osborne. Can I take your coat?'

'I prefer to keep it on,' said Anne, eyeing a nail sticking out of the wall.

'Of course, of course.'

Anne eyed Ricardo covertly as he sat back down and lit a new cigar. She did not care for his light green suit, his multi-coloured tie or his thickly greased hair. It was only the belief that it wouldn't be better anywhere else that stopped her leaving.

'Now, what's the problem?' said Ricardo, sharpening an already short pencil with a blunt knife. The shavings dropped everywhere except into the wastepaper basket. 'Have you lost your dog, your jewellery or your husband?'

'First, Mr Ricardo, I want to be assured of your complete discretion,' Anne began.

'Of course, of course, it goes without saying,' said Ricardo, not looking up from his disappearing pencil.

'Nevertheless, I am saying it,' said Anne.

'Of course, of course.'

Anne thought that if the man said 'of course' once more, she would scream. She drew a deep breath. 'I have been receiving anonymous letters which allege that my husband has been having an affair with a close friend. I want to know who is writing the letters and if there is any truth in the allegations.'

She felt an immense sense of relief at having voiced her

fears for the first time. Ricardo looked at her impassively, as if it was not the first time he had heard such sentiments expressed. He put a hand through his long black hair.

'Right,' he began. 'The husband will be easy. Who's responsible for sending the letters could be a lot harder. You've kept them, of course?'

'Only the last one,' said Anne.

Glen Ricardo sighed and wearily stretched his hand across the table. Anne reluctantly took the letter out of her bag and hesitated for a moment.

'I know how you feel, Mrs Osborne, but I can't do my job with one hand tied behind my back.'

'Of course, Mr Ricardo. I'm sorry.'

Anne couldn't believe she had said 'of course'.

Ricardo read the letter through two or three times before speaking. 'Have all of the letters been typed on the same paper and sent in this sort of envelope?'

'Yes, I think so,' said Anne. 'As far as I can remember.'

'Well, when the next one comes, be sure to—'

'How can you be certain there will be another one?' interrupted Anne.

'There will be, believe me. So be sure to keep it. Now, I'll need some details about your husband. Do you have a photograph?'

'Yes.' Once again she hesitated.

'I don't want to waste my time chasing the wrong man, do I, Mrs Osborne?' said Ricardo.

Anne opened her bag again and passed him a worn photograph of Henry in a lieutenant's uniform.

'Good-looking man,' said the detective. 'When was this photograph taken?'

'About five years ago, I think,' said Anne. 'I didn't know him when he was in the army.'

Ricardo questioned Anne for several minutes on Henry's daily routine. She was surprised to realize how little she knew about his lifestyle, and even less about his past.

'Not a lot to go on, Mrs Osborne, but I'll do the best I can.

My charges are ten dollars a day plus expenses. I'll give you a written report once a week. Two weeks' payment in advance.' His hand reached across the desk again, more eagerly than before.

Anne opened her handbag, took out two crisp $100 bills and passed them across to him. He studied them carefully. Benjamin Franklin gazed imperturbably at Ricardo, who obviously had not seen the great man for some time. Ricardo handed Anne $60 in grubby fives.

'I see you work on Sundays, Mr Ricardo,' said Anne, pleased with her mental arithmetic.

'Of course,' he said. 'After all, that's the most common day for infidelity. Will the same time next week suit you, Mrs Osborne?' he added, as he pocketed the money.

'Of course,' said Anne, and left quickly, so as to avoid having to shake hands with the man a second time.

17

WLADEK FOUND a seat in the workers' carriage.

The first thing he did once the train was under way was to untie the parcel the woman had thrust into his hands. He started rummaging through the contents: apples, bread, nuts, a shirt, a pair of trousers and a pair of shoes. He changed into the new clothes in the nearest lavatory, retaining only his warm 50-rouble coat. After he had returned to his seat, he bit into an apple and smiled. He would save the rest of the food for the long journey to Odessa. Once he had finished the apple, including the core, he turned his attention to the doctor's map.

Odessa was not quite as far from Moscow as Irkutsk, about a thumb's length on the doctor's sketch, 700 miles in reality. As Wladek was studying the rudimentary map, he became distracted by another game of pitch-and-toss that was taking place in the carriage. He folded the parchment, replaced it safely in his pocket and began taking a closer interest in the game. The same routine was being carried out, with only one player consistently winning, while the others lost. Clearly a well organized gang was working the trains. Wladek decided to take advantage of his new-found knowledge.

He edged forward and made a place for himself in the circle of gamblers. Every time the cheat had lost twice in a row, Wladek backed him with one rouble, doubling his stake until he won. The cheat never even glanced in his direction. By the time they reached the next station, Wladek had won fourteen roubles, two of which he used to buy himself another apple and a cup of hot soup. He had won enough to last the entire journey to Odessa, and he smiled at the thought of rejoining the game as he climbed back into the train.

As his foot touched the top step, a fist landed on the side of his head and he was knocked flying into the corridor. His arm was jerked painfully behind his back and his face was pressed hard against the carriage window. His nose was bleeding, and he could feel the point of a knife touching his ear lobe. 'Do you hear me, boy?'

'Yes,' said Wladek, petrified.

'If you go back to my carriage again, I'll cut this ear off. Then you won't be able to hear me, will you?'

'No, sir,' said Wladek.

Wladek felt the knife break the surface of the skin behind his ear and blood began trickling down his neck.

'Let that be a warning to you, boy.'

A knee suddenly came up into his kidneys with so much force that Wladek collapsed to the floor. A hand rummaged inside his coat pockets and removed his recently acquired roubles.

'Mine, I think,' the voice said.

Blood was still pouring from Wladek's nose and from behind his ear. When he summoned the courage to look up, he was alone; there was no sign of the gambler, and the other passengers kept their distance. He tried to stand up, but his body refused to obey the order from his brain, so he remained slumped in the corridor for several minutes. Eventually, when he was able to get to his feet, he walked slowly to the other end of the train, as far away from the gambler's carriage as possible, his limp grotesquely exaggerated. He took a seat in a carriage occupied mostly by women and children, and fell into a deep sleep.

At the next stop, Wladek didn't leave the train, and when it moved off he fell asleep again. He ate, he slept, he dreamed. Finally, after four days and five nights, the train chugged into the terminal at Odessa. The same check at the ticket barrier, but his papers were all in order, so the guard barely gave him a second look. Wladek was now on his own. He still had 150 roubles in the lining of his sleeve, and he didn't intend to waste a single one of them.

He spent the rest of the day walking around the town trying to familiarize himself with its layout, but he was continually distracted by sights he had never seen before: large town houses, shops with plate-glass windows, hawkers selling their colourful trinkets on the streets, gaslights, even a monkey on a stick. He walked on until he reached the harbour. Yes, there it was – the sea. Wladek gazed longingly into the blue expanse: that way lay freedom and escape from Russia. The Baron had told him about the great ships that crossed the high seas delivering their cargoes to foreign lands, but now he was seeing them for the first time. They were much larger than he had imagined, and they stood in a line as far as the eye could see.

As the sun disappeared behind the tall buildings, he decided to look for somewhere to spend the night. The city must have suffered from many invaders, because dilapidated houses were everywhere to be seen. He took a side road and kept walking; he must have been a strange sight, with his sheepskin coat almost touching the ground and the brown paper parcel under his arm. Nowhere looked safe to him until he came across a railway siding in which a solitary burned-out railway carriage stood. He peered inside it cautiously: darkness and silence, no one to be seen. He threw his paper parcel into the carriage, raised his tired body up onto the boards, crawled into a corner and quickly fell asleep.

He woke with a start to find a body was on top of him and two hands around his throat. He could barely breathe.

'Who are you?' growled the voice of a boy who in the darkness sounded no older than himself.

'Wladek Koskiewicz.'

'Where do you come from?'

'Moscow.'

'Well, you're not sleeping in my carriage, Muscovite,' said the voice.

'Sorry,' gasped Wladek. 'I didn't know.'

'Got any money?' The thumbs pressed into Wladek's throat.

'A little.'

'How much?'

'Seven roubles.'

'Hand it over.'

Wladek rummaged in an empty pocket of his overcoat. The boy also stuck a hand inside, reducing the pressure on Wladek's throat.

Wladek immediately jerked his knee into the boy's crotch. His attacker fell back in agony, clutching his groin. Wladek leapt on him, hitting out fiercely. The boy from Odessa was no match for Wladek – sleeping in a derelict railway carriage was five-star luxury compared to living in the dungeons and a Russian labour camp. Wladek stopped only when his adversary was pinned to the floor.

'Get back to the other end of the carriage and stay there,' said Wladek. 'If you so much as move a muscle, I'll kill you.'

The boy scrambled away.

Wladek sat still and listened for a few moments – no movement – then he lay down and was soon sleeping soundly.

When he woke, the sun was shining through the gaps in the roof. He turned over and glanced at his adversary of the previous night. He was lying in a foetal position, staring at him from the other end of the car.

'Come here,' commanded Wladek.

The boy didn't move.

'Come here,' repeated Wladek, a little more sharply.

The boy stood up. It was the first chance Wladek had to look at him properly. They were about the same age, but the other boy must have been a foot taller, with a fresh face and scruffy fair hair.

'First things first,' said Wladek. 'Where do we find something to eat?'

'Follow me,' said the boy, and leapt out of the carriage without another word. Wladek limped after him and up the hill to the town square, where the morning market was being set up. He had not seen such a variety of food since those magnificent banquets in the Baron's castle: row upon row of stalls laden with fruit, vegetables, greens and even his favourite nuts. The other boy could see that Wladek was overwhelmed by the sight.

'Now I'll tell you what we do,' he said. 'I'll go over to the corner stall and steal an orange and then make a run for it. You shout at the top of your voice, "Stop thief!" The stall keeper will chase me, and when he does, you move in and fill your pockets. Don't be greedy – just enough for one meal. I'll see you back here. Got it?'

'Yes, I think so,' said Wladek, trying to sound as confident.

'Right, let's see if you're up to it, Muscovite.' The boy looked at him and sneered, before swaggering towards the corner stall, removing an orange from the top of a pyramid, making some remark to the stall keeper before starting to run slowly. He glanced back at Wladek, who had entirely forgotten to shout 'Stop thief', but the stall owner began to chase him anyway. While everyone's eyes were on his accomplice, Wladek moved in quickly. When the stall keeper looked as if he was about to catch the boy, he lobbed the orange back at him. The man stopped to pick it up, swore, shook his fist and returned to his stall, complaining vociferously to the other merchants on the way.

Wladek was shaking with mirth when a hand was placed firmly on his shoulder. He turned around, horrified at having been caught.

'Did you get anything, Muscovite, or are you only here as a sightseer?'

Wladek burst out laughing with relief and produced three oranges, an apple and a potato from the deep pockets of his coat. The boy smiled.

'What's your name?' said Wladek.

'Stefan.'

'Let's do it again, Stefan.'

'Hold on, Muscovite; don't get too clever. If we do it again, we'll have to go to the other end of the market and wait for at least an hour. You're working with a professional, but don't imagine you won't get caught occasionally.'

The two boys walked slowly to the other end of the market, Stefan moving with a swagger for which Wladek would have traded the three oranges, the apple, the potato and even his 150 roubles, while he limped behind. They mingled with the morning shoppers, and when Stefan decided the time was right, they repeated the escapade. They then returned to the railway carriage to enjoy their captured spoils: six oranges, five apples, three potatoes, a pear, several varieties of nuts, and the special prize, a melon. Stefan had never had pockets big enough to hold a melon.

'Not bad,' said Wladek as he dug his teeth into a potato.

'You eat the skins as well?' asked his new companion.

'I've been places where a potato skin's a luxury,' replied Wladek.

Stefan looked at him with admiration.

'Next problem is, how do we get some money?' said Wladek.

'You expect everything on your first day, don't you?' said Stefan. 'Chain gang on the waterfront will be our best bet. That is, if you're up to some real work, Muscovite.'

'Show me,' said Wladek.

Once they had eaten half the fruit and hidden the rest under the straw in the corner of the carriage, Stefan led Wladek back down to the harbour.

'See that ship over there, the big green one?' said Stefan. 'It's only just docked, so what we'll do is pick up a basket, fill it with grain, climb up the gangplank and then drop the load into the hold. You get a rouble for every four trips you make. Be sure you keep count, Muscovite, because the bastard in charge of the gang will swindle you as soon as look at you and pocket the money for himself.'

The two of them spent the rest of the afternoon humping grain up the gangplank and dropping it into the hold. They made twenty-six roubles between them. After a dinner of stolen nuts, bread and an onion they hadn't intended to take, they slept happily at the same end of the railway carriage.

When Stefan woke the next morning, he found Wladek studying his map.

'What's that?'

'It's a map showing me how to escape from Russia.'

'Why do you want to leave Russia, when you can stay here and team up with me?' said Stefan. 'We could be partners.'

'No, I have to get to Turkey, where I'll be a free man. Why don't you come with me, Stefan?'

'I could never leave Odessa. This is my home, and these are the people I've known all my life. It's not so good, but it might be even worse in Turkey. But if that's what you want, perhaps I can help you.'

'How do I find a ship that's sailing to Turkey?' asked Wladek.

'Easy – I know how to find out where every ship is going. We'll ask One Tooth Joe, who lives at the end of the pier. But you'll have to give him a rouble.'

'I bet he splits the money with you.'

'Fifty-fifty,' said Stefan. 'You're learning fast, Muscovite,' he added as he leapt out of the carriage.

Wladek followed him, again conscious of how easily other boys moved while he limped. When they reached the end of the pier, Stefan led him into a small room full of dust-covered books and old timetables. Wladek couldn't see anyone, but then he heard a voice from behind a large pile of books. 'What do you want, urchin? I don't have time to waste on you.'

'Some information for my companion, Joe. When is the next luxury cruise to Turkey?'

'Money up front,' said an old man whose head appeared from behind the books, a lined, weather-beaten face below a seaman's cap. His black eyes were studying Wladek.

'One Tooth used to be a great sea dog,' said Stefan in a whisper loud enough for Joe to hear.

'None of your cheek, boy. Where's the rouble?'

'My friend carries my purse,' said Stefan. 'Show him the rouble, Wladek.'

Wladek handed over a coin. Joe bit it with his one remaining tooth, shuffled over to the bookcase and pulled out a large green ledger. Dust flew everywhere. He started coughing as he thumbed through the dirty pages, moving a short, stubby, calloused finger down the long columns of names.

'On Thursday the *Renaska* is coming in to pick up coal – probably returning to Constantinople on Saturday. If she can load quickly enough, she may even sail on the Friday night and save herself extra berthing tariffs. She'll dock at Berth Seventeen.'

'Thanks, One Tooth,' said Stefan. 'I'll see if I can bring in some more of my wealthy associates in the future.'

One Tooth Joe raised a fist, cursing, as Stefan and Wladek ran back out onto the wharf.

◄○►

For the next three days the two boys stole food, loaded grain and slept. By the time the Turkish ship docked on Thursday, Stefan had almost convinced Wladek that he should remain with him in Odessa. But Wladek's fear of the Russians finding him and sending him back to the camps outweighed even the attractions of his new life with Stefan.

They stood on the quayside, watching the *Renaska* docking at Berth 17.

'How will I get on board?' asked Wladek.

'Simple,' said Stefan. 'We join the chain gang tomorrow morning. I'll take the place behind you, and when the coal hold is nearly full, you jump in and hide, and I'll pick up your basket and walk down the other side.'

'And collect my share of the money, no doubt,' said Wladek with a grin.

'Naturally,' said Stefan. 'There must be some financial reward for my superior knowledge. How else could I hope to sustain my belief in free enterprise?'

They joined the chain gang at six the next morning, and hauled coal up the gangplank and into the hold until they were both ready to drop, but it wasn't enough. The hold was only half full by nightfall, although Wladek was blacker than he'd ever been in prison. The two boys slept soundly that night. The following morning they started again, and by mid-afternoon, when the hold was almost full, Stefan kicked Wladek's ankle.

'Next time, Muscovite,' he said firmly.

When they reached the top of the gangplank, Wladek threw his head in, dropped his basket on the deck and jumped over the side of the hold.

'Farewell, my friend,' Stefan said, 'and good luck with the

infidel Turks.' He grabbed Wladek's basket and returned down the gangplank, whistling.

Wladek pressed himself into a corner of the hold as the coal continued to come pouring in. The black dust was everywhere: in his nose and mouth, lungs and eyes. With a painful effort he tried to avoid coughing for fear of being heard by one of the ship's crew. Just as he thought he could no longer bear the dust-filled air of the hold and decided to return to Stefan and find some other way of escaping, the hatch above him slammed shut. He coughed luxuriously.

After a few moments, he felt something take a bite at his ankle. His blood went cold as he realized what it had to be; he'd had to deal with too many of the vermin in the dungeons. He threw a piece of coal at the monster and sent it scurrying away, but another one came at him, then another and another. The braver ones went for his legs. They seemed to appear from nowhere; black, large and desperately hungry. He stared down, searching for them. He clambered desperately to the top of the pile of coal and pushed open the hatch. The sunlight came flooding in, and the rats immediately disappeared into their tunnels below the coal. He started to climb out, but the ship was already well clear of the quayside. He fell back into the hold, terrified. If he was discovered, and the captain decided to return to Odessa and hand him over, it would mean a one-way journey back to Camp 201 and the White Russians. He chose to stay with the black rats. As soon as he closed the hatch the red eyes appeared again. As fast as he could throw lumps of coal at the verminous creatures, new ones would appear. Every few minutes he had to open the hatch to let some light in, for light seemed to be his only ally.

For two days and three nights Wladek waged a running battle with the rats, without ever catching a moment of sleep. When the ship finally sailed into Constantinople and a deckhand opened the hold, Wladek was black from his head to his knees with coal dust, and red from his knees to his toes with blood. The deckhand dragged him out. Wladek tried to stand up, but collapsed in a heap on the deck.

18

AFTER WILLIAM read in Kane and Cabot's quarterly trust report that Henry Osborne – 'Henry Osborne', he repeated the name out loud to be sure he wasn't mistaken – was requesting $500,000 to invest in his company, he had a bad day. For the first time in his four years at St Paul's he came second in a maths test. Matthew Lester, who beat him, asked if he was feeling well. He didn't reply.

That evening, William telephoned Alan Lloyd at home. The chairman of Kane and Cabot was not altogether surprised to hear from him after Anne's disclosure about his unhappy relationship with Henry.

'William, dear boy. How are you, and how are things at St Paul's?'

'All's well at this end, thank you, sir, but that's not why I'm calling.'

'No, I didn't imagine it was,' said Lloyd drily. 'What can I do for you?'

'I'd like to see you tomorrow afternoon.'

'On a Sunday, William?'

'Yes, it's the only day I can get away from school and I need to see you as soon as possible,' he said, making the statement sound as though it were a concession on his part, before adding, 'and under no circumstances is my mother to be informed of our meeting.'

'Well, William—' Lloyd began.

William's voice grew firmer. 'I don't have to remind you, Mr

Lloyd, that the investment of my trust money in my stepfather's company, while not actually illegal, would undoubtedly be considered unethical.'

Lloyd was silent for a few moments, wondering if he should try to placate the boy. The boy. Had he ever been a boy?

'Fine, William. Why don't you join me for lunch at the Hunt Club, say one o'clock?'

'I'll look forward to seeing you then, sir.' The line went dead.

At least the confrontation will be on my home ground, thought Alan Lloyd as he replaced the mouthpiece, cursing Mr Bell for inventing the damn machine.

—◦—

Lloyd had chosen the Hunt Club because he did not want the meeting to be too private. The first thing William asked when he arrived was that they might play a round of golf after lunch.

'Delighted, my boy,' said Alan, and reserved a place on the first tee for three o'clock.

He was surprised that William did not raise the subject of Henry Osborne's proposal during lunch. Instead, the boy talked knowledgeably about President Harding's views on tariff reform and the incompetence of Charles G. Dawes as Director of the Budget. Alan began to wonder if William, having slept on it, had changed his mind about discussing Osborne's proposal. Well, if that's the way the boy wants to play it, thought Alan, that's fine by me. He looked forward to a quiet afternoon of golf. After an agreeable lunch and the better part of a bottle of wine – William limited himself to one glass – they changed in the clubhouse and walked across to the first tee.

'Do you still have a nine handicap, sir?' asked William.

'Thereabouts, my boy. Why?'

'Will ten dollars a hole suit you?'

Alan Lloyd hesitated, remembering that golf was the one game that William enjoyed. 'Yes, fine.'

Nothing was said on the first hole, which Alan managed to par while William made a bogey. Alan also won the second and the third quite comfortably, and began to relax, feeling rather pleased with his game. By the time they had reached the fourth tee, they were half a mile from the clubhouse. William waited until Alan was about to begin his backswing.

'I must make it clear,' began William, 'that there are no circumstances under which I would allow you to loan five hundred thousand dollars of my trust money to any company or person associated with Henry Osborne.'

Lloyd hit a bad tee shot that ended up in the left-hand rough. Its only virtue was that it put him far enough away from William, who had made a safe drive right down the middle, to give him a few minutes to think about how to address both William's remark and the ball. By the time they met on the green, Lloyd had played three more shots. He conceded the hole.

'William, you know that, as a trustee, I only have one vote out of three, and you will also be aware that you have no authority over trust decisions until your twenty-first birthday. You must also realize that we shouldn't be discussing this subject at all.'

'I'm fully aware of the legal implications, sir, but as both of the other trustees are sleeping with my stepfather—'

Lloyd's next drive landed in the lake.

'Don't tell me you're the only person in Boston who doesn't know that Millie Preston is having an affair with my stepfather?'

Lloyd conceded the hole.

William continued: 'I want to be certain that I have your vote, and that you will do everything in your power to influence my mother against this loan, even if it means telling her the truth about my stepfather and Mrs Preston.'

William's drive on the sixth was straight down the middle of the fairway. Alan's was even worse than his previous one, and landed in the bunker of an adjacent hole. He shanked his next shot into a bush he had never even realized existed before, and said 'Shit' out loud for only the second time in forty-three years. (He had got a hiding on that occasion as well.)

'That's asking a little too much,' said Alan as he joined up with William on the green.

'It's nothing compared with what I'd do if I couldn't count on your support, sir.'

'I don't think your father would have approved of threats, William,' said Alan as he watched William sink his putt from fourteen feet.

'The only thing my father would not have approved of is Henry Osborne,' retorted William. Lloyd missed his putt from two feet.

'In any case, Mr Lloyd, you must be well aware that my father had a clause inserted in the trust deed that money invested by the trustees should always be a private matter, and the beneficiary should not be made aware that the Kane family was personally involved. It was a rule he never broke in his life as a banker. That way he could always be certain there was no conflict of interest between the bank's investments and those of the family trust.'

'Perhaps your mother feels that the rule can be broken for a member of the family.'

'Henry Osborne is not a member of *my* family, and when I control the trust it will be a rule that I, like my father, will never break.'

'You may live to regret taking such a rigid stance, William. Perhaps you should consider for a moment the consequences of your mother finding out about Mrs Preston and your stepfather.'

'My mother has already lost five hundred thousand dollars of her own money, sir. Isn't that enough for one husband? Why do I have to lose five hundred thousand of mine as well?'

'We don't know that to be the case, William. The investment may yield an excellent return; I haven't yet had a chance to look carefully into Henry's books.'

William winced when Lloyd called his stepfather Henry.

'I can assure you, sir, he's blown nearly every penny of my mother's money. To be exact, he has thirty-three thousand four hundred and twelve dollars left in his account. I suggest you take very little notice of Osborne's books and check a little more thoroughly into his background, past business record and associates. Not to mention the fact that he gambles – heavily.'

On the eighth tee, Alan hit his ball into the same lake on the way back. Once again he conceded the hole.

'How did you come by this information?' asked Alan, fairly certain it had been through Thomas Cohen's office.

'I prefer not to say, sir.'

Alan kept his own counsel; he might need to keep that particular ace up his sleeve to play a little later in William's life.

'If all you claim turns out to be accurate, William, naturally I would have to advise your mother against any investment in Henry's company, and it would also be my duty to discuss the matter frankly with Henry.'

'So be it, sir.'

Alan hit a better shot, but he knew it was too late to recover.

William continued, 'It may also interest you to know that Osborne needs the five hundred thousand from my trust not for the hospital contract, but to clear a long-standing debt in Chicago. I take it you were not aware of that, sir?'

Alan said nothing; he certainly had not been aware of it. William won the hole.

By the time they reached the eighteenth, Alan was eight holes down, and was about to complete the worst round he cared to remember. He had a five-foot putt that would at least enable him to halve the final hole.

'Do you have any more bombshells for me?' he asked.

'Before or after you take your putt, sir?'

Alan laughed and decided to call his bluff. 'Before, William,' he said, leaning on his club.

'Osborne won't be awarded the hospital contract. It's thought by those who matter that he's been bribing a junior councillor on the planning committee. Nothing will be made public, but his company has already been removed from the shortlist. The contract will be awarded to Kirkbride and Carter. That last piece of information, sir, is confidential. Even Kirkbride and Carter will not be informed until a week on Thursday, so I'd be obliged if you would keep it to yourself.'

Alan missed his putt. William holed his, walked over and shook Lloyd warmly by the hand.

'Thank you for the game, sir. I think you'll find you owe me ninety dollars.'

Lloyd took out his wallet and handed over a hundred-dollar bill. 'William, I think the time has come for you to stop calling me "sir". My name, as you well know, is Alan.'

'Thank you, Alan.' William handed him ten dollars.

19

WHEN WLADEK came to, he found himself on a bed in a small room with three men in long white coats studying him carefully, speaking a tongue he had never heard before. How many languages were there in the world?

He tried to sit up, but the oldest of the three men, with a thin, lined face and a goatee beard, pushed him firmly back down. He addressed Wladek in the strange tongue. Wladek shook his head. The man then tried Russian. Wladek shook his head again – that would be the quickest way back to where he had come from. The next language the doctor tried was German, and Wladek realized that his command of the language was greater than his inquisitor's.

'Ah, so you're not Russian then?' said the inquisitor.

'No.'

'What were you doing in Russia?'

'Trying to escape.'

'Ah.' The man turned to his companions and seemed to report the conversation in their own tongue. The three left the room.

A nurse came in and scrubbed Wladek clean, taking little interest in his cries of pain. She didn't like dirty objects in her hospital. She finally covered his legs in a thick brown ointment and left him to sleep again. When he awoke for the second time, he was alone. He stared up at the white ceiling, thinking about his next move.

He climbed out of the bed and crossed the room to the window. It looked out onto a marketplace, not unlike the one in

Odessa, except that the men wore long white robes and had darker skins. They also wore colourful objects on their heads that looked like small, upside-down red flowerpots, and had open sandals on their feet. The women were all in black; even their faces were covered. All he could see were their black eyes. Wladek watched the bustle in the marketplace as the women bargained for their daily food; that seemed to be one thing that was international.

It was several minutes before he noticed that running down the side of the building was an iron fire escape that reached the ground. He walked cautiously to the door, opened it and peered into the corridor. People were walking up and down, but none of them showed any interest in him. He closed the door gently, searched for his belongings, which he found in a closet in the corner of the room, and dressed quickly. His clothes were still black with coal dust, and felt gritty on his clean skin. He returned to the window, eased it open, clambered out onto the fire escape and started to climb down towards freedom. The first thing that hit him was the heat. He wished he wasn't wearing the heavy overcoat.

Once his feet touched the ground he tried to run, but his legs were so weak that he could only walk slowly. How he prayed he would wake up one day and his limp would somehow have miraculously disappeared. He did not look back at the hospital until he was lost in the throng of the marketplace.

The stalls were piled high with tempting food, and he decided to buy an orange and some nuts. He reached into the lining in his suit, but his money was no longer there. Far worse, he realized that the silver band had also gone. The men in the white coats must have stolen his possessions. He thought about going back to the hospital to retrieve them, but decided against it until he'd had something to eat. Perhaps there were still come coins in the large overcoat pockets. He searched around, and immediately found the three 50-rouble notes and some coins. They were wrapped together with the doctor's map and the silver band. Wladek was overjoyed. He slipped on the silver band, and pushed it above his elbow.

He chose the largest orange he could see, and a handful of nuts. The stall keeper said something to him that he could not understand. Wladek felt the easiest way around the language barrier was to hand over some money. The stall keeper looked at the 50-rouble note, laughed and threw his arms in the air. 'Allah!' he cried. He snatched the nuts and the orange from Wladek and waved him away.

Wladek walked off in despair: a different language meant a different currency. In Russia he had been poor; here he was penniless. He would have to steal some food; if he was likely to be caught, he would throw it back at the stall keeper. He walked to the other end of the marketplace in the same confident way as Stefan, but he couldn't imitate the swagger, and he certainly didn't feel the same confidence. He chose the end stall, and when he was sure no one was watching, he picked up an orange and started to run. Suddenly there was uproar; it seemed as if half the city was chasing him.

A large, athletic man jumped on the limping Wladek and threw him to the ground. Six or seven others seized hold of different parts of his body, and a larger group followed as he was dragged back to the stall, where a policeman awaited them. There was a shouted exchange and much movement of arms between the stall owner and the policeman. The policeman finally turned to Wladek and shouted at him too, but Wladek couldn't understand a word he was saying. The officer shrugged his shoulders and grabbed Wladek by the ear. People continued to bawl at him as he was marched off, while others spat on him.

When Wladek arrived at the police station he was thrown into a tiny cell, already occupied by twenty or thirty criminals – thugs, thieves, he knew not what. He did not speak, and they showed no desire to talk to him. He remained with his back to a wall for a day and a night, frightened to move. The smell of excrement made him vomit until there was nothing left in him. He had never thought the day would come when the dungeons in the Baron's castle would seem too crowded and powerful.

The following morning Wladek was dragged from the basement by two guards and marched into a room where he was lined up with several other prisoners. They were then all roped to each other round the waist and led out into the street. A large crowd had gathered, and their loud cheer of welcome made Wladek feel they had been waiting some time for the prisoners to appear. The crowd followed them all the way to the marketplace, screaming, clapping and chanting – but Wladek had no idea why they seemed so excited. The prisoners came to a halt when they reached the market. The first man was untied and taken to the centre of the square, which was crammed with hundreds of people, all baying for blood.

Wladek watched the scene in disbelief. Once a prisoner reached the middle of the square, he was knocked to his knees by the guard. His right hand was strapped to a wooden block by a giant of a man, who then raised a large sword above his head and brought it down with terrible force, aiming at the prisoner's wrist. On his first attempt he managed to catch only the tips of the fingers. The prisoner screamed with pain as the sword was raised again. This time the sword hit the wrist but did not finish the job properly, and the hand dangled from the prisoner's arm, blood pouring out onto the dust. The sword was raised a third time, and when it came swinging down, the prisoner's hand finally fell to the ground. The crowd roared its approval. The prisoner was at last released and slumped in a heap, unconscious. He was dragged off by a bored guard and left on the edge of the crowd. A weeping woman – his wife, Wladek presumed – hurriedly tied a tourniquet of dirty cloth around the bloody stump. The second prisoner died of shock before the fourth blow was administered. The giant swordsman was not interested in death, so he continued his commission; he was only paid to remove hands.

Wladek looked around in terror and retched; he would have vomited if there had been anything left in his stomach. He searched in every direction for help or some means of escape; no one had warned him that under Islamic law the punishment for trying to escape would be the loss of a foot. His eyes darted around the mass of faces, stopping only when he saw a man dressed in a dark suit, white shirt and tie, standing some twenty yards from Wladek and watching the spectacle with obvious disgust. He did not once look in Wladek's direction, nor did he hear his shouts for help in the uproar that followed every time the sword was brought down. Was he French, German, English, or perhaps even Polish? Wladek could not tell, but for some reason he was there to witness the macabre spectacle.

Wladek stared at him, willing him to look his way. He waved his free arm, but still could not gain the foreigner's attention. The guards untied the man two in front of Wladek and dragged him towards the block. The sword was raised again, the crowd cheered, and the man in the dark suit turned his eyes away in horror. Wladek continued to wave frantically at him.

The man stared at Wladek, then turned to talk to a companion whom Wladek had not noticed. The guard was now struggling with the prisoner immediately in front of Wladek. He strapped the man's hand on the block; the sword went up and removed it in one blow. The crowd seemed disappointed, hardly raising a cheer. Wladek stared again at the two foreigners, both of whom were now studying him more closely. He willed them to do something, but they only continued to stare.

The guard came over, ripped off Wladek's 50-rouble overcoat and threw it on the ground. He then undid his cuff and rolled up his sleeve. Wladek struggled helplessly as he was dragged across the square. He was no match for the burly guard. When he reached the block, he was kicked in the back of the knees and collapsed to the ground. The strap was fastened over his right wrist. There was nothing left for him to do but close his eyes as the sword was raised high in the air. He waited in agony for the terrible blow, but there was a sudden hush as the Baron's silver band slid from his elbow down to his wrist and onto the block. An eerie silence fell over the crowd as it shone brightly in the sunlight.

The executioner hesitated, then slowly lowered his sword as he studied the silver band. Wladek opened his eyes as the guard tried to pull the band off his wrist, but he couldn't get it past the leather strap. A man in uniform ran quickly up to the block. He too studied the band and its inscription, before running across to another man, who must have been of higher authority, because he took his time as he strolled over. The sword was still resting on the ground and the crowd was beginning to jeer and hoot. The second officer also tried to pull the silver band off, but could not get it over the block and he didn't have the authority to undo the strap. He shouted at Wladek, who did not understand what he was saying, and replied in Polish, 'I do not speak your language.'

The officer looked surprised and threw his hands in the air shouting 'Allah!' then walked slowly towards the two men wearing western suits. Wladek prayed to God – in such situations any man prays to any god, be he a Muslim or a Christian. One of the two men joined the Turkish officer and they walked towards the block. The foreigner knelt on one knee by Wladek's side, studied the silver band, then looked carefully at him. Wladek waited. He could speak five languages, and prayed that the man knew one of them. His heart sank when the man turned to the officer and addressed him in his own tongue. The crowd was now booing and throwing rotten fruit at the block. The officer was nodding his agreement. The foreigner turned round and knelt by Wladek's side. 'Do you speak English?'

Wladek heaved a sigh of relief. 'Yes, sir, not bad. I am Polish citizen.'

'How did you come into possession of that silver band?'

'It belong my father, sir. He die in dungeon by the Germans in Poland, and I captured and sent to prison camp in Russia. I escape and come here by ship. I have no food for days. When stall keeper no accept my roubles for orange, I take one because I very, very hungry.'

The Englishman rose, turned to the officer and spoke to him very firmly. The latter, in turn, addressed the executioner, who looked doubtful, but when the officer repeated the order a little louder, he bent down and reluctantly undid the leather strap. Wladek retched again. The Englishman handed each man a silver coin, as the crowd continued to protest. They had been robbed of a hand.

'Come with me,' said the Englishman. 'And quickly, before they change their minds.'

Still in a daze, Wladek grabbed his coat and followed. The crowd booed and jeered, continuing to throw rotten vegetables and fruit at him as he departed. The swordsman strapped the next prisoner's hand to the block and with his first blow only managed to remove a thumb. This seemed to pacify the mob.

‑‹○›‑

The Englishman moved swiftly through the bustling crowd and out of the square, where he was joined by his companion.

'What's happening, Edward?'

'The boy says he's a Pole and has escaped from Russia. I told the official in charge he was English, so now he's our responsibility. Let's get him to the consulate and find out if his story bears any resemblance to the truth.'

Wladek struggled to keep up with the two men as they hurried down the Street of Seven Kings. He could still faintly hear the mob behind them, screaming their approval every time the sword came down.

The two Englishmen led Wladek through an archway and across a pebbled courtyard towards a large grey building. On the door were the welcoming words, BRITISH CONSULATE. Once he was inside the building, Wladek began to feel safe for the first time. He followed the two men down a long hall with walls covered in paintings of men in strange uniforms. At the far end was a magnificent portrait of an old man in a blue uniform adorned with medals. His fine beard reminded Wladek of the Baron. A soldier appeared from nowhere and saluted.

'Take this boy, Corporal Smithers, and see that he gets a bath. Then find him some clothes and feed him in the kitchen. When he's eaten and smells a little less like a walking pigsty, bring him to my office.'

'Yes, sir,' the corporal said, and saluted again. 'Come with me, laddie.'

Wladek followed the soldier obediently, almost having to run to keep up with him. He was taken to a little bedroom in the basement. It only had one tiny window. no chance of escape. The corporal told him to get undressed, then left him on his own. He returned a few minutes later, only to find Wladek still sitting on the edge of the bed fully dressed, dazedly twisting the silver band around and around his wrist.

'Hurry up, lad. You're not on a rest cure.'

'Sorry, sir,' Wladek said.

'Don't call me sir, lad. I'm Corporal Smithers. You call me Corporal.'

'I am Wladek Koskiewicz. You call me Wladek.'

'Don't try to be funny with me, lad. We've got enough funny people in the British army without you wishing to join the ranks.'

Wladek did not understand what the soldier meant. He undressed quickly.

'Follow me at the double.'

Another soothing bath with hot water and soap brought back memories of his Russian protectress, and of the son he might have become, but for her husband. The soldier was back at the door with a set of clothes, strange, but clean and fresh-smelling. Whose son had they belonged to?

Corporal Smithers escorted Wladek to the kitchen and left him with a plump, pink-faced cook, with the friendliest face Wladek had seen since leaving Poland. She reminded him of his *niania*. Wladek could not help wondering what would happen to her waistline after a few weeks in Camp 201.

'Hello,' she said with a beaming smile. 'What's your name, then?'

Wladek told her.

'Well, Wladek, it looks as though you could do with a good British meal inside of you – none of that Turkish rubbish. We'll start with some hot soup and beef. You'll need something substantial if you're to face Mr Prendergast.' She laughed. 'Just remember, his bite's not as bad as his bark. Although he's English, his heart's in the right place.'

'You are not English, Mrs Cook?' asked Wladek, surprised.

'Good Lord no, laddie, I'm Scottish. There's a world of difference. We hate the English more than the Germans do,' she said, laughing. She set a dish of steaming soup, thick with meat and vegetables, in front of Wladek. He had entirely forgotten that food could smell and taste so good. He ate slowly, fearing that this might be his last good meal for a very long time.

The corporal reappeared. 'Have you had enough to eat, my lad?'

'Yes, thank you, Mr Corporal.'

The corporal gave Wladek a suspicious look, but saw no trace of cheek in the boy's expression. 'Good. Then let's be moving. Can't be late on parade for Mr Prendergast.'

The corporal disappeared through the kitchen door. Wladek glanced at the cook. He always hated saying goodbye to someone he had just met, especially when the person had been so kind.

'Off you go, laddie, if you know what's good for you.'

'Thank you, Mrs Cook,' said Wladek. 'Your food is best I can ever remember.'

She smiled at him. He again had to trot to keep up with the corporal, who came to a brisk halt outside a door and Wladek nearly ran into him.

'Look where you're going, lad.' The corporal gave a short *rap-rap* on the door.

'Come,' said a voice.

The corporal opened the door and saluted. 'The Polish boy, sir, as you requested, scrubbed, dressed and fed.'

'Thank you, Corporal. Perhaps you would be kind enough to ask Mr Grant to join us.'

Edward Prendergast looked up from his desk. He waved Wladek to a seat and continued to work on some papers. Wladek sat looking at him, and then at the paintings on the wall. More men in uniform, but that old bearded gentleman still had the biggest portrait, this time wearing khaki. A few minutes later the other Englishman he'd seen in the market square walked in to join them.

'Thank you for joining us, Harry. Have a seat, old chap.' Mr Prendergast turned to Wladek. 'Now, my boy, let's hear your story from the beginning, with no exaggerations, only the truth. Do you understand?'

'Yes, sir.'

Wladek began with his days at the trapper's cottage in Poland. It took him some time to find the right English words. The two Englishmen occasionally stopped him and asked a question, nodding to each other once he'd given his answer. After an hour of talking, Wladek's life history had reached the point where he was in the office of Mr Edward Prendergast, His Britannic Majesty's Second Consul to Turkey.

'I think, Harry,' said Prendergast, 'it's our duty to inform the Polish delegation immediately, and then hand young Koskiewicz over to them. Given the circumstances he must be their responsibility.'

'I agree,' said the man called Harry. 'You know, my boy, you had a narrow escape today. The Sharia – that is, the old Islamic law which provides for cutting off a hand for theft – was in theory officially abandoned years ago. In fact, it's a crime under the Ottoman Penal Code to inflict such a punishment. Nevertheless, in practice the barbarians still continue administering it.' He shrugged.

'Why not my hand?' asked Wladek, holding onto his wrist.

'I told them they could cut off all the Muslim hands they wanted, but not an Englishman's,' the Second Consul interjected.

'Thank God,' Wladek said faintly.

'Edward Prendergast, actually,' the Second Consul said, smiling for the first time. 'You can spend the night here, and then we'll take you to your own delegation tomorrow. The Polish Consul is a good fellow, considering he's a foreigner.' He pressed a button, and the corporal reappeared immediately.

'Sir.'

'Corporal, take young Koskiewicz to his room, and in the morning see he's given breakfast and returned to me at nine sharp.'

'Sir. This way, lad, at the double.'

Wladek was led away by the corporal. He had not even had time to thank the two Englishmen who had saved his hand – and perhaps his life. Back in the clean little room, with its small bed neatly turned down as if he were an honoured guest, he undressed, threw the pillow on the floor and slept soundly until the morning light shone through the tiny window.

'Rise and shine, lad, sharpish.'

It was the corporal once again, his uniform immaculately smart and knife-edge pressed, looking as though he had never been to bed. For an instant Wladek, surfacing from sleep, thought himself back in Camp 201, as the corporal's banging on the end of the metal bed frame with his cane resembled the noise of the prison triangle that Wladek had grown to hate. He slid out of bed and reached for his clothes.

'Wash first, my lad, wash first. We don't want your horrible smells worrying Mr Prendergast so early in the morning, do we?'

Wladek was unsure which part of himself to wash, as he'd never been so clean in his life. He noticed that the corporal was staring at him.

'What's wrong with your leg, lad?'

'Nothing, nothing,' said Wladek, turning away from the staring eyes.

'Right. I'll be back in three minutes. Three minutes, do you hear, my lad? Be sure you're ready.'

Wladek washed his hands and face and then dressed quickly. He was sitting on the end of the bed, holding his long sheepskin coat, when the corporal returned to take him to the Second Consul. Mr Prendergast welcomed him, and seemed to have softened considerably since their meeting the previous day.

'Good morning, Koskiewicz,' he said.

'Good morning, sir.'

'Did you enjoy your breakfast?'

'I no had breakfast, sir.'

'Why not?' asked the Second Consul, looking towards the corporal.

'Overslept, I'm afraid, sir. He would have been late for you.'

'Well, we must see what we can do about that. Corporal, will you ask Mrs Henderson to rustle up an apple or something?'

'Yes, sir.'

Wladek and the Second Consul walked slowly along the corridor towards the front door of the consulate and across the pebbled courtyard to a waiting car, one of the few in Turkey. It was Wladek's first journey in such a vehicle. He was sorry to be leaving the British Consulate. It was the only place in which he'd felt safe for years. He wondered if he was ever going to sleep more than one night in the same bed for the rest of his life. The corporal ran down the steps and took the driver's seat. He passed Wladek an apple and some warm fresh bread.

'See there are no crumbs left in the car, lad. The cook sends her compliments.'

The drive through the hot, busy streets was conducted at walking pace as the Turks made no attempt to clear a path for the English camel on wheels. Even with all the windows open Wladek was sweating from the oppressive heat. Mr Prendergast, seated in the back, remained quite cool and unperturbed. Wladek lowered his head for fear that someone who had witnessed the previous day's events might recognize him and stir the mob to anger again. When the little black Austin came to a halt outside a small, decaying building marked KONSULAT POLSKI, Wladek felt a twinge of excitement mingled with disappointment.

The three of them climbed out.

'Where's the apple core, boy?' demanded the corporal.

'I eat him.'

The corporal laughed, and knocked on the door. A friendly-looking little man with dark hair and a firm jaw answered it. He was in shirt sleeves, and deeply tanned by the Turkish sun. He addressed them in Polish, the first words Wladek had heard in his native tongue since leaving the labour camp. Wladek answered quickly, explaining his presence. His fellow countryman turned to the British Second Consul.

'This way, Mr Prendergast,' he said in perfect English. 'It was good of you to bring the boy over personally.'

A few diplomatic niceties were exchanged before Prendergast and the corporal took their leave. Wladek gazed at them, fumbling for an English expression more adequate than 'Thank you'.

Prendergast patted him on the head as he might a cocker spaniel. And as the corporal closed the door, he turned and winked at Wladek. 'Good luck, my lad. God knows you deserve it.'

The Polish Consul introduced himself as Pawel Zaleski. Once

again Wladek was required to recount the story of his life, finding it easier in Polish than he had in English. Zaleski listened in silence, shaking his head sorrowfully.

'My poor child,' he said. 'You have borne more than your share of our country's suffering for one so young. And now what are we to do with you?'

'I must return to Poland and reclaim my castle,' said Wladek.

'Poland,' said the Consul. 'Where's that? The region where you lived remains in dispute, and there is still heavy fighting going on between the Poles and the Russians as they attempt to agree on a border. General Pilsudski is doing all he can to protect the territorial integrity of our fatherland. But it would be foolish for any of us to be optimistic. There is little left for you now in Poland. No, your best plan would be to start a new life in England or America.'

'But I don't want to go to England or America. I am Polish.'

'You will always be Polish, Wladek – no one can take that away from you, wherever you decide to settle. But you must be realistic about your future while you're still so young.'

Wladek lowered his head in despair. Had he gone through all this only to be told he could never return to his homeland, never see his castle again? He fought back the tears.

The Consul put his arm around the boy's shoulders. 'Never forget that you are one of the lucky ones who escaped and came out alive. You only have to remember your loyal friend Dr Dubien to be aware of what your life might have been like.'

Wladek didn't speak.

'Now you must put all thoughts of the past behind you and think only of the future, Wladek. Perhaps in your lifetime you will see Poland rise again, which is more than I dare to hope for.'

20

ALAN LLOYD arrived at the bank on Monday morning with a little more to do than he had anticipated before his meeting with William. He immediately put five departmental managers to work on checking the accuracy of William's allegations. He feared he already knew what their enquiries would reveal, and because of Anne's relationship with the bank, he made sure that no department was aware of what the others were up to. His instructions to each manager were clear: all reports were to be strictly confidential, and for the chairman's eyes only.

By Wednesday, he had five preliminary reports on his desk. They all seemed to confirm William's judgement, although each manager had asked for more time to verify some details. Alan decided against discussing the matter with Anne until he had more concrete evidence to go on. The best he felt he could do for the time being was to take advantage of a buffet supper the Osbornes were giving on Friday evening, when he could advise Anne against taking any immediate decision on the loan.

—◦—

When Alan arrived at Anne's home – he could never think of it as Osborne's – he was shocked to see how tired and pale she looked, which made him decide to soften his approach even more. He finally managed to catch her alone, but they only had a few moments together. If only she were not having a baby just at the time all this was going on, he thought.

Anne smiled at him. 'How kind of you to come, Alan, when you must be so busy at the bank.'

'I couldn't afford to miss one of your parties, my dear. They're still the most sought-after invitation in Boston.'

She smiled. 'I wonder if you ever say the wrong thing.'

'All too frequently. Anne, have you had time to give any more thought to the matter we discussed last week?'

'No, I am afraid I haven't. I've been up to my ears preparing for this evening, Alan. How did Henry's accounts look?'

'Fine, but we only have one year's figures to go on, so I think we ought to bring in our own accountants to double-check them over. It's standard banking policy to do that with any company that's been operating for less than three years. I'm sure Henry would understand our position.'

'Anne, darling, lovely party,' interrupted a loud voice over Alan's shoulder. He did not recognize the face; presumably one of Henry's political friends. 'How's the little mother-to-be?' continued the effusive voice.

Alan slipped away, hoping he had bought a little time for the bank. There were a lot of local politicians from City Hall at the party, and even a couple of congressmen, which made him wonder if William would turn out to be wrong about the hospital contract. Not that the bank intended to investigate that: after all, the official announcement from City Hall was due in a week's time. He picked up his black overcoat from the cloakroom and slipped out.

'If I can just hold on until this time next week,' he said out loud as he walked back down Chestnut Street to his own house.

During the party, Anne found herself watching Henry whenever he was near Millie Preston. There was certainly no outward sign of anything between them; in fact, Henry spent far more time with John Preston. Anne began to wonder if she had misjudged her husband, and thought about cancelling her appointment with Glen Ricardo. The party finally came to an end two hours later than Anne had anticipated; she only hoped it meant that the guests had all enjoyed themselves and Henry would benefit.

'Great party, Anne, thanks for inviting us.' It was the loud voice again, the last person to leave. Anne couldn't remember his name – something to do with City Hall. He disappeared down the drive.

Anne climbed the stairs slowly and started to undo her dress even before she had reached the bedroom, promising herself that she wouldn't give any more parties before the baby was due in ten weeks' time.

Henry joined her a moment later. 'Did you get a chance to have a word with Alan, darling?' he asked, trying to sound casual.

'Yes, I did,' replied Anne. 'He said your books look fine, but as the company can only produce one year's figures, the bank's accountants have to double-check. Apparently that's standard banking policy.'

'Standard banking policy be damned. Can't you feel William's presence behind all this? He's trying to hold up the loan, Anne.'

'How can you say that? Alan didn't even mention William.'

'Didn't he?' said Henry, his voice rising. 'So he didn't bother to tell you that William had lunch with him on Sunday, and they played a round of golf at his club?'

'What?' said Anne. 'I don't believe it. William would never come to Boston without seeing me. You must be mistaken, Henry.'

'My dear, half your set was there, and I can't imagine that William travelled fifty miles just to play a round of golf with Alan Lloyd. Some time, Anne – and very soon – you're going to have to decide whether you trust William more than your husband. Don't you understand that I must have the money by next Wednesday, because if I can't show City Hall I'm good for that amount, I'll be disqualified. Disqualified because a schoolboy doesn't approve of your being married to someone other than his father. Please, Anne, you must call Alan tomorrow and tell him to transfer the money.'

His insistent voice boomed in Anne's head, making her feel faint and dizzy.

'No, not tomorrow, Henry. Can it wait until Monday?'

Henry smiled and strolled over to join her as she stood naked, looking at herself in the mirror. He ran his hand over her bulging stomach. 'I just want this little fellow to be given the same opportunities as William.'

◄○►

The following morning Anne told herself a hundred times that she would not go to see Glen Ricardo, but just before noon she found herself flagging down a cab. Twenty minutes later she was climbing the creaky wooden stairs, apprehensive of what she was about to learn. She hesitated before knocking on the door and even thought about turning back.

'Come in.'

She opened the door.

'Ah, Mrs Osborne, how nice to see you again. Do have a seat.'

Anne remained standing.

'The news, I'm afraid, is not good,' said Ricardo, pushing his hand through his long, dark hair.

Anne's heart sank, and she collapsed into the nearest chair.

'Mr Osborne has not been seen with Mrs Preston, or any other woman, during the past week.'

'But you said the news wasn't good,' said Anne.

'Of course, Mrs Osborne. I assumed you were looking for grounds for divorce. Angry wives don't normally come to me hoping I'll prove their husbands are faithful.'

'No, no,' said Anne, with relief. 'It's the best piece of news I've had in weeks.'

'Oh, that's good,' said Ricardo, slightly taken aback. 'Then let's hope the second week also reveals nothing.'

'You can stop your investigation now, Mr Ricardo. I'm confident you won't find anything of any consequence next week.'

'I don't think that would be wise, Mrs Osborne. To make a final judgement on only one week's observation would, in my experience, be premature to say the least.'

'All right, if you think it will prove the point, but I'm still confident you won't uncover anything new.'

'In any case,' continued Ricardo, puffing away at his cigar, which looked bigger, and smelled better, to Anne than the one he had smoked at their previous meeting, 'you've already paid for the two weeks.'

'What about the letters?' asked Anne. 'I suppose they must have come from someone jealous of my husband's achievements.'

'Well, as I pointed out to you when we last met, Mrs Osborne, tracing the sender of anonymous letters is never easy. However, I have been able to locate the shop where the stationery was purchased, as the brand is fairly unusual. But for the moment I have nothing further to report on that front. Again, I may have a lead for you next week. Have you had any more letters?'

'No, I haven't.'

'Good. Then it all seems to be working out for the best. Let's hope, for your sake, that the next meeting will be our last.'

'Yes,' said Anne happily, 'let's hope so. Can I settle your expenses next week?'

'Of course, of course.'

Anne had nearly forgotten the phrase, but this time it only made her laugh. She agreed to see Ricardo for what she felt certain would be their last meeting, on Thursday. As she was being driven home Anne decided that Henry must be given the $500,000 and the chance to prove William and Alan wrong. She still hadn't recovered from the discovery that William had come to Boston without letting her know. She felt Henry had every right to feel that her son was trying to work behind their backs.

Henry was delighted when Anne told him over supper of her decision on the loan, and he produced the legal documents for her signature the following morning. Anne couldn't help thinking that he must have had them prepared for some time, especially as Millie Preston had already signed. Or was she being overly suspicious again? She dismissed the idea and added her signature.

◄○►

She was fully prepared for Alan Lloyd when he telephoned on Monday morning.

'Anne, why don't we just hold things up until Thursday. Then, at least, we'll know who's been awarded the hospital contract.'

'No, Alan, I've made up my mind. Henry needs the money

now. He has to prove to City Hall that he's financially capable of fulfilling the contract, and you already have the signatures of two trustees, so the decision is not yours to make.'

'The bank could always guarantee Henry's position without actually passing over the money,' said Alan. 'I'm sure City Hall would find that acceptable. In any case, I still haven't had enough time to check over his company's accounts.'

'But you did find enough time to have lunch and play a round of golf with William last Sunday without bothering to tell me.'

There was a momentary silence on the other end of the line.

'Anne, I—'

'Don't say you didn't have the opportunity to inform me. You came to our party on Friday evening, and could easily have mentioned it to me then. You chose not to, although you did find enough time to advise me to postpone judgement on the loan to Henry.'

'Anne, I'm sorry. I can understand how that might look and why you're upset, but there was a reason, believe me. May I come around and explain everything to you?'

'No, Alan, you can't. You're all ganging up against my husband. None of you wants to give him the chance to prove himself. Well, I'm going to allow him that chance.'

Anne put the telephone down, pleased with herself, feeling she had been loyal to Henry in a way that fully atoned for her ever having doubted him in the first place.

Alan Lloyd rang back, but Anne instructed the maid to say she was out for the rest of the day. When Henry returned home that night, he was delighted to hear how firm Anne had been with Alan.

'It will all turn out for the best, my darling, you'll see. On Thursday morning I'll be awarded the contract and you can kiss and make up with Alan; still, you'd better keep out of his way until then. If you like, we can have a celebration lunch at the Grand on Thursday, and wave at him from the other side of the room.'

Anne smiled. She couldn't help remembering that she was meant to be seeing Glen Ricardo at twelve o'clock that day. Still, that would give her easily enough time to be at the Grand Hotel by one, when she could celebrate both triumphs.

—◦—

Alan tried repeatedly to reach Anne, but the maid always had a ready excuse. As the loan document had been signed by two trustees, he could not hold up payment for more than twenty-four hours. The wording was typical of any legal agreement drawn up by Richard Kane; there were no loopholes to crawl through. When the cheque for $500,000 left the bank by special messenger on Tuesday afternoon, Alan wrote a long letter to William, explaining why he'd been left with no choice but to transfer the money, withholding only the unconfirmed findings of his departmental reports. He sent a copy of the letter to each director of the bank, conscious that although he had behaved with the utmost propriety, he had laid himself open to accusations of concealment.

William received Alan Lloyd's letter at St Paul's on the Thursday morning while he was having breakfast with Matthew.

—◦—

Breakfast at Beacon Hill on Thursday morning was the usual eggs and bacon, hot toast, cold oatmeal and a pot of steaming coffee. Henry was simultaneously tense and jaunty, snapping at the maid, joking with a junior city official who telephoned to confirm that the name of the company that had won the hospital contract would be announced by the mayor at a press conference at ten o'clock.

Anne was almost looking forward to her last meeting with Glen Ricardo. She flicked through *Vogue*, trying not to notice that Henry's hands were trembling as he read the pages of the *Boston Globe*.

'What are you going to do this morning?' Henry asked, trying to make conversation.

'Oh, nothing much before we have our celebration lunch. Do you still plan to name the children's wing in memory of Richard?' Anne asked.

'Not in memory of Richard, my darling. This will be my

achievement, so I shall name it in your honour. The Mrs Henry Osborne wing,' he added grandly.

'What a nice idea,' Anne said, putting her magazine down and smiling at him. 'You mustn't let me drink too much champagne at lunch. I have an appointment with Dr MacKenzie later this afternoon, and I don't think he'd approve if I arrived drunk only a few weeks before the baby is due. When will you know for certain that the contract is yours?'

'I already know,' Henry said. 'The clerk I just spoke to was one hundred per cent confident, but it won't be official until ten o'clock.'

'The first thing you must do, Henry, is phone Alan and tell him the good news. I'm beginning to feel quite guilty about the way I treated him on Monday.'

'No need for you to feel any guilt, darling. After all, he didn't bother to keep you informed about his meeting with William.'

'No, but he tried to explain later, Henry, and I didn't give him the chance.'

'All right, all right, anything you say. If it'll make you happy I'll phone him at five past ten, and then you can write and tell William I've made him another million.' He looked at his watch. 'I'd better be going. Wish me luck.'

'I thought you didn't need any luck,' said Anne.

'I don't, I don't, it's just an expression. See you at the Grand at one o'clock.' He kissed her on the forehead. 'By tonight you'll be able to laugh about Alan, William and contracts, and treat them all as problems of the past, believe me. Goodbye, my darling.'

—◦—

An uneaten breakfast was laid out in front of Alan Lloyd. He was reading the financial pages of the *Boston Globe*, noting a small paragraph in a right-hand column reporting that at ten o'clock that morning the mayor would be announcing which company had been awarded the $5 million hospital contract.

Alan had already decided what course of action he must take if Henry failed to secure the contract and everything that William had warned him about turned out to be accurate. He would do exactly what Richard would have done in the circumstances: act only in the best interests of the bank. The latest departmental reports on Henry's personal finances had disturbed him greatly. Osborne was indeed a heavy gambler, and no trace could be found to show that the trust's $500,000 had been deposited with his company.

Alan sipped his orange juice, leaving the rest of his breakfast untouched. He apologized to his housekeeper and walked to the bank. It was a bright, sunny day.

◄○►

'William, do you feel up to a game of tennis this afternoon?'

Matthew waited for William to reply, but he continued to read the letter from Alan Lloyd.

'What did you say?'

'Are you going deaf, or already suffering from senile dementia?' Still no reply. Matthew tried again. 'Am I going to be allowed to beat you black and blue on the tennis court this afternoon?'

'No, not this afternoon, Matthew. I have more important matters to attend to.'

'Naturally, old buddy, I forgot that you'll be off on your weekly visit to the White House to advise President Harding on the nation's fiscal problems. Mind you, you couldn't do any worse than that posturing fool, Charles G. Dawes.' William didn't respond. 'Tell the president you'll continue to advise him as long as he appoints Matthew Lester to be the next Attorney General.'

There was still no response from William.

'I know the joke was pretty weak, but I thought it at least worthy of comment,' said Matthew, looking more carefully at his silent friend. 'It's the eggs, isn't it? Taste as though they've come out of a Russian prisoner-of-war camp.'

'Matthew, I need your help,' said William as he placed Alan's letter back in its envelope.

'You've had a letter from my sister, and she thinks you're more sexy than Rudolph Valentino.'

William stood up. 'Quit kidding, Matthew. If your father's

bank was being robbed, would you sit around making jokes about it?'

The expression on William's face left Matthew in no doubt that he was serious. 'No, I wouldn't,' he said quietly.

'Right. Then let's get moving, and I'll explain everything on the way,' said William.

'On the way to where?' asked Matthew innocently.

'Boston.'

—◁◦▷—

Anne left Beacon Hill a little after ten to do some shopping before going on to her meeting with Glen Ricardo.

The telephone rang as she disappeared down Chestnut Street. The maid answered it, looked out the window, but her mistress was already out of sight. If Anne had taken the call she would have learned City Hall's decision on the hospital contract; instead she bought some silk stockings and tried out a new perfume. She arrived at Glen Ricardo's office a little after twelve, hoping her new perfume might counter the smell of stale cigar smoke.

'I hope I'm not late, Mr Ricardo,' she began briskly.

'Please have a seat, Mrs Osborne.'

Ricardo didn't look particularly cheerful, but then he never did, thought Anne. She noticed that he was not smoking his usual cigar. He opened a smart brown file, the only new thing Anne could see in the office, and extracted some papers.

'Let's start with the anonymous letters, shall we, Mrs Osborne?'

Anne did not like the tone of his voice.

'Yes, all right,' she managed.

'They are being sent by a Mrs Ruby Flowers.'

'Who? Why?' said Anne, impatient for answers she did not want to hear.

'I suspect one of the reasons is that Mrs Flowers is at present suing your husband.'

'Well, that explains everything,' said Anne. 'She must want revenge. How much does she claim Henry owes her?'

'She is not alleging debt, Mrs Osborne.'

157

'Well, what is she alleging?'

Ricardo pushed himself up from the chair, as if it required the full strength of both his arms to raise his tired frame. He walked across to the window and looked out over the crowded Boston harbour.

'She is suing him for breach of promise, Mrs Osborne.'

'But that's not possible,' said Anne.

'It appears that they were engaged to be married when Mr Osborne first met you, and that the engagement was suddenly terminated for no apparent reason.'

'Gold digger. She must have wanted Henry's money.'

'No, I don't think so. You see, Mrs Flowers is quite well off. Not in your class, of course, but well off by most people's standards. Her late husband owned a soft drink bottling company and left her everything.'

'Her late husband? How old is she?'

Ricardo walked back to the table and flicked over a page or two of his file before his thumb started moving down the page.

'She'll be fifty-three in July.'

'Oh, my God,' said Anne. 'The poor woman. She must hate me.'

'Possibly she does, Mrs Osborne, but that won't help us. Now I must turn to your husband's other activities.'

The nicotine-stained finger turned over some more pages.

Anne began to feel sick. Why had she returned? Why hadn't she left well enough alone? She didn't have to know. She didn't want to know. She wanted to get up and leave. How she wished Richard was by her side. She found herself unable to move, transfixed by Ricardo and the contents of his smart new file.

'On two occasions last week Mr Osborne spent over three hours with Mrs Preston.'

'But that doesn't prove anything,' began Anne desperately. 'I know they were discussing a very important financial transaction.'

'In a small hotel on La Salle Street, at eight o'clock in the evening.'

Anne didn't interrupt again.

'On both occasions they were seen walking into the hotel, whispering and laughing. It's not conclusive, of course, but we have photographs of them entering and leaving the hotel together.'

'Destroy them,' Anne said quietly.

Glen Ricardo blinked. 'As you wish, Mrs Osborne. I'm afraid there's more. My enquiries show that Mr Osborne was never at Harvard, nor was he an officer in the American Armed Forces. There was a Henry Osborne at Harvard who, it turns out, was five foot five, sandy-haired and came from Alabama. He was killed on the Somme in 1917. I've also discovered that your husband is considerably younger than he claims, that his real name is Vittorio Togna and that he has served—'

'Stop. I don't want to hear any more,' said Anne, tears flooding down her cheeks. 'I don't want to hear any more.'

'Of course, Mrs Osborne, I understand. I'm sorry my news is so distressing. In my job sometimes . . .'

Anne fought for a measure of self-control. 'Thank you, Mr Ricardo. I appreciate all you have done. How much do I owe you?'

'You have already paid for the two weeks in advance. My expenses came to seventy-three dollars.'

Anne passed over a hundred-dollar bill and rose from her chair.

'Don't forget your change, Mrs Osborne,' Ricardo said as she turned to leave.

Anne didn't seem to hear him.

'Are you feeling all right, Mrs Osborne? You look a little pale. Can I get you a glass of water, or something stronger?'

'No, thank you, I'm fine,' lied Anne.

'Perhaps you would allow me to drive you home?'

'No, thank you, Mr Ricardo, I'll be able to get myself home.' She turned and smiled at the private detective. 'It was kind of you to offer.'

Glen Ricardo closed the door quietly behind his client, walked slowly across to the window, bit the end off his last big cigar and spat it out. He cursed his job as he watched Mrs Osborne climb into a taxi. Such a nice lady.

—◁◦▷—

Anne paused at the bottom of the litter-strewn staircase, clinging to the banister, almost fainting. The baby kicked inside her, making her feel nauseous. She found a cab on the corner of the block and fell into the back; she was unable to stop herself from sobbing, unsure of what to do next. As soon as she was dropped off at the Red House she went to her bedroom before any of the staff could see her distress. The telephone was ringing as she entered the room. She picked it up, more out of habit than from any curiosity as to who it might be.

'Could I speak to Mrs Osborne, please?'

She recognized Alan's clipped tones at once. Another tired, weary voice.

'Hello, Alan. This *is* Anne.'

'Anne, my dear, I was sorry to hear this morning's news.'

'How do you know about it, Alan? How can you possibly know? Who told you?'

'City Hall phoned me and gave me the details soon after ten. I tried to call you, but your maid said you'd already left to do some shopping.'

'Oh, my God,' said Anne, 'I'd completely forgotten about the contract.' She sat down, breathing heavily.

'Are you all right, Anne?'

'Yes, I'm fine,' she said, trying unsuccessfully to hide the sobbing in her voice. 'What did City Hall have to say?'

'The hospital contract was awarded to a firm called Kirkbride and Carter. Apparently Henry wasn't even placed in the top three. I've been trying to reach him all morning, but it seems he left his office soon after ten, and he hasn't been seen since. I don't suppose you know where he is, Anne?'

'No, I haven't any idea.'

'Do you want me to come around, my dear? I could be with you in a few minutes.'

'No, thank you, Alan.' Anne paused to draw a shaky breath.

'Please forgive me for the way I've treated you these past few days. If Richard were still alive, he would never forgive me.'

'Don't be silly, Anne. Our friendship has lasted for far too many years for a little thing like that to be of any importance.'

The kindness of his words triggered off a fresh bout of weeping. Anne staggered to her feet.

'I must go, Alan. I can hear someone at the front door – it may be Henry.'

'Take care, Anne, and don't worry. As long as I'm chairman, the bank will always support you. Don't hesitate to call if there's anything I can do.'

Anne put the telephone down. The effort of breathing became overwhelming, and the vigorous contractions made her feel sick. She sank to the floor.

A few moments later the maid knocked quietly on the door. She looked in to see her mistress lying on the floor. She rushed in, William by her side. It was the first time he had entered his mother's bedroom since her marriage to Henry Osborne. Anne was shaking uncontrollably, unaware of their presence. Little flecks of foam spattered her lips. In a few seconds the attack passed, and she lay moaning quietly.

'Mother,' William said urgently, 'what's the matter?'

Anne opened her eyes and stared wildly at her son. 'Richard,' she said, 'thank God you've come.'

'It's William, Mother.'

Her gaze faltered. 'I have no more strength left, Richard. I must pay for my mistake. Forgive . . .'

Her voice trailed off to a groan as another spasm overcame her.

'What's happening?' said William helplessly.

'I think it must be the baby,' the maid said, 'though it isn't due for two months.'

'Get Dr MacKenzie on the phone immediately,' said William as he ran to the bedroom door. 'Matthew!' he shouted. 'Come up quickly.'

Matthew bounded up the stairs and joined William in the bedroom.

'Help me get my mother down to the car.'

The two boys picked Anne up and carried her gently downstairs and out to the car. She was panting and groaning, clearly in considerable pain. William ran back into the house and grabbed the phone from the maid while Matthew waited in the car.

'Dr MacKenzie.'

'Yes, who's this?'

'My name is William Kane – you won't know me, sir.'

'Don't know you, young man? I delivered you. What can I do for you?'

'I think my mother is in labour. I'm driving her to the hospital immediately. We should be there in a few minutes.'

Dr MacKenzie's tone changed. 'All right, William, don't worry. I'll be waiting for you, and everything will be prepared and ready by the time you arrive.'

'Thank you, sir.' William hesitated. 'She seemed to have had some sort of a fit. Is that normal?'

William's words chilled the doctor. He too hesitated.

'Well, not quite normal. But your mother will be just fine once she's had the baby. Get her here as quickly as you can.'

William put down the phone, ran out of the house and jumped into the Rolls-Royce. Matthew, having only had one lesson on his father's Rolls, drove the car in fits and starts, never once getting out of first gear. He didn't stop for anything until they reached the hospital entrance. The two boys lifted Anne gently out of the car and placed her on a waiting stretcher. A nurse quickly guided them through to the maternity unit, where Dr MacKenzie was standing in the doorway of one of the delivery rooms. He took over, and asked them to remain outside.

William and Matthew sat in silence on a small bench in the corridor and waited. Frightening cries and screams, unlike any sound they had ever heard before, came from the delivery room – to be succeeded by an even more frightening silence. For the first time in his life William felt totally helpless. The two boys sat on the bench for over an hour, not a word passing between them. Eventually a tired Dr MacKenzie emerged. When they rose the doctor looked at Matthew. 'William?' he asked.

'No, sir, I'm Matthew Lester. This is William.' The doctor turned and put a hand on William's shoulder. 'William, I'm so sorry. Your mother died a few minutes ago ... and the child, a little girl, was stillborn.'

William's legs gave way and he sank back onto the bench.

'We did everything in our power to save them, but it was too late.' He shook his head wearily.

William sat in silence. At last he whispered, 'How *could* she die? How could you *let* her die?'

The doctor sat down on the bench beside him. 'She wouldn't listen,' he said. 'I warned her repeatedly after her miscarriage not to have another child, but after she married again, she and your stepfather never took my warnings seriously. When you brought her in today, for no apparent reason her blood pressure had soared to the level where eclampsia ensues.'

'Eclampsia?'

'Convulsions. Sometimes patients can survive several attacks. Sometimes they simply – stop breathing.'

William began to cry and let his head fall into his hands. No one spoke for several minutes. William eventually stood up and Matthew guided him gently along the corridor. The doctor followed them. When they reached the entrance, he looked at William.

'Her blood pressure went up so suddenly. That's most unusual, and she didn't put up a real fight, almost as if she no longer cared. Strange – had something been troubling her lately?'

William raised his tear-streaked face. 'Not *something*,' he said with passion. 'Some*one*.'

—◦—

Alan Lloyd was sitting in a corner of the drawing room when the two boys arrived back at the Red House. He rose as they entered.

'William,' he said immediately. 'I blame myself for authorizing the loan.'

William stared at him, not taking in his words.

Matthew stepped into the silence. 'I don't think that's

important any longer, sir,' he said quietly. 'William's mother has just died giving birth to a stillborn child.'

Alan Lloyd turned ashen, steadied himself by grasping the mantelpiece and turned away. It was the first time either of them had seen a grown man weep.

'It's my fault,' said the banker. 'I'll never forgive myself. I didn't tell her everything I knew. I loved her so much that I never wanted her to be distressed.'

His anguish enabled William to be calm.

'It wasn't your fault, Alan,' he said firmly. 'You did everything in your power, I know that, and now it's me who's going to need your help.'

Alan Lloyd braced himself. 'Has Osborne been informed about your mother's death?'

'I neither know nor care.'

'I've been trying to reach him all day about the hospital contract. He left his office soon after ten this morning and he hasn't been seen since.'

'He'll turn up sooner or later,' William said grimly.

◄○►

After Alan Lloyd had left, William and Matthew sat together in the drawing room for most of the night, dozing off and on, rarely speaking. At four o'clock in the morning, as William counted the chimes of the grandfather clock, he thought he heard a noise in the street. He looked up to see Matthew staring out of the window, and walked stiffly across to join him. They both watched Henry Osborne stagger across Louisburg Square, a bottle in one hand, a bunch of keys in the other. He fumbled with his keys for some time and finally stepped into the hallway, blinking dazedly at the two boys.

'I want Anne, not you. Why aren't you at school? I don't want you,' he said, his voice thick and slurred, as he pushed past William and walked into the drawing room. 'Where's Anne?'

'My mother is dead,' said William quietly.

Osborne looked at him, disbelief etched on his face. He

walked across to the sideboard and poured himself a whiskey, which caused William to lose his self-control.

'Where were you when she needed a husband?' he shouted.

Osborne didn't let go of the bottle. 'What about the baby?'

'Stillborn, a little girl.'

Osborne slumped into a chair, drunken tears starting to run down his face. 'She lost my little baby?'

William was nearly incoherent with rage. 'Your baby? Stop thinking about yourself for a change!' he shouted. 'You know Dr MacKenzie advised her against becoming pregnant again.'

'Expert in that as well, are we, like everything else? If you'd minded your own fucking business, I could have taken care of my own wife without your interference.'

'And her money, it seems.'

'Money. You tightfisted little bastard. I bet losing that hurts you more than losing your mother.'

'Get up!' William shouted at him.

Osborne dragged himself up and smashed the bottle on the edge of a table, splashing whiskey onto the carpet. He swayed towards William, the broken bottle in his raised hand. William stood his ground. Matthew came between them and easily removed the bottle from the drunken man's grasp.

William pushed his friend aside and advanced until his face was only inches away from Osborne's.

'Now, you listen to me, and listen carefully. I want you out of this house immediately. If I ever hear from you again I shall instigate a full legal inquiry into what has happened to my mother's half-million dollar investment in your firm, and I shall reopen my enquiries about who you really are and your past activities in Chicago. If, on the other hand, I do not hear from you again, ever, I shall consider the matter closed. Now get out before I do something I'll regret.'

Osborne staggered out of the room. Neither of them heard his threat as the door slammed.

—◇—

The next morning William visited the bank. He was immediately shown into the chairman's office. Alan Lloyd was placing some documents into a briefcase. He handed a piece of paper to William without speaking. It was a short letter to all board members tendering his resignation as chairman of the bank.

'Could you ask your secretary to join us?' asked William quietly.

'As you wish.'

Alan pressed a button on the side of his desk, and a middle-aged, conservatively dressed woman entered the room.

'Good morning, Mr Kane,' she said when she saw William. 'I was so sorry to hear about your mother.'

'Thank you,' said William. 'Has anyone else seen this letter?'

'No, sir,' said the secretary. 'I was about to type twelve copies for Mr Lloyd to sign.'

'Well, don't,' said William, 'and please forget that it ever existed.'

She stared into the blue eyes of the sixteen-year-old boy. So like his father, she thought. 'Yes, Mr Kane.' She left, closing the door. Alan Lloyd looked puzzled.

'Kane and Cabot does not need a new chairman at the moment, Alan,' said William. 'You did nothing my father would not have done in the same circumstances.'

'It's not as easy as that,' Alan said.

'It is as easy as that,' said William. 'We can discuss this again when I'm twenty-one, and not before. Until then I would be obliged if you would run my bank with your usual prudence and wisdom. I want nothing of what has happened to be discussed outside this office. You will destroy any information you have on Henry Osborne, and consider the matter closed.'

William tore up the letter of resignation and dropped the pieces into the fire. He put his arm around Alan's shoulders.

'I have no family now, Alan, only you. For God's sake, don't desert me.'

―◇―

When William returned to Beacon Hill, Grandmother Kane and Grandmother Cabot were sitting in silence in the drawing room.

They rose as he entered the room. It was the first time William realized he was now the head of the Kane family.

The funeral took place quietly four days later at St Paul's Episcopal Cathedral. No one but family and close friends was invited; the only notable absentee was Henry Osborne. As the mourners departed, they paid their respects to William. The grandmothers stood a pace behind him, like sentinels, watching, approving the calm and dignified way in which he conducted himself. When everyone had left, William accompanied Alan Lloyd to his car.

The chairman was delighted by William's request.

'As you know, Alan, my mother always intended to build a children's wing for Massachusetts General, in memory of my father. I would like her wish to be carried out.'

21

WLADEK REMAINED at the Polish consulate in Constantinople for over a year, rather than the few days he had originally anticipated. He worked day and night with Pawel Zaleski, becoming an indispensable aide, colleague and close friend. Nothing was too much trouble for him, and Zaleski soon began to wonder how he would manage when Wladek left. The young man visited the British Consulate once a week to eat in the kitchen with Mrs Henderson, the Scottish cook, and on one occasion with His Britannic Majesty's Second Consul, in the dining room.

Around them the old Islamic traditions were being swept away, and the Ottoman Empire was beginning to totter. Mustafa Kemal was the name on everyone's lips. The sense of impending change only made Wladek more restless. His mind returned continually to the Baron and those he had loved at the castle. The necessity of surviving from day to day in Russia had kept them from his mind, but in Turkey they rose up before him, a silent procession: the Baron, Leon, Florentyna . . . Sometimes he could see them laughing and happy – Leon swimming in the river, Florentyna playing cat's cradle in her bedroom, the Baron's face strong and proud in the evening candlelight – but always the well-remembered, well-loved faces would melt away, and try as he might to hold them firm, it was always the last time he'd seen them that came back again and again: Leon lying dead in the castle grounds, Florentyna bleeding in agony, the Baron blind and broken.

Wladek began to feel that he could never return to a land

peopled by such ghosts until he had made something of his own life. With that single thought in mind he set his heart on emigrating to America, as his countryman Tadeusz Kosciuszko, of whom the Baron had told so many enthralling tales, had done long before him. The United States, described by Pawel Zaleski as the 'New World'. The name inspired Wladek with hope for the future, and perhaps even a chance to return one day to Poland in triumph.

It was Pawel who supplied the money for an immigrant passage to the United States. They were difficult to come by, and had to be arranged at least a year in advance. It seemed to Wladek as though the whole of Eastern Europe was trying to escape and start afresh in the New World.

◄o►

In the spring of 1921, Wladek Koskiewicz boarded the SS *Black Arrow*, bound for Ellis Island, New York. He took with him one suitcase, containing all his belongings, and a set of papers issued by Pawel Zaleski.

The Polish Consul accompanied him to the wharf embraced him affectionately and bade him farewell. 'Go with God, my child.'

The traditional Polish response came naturally from the recesses of Wladek's memory. 'Remain with God,' he replied.

As he reached the top of the gangplank, Wladek recalled his terrifying journey from Odessa to Constantinople a year before. This time there wasn't a lump of coal in sight, only emigrants wherever he looked – Poles, Lithuanians, Estonians, Ukrainians, Slavs, and others whose racial background he hadn't come across. He clutched his suitcase and waited in line, the first of many long waits he would have to endure before being allowed to enter the United States.

His papers were carefully scrutinized by an official checking for Turks trying to avoid military service, but Pawel Zaleski's documents were impeccable. Wladek invoked a silent blessing on his fellow countryman, as he watched others being turned back.

Next came a vaccination, followed by a cursory medical

examination which, had he not been well fed for the past year, Wladek might have failed. At last, with all the checks completed, he was allowed to go below to the steerage quarters where there were separate compartments allocated for males, females and married couples. Wladek made his way to the male quarters, where he found a group of Poles occupying a large block of iron berths, each containing four two-tiered bunk beds. Each bunk had a thin straw mattress, a light blanket and no pillow. Having no pillow didn't concern Wladek, who had never been able to sleep on one since leaving Camp 201.

He selected a bunk below a boy who looked roughly his own age.

'I'm Wladek Koskiewicz.'

'I'm Jerzy Nowak from Warsaw,' volunteered the boy in Polish, 'and I'm going to make my fortune in America.' The boy thrust out his hand.

Wladek and Jerzy spent the time before the ship sailed telling each other of their experiences, both pleased to have someone to share their loneliness with, neither willing to admit his total ignorance of what to expect when they reached the shores of America. Jerzy, it turned out, had lost both his parents in the war but had few other claims of interest. He became entranced by Wladek's stories: the son of a baron, brought up in a trapper's cottage, imprisoned by the Germans and the Russians, escaped from Siberia and then from a Turkish executioner thanks to the silver band left to him by his father. It seemed to Jerzy that Wladek had packed more into his fifteen years than he could hope to manage in a lifetime.

The following morning the *Black Arrow* sailed. Wladek and Jerzy leaned over the rail and watched Constantinople slip away in the blue distance of the Bosphorus. After the calm of the Sea of Marmara, the choppiness of the Aegean afflicted most of the passengers with a horrible abruptness. The two washrooms for the steerage passengers, with ten basins apiece, six toilets and cold saltwater taps, caused queues during waking hours and a continual disruption at night. After a couple of days the stench of their quarters reminded Wladek of the dungeons in Slonim castle.

Food was served on long wooden tables in a large, filthy dining hall: warm soup, potatoes, fish, boiled beef and cabbage, brown or black bread. Wladek had tasted worse food, but not since leaving Siberia, and he was glad of the provisions Mrs Henderson had packed for him: sausages, nuts and even a little brandy. He and Jerzy shared their feast huddled in the corner of their berth. They ate together, explored the ship together and, at night, slept one above the other.

On the third day at sea, Jerzy brought a Polish girl to their table for supper. Her name, he informed Wladek casually, was Zaphia. It was the first time in his life that Wladek had ever looked at a girl twice, and from that moment he couldn't stop looking at her. She rekindled his memories of Florentyna. The warm grey eyes, the long fair hair that fell onto her shoulders, the soft, gentle voice. He found he wanted to touch her. She occasionally smiled across at Wladek, who was miserably aware of how much better looking Jerzy was than he. He tagged along when Jerzy escorted her back to the women's quarters.

Jerzy turned on him afterwards, mildly irritated. 'Can't you find a woman of your own? This one's mine.'

Wladek didn't admit that he had no idea how to find a woman of his own.

'There will be enough time for girls when we reach America,' he said scornfully.

'Why wait for America? I intend to have as many on this ship as possible.'

'How will you manage that?' asked Wladek, intent on acquiring knowledge without admitting to his ignorance.

'We have twelve more days on this awful old tub, and by the time we reach America, I intend to have had twelve women,' boasted Jerzy.

'What can you do with twelve women?' asked Wladek.

'Fuck them, of course.'

Wladek looked perplexed.

'Good God,' said Jerzy. 'Don't tell me the man who survived the Germans, escaped from the Russians, killed a man at the age of twelve and narrowly missed having his hand chopped off by a

bunch of savage Turks has never bedded a woman?' He laughed
so loud that a multilingual chorus from the surrounding bunks
told him to shut up.

'Well,' Jerzy continued in a whisper, 'the time has come to
broaden your education, because at last I've found something I
can teach you.' He peered over the side of his bunk, although he
could not see Wladek's face in the dark. 'Zaphia's an understanding sort of girl. I don't doubt she could be persuaded to expand
your education a little. I'll see if I can arrange it.'

Wladek didn't reply.

No more was said on the subject, but the next day Zaphia
began to show a little more interest in Wladek. She sat next to
him at mealtimes, and they talked for hours of their experiences
and expectations. She was an orphan from Poznan, on her way
to join cousins in Chicago. Wladek told her that he was going to
New York, and would probably live with Jerzy.

'I hope New York is not far from Chicago,' said Zaphia.

'You can come and see me when I am the mayor,' said Jerzy
expansively.

She sniffed disparagingly. 'You're too Polish, Jerzy. You can't
speak good English like Wladek.'

'I'll learn,' Jerzy said confidently. 'And I'll start by making my
name American. From today I will be George Novak. Then I'll
have no trouble. Everyone in the United States will think I'm
American. What about you, Wladek Koskiewicz? Nothing much
you can do with a name like that?'

Wladek looked at the newly christened George in silent
resentment of his own name. Unable to adopt the title to which
he felt himself the rightful heir, he hated the name Koskiewicz,
which only reminded him of his illegitimacy.

'I'll manage,' he said. 'I'll even help you with your English if
you like.'

'And I'll help you find a girl.'

Zaphia giggled. 'You needn't bother, he's found one.'

Jerzy, or George, as he now insisted they call him, retreated
after supper each night into one of the tarpaulin-covered lifeboats
with a different girl. Wladek longed to know what he got up to,

even though some of the women George selected were not merely filthy, but would clearly have been unattractive even when scrubbed.

One night after supper, when George had disappeared again, Wladek and Zaphia sat out on deck. She placed an arm around his neck and began to kiss him. He pressed his mouth firmly against hers; it felt horribly unfamiliar, and he didn't know what to do next. To his surprise and embarrassment, her tongue parted his lips. After a few moments of apprehension, Wladek found her open mouth intensely exciting, and was alarmed to find his penis stiffening. He tried to draw away, not wishing to embarrass her, but she didn't seem to mind. She began to press her body gently and rhythmically against his, and pulled his hands down to her buttocks. His swollen penis throbbed against her stomach, giving him almost unbearable pleasure. She disengaged her mouth and whispered in his ear.

'I think the time has come to take your clothes off, Wladek.' She detached herself, and burst out laughing when he didn't move. 'Well, maybe tomorrow,' she said, pushing herself up off the deck before kissing him.

Wladek stumbled back to his bunk in a daze, determined not to make a fool of himself a second time. No sooner had he settled in his berth, imagining what might have happened if he'd taken off his trousers, than a large hand grabbed him by the hair and pulled him out of his bunk and onto the floor. In an instant, any thoughts of Zaphia vanished. Two men he had never seen before towered above him. They dragged him to a far corner and pushed him up against the wall. One of them clamped his hand firmly over Wladek's mouth, and held a knife to his throat.

'Don't make a sound, Polack' whispered the man holding the knife, as he pushed the blade against Wladek's skin. 'All we want is the silver band.'

The realization that his treasure might be stolen was almost as horrifying to Wladek as the thought of losing his hand. Before he could respond, the other man wrenched the band from his wrist.

Suddenly someone leapt onto the back of the man holding the knife. This gave Wladek the chance to punch the one who was holding him pinned to the wall. The sleepy emigrants around them began to wake and take an interest in what was going on. The two intruders were no match for the Poles, and escaped as quickly as they could, but not before George had managed to stick the knife into the side of one of them.

'Go to the cholera!' shouted Wladek at his retreating back.

'I don't think they'll be back in a hurry,' said George. He looked down at the silver band lying in the sawdust on the floor. 'It's magnificent,' he said almost reverently. 'There will always be men who will go after such a prize.'

Wladek picked up the band and slipped it back onto his wrist.

'You nearly lost it that time,' said George. 'Lucky for you I was a little late getting back tonight.'

'Why were you late?' asked Wladek.

'I found some other idiot in my lifeboat tonight, already with his pants down. I soon got rid of him.'

'How did you manage that?' asked Wladek as he climbed back into his bunk.

'I told him the girl he was on top of had the pox. I've never seen anyone get dressed so quickly.'

'What do you do when you're in the lifeboat?' asked Wladek.

'Fuck them silly – what do you think I do?' With that George rolled over and went to sleep.

Lying in his bunk, unable to sleep, Wladek touched the silver band and thought about what George had said, wondering what it would be like to 'fuck' Zaphia.

The next morning the ship was hit by a storm, and all the passengers were ordered below decks. The stench of so many bodies in close proximity, intensified by the ship's heating system, seemed to permeate every inch of their quarters, and few escaped being violently sick.

'The worst of it is,' groaned George, 'now I won't be able to make it a round dozen.'

When the storm abated, anyone who could still move headed for the decks. Wladek and George made their way around the crowded gangways, thankful to gulp the fresh sea air. Many of the girls smiled at George, but not one of them gave Wladek a second look. A dark-haired girl, her cheeks made pink by the wind, smiled when she passed George. He turned to Wladek.

'I'll have her tonight.' Wladek stared at the girl and noticed the way she looked at George. 'Tonight,' he repeated as the girl passed within earshot. She pretended not to hear him, and walked away a little too quickly.

'Turn round, Wladek, and see if she's still looking at me.'

Wladek turned around. 'Yes, she is,' he said, surprised.

'She's mine tonight,' said George. 'Have you had Zaphia yet?'

'No,' said Wladek. 'Tonight.'

'About time. After all, you're never going to see her again once we've reached New York.'

George arrived at supper that night with the dark-haired girl who they'd seen on deck. Wladek and Zaphia left them, went onto the deck and strolled around the ship several times. Wladek glanced sideways at her pleasing figure. It had to be now or never. He led her to a shadowy corner near one of the lifeboats, and started to kiss her. She responded by opening her mouth, then leant back a little until her shoulders were resting against the tarpaulin. They heard groans coming from inside the lifeboat. It didn't help. Wladek moved towards her, and she drew his hands slowly up to her breasts. He touched them tentatively, surprised by their softness. She undid a couple of buttons on her blouse and slipped his hand inside. His first feel of her naked flesh was delicious.

'Christ, your hand is frozen,' Zaphia said.

Wladek pulled her towards him, his mouth dry, his breath heavy. She parted her legs a little and Wladek fell clumsily against her, aware of several layers of clothing. She moved in sympathy with him for a couple of minutes, then pushed him away.

'Not here on the deck,' she said. 'Let's find a boat.'

The first three boats they checked were already occupied, but they finally found an empty one and wriggled under the tarpaulin. In the pitch darkness, Wladek could hear her making some adjustments to her clothing, she then pulled him gently on top of her. It took her very little time to bring Wladek to his earlier pitch of excitement, despite the remaining layers of clothing. He thrust himself between her legs, and was on the point of orgasm when she again pushed him away.

'Why don't you undo your trousers?' she whispered.

He hurriedly undid his fly buttons and thrust himself inside her. He came almost immediately, and quickly withdrew, feeling the sticky sperm running down the inside of his thigh. He lay dazed, shocked by the abruptness of the act, painfully aware that the wooden notches of the lifeboat were digging uncomfortably into his elbows and knees.

'Was that the first time you've made love to a girl?' asked Zaphia, wishing he would climb off her.

'No, of course not.'

'Do you love me, Wladek?'

'Yes, I do,' he said. 'And as soon as I've settled in New York, I'll come and find you in Chicago.'

'I'd like that, Wladek,' she said as she buttoned up her dress. 'I love you, too.'

'Did you fuck her?' was George's first question on Wladek's return.

'Yes.'

'Was it good?'

'Not bad,' said Wladek, 'but I've had better.'

◄○►

In the morning they were awakened by the noise of other passengers already celebrating their last day on board the *Black Arrow*. Some of them had been on deck long before sunrise, hoping to catch the first sight of land.

Wladek packed his few belongings in his suitcase, put on his only suit and cap, and joined Zaphia and George on deck. The three of them peered into the distance, waiting in silence for their first glimpse of the United States of America.

'There it is!' shouted a passenger from a deck above them, and cheering broke out as more and more passengers spotted the grey strip of Long Island on the horizon.

A little tug bustled up to the side of the *Black Arrow* and guided her between Brooklyn and Staten Island and on into New

York Harbor. The Statue of Liberty seemed to welcome them, her lamp lifted high into the early morning sky. Wladek gazed in awe at the emerging skyline of Manhattan.

Finally they moored near the turreted and spired red brick buildings of Ellis Island. The first- and second-class passengers who had private cabins and their own separate decks disembarked first. Wladek hadn't caught a glimpse of them until that morning. Their bags were carried for them by porters, and they were greeted by smiling faces at the dockside. Wladek knew there would be no smiling faces to greet him.

After the favoured few had disembarked, the captain announced over the loudspeaker that the rest of the passengers would not be leaving the ship for several hours. A groan of disappointment went up as the message was translated into various languages. Zaphia sat down on the deck and burst into tears. Wladek tried to comfort her. Eventually an immigration official came around with numbered labels which he hung round the passengers' necks. Wladek's was B.127; it reminded him of the last time he was a number. Would America turn out to be even worse than the Russian camps?

In the middle of the afternoon – they had been offered no food, nor further information – an announcement over a loudspeaker told them they could disembark. Wladek, George and Zaphia joined the others as they shuffled slowly down the gangplank to set foot on American soil for the first time. Immediately the men were separated from the women and sent off to a different shed. Wladek kissed Zaphia and didn't want to let her go, holding up the line. An official parted them.

'All right, let's get moving,' he said. 'You'll be able to meet up on the other side.' Wladek lost sight of Zaphia as he and George were pushed forward.

They spent their first night in America in a damp shed. They were unable to sleep as interpreters moved among the crowded rows of bunks, offering assistance to the bewildered immigrants. In the morning they were lined up for medical examinations. Wladek was told to climb a steep flight of stairs, an exercise the blue-uniformed doctor made him repeat twice, observing his limp carefully. Wladek tried very hard to minimize it, until finally the doctor was satisfied. Wladek was next made to remove his cap and his stiff collar so that his face, eyes, hair, hands and neck could be examined carefully. The man standing behind him had a harelip; the doctor stopped him immediately, put a chalk cross on his right shoulder and sent him to the other end of the shed.

After the physical was over, Wladek joined George to stand in another long line outside the Public Examination room, where each person was interviewed for about five minutes. Wladek could only wonder what they were being asked.

It was three more hours before George was ushered into the tiny cubicle. When he came out, he grinned at Wladek. 'Easy,' he said, 'even for someone as dumb as you.'

Wladek could feel the palms of his hands sweating as he stepped forward and followed an official into a small, undecorated cubicle. There were two examiners seated behind a desk, writing furiously on what looked like official papers.

'Do you speak English?' asked the first.

'Yes, sir, I do quite good,' replied Wladek, wishing he had practised his English more on the voyage.

'What is your name?'

'Wladek Koskiewicz, sir.'

The second man passed him a big black book. 'Do you know what this is?'

'Yes, sir, the Bible.'

'Do you believe in God?'

'Yes, sir, I do.'

'Put your hand on the Bible and swear that you will answer our questions truthfully.'

Wladek placed his right hand on the Bible and said, 'I promise I tell the truth.'

'What is your nationality?'

'Polish.'

'Who paid for your passage?'

'I paid from my money that I earn in Polish consulate in Constantinople.'

The first official studied Wladek's papers, nodded and then asked, 'Do you have a home to go to?'

'Yes, sir. I go stay at Mr Peter Novak. He my friend's uncle. He live in New York.'

'Good. Do you have a job to go to?'

'Yes, sir. I go work in bakery of Mr Novak.'

'Have you ever been arrested?' asked the other man.

Russia flashed through Wladek's mind. That couldn't count. Turkey – he wasn't going to mention that.

'No, sir, never.'

'Are you an anarchist?'

'No, sir.'

'Are you a communist?'

'No, sir. I hate communists – they kill my sister.'

'Are you willing to abide by the laws of the United States of America?'

'Yes, sir.'

'Have you any money?'

'Yes, sir.'

'May we see it?'

'Yes, sir.' Wladek placed a bundle of bills and a few coins on the table.

'Thank you,' said the examiner. 'You may put the money back in your pocket.'

'What is twenty-one plus twenty-four?' the second examiner asked.

'Forty-five,' said Wladek without hesitation.

'How many legs does a cow have?'

Wladek could not believe his ears. 'Four, sir,' he said, wondering if it was a trick question.

'And a horse?'

'Four, sir,' said Wladek, still in disbelief.

'Which would you throw overboard if you were out at sea in a small boat which needed to be lightened, bread or money?'

'The money, sir,' said Wladek.

'Good.' The examiner picked up a card marked 'Admitted'

and handed it to Wladek. 'After you've changed your money for dollars, show this card to the Immigration Officer. Tell him your full name and he will give you a registration card. You will then be given an entry certificate. If you do not commit a crime for five years, then pass a simple reading and writing examination in English and agree to obey the Constitution, you will be allowed to apply for full United States citizenship. Good luck, Wladek.'

'Thank you, sir.'

At the money-exchange counter Wladek handed in a year's worth of Turkish savings along with three 50-rouble notes. He was given $47 and 20 cents in exchange for the Turkish money, but was told the roubles were worthless. He thought of Dr Dubien and his fifteen years of diligent saving.

The final step was to see the Immigration Officer, who was seated behind a counter near the exit barrier, directly under a picture of President Harding. Wladek and George walked across and stood in front of him.

'Full name?' the officer asked George.

'George Novak,' came the firm reply. The officer wrote the name on a card.

'And your address?' he asked.

'286 Broome Street, New York.'

The officer passed George a card. 'This is your immigration certificate: MDL21871707 – George Novak. Welcome to the United States, George. I'm from Poland too. I have a feeling you'll do well in America. Many congratulations, and good luck, George.'

George smiled and shook hands with the officer, then stood to one side and waited for his friend. The official turned his attention to Wladek, who passed over the card marked 'Admitted.'

'Full name?' asked the officer.

Wladek hesitated.

'What's your name?' repeated the man, a little louder.

Wladek couldn't get the words out. How he hated that peasant name.

'For the last time, what's your name?' the man insisted.

George was staring at Wladek. So were several others who

were waiting in line behind him. Wladek still didn't speak. The officer reached across and grabbed his wrist, looked closely at the inscription on the silver band, wrote something down on a card and passed it to Wladek.

'This is your immigration certificate, MDL21871708 – Baron Abel Rosnovski. Welcome to the United States. Many congratulations, and good luck, Abel.'

PART TWO

1923-1928

22

IN SEPTEMBER 1923 William was elected president of the senior class of St Paul's, exactly thirty-three years after his father had held the same office.

William did not win the election by virtue of being the finest athlete or the most popular boy in the school. Matthew Lester, his closest friend, would undoubtedly have won any contest based on those criteria. It was simply that William was the most impressive boy in the school and for that reason Matthew could not be persuaded to run against him.

St Paul's also entered William's name as its candidate for the Hamilton Memorial Mathematics Scholarship to Harvard, and William worked single-mindedly towards that goal every waking hour.

When he returned to the Red House for Christmas, he was looking forward to an uninterrupted period in which to get to grips with *Principia Mathematica*. But it was not to be, as there were several invitations to parties and balls awaiting his arrival. To most of them he was able to reply with a tactful message of regret, but one was absolutely inescapable. The grandmothers had arranged a ball, to be held at the Red House. William wondered how old he would have to be before he could defend his home against invasion from the two great ladies, and decided that time had not yet come. He had few close friends in Boston, but that did not inhibit the grandmothers in their compilation of a formidable guest list.

To mark the occasion they presented William with his first

tuxedo, in the latest double-breasted style; he received the gift with a pretence of indifference, but later swaggered around his bedroom, admiring his image in the mirror.

The next day he put through a long-distance call to New York and asked Matthew to join him for the 'ghastly affair'. Matthew's sister wanted to come as well, but her mother didn't think it would be 'suitable' unless she was accompanied by a chaperone.

William was standing on the platform when Matthew stepped off the train.

'Come to think of it,' said Matthew as the chauffeur drove them to Beacon Hill, 'isn't it time you got yourself laid, William? There must be one girl in Boston with absolutely no taste.'

'Why, have you had a girl, Matthew?'

'Sure, last December in New York.'

'What was I doing at the time?'

'Probably touching up Bertrand Russell.'

'You never told me about her.'

'Nothing much to tell. It all happened at the bank's Christmas staff party. Actually, to put the incident in its proper perspective, I was taken advantage of by one of the directors' secretaries, a comely lady called Cynthia with large breasts that wobbled when . . .'

'Did you enjoy it?'

'Yes, but I'm not sure Cynthia did. She was far too drunk to realize I was there at the time. Still, you have to begin somewhere, and she was willing to give the boss's son a helping hand.'

A vision of Alan Lloyd's prim, middle-aged secretary flashed across William's mind.

'I don't think my chances of initiation by the chairman's secretary are all that promising,' he mused.

'You'd be surprised,' said Matthew knowingly. 'The ones who go around with their legs clamped together are often the ones who can't wait to get them apart.'

'Matthew, on the basis of one drunken experience, you are hardly entitled to consider yourself an oracle,' said William, as the car drew up outside the Red House.

'Oh, such jealousy, and from one's dearest friend,' Matthew sighed mockingly, as they entered the house. 'Wow! You've certainly made some changes since I was last here,' he added, admiring the modern cane furniture and the new paisley wallpaper. Only the maroon leather chair remained firmly rooted in its usual spot.

'The place needed brightening up a little,' said William. 'It was like living in the Stone Age. Besides, I didn't want to be reminded of ... Come on, this is no time to hang around discussing interior decoration.'

'What time are the guests expected for your little party?'

'Ball, Matthew – the grandmothers insist on calling it a ball.'

'There's only one thing that can be described as a ball on these occasions.'

William laughed and looked at his watch. 'They should start arriving in a couple of hours. Time for a bath and to get changed. Did you remember to bring a tuxedo?'

'Yes. But if I hadn't I could always wear my pyjamas. I usually leave one or the other behind, but I've never yet managed to forget both.'

'I don't think the grandmothers would approve of you turning up for the ball in your pyjamas.'

◄○►

The caterers arrived at six o'clock, twenty-three of them in all, and the grandmothers at seven to oversee the preparations, regal in long black lace dresses that swept along the floor. William and Matthew joined them in the drawing room a few minutes before eight. William was about to remove an inviting red cherry from the top of a magnificent iced cake when he heard Grandmother Kane's sentinel voice behind him.

'Don't touch the food, William, it's not for you.'

He swung around. 'Then who is it for?' he asked, as he kissed her slowly.

'Don't be fresh, William. Just because you're over six feet doesn't mean I wouldn't spank you.'

Matthew laughed.

'Grandmother, may I introduce my closest friend, Matthew Lester?'

Grandmother Kane subjected Matthew to a careful appraisal through her pince-nez before venturing: 'How do you do, young man?'

'It's an honour to meet you, Mrs Kane. I believe you knew my grandfather.'

'Knew your grandfather? Caleb Longworth Lester? He proposed marriage to me once, over fifty years ago. Of course, I turned him down. I told him he drank too much and that it would lead him to an early grave. I was proved right, so don't follow his example, either of you. Remember, alcohol dulls the brain.'

'We hardly get much chance, with Prohibition,' remarked Matthew innocently.

Mrs Kane ignored the comment, and turned her attention to the guest list.

The guests began to appear soon after eight, many of them complete strangers to their host, although he was delighted to see Alan Lloyd among the early arrivals.

'You're looking well, my boy,' Alan said, finding himself looking up at William for the first time.

'You too, sir. It was kind of you to come.'

'Kind? Have you forgotten that the invitation came from your grandmothers? I'm possibly brave enough to refuse one of them, but both . . .'

'You too, Alan?' William laughed. 'Can you spare a moment?' He guided the chairman towards a quiet corner, where he wasted no more time on small talk. 'I want to change my investment plan slightly, and start buying Lester's Bank stock whenever it comes on the market. I'd like to be holding about five per cent of the company by the time I'm twenty-one.'

'That won't be easy,' responded Alan. 'Lester's stock doesn't often come on the market, because it's all in private hands. But I'll see what I can do. May I enquire what is going on in that mind of yours, William?'

'Well, my long-term plan is—'

'William!' William turned to see Grandmother Cabot bearing down on them, a determined look on her face. 'William, this is a ball, not a board meeting, and I haven't seen you on the dance floor once this evening.'

'Quite right,' said Alan. 'You come and sit down with me, Mrs Cabot, while I kick the boy out into the real world. We can watch the dancing and enjoy the music.'

'Music? That's not music, Alan. It's nothing more than a cacophony of sound with no suggestion of melody.'

'My dear grandmother,' said William, 'that is "Yes, We Have No Bananas", the latest hit song by—'

'Then the time has come for me to depart this world,' said Grandmother Cabot, wincing.

'Never,' said Alan Lloyd gallantly.

William left them, and danced with a couple of girls he had a vague recollection of meeting in the past, although he needed to be reminded of their names. When he spotted Matthew sitting on a sofa in a corner he was glad of the excuse to escape the dance floor. He did not notice the girl sitting next to his friend until he was almost on top of them. When she looked up he felt his knees give way.

'Do you know Abby Blount?' asked Matthew casually.

'No,' said William, unable to take his eyes off her.

'This is your host, Mr William Lowell Kane.'

The girl cast her eyes demurely downward as William sat beside her. Matthew had noted the look on William's face, and left them to go off in search of some punch.

'How is it I've lived in Boston all my life and we've never met?' William asked.

'We did meet once before, Mr Kane,' said Abby. 'On that occasion you pushed me into the pond on the Common. We were both three at the time. That was fourteen years ago, and I still haven't forgiven you.'

'I'm sorry,' said William, after a pause during which he was unable to think of a more witty reply.

Abby smiled, trying to put him at ease. 'What a lovely house you have, William,' she said.

There was another long pause. 'Thank you,' said William weakly. He glanced, trying not to look as if he was staring at her. She was slim – oh, so slim – with huge brown eyes, long eyelashes and a profile that would have made any man look a second time. Her auburn hair was bobbed in a style he had hated until that moment.

'Matthew tells me you're going to Harvard next year,' she tried again.

'Yes, I am. I mean, would you like to dance?'

'Thank you,' she said.

The steps that had come so easily a few minutes before now seemed to forsake him. He trod on Abby's toes and continually propelled her into other dancers. He apologized, and she smiled. He held her a little more closely during the fourth dance.

'Do we know that young woman who seems to have monopolized William for the past hour?' Grandmother Cabot asked suspiciously.

Grandmother Kane picked up her pince-nez and studied the girl accompanying William through the open bay windows and out onto the lawn.

'Abigail Blount,' Grandmother Kane declared.

'Admiral Blount's granddaughter?' enquired Grandmother Cabot.

'Yes.'

Grandmother Cabot gave a slight nod, showing a degree of approval.

William guided Abby to the far end of the garden, and stopped by a large chestnut tree that he had only used in the past for climbing.

'Do you always try to kiss a girl the first time you meet her?' asked Abby.

'To be honest,' said William, 'I've never kissed a girl before.'

Abby laughed. 'I'm very flattered.'

She offered him her pink cheek, but then said it was too cold to stay outside and insisted on being taken back indoors. The grandmothers observed their return with undisguised relief.

After all the guests had left, the two boys walked around the garden, chatting about the evening.

'Not a bad party,' said Matthew. 'Almost worth the trip from New York to the provinces, despite your stealing my girl.'

'Do you think she'll help me lose my virginity?' asked William, ignoring Matthew's mock accusation.

'Well, you've got two weeks to find out. But I suspect you'll discover she hasn't lost hers yet.'

'How can you be so sure?' asked William.

'Just the way she looked at you. Virgins always blush. I'm willing to bet you five dollars she doesn't succumb even to the charms of William Lowell Kane.'

The two men shook hands.

—◇—

William planned his campaign carefully. Losing his virginity was one thing, but losing five dollars to Matthew Lester was quite another. He saw Abby almost every day after the ball, taking advantage for the first time of owning his own home and car. He began to feel he would do better without the discreet but persistent chaperonage of Abby's parents, who seemed always to be in the middle distance, and he was not any nearer his goal when the last day of the holidays dawned.

Determined not to lose his five dollars, he sent Abby a dozen roses that morning, took her out to an expensive dinner at Joseph's in the evening and finally succeeded in coaxing her back to the Red House that night.

'How did you get hold of a bottle of whiskey?' asked Abby.

'It's not difficult if you know the right people,' William boasted.

The truth was that he had hidden a bottle of Henry Osborne's bourbon in his bedroom soon after he had departed, and was now glad he hadn't poured it down the drain as he'd originally planned.

The alcohol made William gasp and Abby's eyes water. He sat down beside her and put his arm confidently around her shoulder. She settled into it.

'Abby, I think you're terribly pretty,' he murmured at her auburn curls.

She gazed at him earnestly, her brown eyes wide open. 'Oh, William,' she breathed. 'And I think you're just wonderful.'

She leaned back, closed her eyes and allowed him to kiss her on the lips for the first time. Thus emboldened, William slipped a tentative hand from her wrist onto her breast. He left it there like a traffic cop halting an advancing stream of automobiles. She indignantly pushed it away to allow the traffic to move on.

'William, you mustn't do that.'

'Why not?' said William, struggling vainly to retain the initiative.

'Because you can't tell where it might end.'

'I've got a fair idea.'

Before he could renew his advances, Abby rose hastily from the sofa and smoothed her dress.

'I think I ought to be getting home, William.'

'But you've only just arrived.'

'Mother will want to know what I've been doing.'

'You'll be able to tell her – nothing.'

'And I think it's best it stays that way,' she replied.

'But I'm going back tomorrow,' – he avoided saying 'to school' – 'and I won't see you for three months.'

'Well, you can write to me, William.'

Unlike Valentino, William knew when he was beaten. 'Yes, of course I will,' he said. He rose, straightened his tie, took Abby by the hand and drove her home.

The following day, back at St Paul's, Matthew Lester accepted the proffered five-dollar bill with his eyebrows raised in mock astonishment.

'Say one word, Matthew, and I'll chase you right around the school with a baseball bat.'

'I can't think of any words that would truly express my deep feeling of sympathy for you.'

'Matthew,' he warned, 'right around the school.'

—◦—

William became aware of his housemaster's wife during his last term at St Paul's.

Mrs Raglan was a good-looking woman, a little slack around the stomach, and her hips could have been slimmer, but she carried her splendid bosom well, and the thick dark hair piled on top of her head was no more streaked with grey than was becoming. One Saturday when William had sprained his wrist on the hockey field, Mrs Raglan bandaged it for him in a cool compress, standing a little closer than was necessary, allowing William's arm to brush against her breast. He enjoyed the sensation. On another occasion, when he had a fever and was confined to the sick room for a few days, she brought him his meals herself and sat on his bed, her body touching his legs through the thin covering while he ate. He enjoyed that too.

She was rumoured to be Rags Raglan's second wife. None of the boys could imagine how Rags had managed to secure even one spouse, and Mrs Raglan occasionally indicated by the subtlest of sighs and silences that she shared something of their incredulity at her fate.

As part of his duties as house captain, William was required to report to Rags every night at ten-thirty once he had completed the lights-out round and was about to go to bed himself. One Monday evening when he knocked on Rags's door, he was surprised to hear Mrs Raglan's voice bidding him to enter. She was lying on a chaise longue dressed in a loose silk robe of faintly Japanese appearance.

William kept a firm grasp on the cold doorknob. 'All the lights are out and I've locked the front door, Mrs Raglan. Good night.'

She swung her legs onto the ground, and a pale flash of stockinged thigh appeared momentarily from under the draped silk.

'You're always in such a hurry, William. You can't wait for your life to begin, can you?' She walked over to a side table. 'Why don't you stay and have some hot chocolate? Silly me, I made enough for two. I quite forgot that Mr Raglan won't be back until Saturday morning.' There was a definite emphasis on the word 'Saturday'.

She carried a steaming cup over to William and looked at him to see whether the significance of her remarks had registered. Satisfied, she smiled and passed him the cup, allowing their hands to touch. He stirred the hot chocolate vigorously.

'Gerald is attending a conference,' she continued. It was the first time he had ever heard Mr Raglan's first name. 'Do shut the door, William, and come and sit down.'

William hesitated; he shut the door, but he did not feel he could sit in Rags's chair, nor did he want to sit next to Mrs Raglan. He decided Rags's chair was the lesser of two evils, and moved towards it.

'No, no,' she said, and patted the seat beside her.

William shuffled across and sat down nervously by her side, staring into his cup for inspiration. Finding none, he gulped the contents down, burning his tongue. He was relieved when Mrs Raglan stood up. She refilled his cup, ignoring his murmured protest, then moved silently across the room, wound up the Victrola and placed the needle on a record. He was still looking at the floor when she returned.

'You wouldn't let a lady dance by herself, would you, William?'

She began swaying in time to the music. William stood up and put his arm formally around her waist, as if they were in the middle of a crowded dance floor. Rags could have fitted in between them without any trouble. After a few bars she moved closer to William, and he stared over her right shoulder fixedly to indicate that he had not noticed that her left hand had slipped from his shoulder to the small of his back. When the music stopped, William assumed he would have a chance to return to the safety of his hot chocolate, but she had turned the record over and was back in his arms before he could sit down.

'Mrs Raglan, I think I ought to—'

'Relax a little, William.'

At last he found the courage to look into her eyes. He tried to reply, but he couldn't speak. Her hand was now exploring his back, and he felt her thigh move gently against his groin. He tightened his hold around her waist.

'That's better,' she said.

They circled the room, closely entwined, slower and slower, keeping time with the music as the record gently ran down. When it stopped she slipped away and switched off the light. William stood in the near dark, not moving, hearing the rustle of silk as he watched her discard her clothes.

The crooner had completed his song, and the needle was still scratching as the record continued to spin. William stood motionless in the middle of the room. Mrs Raglan took off his jacket, then led him back to the chaise longue. He groped for her in the dark, his shy novice's fingers encountering several parts of her body that did not feel at all as he had imagined they would. He withdrew them hastily to the comparatively familiar territory of her breasts. Her fingers exhibited no such reticence, and he began to feel sensations he had never dreamed possible. He wanted to shout out loud but checked himself, fearing it would wake the boys sleeping above him. She undid his fly buttons, and began to pull off his trousers.

William wondered how to enter her without showing his total lack of experience. It was not as easy as he had expected, and he grew more desperate by the second. Then her fingers moved across his stomach and guided him expertly. But before he could enter her, he had an orgasm.

'I'm so sorry,' said William, not sure what to do next. He lay silently on top of her for some time before she spoke.

'It will be better tomorrow, William. Don't forget, Rags is not back until Saturday.'

The sound of the scratching record returned to his ears.

Mrs Raglan remained in William's mind until lights out the next day. That night, she sighed. On Wednesday she panted. On Thursday she moaned. On Friday she cried out.

On Saturday morning, Rags Raglan returned from his conference, by which time William's education was complete.

—◦—

At the end of the Easter vacation, on Ascension Day, to be unfair, Abby Blount finally succumbed to William's charms. It cost Matthew five dollars and Abby her virginity. She was, after Mrs

Raglan, something of an anticlimax. It was the only event worthy of mention that happened during the entire break, because Abby was whisked off to Palm Beach with her parents, and William spent most of his time shut away with his books, at home to no one other than the grandmothers and Alan Lloyd. As Rags Raglan attended no further conferences, when William returned to St Paul's he continued to concentrate on his books.

He and Matthew would sit in their study for hours, never speaking unless Matthew had some mathematical equation he was quite unable to solve. When the long-awaited examinations finally took place, they lasted for one brutal week. The moment they were over, both young men felt relaxed, but as the days slipped by and they waited and waited to learn their results, they became less sanguine.

The Hamilton Memorial Mathematics Scholarship to Harvard was based entirely on the final examination results, and was open to every schoolboy in America. William had no way of judging how tough his opposition might be. When, a month later, he'd still heard nothing, he began to assume the worst, and even wondered if Harvard would offer him a place at all.

William was out playing baseball with some other seniors who were trying to kill the last few days of term before leaving school when the telegram arrived; those warm summer evenings when boys are most likely to be expelled for drunkenness, breaking windows or trying to get into bed with one of the masters' daughters, if not their wives.

William was declaring in a loud voice, to those who cared to listen, that he was about to hit his first home run. 'The Babe Ruth of St Paul's!' declared Matthew. Much laughter greeted this unlikely claim. When the telegram was handed to William by a second-former, home runs were quickly forgotten. He dropped his bat and tore open the little yellow envelope. The pitcher and fielders waited impatiently as he read the communication slowly.

'Are the Red Sox offering you a contract?' shouted the first baseman, the arrival of a telegram being an uncommon occurrence during a baseball game.

Matthew strolled across from the outfield to join his friend, trying to make out from his expression if the news was good or bad. William passed the telegram to him. He read it, leapt high into the air, dropped the piece of paper on the ground and accompanied William as he raced around the bases even though he hadn't actually hit the ball. The catcher picked up the telegram, read it and threw his glove into the bleachers with gusto. The little piece of yellow paper was then passed eagerly from player to player. The last to read it was the second-former, who, having caused so much happiness while receiving no thanks, decided the least he deserved was to know the contents.

The telegram was addressed to Mr William Lowell Kane. It read: 'Congratulations on winning the Hamilton Memorial Mathematics Scholarship to Harvard, full details to follow. Abbot Lawrence Lowell, President.' William never did get his home run, as he was heavily set upon by several fielders before he reached home plate.

Matthew looked on with delight as he revelled in his closest friend's success, but he was sad to think that it meant they might be parted. William felt it, too, but said nothing; they had to wait another nine days to learn that Matthew had also been offered a place at Harvard.

Upon the heels of that news, another telegram arrived, this one from Charles Lester, congratulating his son and inviting him and William to tea at the Plaza Hotel in New York. Both grandmothers sent congratulations to William, but as Grandmother Kane informed Alan Lloyd, somewhat testily, 'The boy has done no less than was expected of him and no more than his father did before him.'

◄○►

The two young men sauntered down Fifth Avenue on a balmy afternoon. Girls' eyes were drawn to the handsome pair, who affected not to notice. They removed their straw boaters as they entered the Plaza at three fifty-nine and strolled nonchalantly into the Palm Court where the family group was awaiting them. William's grandmothers flanked another old lady, who he assumed was the Lesters' equivalent of Grandmother Kane. Mr and Mrs

Charles Lester, their daughter Susan, whose eyes never left William, and Alan Lloyd completed the party, leaving two vacant chairs for William and Matthew.

Grandmother Kane summoned the nearest waiter with an imperious gloved hand. 'A fresh pot of tea and more cakes, please.'

The waiter hurried off to the kitchen. 'A pot of tea and cream cakes, madam,' he said on his return.

'Your father would have been proud of you, William,' the older man was saying to the taller of the two youths.

The waiter wondered what it was that the good-looking young man had achieved to elicit such praise.

William would not have noticed the waiter at all had it not been for the silver band around his wrist. The piece might easily have come from Tiffany's; the incongruity of it puzzled him.

'William,' said Grandmother Kane. 'Two cakes are quite sufficient; this is not your last meal before you go to Harvard.'

He smiled at the old lady with affection, and quite forgot about the silver band.

23

THAT NIGHT, Abel lay awake in his small room at the Plaza, thinking about the young man he'd served that afternoon, whose father would have been proud of him. He realized for the first time in his life exactly what he hoped to achieve. He wanted to be thought of as an equal by the Williams of this world.

Abel had had quite a struggle on his arrival in New York. He had been obliged to share a single small room with George and two of his cousins. As there were only two beds, he could only sleep when one of them was unoccupied. George's uncle had been unable to offer him a job, and after a few anxious weeks during which most of his savings were spent on keeping himself alive while he searched from Brooklyn to Queens, he finally found work in a large meat packers' on the Lower East Side. They paid $9 for a six-and-a-half-day week, and allowed him to sleep above the premises. The warehouse was in the heart of an almost self-sufficient little Polish community, but Abel rapidly became impatient with the insularity of his fellow countrymen, many of whom made no effort to speak English.

He saw George and his constant succession of girlfriends regularly at weekends, but spent most of his evenings during the week at night school improving his ability to read and write English. Within two years he had made himself fluent in his new tongue, retaining only the slightest trace of an accent. He now felt ready to leave the meat packers' – but for what, where and how?

Three months later, he found out.

Abel was dressing a leg of lamb one morning when he overheard one of the shop's biggest customers, the catering manager of the Plaza Hotel, grumbling to the butcher that he'd had to fire a junior waiter for petty theft.

'How can I find a replacement at such short notice?' the manager complained.

The butcher had no solution to offer. Abel did. He put on his only suit, walked forty-seven blocks uptown and was offered the job of junior waiter in the Palm Court, at $10 a week, with a room provided.

Once he had settled in at the Plaza, he enrolled for a night course in advanced English at Columbia University. He worked conscientiously every evening, secondhand *Webster's* open in one hand, pen scratching away with the other. During the mornings, between serving breakfast and setting up for lunch, he would copy out the editorials from *The New York Times*, looking up in his dictionary any word he didn't know the meaning of.

For the next two years Abel worked night and day at the Plaza – overtime was a word he didn't need to look up in his dictionary – until he was promoted to become a waiter in the Oak Room. He now made about twenty-five dollars a week, including tips. In his own world, he lacked for nothing.

Abel's teacher at Columbia was so impressed by his diligent pupil that he advised him to enrol for a further course, which would be a first step towards taking a Bachelor of Arts degree. He switched his spare-time reading from linguistics to economics, and started copying out the editorials in *The Wall Street Journal* instead of those in *The Times*. His new studies totally absorbed him and, with the exception of George, he quickly lost touch with the Polish friends of his early days in New York.

Each day Abel would carefully study the list of those who had reserved tables in the Oak Room – the Bakers, Loebs, Whitneys, Morgans and Phelpses – and try to work out why the rich were different. He read H. L. Mencken, *The American Mercury*, Scott Fitzgerald, Sinclair Lewis and Theodore Dreiser in his endless quest for knowledge. He studied *The Wall Street Journal* while the other waiters flipped through the *Mirror*, and read *The New*

York Times in his hour-long break while they dozed. He was not sure where his newly acquired knowledge would take him, but he never doubted the Baron's maxim that there was no substitute for a good education.

One Monday in August 1926 – he remembered the occasion well because it was the day Rudolph Valentino died, and many of the ladies shopping on Fifth Avenue wore black – Abel was serving one of the corner tables, which were always reserved for important businessmen who wished to lunch in privacy without being overheard. He enjoyed serving there, as he often picked up pieces of inside information from the conversation. After the restaurant had closed for the afternoon, Abel would check the stock prices of the diners' companies, and if the tone of the conversation had been optimistic, he would invest a small amount of money in the company. If the host had ordered cigars at the end of the meal, Abel would make a larger investment. Seven times out of ten, the value of the stock he had selected doubled within six months, the period he would allow himself to hold on to any stock. Using this system, he lost money on only three occasions during the four years he worked at the Plaza.

What was unusual about this particular day was that the two diners at the corner table ordered cigars even before they sat down. Later they were joined by more guests, who ordered more cigars and bottles of champagne. Abel looked up the name of the host in the maître d's reservation book. Woolworth. Abel had seen the name in the financial columns quite recently, but he could not immediately remember why. The other guest was a Mr Charles Lester, a regular patron of the Plaza, who Abel knew to be a distinguished banker. The diners showed absolutely no interest in their unusually attentive waiter, which allowed Abel to listen intently. Abel could not discover any specific details, but he gathered that some sort of deal had been closed that morning, and would be announced after close of business that evening. Then he remembered. He had seen the name in *The Wall Street Journal*. Mr Woolworth's father had started the first five and dime store; now the son was trying to raise money to expand. While the guests were enjoying their desserts – most of them had chosen the strawberry cheesecake (Abel's recommendation) – he took the opportunity to leave the dining room for a few moments to call his broker on Wall Street.

'What is Woolworth trading at?' he asked.

There was a pause at the other end of the line. 'Two and one-eighth. Quite a lot of movement lately; don't know why, though,' came the reply.

'Buy up to the limit on my account until you hear an announcement from the company later today.'

'What will the announcement say?' asked the puzzled broker.

'I am not at liberty to reveal that,' replied Abel.

The broker was suitably impressed: Abel's record in the past had led him not to enquire too closely about the sources of his information. Abel hurried back to the Oak Room in time to serve the guests' coffee. They lingered over brandies for some time, and Abel only returned to the table as they were preparing to leave. The man who picked up the check thanked Abel for his attentive service and, turning so that his friends could hear him, said, 'Do you want a tip, young man?'

'Thank you, sir,' said Abel.

'Buy Woolworth stock.'

The guests all laughed. Abel laughed as well, took the $5 bill the man held out and thanked him. He also took a further $2,412 profit on Woolworth stock over the next six weeks.

—◇—

Abel was granted full United States citizenship a few days after his twenty-first birthday, and decided the occasion ought to be celebrated. He invited George and his latest love, Monika, and a girl called Clara, one of George's ex-loves, to see John Barrymore in *Don Juan*, and then on to Bigo's for dinner. George was still an apprentice in his uncle's bakery, working for eight dollars a week, and although Abel still looked upon him as his closest friend, he was aware of the growing difference between the penniless George and himself. Abel now had over $8,000 in his bank account and was in his last year at Columbia University studying for a BA in economics. He knew exactly where he was going, whereas George had stopped telling everyone he would be the mayor of New York one day.

The four of them had a memorable evening, mainly because Abel knew exactly what to expect from a good restaurant. His guests all had a great deal too much to eat and drink, and when the bill was presented, George was shocked to see that it came to more than he earned in a month. Abel paid without comment. If you have to pay a bill, always make it look as if the amount is of no consequence. If it is, don't go to the restaurant again. Whatever you do, don't complain or look surprised – that was something else the rich had taught him.

When the party broke up at about two in the morning, George and Monika returned to the Lower East Side. Abel felt he had earned Clara and invited her back to the Plaza. He smuggled her through the service entrance into a laundry elevator and then up to his room. She did not require much enticement, and Abel didn't waste any time on foreplay, mindful that he had to catch some sleep before reporting for breakfast duty. He rolled over at three o'clock, fully satisfied, and sank into an uninterrupted sleep until his alarm rang at 6 a.m. This left him just enough time to make love to Clara a second time before he got dressed.

Clara regarded him sullenly as he put on his white bow tie, before giving her a perfunctory goodbye kiss.

'Be sure you leave the way you came in, or you'll get me into a load of trouble,' he said. 'When will I see you again?'

'You won't,' said Clara stonily.

'Why not?' asked Abel, surprised. 'Something I did?'

'No, something you didn't do.' She jumped out of bed and started to dress quickly.

'What didn't I do? You wanted to go to bed with me, didn't you?'

She turned around and faced him. 'I thought I did, until I realized you have only one thing in common with Rudolf Valentino – you're both dead. You may be the smartest thing the Plaza has seen in a bad year, but in bed, I can tell you, you're a non-event.' Fully dressed now, Clara paused by the door, composing her parting thrust. 'Tell me, have you ever persuaded any girl to go to bed with you a second time?'

Stunned, Abel stared as the door slammed behind her. He spent the rest of the day thinking about Clara's accusation. He couldn't think of anyone he could discuss it with; George would only have laughed at him, and the staff at the Plaza all thought he knew everything. He decided that this problem, like any other he had encountered in his life, could be overcome with study or experience.

After lunch that day he visited Scribner's on Fifth Avenue. The bookstore had in the past solved all his economics and linguistic problems, but he couldn't find anything on its shelves that looked as if it might even begin to help his sexual ones. The books on etiquette were useless as he knew how to hold a knife and fork, and *The Moral Dilemma* turned out to be utterly inappropriate.

Abel left the store without making a purchase, and spent the rest of the afternoon in a dingy Broadway fleapit, not watching the movie but still going over what Clara had said. The film, a love story starring Greta Garbo and Errol Flynn, did not reach the kissing stage until the final reel, and provided no more insight than Scribner's had.

When Abel left the movie house it was early evening, and there was a cool breeze blowing down Broadway. It still surprised Abel that any city could be almost as noisy and bright by night as it was by day. He started walking uptown towards Fifty-Ninth Street, hoping the fresh air would clear his mind. He stopped on the corner of Fifty-Second to buy an evening paper, so he could check the closing stock prices.

'Looking for a girl?' asked a voice from the corner by the newsstand.

Abel turned around. She must have been about thirty-five, heavily made up and wearing the latest fashionable shade of pink lipstick. Her white silk blouse had a couple of buttons undone, and she wore a long black skirt, black stockings and black shoes.

'Only five dollars, worth every penny,' she said, pushing her hip out at an angle, allowing the slit in her skirt to part and reveal the top of her stockings.

'Where do we go?' asked Abel.

'I have a little place of my own on the next block.'

She inclined her head, indicating the direction she meant, and for the first time he saw her face clearly under the streetlight. She was not unattractive. Abel nodded his agreement, and she took his arm.

'If the police stop and question us,' she said, 'you're an old friend, and my name's Joyce.'

They walked to the next block and entered a squalid little apartment building. Abel was horrified by the dingy room, with its single bare lightbulb, one chair, a wash basin and a crumpled double bed, which had obviously already been occupied several times that day.

'You live here?' he asked incredulously.

'Good God, no. I only use this place for work.'

'Why do you do this?' asked Abel, wondering still if he wanted to go through with his plan.

'I have two children to bring up and no husband. Can you think of a better reason? Now, do you want me or not?'

'Yes, but not the way you think,' said Abel.

She eyed him warily. 'Not one of those weird ones, an admirer of the Marquis de Sade, are you?'

'Certainly not,' said Abel.

'You're not gonna burn me with cigarettes?'

'No, nothing like that. I just need to be taught how to make love. I want lessons.'

'Lessons? Are you joking? What do you think this is, baby, a fucking night school?'

'Something like that,' said Abel. He sat down on the corner of the bed and told her what Clara had said that morning. 'Do you think you can help?'

The lady of the night studied Abel more carefully, wondering if it was April 1st.

'Sure,' she said finally, 'but it's still going to cost you five dollars for thirty minutes.'

'More expensive than a BA from Columbia,' said Abel. 'How many lessons do you think I'll need?'

'Depends how quick a learner you are, doesn't it?' she said.

'Well, let's start right now,' said Abel, taking a five-dollar bill out of an inside pocket. She tucked it into the top of her stocking, a sure sign she never took them off.

'Clothes off first, baby,' she said. 'You won't learn much fully dressed.'

When he was naked, she looked at him critically. 'You're not exactly Douglas Fairbanks, are you? Don't worry about it – it doesn't matter what you look like once the lights are out; it only matters what you can do.'

Abel listened carefully as she told him how to treat a lady. She was surprised to find that he really didn't want her, and was even more surprised when he continued to turn up every afternoon for the next three weeks. 'When will I know I've made it?' he asked her one evening.

'You'll know, baby,' replied Joyce. 'If you can make me come, you can make an Egyptian mummy come.'

She taught him first where the sensitive parts of a woman's body were, and then to be patient in his lovemaking – and the signs that would show when he was pleasing her. How to use his tongue and lips in every place other than a woman's mouth.

Abel listened carefully, and followed her instructions to the letter, to begin with, a little too mechanically. Despite her assurance that he was improving out of all recognition, he had no real idea if she was telling him the truth, until one afternoon about three weeks and $110 later, when to his surprise and delight Joyce suddenly came alive in his arms. She held his head close to her as he gently licked her nipples. As he stroked her between her legs, he discovered she was wet – for the first time – and after he had entered her she moaned, a sound he had never experienced before and found intensely exciting. She clawed at his back, commanding him not to stop. The moaning continued, sometimes loud, sometimes soft. Finally she cried out sharply, clung onto him and then relaxed.

When she had caught her breath, she said, 'Baby, you just graduated top of the class.'

Abel hadn't even come.

◄○►

Abel celebrated being awarded his degree by paying scalper's prices to see Babe Ruth's New York Yankees defeat the Pittsburgh Pirates in the World Series decider. He invited George, Monika and a reluctant Clara to be his guests for the evening. After the game, Clara felt it was nothing less than her duty to go to bed with Abel; after all, he had spent a month's wages on her.

The following morning, just before she left, Clara said, 'When will I see you again?'

◄○►

Once Abel had graduated from Columbia, he quickly became dissatisfied with his life at the Plaza, but he could not figure out how to take advantage of his new qualifications.

Although he served some of the wealthiest and most successful men in America, he was unable to approach any of them directly; to do so might well cost him his job. In any case, customers like that were unlikely to pay any attention to the aspirations of a waiter.

On one occasion, when Mr and Mrs Ellsworth Statler came to lunch at the Plaza's Edwardian Room, he thought his chance had come. He did everything he could think of to impress the famous hotelier, and the meal went without a hitch. As he left, Statler thanked Abel warmly and tipped him $10, but he didn't say another word. As Abel watched him disappear through the Plaza's revolving doors, he couldn't help wondering if he was ever going to get a break.

When he returned to his post, Sammy, the headwaiter, tapped him on the shoulder. 'What did you get from Mr Statler?'

'Nothing,' said Abel.

'He didn't tip you?'

'Oh, yes, sure,' said Abel. 'Ten dollars.' He handed the money over.

'That's more like it,' said Sammy. 'I was beginning to think you was double-dealing me, Abel. Ten dollars, that's good even for Mr Statler. You must have impressed him.'

'No, I didn't.'

'What do you mean?'

'It doesn't matter,' said Abel as he walked away.

'Wait a moment, Abel. The gentleman at table seventeen, Mr Leroy, wants to speak to you personally.'

'What about?'

'How should I know? He probably heard you're a big shot and hopes you'll give him some financial advice.'

Abel glanced over at table 17, strictly for the meek or the unknown, because it was placed near the swinging doors into the kitchen and was always the last to be occupied. Abel usually tried to avoid serving any of the tables at that end of the room.

'Who is he?' he asked.

'I don't know,' said Sammy, not bothering to look up. 'I'm not in touch with the life story of every customer the way you are. Give them a good meal, make sure you get a big tip and hope they come again. You may think that's a simple philosophy, but it's good enough for me. Maybe they forgot to teach you the basics at Columbia. Now get your butt over there, and if it's a tip, be sure to bring it straight back to me.'

Abel smiled at Sammy and went over to 17. There were two people seated at the table – a man in a colourful checked jacket, which Abel would have described as lurid, and an attractive young woman with a mop of curly blonde hair, which momentarily distracted him. Abel assumed she was the checked jacket's New York girlfriend. He put on his 'sorry smile', betting himself a silver dollar that the man was going to make a big fuss about being placed next to the kitchen doors and try to get his table changed to impress the stunning blonde. No one liked being near the smell of the kitchen and the continual banging of waiters' heels on the doors, but it was impossible to avoid using the table when the hotel was packed with residents and regulars, who looked upon visitors as nothing more than intruders. Why did Sammy always leave the tricky customers for him?

Abel approached the checked jacket cautiously. 'You asked to speak to me, sir?'

'Sure did,' said a Texan accent. 'My name is Davis Leroy, and this is my daughter, Melanie.'

Abel turned his attention to Melanie, which was a foolish mistake, because he couldn't take his eyes off her.

'I've been watching you, Abel, for the past five days,' Leroy continued in his Texan drawl. 'I've been very impressed by what I've seen. You've got class, real class, and I'm always on the look-out for that. Ellsworth Statler was a fool not to offer you a job on the spot.'

Abel took a closer look at Mr Leroy. His purple cheeks left him in no doubt that he hadn't taken much notice of Prohibition, and the empty plate in front of him accounted for his basketball belly, but neither the name nor the face meant anything to him. At a normal lunchtime, Abel would be familiar with the background of most guests occupying the thirty-nine tables in the Edwardian Room. But Mr Leroy remained a blank.

Leroy was still talking. 'Now, I'm not one of those multimillionaires who have to sit at your corner tables when they eat at the Plaza.'

Abel was impressed. The average customer wasn't supposed to appreciate the relative merits of the various tables.

'But I'm not doing so badly for myself. In fact, my best hotel may well grow to be as impressive as this one someday, Abel.'

'I'm sure it will, sir,' said Abel, playing for time. Leroy, Leroy, Leroy. The name still didn't mean a thing.

'Lemme git to the point, son. The number one hotel in my group needs a new assistant manager in charge of the restaurants. If you're interested, join me in my room when you get off duty.'

He handed Abel an unembossed card.

'Thank you, sir,' said Abel, glancing at it: 'Davis Leroy. The Richmond Group of Hotels, Dallas.' Underneath was inscribed the motto: 'One day a hotel in every state.' The name still meant nothing to him.

JEFFREY ARCHER

'I look forward to seeing you,' said Leroy.

'Thank you, sir,' said Abel. He smiled at Melanie, who didn't return the compliment. He went back to Sammy, who, head down, was still counting his takings.

'Ever heard of the Richmond Group of Hotels, Sammy?'

'Sure, my brother was a junior waiter in one once. Must be about eight or nine of them, mostly in the south, run by some crazy Texan, but I can't remember the guy's name. Why you want to know?' asked Sammy suspiciously.

'No particular reason,' said Abel.

'There's always a reason with you, Abel. What did table seventeen want?'

'Grumbling about being placed so near the kitchen. Can't say I blame him.'

'What does he expect me to do, put him out on the veranda? Who does the guy think he is, John D. Rockefeller?'

Abel left Sammy to his counting, and cleared his tables as quickly as possible. Then he went to his room to begin checking on the Richmond Group. A few calls and he'd learned enough to satisfy his curiosity. The group turned out to have eleven hotels in all, the most impressive one a 342-room deluxe establishment in Chicago, the Richmond Continental. Abel decided he had nothing to lose by paying a call on Mr Leroy and Melanie. He checked Leroy's room number – 85 – one of the better small rooms. He knocked on the door a little before four o'clock, and was disappointed to discover that Melanie was not with him.

'Glad you could drop by, Abel. Take a seat.'

It was the first time Abel had sat down with a guest in the four years he had worked at the Plaza.

'How much are you paid?' asked Leroy.

The suddenness of the question took Abel by surprise.

'I take in around twenty-five dollars a week with tips.'

'I'll start you at thirty-five a week, and you can be in charge of tips.'

'Which hotel?' asked Abel.

'If I'm a good judge of character, Abel, I'd say you got off table duty about three-thirty and took the next thirty minutes finding out which hotel I had in mind. Am I right?'

Abel was beginning to like the man. 'The Richmond Continental in Chicago?' he ventured.

Leroy laughed. 'I was right about you.'

Abel's mind was working fast. 'How many people would be above me?'

'Only the manager and me. The manager's old school, and near retirement; and as I've got ten other hotels to worry about, I don't think you'll have too much trouble from me. Although I must confess Chicago is my favourite, my first hotel in the north. And since Melanie's at school there, I find I spend more time in the Windy City than I ought to.'

Abel was still thinking.

'Don't ever make the mistake most New Yorkers do, of underestimating Chicago. They think it's only a postage stamp on a very large envelope, and they're the envelope.'

Abel smiled.

'The hotel's a little run-down at the moment,' Leroy admitted. 'The last assistant manager left without giving notice, so I need a good man to take his place. Now listen, Abel, I've watched you carefully for the past five days, and I know you're that man. Do you think you'd be interested in moving to Chicago?'

'Forty dollars a week and ten per cent of any increased profits, and I'll take the job.'

'What?' said Davis, flabbergasted. 'None of my managers are paid on a profit basis. The others would raise hell if they ever found out.'

'I'm not going to tell them if you don't,' said Abel.

Davis didn't reply for some time. 'Now I know I chose the right man, even if he strikes a harder bargain than a Yankee with six daughters.' He slapped the side of his chair. 'I agree to your terms, Abel.'

'Will you be requiring references, Mr Leroy?'

'References? I know your background and your history from the moment you left Europe right through to getting a degree in economics at Columbia. What do you think I've been doing the last few days? I wouldn't put someone who needed references in as the number two in my best hotel. When can you start?'

—<o>—

Leaving New York City and the Plaza Hotel, his first real home since leaving the Baron, turned out to be more of a wrench than Abel had anticipated. Saying goodbye to George, Monika and his few friends from Columbia left him wondering if he'd made the right decision. Sammy and the other waiters threw a farewell party for him.

'I'm sure we haven't heard the last of you, Abel Rosnovski,' said Sammy. 'In fact, I wouldn't be surprised if you were after my job.'

—<o>—

Abel loved Chicago from the moment he stepped off the train, but the feeling was not extended to the Richmond Continental, despite the hotel being well placed on Michigan Avenue, in the heart of one of the fastest-growing cities in America. This pleased Abel, who was familiar with Ellsworth Statler's maxim that only three things really mattered about a hotel: position, position and position.

He soon discovered that position was about the only thing the Richmond had going for it. Davis Leroy had understated the case when he said the hotel was a little run-down. Desmond Pacey, the manager, wasn't old school, as Leroy had suggested, he was just plain lazy, and didn't endear himself to Abel when he put his new assistant manager in a tiny room in the staff annexe across the street, and not in the main hotel. A quick check on the Richmond's books revealed that the daily occupancy rate was running at less than 40 per cent, and the restaurant was never more than half full, not least because the food was inedible. The staff spoke half a dozen languages between them, none of which seemed to be English, and they certainly showed no sign of welcoming the Polack from New York. It was not hard to see why the last assistant manager had left in such a hurry. If the

Richmond was Davis Leroy's finest hotel, Abel feared for the other ten in the group, even if his new employer did have deep Texan pockets.

The one piece of good news that Abel discovered in his first week in Chicago was that Melanie Leroy was an only child.

24

WILLIAM AND MATTHEW started their freshman year at Harvard in the fall of 1924.

William accepted the Hamilton Memorial Mathematics Scholarship and, despite his grandmothers' disapproval, at a cost of $290, treated himself to 'Daisy', the latest Model T Ford which became the first real love of his life. He painted Daisy bright yellow, which halved her value but doubled the number of his girlfriends. Calvin Coolidge won a landslide victory to return to the White House – much to the disappointment of the grandmothers, who both voted for John W. Davis – and the volume on the New York Stock Exchange reached a five-year record of 2,336,160 shares.

Both young men – 'We can no longer refer to them as children,' pronounced Grandmother Cabot – had been looking forward to going to college. After an energetic summer of chasing golf balls and girls, both with handicaps, they were finally ready to get down to more serious pursuits. William started work on the day he arrived in their new room on the 'Gold Coast', a considerable improvement on their small study at St Paul's, while Matthew went in search of the university rowing club. He was elected to captain the freshman crew, and William left his books every Sunday afternoon to watch his friend from the banks of the Charles River. He secretly enjoyed Matthew's success, but was outwardly scathing.

'Life is not about eight muscle-bound men pulling unwieldy pieces of misshapen wood through choppy water while one smaller man bellows at them,' he declared haughtily.

'Tell Yale that,' said Matthew.

William, meanwhile, quickly demonstrated to his mathematics professors that, like Matthew, he was several strokes ahead of the field. He became chairman of the freshman Debating Society, and talked his great-uncle, President Lowell, into introducing the first university insurance plan, where students graduating from Harvard would take out a life policy for $1,000, naming the university as the beneficiary. William estimated that if 40 per cent of the alumni joined the scheme, Harvard would have a guaranteed income of about $3 million a year from 1950 onward. His great-uncle was impressed, and gave the scheme his full backing. A year later he invited William to join the board of the University Fund Raising Committee. William accepted with pride, not realizing that the appointment was for life.

President Lowell informed Grandmother Kane that he had captured one of the finest financial brains of his generation free of charge. Grandmother Kane testily told her cousin, 'Everything has a purpose, and this will teach William to read the fine print.'

—◦—

Almost as soon as the sophomore year began, it became time to choose (or be chosen for) one of the Finals Clubs that dominated the social landscape of the most successful at Harvard. William was 'punched' for the Porcellian, the oldest, most exclusive and least ostentatious of such clubs. In the clubhouse on Massachusetts Avenue, incongruously situated above a cheap Hayes-Bickford cafeteria, he would sit in a comfortable armchair, considering the four-colour map problem, discussing the implications of the Loeb-Leopold case and idly watching the street below through the conveniently angled mirror while listening to the large, newfangled radio set.

When the Christmas vacation came, William was persuaded to go skiing with Matthew in Vermont, and spent a week panting uphill in the footsteps of his fitter friend.

'Tell me, Matthew, what is the point of sponding an hour climbing up a hill only to come back down the same hill in a matter of seconds at considerable risk to life and limb?'

Matthew grunted. 'It sure gives me a bigger kick than graph theory, William. Why don't you just admit you're not very good at either the going up or the coming down?'

They both did enough work during their sophomore year to get by, although their interpretations of 'getting by' were wildly different. For the first two months of the summer vacation they worked as junior management clerks in Charles Lester's bank in New York, Matthew's father having long since given up the battle of trying to keep William off the premises.

When the dog days of August arrived, they spent most of their time dashing about the New England countryside in 'Daisy', sailing on the Charles River with as many different girls as possible and attending any house party to which they could get themselves invited. They were fast becoming the most respected personalities of the university, known to the cognoscenti as the Scholar and the Sweat. It was perfectly understood in Boston society that the girl who married William Kane or Matthew Lester would have no fears for her future, but as fast as hopeful mothers appeared with their fresh-faced daughters, Grandmother Kane and Grandmother Cabot unceremoniously dispatched them.

—◇—

On April 18, 1927, William celebrated his twenty-first birthday by attending the final meeting of the trustees of his estate. Alan Lloyd and Tony Simmons had prepared all the documents for his signature.

'Well, William dear,' said Millie Preston, as if a great burden had been lifted from her shoulders, 'I'm sure you'll be able to do every bit as well as we did.'

'I hope so, Mrs Preston,' William replied. 'But if ever I need to lose half a million overnight, I'll give you a call.'

Millie Preston turned bright red, and never spoke to William again.

The trust now showed a balance of over $32 million, and William already had plans for further growth. But he had also set himself the target of making a million dollars in his own right before he left Harvard. It was not a large sum compared with the amount in his trust, but his inherited wealth meant far less to him than the balance in his personal account at Lester's.

That summer, the grandmothers, fearing a fresh outbreak of predatory girls, dispatched William and Matthew on the grand tour of Europe. This turned out to be thoroughly worthwhile for both of them. Matthew, surmounting all language barriers, found a beautiful girl in every major European capital – love, he assured William, was an international commodity. William secured introductions to directors of most of the major European banks – money, he assured Matthew, was also an international commodity, and a far less capricious one.

From London to Berlin to Rome, the two young men left a trail of broken hearts and suitably impressed bankers. When they returned to Harvard in September, they were both ready to hit the books for their final year.

<o>

In the bitter winter of 1927, Grandmother Kane died, aged eighty-five, and William wept for the first time since his mother's death.

'Come on,' said Matthew, after bearing with his depression for several days. 'She had a good life, and waited a long time to discover whether God's a Cabot or a Lowell.'

William missed the shrewd observations he hadn't fully appreciated in his grandmother's lifetime, and arranged a funeral she would have been proud to attend. The great lady may have arrived at the cemetery in a Packard hearse ('An outrageous contraption – over my dead body'), but her only criticism of William's arrangements for her departure would have concerned this unsound mode of transport. Her death drove William to work with even more purpose during his final year at Harvard, and he dedicated himself to winning the university's top mathematics prize in her memory.

Grandmother Cabot died five months after Grandmother

Kane – probably, said William, because there was no one left for her to talk to.

–◁◦▷–

In February 1928, William received a visit from the captain of the university Debating Team. There was to be a full-dress debate the following month on the motion 'Socialism or Capitalism for America's Future', and he asked William to represent capitalism.

'What if I told you I was only willing to speak on behalf of the downtrodden masses?' William enquired of the surprised captain, slightly nettled by the thought that outsiders assumed they knew his ideological position simply because he had inherited a famous name and a prosperous bank.

'Well, I must say, William, we did think your preference would be for, er – '

'It is. I accept your invitation. I take it that I am at liberty to select my partner?'

'Naturally.'

'Good. Then I choose Matthew Lester. May I know who our opponents will be?'

'Not until the day before the debate, when the posters revealing the names will go up in the Yard.'

For the next month Matthew and William read the leaders in all the leading journals of the Left and Right at breakfast, and spent the evenings in strategy sessions for what the campus was beginning to call 'The Great Debate'. William decided that Matthew should lead off.

As the day approached, it became clear that all of the politically motivated students, professors and even some Boston and Cambridge notables would be attending. On the morning before, William and Matthew walked over to the Yard to discover who their opponents would be.

'Leland Crosby and Thaddeus Cohen. Either name ring a bell with you, William? Crosby must be one of the Philadelphia Crosbys, I suppose.'

'That's right. "The Red Maniac of Rittenhouse Square" as his aunt once described him. He's the most committed revolutionary on campus. He's loaded, and he spends most of his money on the popular radical causes. I can hear his opening already.' William parodied Crosby's grating tone: '"I know at first hand the rapacity and the utter lack of social conscience of the American moneyed class." If everyone in the audience hadn't already heard his views fifty times, he'd make a formidable opponent.'

'And Cohen?'

'Never heard of him. Probably a Jew.'

The following evening they made their way through the snow and biting wind, heavy overcoats flapping behind them, as they passed the gleaming columns of the Widener Library – like William's father, the donor's son had gone down on the *Titanic* – to Boylston Hall.

'With weather like this, at least if we take a hiding, there shouldn't be many to tell the tale,' said Matthew hopefully.

But as they rounded the north end of the library they saw a steady stream of stamping, huffing figures ascending the steps and filing into the hall. After they had taken their seats on the podium William picked out some people he recognized in the packed audience: President Lowell, sitting discreetly in a middle row; ancient Newbury St John, professor of botany; a pair of Brattle Street bluestockings he recognized from Red House parties; and, to his right, a group of Bohemian-looking young men and women, some not even wearing ties, who turned and began to clap as their spokesmen – Crosby and Cohen – walked onto the stage.

Crosby was the more striking of the two, tall and thin almost to the point of caricature, dressed absentmindedly – or very carefully – in a shaggy tweed suit with a stiffly pressed shirt and a pipe dangling from his lower lip. Thaddeus Cohen was shorter, and wore rimless spectacles and an almost too perfectly cut dark worsted suit. William could have sworn he'd seen that face before.

The bells of Memorial Church sounded vague and distant as they rang out seven times.

The four speakers stood, hands clasped anxiously before them, as the rules of the debate were spelled out. 'The first speaker will be Mr Leland Crosby, Junior,' announced the captain of debaters.

Crosby's speech caused William little anxiety. He had anticipated the strident tone Crosby would take, the overstressed, nearly hysterical points he would emphasize. He recited the incantations of American radicalism – Haymarket, Money Trust, Standard Oil, even Cross of Gold. William didn't think Crosby had done more than make an exhibition of himself, although he garnered the expected applause from his own little clique. When he sat down he had clearly won few new supporters, and it looked as though he might have lost a few old ones.

Matthew spoke well and to the point, charming his listeners by appearing to be the incarnation of liberal tolerance. William pumped his hand warmly when he returned to his seat to loud applause.

'It's all over bar the shouting,' he whispered, but that was before they'd heard Thaddeus Cohen.

The young unknown took everyone by surprise. He had a pleasant, diffident manner and a sympathetic style. His references and quotations were catholic, pointed and illuminating. Without patronizing the audience, he conveyed a moral earnestness that made a failure to support those less fortunate than oneself seem to be irrational. He was willing to admit the excesses of the Left and the inadequacy of some of its leaders, but he didn't leave the audience in any doubt that, in spite of its dangers, there was no alternative to socialism if the lot of mankind was ever to be improved. 'Equality in the end is more important than equity.' He sat down to loud applause from both sides.

William was flustered. A surgically logical attack on his adversaries would be useless against Cohen's gentle and persuasive presentation. But to outdo him as a spokesman of hope and faith in the human spirit might also be impossible. He concentrated first on refuting some of Crosby's more outrageous claims, then attempted to counter Cohen's arguments with a declaration of his faith in the ability of the American system to produce the best results through competition, both intellectual and economic. He felt he had played a good defensive game, but no more, and sat down feeling that he had been well beaten by Cohen.

Crosby was their opponents' rebuttal speaker. He began

ferociously, sounding as if he now needed to beat Cohen even more than William or Matthew, demanding if anyone present could identify the *enemy of the people* among us tonight. He glared around the room for several long seconds as the audience squirmed in embarrassed silence, and even his most ardent supporters studied their shoes. Then he learned forward and roared:

'He stands before you. He has just spoken in your midst. His name is William Lowell Kane.' Gesturing with one hand towards William – but without looking at him – he thundered: 'His bank owns mines in which the workers die to give its owners an extra million a year in dividends. His bank supports the bloody, corrupt dictatorships of Latin America. Through his bank, the American Congress is bribed into crushing the small farmer. His bank . . .'

The tirade went on for several minutes. William sat in stony silence, occasionally jotting down a comment on his yellow legal pad. A few members of the audience had begun shouting, 'No!' Crosby's supporters shouted 'Yes!' loyally back. The society officials began to look nervous.

Crosby's allotted time was almost up. He finally raised his fist and said, 'Ladies and gentlemen, I suggest that not more than two hundred yards from this very room we have the answer to the plight of America. There stands the Widener Library, the greatest private library in the world. Poor and immigrant scholars pass through its doors, along with the best-educated Americans, to increase their knowledge of the world. But why does it exist? Because one rich playboy had the misfortune to set sail sixteen years ago on a pleasure boat called the *Titanic*. I suggest, ladies and gentlemen, that not until the people of America hand each and every member of the ruling class a ticket for his own private cabin on the *Titanic* of capitalism, will the hoarded wealth of this great continent be freed, and devoted to the service of liberty, equality and progress.'

As Matthew listened to Crosby's speech, his sentiments changed from consternation that with this blunder the victory had been handed to his side, to rage at the reference to the *Titanic*. He had no idea how William would respond to such provocation.

When a measure of silence had been restored, the debating captain walked to the lectern and said, 'Mr William Lowell Kane.'

William walked slowly to the lectern and looked out over the audience. An expectant hush filled the room.

'It is my opinion that the views expressed by Mr Crosby do not merit a response.'

He sat down. There was a moment of surprised silence – followed by thunderous applause.

The captain returned to the lectern, but appeared uncertain what to do next. A voice from behind him broke the tension.

'If I may, Mr Chairman, I would like to ask Mr Kane if I might use his rebuttal time.' It was Thaddeus Cohen.

William nodded his agreement.

Cohen walked to the lectern and blinked at the audience disarmingly. 'It has long been true,' he began, 'that the greatest obstacle to the success of democratic socialism in the United States has been the extremism of some of its exponents. Nothing could have better exemplified this unfortunate fact more clearly than my colleague's rebuttal speech tonight. The propensity to damage the progressive cause by calling for the physical extermination of those who oppose it might be understandable in a battle-hardened immigrant, a veteran of foreign struggles fiercer than our own. In America it is inexcusable. Speaking for myself, I extend my sincere apologies to Mr Kane.'

This time the applause was instantaneous. Virtually the entire audience rose to its feet and cheered.

It was no surprise to either William or Matthew that they won the debate by a margin of more than 150 votes. As the audience filed out of the hall, talking animatedly at the tops of their voices, William walked across to shake hands with Thaddeus Cohen.

'How did you know my father was on the *Titanic*?' he asked.

'Because my father told me years ago.'

'Of course,' said William. 'You must be Thomas Cohen's son. Why don't you join us for a drink?'

'Thank you,' said Cohen. The three of them set off together across Massachusetts Avenue, barely able to see where they were going in the driving snow. They came to a halt outside a big black door almost directly opposite Boylston Hall. William opened it with his key, and the three entered the vestibule.

Before the door was closed behind him, Cohen spoke. 'I'm afraid I won't be welcome here.'

William looked startled for a moment. 'Nonsense. You're with me.'

Matthew gave his friend a cautionary glance, but saw that William was determined.

They went up the stairs and into a large room, comfortably but not luxuriously furnished, in which there were about a dozen young men sitting in armchairs or standing in knots of two or three. As soon as William appeared in the doorway, the congratulations began.

'You were magnificent, William. That's exactly the way to treat that sort of people.'

'Enter in triumph, the Bolski slayer.'

Cohen hung back, but William had not forgotten him.

'Gentlemen, may I present my worthy adversary, Mr Thaddeus Cohen.'

Cohen stepped forward hesitantly.

All conversation ceased. A number of heads were averted, as if they were looking at the elm trees in the Yard, their branches weighed down with snow.

There was the creak of a floorboard as one young man left the room by the far door. Moments later there was another departure. Without haste, without a word being spoken, every other member filed out. The last to leave gave William a long look, then turned on his heel and disappeared through the door.

Matthew gazed at his companions in dismay. Thaddeus Cohen had turned a dull red, and stood with his head bowed. William's lips were drawn together in the same tight, cold fury that had been apparent when Crosby had made his reference to the *Titanic*.

Matthew touched his arm. 'We'd better leave.'

The three trudged off to William's rooms and silently drank some indifferent brandy, and exchanged stories that no one listened to.

When William woke in the morning, an envelope had been pushed under his door. He tore it open to find a short note from the chairman of the Porcellian Club, informing him that he hoped 'there will not be a recurrence of last night's unfortunate incident'.

By lunchtime the chairman had received two letters of resignation.

-◄०►-

After several studious months, William and Matthew were almost ready – no one ever thinks they are entirely ready – for their final examinations. For six days they answered questions and filled pages and pages of the little blue examination books, and once they had written their last line they waited patiently, but not in vain.

A week after the exams it was announced that William had won the President's Mathematics Prize. Matthew had managed a 'gentleman's C', which came as a relief to him, and as no great surprise to anyone. Neither had any interest in prolonging their education, both wishing to join the 'real' world as quickly as possible.

William's bank account in New York edged over the million-dollar mark eight days before he left Harvard. For the first time he discussed with Matthew his long-term plan to gain control of Lester's Bank by merging it with Kane and Cabot. Matthew was enthusiastic about the idea, and confessed, 'That's about the only way I'll ever improve on what my old man has achieved in his lifetime.'

In June 1928, Alan Lloyd, now in his sixtieth year, travelled to Harvard for graduation day. How William wished his father was alive to witness the presentation ceremony.

Afterwards, he took Alan for tea on the square. The banker looked at the tall young man with affection.

'And what do you intend to do now that you've put Harvard behind you?'

'I'm going to join Charles Lester's bank in New York. I want to gain some more experience before I come to Kane and Cabot in a few years' time.'

'But you've been practically living in Lester's Bank since you were twelve years old, William. Why don't you come straight to us? We would make you a director immediately.'

No reply was forthcoming.

'Well, I must say, William, it's most unlike you to be rendered speechless by anything.'

'But I never imagined you'd invite me to join the board before my twenty-fifth birthday. My father . . .'

'It's true that your father was twenty-five when he was elected. But that's no reason why you shouldn't join the board before then if the other directors support the idea, and I know they do. In any case, there are personal reasons why I'd like to see you take your place on the board as soon as possible. When I retire from the bank in five years' time, we must be sure to elect the right chairman. You'll be in a stronger position to influence that decision if you've been working for Kane and Cabot during those years, rather than as a glorified functionary at Lester's. Well, my boy. Will you join the board?'

It was the second time that day that William had wished his father was still alive.

'I should be delighted to accept, sir.'

'That's the first time you've called me "sir" since we played golf together, and I didn't win on that occasion.'

William smiled.

'Good,' said Alan, 'that's settled, then. You'll be a junior director in charge of investments, working directly under Tony Simmons.'

'Can I appoint my own assistant?' asked William.

'Matthew Lester, no doubt?'

'Yes.'

'No. I don't want him doing to our bank what you intended to do to theirs.'

William didn't comment, but he never underestimated Alan Lloyd again.

PART THREE

1928–1932

25

IT TOOK ABEL about three months to appreciate the full extent of the problems facing the Richmond Continental, and why the hotel was losing so much money.

The simple conclusion he came to after twelve weeks of keeping his eyes wide open and his mouth shut, while at the same time allowing the staff to believe he was half asleep, was that the hotel's profits were, quite simply, being stolen. The Richmond staff were working a cooperative on a scale that even Abel had not previously come across. The system did not, however, take into account a new assistant manager who'd had to steal bread from the Russians to stay alive. Abel's first problem was not to let anybody know how much he knew until he'd had a chance to check on every department in the hotel. It didn't take him long to figure out that each one of them had perfected its own system for stealing.

Deception started at the front desk, where the clerks were registering only eight out of every ten guests, and pocketing any cash payments from the remaining two. The routine they were using was a simple one. If anyone had tried it at the Plaza in New York, they would have been found out within minutes, and fired the same day. The head desk clerk would select an elderly couple from another state who had booked in for only one night, and who had never stayed at the hotel before. He would then illicitly make sure they had no business connection in that city, and then simply fail to register them. If they paid cash the following morning, the money was pocketed. Provided they had not signed the register, there was no record to show that they had ever stayed at the hotel. Abel had long thought that all hotels should be required to register every guest, as the Plaza did.

In the dining room the system had been refined. All cash payments from any non-resident guests for lunch or dinner were immediately siphoned off. Abel had anticipated this, but it took him a little longer to check through the restaurant bills and establish that the front desk was working with the dining-room staff to ensure there were no restaurant bills for those guests they had already chosen not to register. In the bar it was even more blatant. The barman was bringing in his own bottles of liquor and pocketing the cash while the hotel's own bottles remained unopened. Over and above all this, there was a steady trail of fictitious breakages and repairs, missing equipment, disappearing food and lost bed linen – even an occasional mattress had gone astray. Abel concluded that more than half of the Richmond's staff were involved in the conspiracy, and that not one department had a completely clean record.

When he'd first arrived at the hotel, he had wondered why the manager, Desmond Pacey, hadn't noticed what was going on under his nose. He wrongly assumed that the man was just lazy, and could not be bothered to follow up minor peccadilloes. Even Abel was slow to realize that the manager was in fact the mastermind behind the entire operation, and the reason it worked so well. Pacey had been employed by the Richmond Group for more than thirty years. There was not a single hotel in the group in which he had not held a senior position at one time or another, which made Abel fearful for the solvency of the entire chain. Moreover, Pacey was a close friend of Leroy, and had become his most trusted lieutenant. Abel calculated that the Chicago Richmond was losing more than $30,000 a year in theft alone, a situation that could be remedied overnight by firing a large portion of the staff, starting with Desmond Pacey. This posed a problem, because in thirty years Davis Leroy had rarely fired anyone. He simply tolerated their indiscretions, hoping that in time they would leave. As far as Abel could determine, Richmond

Group staff went on robbing the chain blind until they reluctantly retired.

Abel decided that the only way he could reverse the hotel's fortunes was to have a showdown with Davis Leroy, but not until he had all the details documented. On his next free weekend Abel boarded the Great Express from Illinois Central to St Louis and on, via the Missouri Pacific, to Dallas. Under his arm was a 200-page report that had taken him three months to compile in his attic room in the hotel annexe. When Davis Leroy had finished reading through the mass of evidence, he sat staring at Abel in disbelief.

'These people are my friends,' were his first words. 'Some of them have been with me for thirty years. Hell – there's always been a little pilfering in the hotel business, but now you tell me they've been systematically robbing me behind my back?'

'In one or two cases, I suspect every day for the past thirty years,' said Abel.

'So what am I expected to do about it?'

'I can stop the rot if you're willing to sack Desmond Pacey, and give me the authority to remove anyone who has been working with him.'

'Well now, Abel, I wish it was as simple as that.'

'It's just that simple,' said Abel. 'And if you won't let me deal with the culprits, you can have my resignation before I get back on the train to Chicago, because I have no interest in being a part of the most corruptly run hotel in America. I'm only surprised Al Capone isn't a director.'

'Couldn't we just demote Desmond Pacey to assistant manager? Then I could make you manager and the problem would simply go away. After all, he's due to retire in a couple of years' time.'

'Just long enough to bankrupt you,' said Abel. 'And what's worse, I suspect all your other hotels are being run in the same cavalier way. If you want things to change in Chicago, you'll have to make a firm decision about Pacey right now, or you can go to the wall on your own, because I've got better things to do with my life.'

'Us Texans have a reputation for speaking our mind, Abel, but we're sure not in your class. Okay, okay, I'll give you the authority to sack Pacey, which means you're now the manager of the Chicago Richmond. Congratulations, my boy,' continued Leroy, standing up and slapping his new manager on the back. 'Don't think I'm ungrateful. You've done a swell job in Chicago, and from now on I'll look upon you as my right-hand man. To be honest with you, Abel, I've been doing so well on the Stock Market I hadn't even noticed the losses in the group, so thank God I have one honest friend. Why don't you stay overnight and join me for dinner?'

'I'd be delighted, Mr Leroy. I was hoping to spend the night at the Dallas Richmond so I can find out what they've been up to.'

'You're not going to let anyone off the hook, are you, Abel?'

'Not if I find out they've been educated at the same business school as Desmond Pacey.'

That evening, Abel and Davis Leroy ate two huge steaks, and drank a little too much whiskey, which the Texan insisted was no more than southern hospitality. He also admitted to Abel that he had been considering inviting someone to take charge of the Richmond Group, so that he could take life a little easier.

'Are you sure you want a dumb Polack in charge?' slurred Abel.

'Abel, it's me who's been dumb. If you hadn't smoked out those thieves, I might have gone under. But now that I know the truth, we'll lick the bastards together, and I'm going to give you the chance to put the Richmond Group back on the map.'

Abel shakily raised his glass. 'I'll drink to that – and to a long and successful partnership.'

'Go get 'em, boy.'

Abel spent the night at the Dallas Richmond, giving a false name and pointedly telling the desk clerk he would be staying only one night. In the morning, he watched the hotel's only copy of the receipt for his cash payment disappear into the wastepaper basket. His suspicions were confirmed. The problem was obviously not Chicago's alone, but had permeated the entire group.

He decided he would have to get Chicago sorted out before he could take on any other Desmond Paceys, and called Davis Leroy to tell him that the disease had spread to more than one limb.

Abel travelled back the way he had come. The Mississippi Valley lay sullen beyond the train windows, devastated by the floods of the previous year. Abel could only think about the devastation he was going to cause once he was back at the Chicago Richmond.

When he walked through the revolving doors of the hotel, there was no sign of the night porter, and only one clerk was on duty. He decided to let them all have a good night's rest before he bade them farewell. A young bellboy opened the front door of the annexe for him.

'Have a good trip, Mr Rosnovski?'

'Yes, thank you. How have things been here?'

'Oh, very quiet.'

You may find it even quieter this time tomorrow, thought Abel, when you're the only member of the staff who still has a job.

Abel unpacked and ordered a light meal from room service. It took more than an hour to arrive, and when it did, it was cold. When he had finished his coffee, he took a cold shower and went over his plan for the following day. He had picked a good time of year for his massacre. It was early February, and the hotel only had about 25 per cent occupancy. He was confident that he could run the Richmond with about half its present staff. He climbed into bed, threw the pillow on the floor and slept, like his unsuspecting staff, soundly.

--<o>--

Desmond Pacey, known to everyone at the Richmond as Lazy Pacey, was sixty-three years old. He was considerably overweight, and rather slow of movement on his short legs. He had seen seven assistant managers come and go during his time at the Richmond. Some had been greedy, and had wanted too much of the 'take' while others couldn't seem to understand how the system worked. The Polack, he decided, was just plain dumb. Like all Polacks. Pacey hummed to himself as he strolled towards

Abel's office for their daily ten o'clock meeting. It was seventeen minutes past ten.

'Sorry to have kept you waiting,' he said, not sounding at all sorry. 'I was held up with something at the front desk – you know how it is.'

Abel knew exactly how it was at the front desk. He slowly opened the drawer of his desk and laid out forty crumpled hotel bills, some of them torn into pieces; bills he had recovered from wastepaper baskets and ashtrays, bills for those guests who'd paid cash and had never been registered. He watched the fat little manager trying to read them upside down, slowly becoming aware what they were.

Not that Pacey cared much. There was nothing for him to worry about. If the stupid Polack had caught on to the system, he could either take his cut or leave. Perhaps a nice room in the hotel would keep him quiet.

'So, what you got for me today, Abel?' he asked just as he was about to sit down.

'You're fired, Mr Pacey. I want you off the premises within the hour.'

Desmond Pacey didn't respond immediately, because he couldn't believe what he'd heard.

'What was that you said? I don't think I heard you right.'

'You heard me just fine,' said Abel. 'You're fired.'

'You can't fire me. I'm the manager. I've been with the Richmond Group for over thirty years. If there's any firing to be done, I'll do it. Who in God's name do you think you are?'

'I'm the new manager.'

'You're *what*?'

'The new manager,' Abel repeated. 'Mr Leroy appointed me yesterday, and my first executive decision is to fire you, Mr Pacey.'

'What for?'

'For larceny.' Abel turned the bills around so that Pacey could see them more clearly. 'Every one of these guests paid their bill, but not one penny of the money reached the Richmond account. And they all have one thing in common – your signature is on them.'

'That doesn't prove anything.'

'I know. You've been running a good system. Well, you can go and run it somewhere else, because your luck's run out here. There's an old Polish saying, Mr Pacey: *The pitcher carries water only until the handle breaks*. The handle has just broken. You're fired.'

'You don't have the authority to fire me,' spluttered Pacey, sweat peppering his forehead. 'Davis Leroy is a close personal friend of mine. He's the only man who can fire me. You only turned up a few months ago. I'll have you thrown out of this hotel with one phone call.'

'Go ahead,' said Abel. He picked up the telephone and asked the operator to get Davis Leroy in Dallas. The two men waited, staring at each other. Sweat began to trickle down to the tip of Pacey's nose. For a second, Abel wondered if Leroy might change his mind.

'Good morning, Mr Leroy, it's Abel Rosnovski calling from Chicago. I've just fired Desmond Pacey, and he wants a word with you.'

Shakily, Pacey took the telephone. He listened for a few moments.

'But Davis, I . . . What could I do . . . ? I swear to you it isn't true . . . There must be some mistake—'

Abel heard the line click.

'One hour, Mr Pacey,' said Abel, 'or I'll hand these bills to the Chicago Police Department.'

'Now wait a moment,' Pacey said. 'Don't act so hasty.' His tone and attitude had suddenly changed. 'We could bring you in on the whole operation. You could make a very steady little income if we ran this hotel together, and no one would be any the wiser. The money would be far more than you're making as assistant manager, and we all know Davis can afford the losses—'

'I'm not the assistant manager any longer. Get out, Mr Pacey, before I throw you out.

'You fucking bastard,' said the ex-manager, realizing his last card had been trumped. 'You better keep your eyes wide open,

235

Polack, because I'm going to cut you down to size.' He slammed the door as he left.

By lunchtime, Pacey had been joined on the street by the headwaiter, head chef, senior housekeeper, chief desk clerk, head porter and seventeen other members of the Richmond staff who Abel felt were past redemption. In the afternoon he called a meeting of the remainder of the employees, explained to them in detail what he had done, and assured them that their jobs were not in any danger.

'But if I find *one dollar*,' said Abel, 'I repeat, *one dollar* misplaced, the person involved will be fired on the spot, without references. Do I make myself clear?'

No one spoke.

Several other members of staff left during the next few weeks, once they realized that Abel Rosnovski did not intend to continue Desmond Pacey's system on his own behalf. They were quickly replaced.

―◦―

William started work as a junior director of Kane and Cabot in September 1928. He began his banking career in a small office next to Tony Simmons, the bank's Investment Director. From the day William arrived he knew, even though nothing was said, either discreetly or indiscreetly, that Simmons was hoping to succeed Alan Lloyd as chairman of the bank.

The bank's entire investment programme was Simmons's responsibility. He delegated some part of his portfolio to William, in particular private investment in small businesses, land and any other outside entrepreneurial activities. Among William's duties was the compilation of a monthly report for the board on any investments he wished to recommend. The seventeen board members met once a month in a larger oak-panelled room, dominated at both ends by portraits, one of William's father, the other of his grandfather. William had never known his grandfather, but had always suspected he must have been one hell of a man to have married Grandmother Kane. There was ample room left on the walls for his own portrait.

William conducted himself with caution during his early months at the bank, and his fellow board members soon came to respect his judgement, and almost invariably accepted his investment recommendations. On the rare occasions when they didn't follow his advice, they lived to regret it. On the first occasion, a Mr Mayer sought a loan from the bank to invest in 'talking pictures', but the board refused to believe that the concept had any merit or future. Another time, a Mr Paley came to William with an ambitious plan for a radio network. Alan Lloyd, who had about as much respect for telegraphy as for telepathy, would have nothing to do with the scheme. The board supported his view. Louis B. Mayer later founded MGM, and William Paley became Chief Executive of CBS. William backed his own judgement and supported both men with his own money, without informing either the bank or the recipients. It was a personal matter.

One of the more unpleasant aspects of William's day-to-day duties was handling the liquidations and bankruptcies of clients who had borrowed large sums from the bank and had subsequently found themselves unable to repay their loans. William was not by nature a soft man, as Henry Osborne had learned to his cost, but insisting that old and respected clients liquidate their stocks, and even sell their homes, was always a disagreeable experience. He soon learned that these clients fell into two distinct categories – those who looked upon bankruptcy as an excuse to avoid their responsibilities, and those who were appalled by the very thought of it, and would spend the rest of their lives trying to repay every penny they had borrowed. William found it easy to be tough with the first category, but was far more lenient with the second, often with the grudging support of Tony Simmons.

The customer who had requested to see him that morning clearly fell into the second category. Max Brookes, had borrowed more than a million dollars from Kane and Cabot to invest in the Florida land boom of 1925, an investment William would never have supported had he been advising the bank at that time. Max Brookes was however celebrated in Massachusetts as one of the intrepid breed of balloonists and flyers, and a close friend of

Charles Lindbergh. His tragic death, when the small plane he was piloting crashed into a tree only a hundred yards after take-off, was reported in the press across the length and breadth of America, making him a national hero.

William, acting for the bank, immediately took over the Brookes estate, which was already insolvent. He closed the account, and tried to cut the bank's losses by selling off the land Brookes owned in Florida, except for two acres on which the family home stood. The bank's loss still turned out to be over $300,000.

Once William had liquidated everything the bank held in Max Brookes's name, he turned his attention to Mrs Brookes, who had signed a personal guarantee for her late husband's debts. Although William always tried to secure such a guarantee on any loans granted by the bank, he never recommended undertaking such an obligation to his friends, however confident they might feel about a venture, as failure invariably caused great distress to the guarantor and, more importantly, to his or her family.

William wrote a formal letter to Mrs Brookes, suggesting she make an appointment to discuss her position. He knew from the Brookes file that she was only twenty-two years old, and a member of an old and distinguished Boston family – daughter of Andrew Higginson and great-niece of Henry Lee Higginson, founder of the Boston Symphony. He also noted that she had substantial assets of her own. He did not relish the thought of requiring her to make them over to the bank, so he steeled himself for an unpleasant encounter.

The morning had begun badly, after a heated disagreement with Simmons about a substantial investment in copper and tin that he wished to recommend to the board. Industrial demand for the two metals was rising steadily, and William was convinced that a world shortage was certain to follow, which would guarantee the bank a handsome profit. Simmons did not agree with William's judgement, feeling the bank should invest more heavily in the stock market, and the matter was still uppermost in William's mind when his secretary ushered Mrs Brookes into his office.

With one tentative smile, she removed copper, tin and all other world shortages from his mind. Before she could sit down, he jumped up and walked around from the other side of his desk and settled her into a chair, simply to assure himself that she would not vanish like a mirage on closer inspection. William had never come across a woman he considered half as beautiful as Katherine Brookes. Her long fair hair fell in loose and wayward curls onto her shoulders, and little wisps escaped enchantingly from her hat and clung around her temples. The fact that she was in mourning in no way detracted from the beauty of her slim figure, and her fine bone structure ensured that she was someone whose beauty would turn to elegance over the years. Her brown eyes were enormous. They were also clearly apprehensive about what he had planned for her.

William strove for a businesslike tone of voice. 'Mrs Brookes, may I say how sorry I was to learn of your husband's death – a man we all admired – and how much I regret the necessity of asking you to come here today.'

Two lies in a single sentence, both of which would have been true five minutes before. He waited to hear her speak.

'Thank you, Mr Kane. I am well aware of my obligations to your bank,' she said, in a soft, gentle voice, 'and I can assure you I will do everything in my power to meet them.'

William said nothing, hoping she would go on speaking. When she did not, he outlined the disposition of Max Brookes's estate – very slowly. She listened with downcast eyes.

'Now, Mrs Brookes, you acted as guarantor for your late husband's loan, and that brings us to the question of your personal assets.' He consulted his file. 'You have eighty thousand dollars in investments – your family money, I believe – and seventeen thousand four hundred and fifty-six dollars in your checking account.'

She looked up. 'Your knowledge of my financial position is more detailed than mine, Mr Kane. You should, however, add Buckhurst Park, our home in Florida, which was in Max's name. I also have some quite valuable jewellery of my own. If I were to realize all of my assets, that would just about cover the three hundred thousand dollars you still require, and I've already made arrangements to do so.' There was only the slightest tremor in her voice.

'Mrs Brookes, the bank has no desire to relieve you of your every last possession. With your agreement, we would like to sell your stocks and bonds. Everything else you mentioned, including the house, we feel should remain in your possession.'

She hesitated. 'I appreciate your generosity, Mr Kane. However, I have no wish to remain under any obligation to your bank, or to leave my husband's name under a cloud.' The little tremor again, but quickly suppressed. 'In any case, I've already decided to sell the house in Florida and return to my parents' home as soon as possible.'

William's pulse quickened when he realized that she would be coming back to Boston. 'In that case, perhaps we can reach some agreement about the proceeds of the sale.'

'Of course,' she said flatly. 'After all, the bank is entitled to the entire amount.'

William played for another meeting. 'Don't make too hasty a decision, Mrs Brookes. I think I should consult my colleagues, and discuss their response with you at a later date.'

She shrugged slightly. 'As you wish, Mr Kane. I don't really care about the money either way, and I wouldn't want to put you to any inconvenience.'

William blinked. 'Mrs Brookes, I must confess to being surprised by your equanimity under such difficult circumstances. At least allow me the pleasure of taking you to lunch.'

She smiled, revealing an unexpected dimple in her right cheek. William gazed at it in fascination, and did his utmost to provoke its reappearance over a long lunch at the Ritz-Carlton Hotel at his father's old table. By the time he returned to his desk, it was well past three o'clock.

'Long lunch, William,' commented Simmons.

'Yes. The Brookes business turned out to be far trickier than I had anticipated.'

'It looked fairly straightforward to me when I glanced through the papers,' said Simmons. 'She isn't complaining about our offer, is she? I thought we were being rather generous, all things considered.'

'Yes, she thought so, too. I had to talk her out of divesting herself of her last dollar to swell our reserves.'

Simmons stared. 'That doesn't sound like the William Kane we know. Still, there's never been a better time for the bank to be magnanimous.'

William grimaced. Since the day of his arrival, he and Simmons had been in disagreement about where the stock market was heading. The Dow Jones had been moving steadily upward since Herbert Hoover's election to the White House in November 1928. In fact, ten days later, the New York Stock Exchange posted a record volume of sales, over six million shares were traded in one day. But William was convinced that the upward trend, fuelled by a large influx of borrowed money could only result in inflation to the point of instability. Simmons, on the other hand, was confident that the boom would continue, and when William urged caution at board meetings he was invariably overruled. However, that did not prevent him from selling some of his own stock and reinvesting it in land, gold, commodities and even in some carefully selected paintings – Manet, Monet and Matisse, although he still wasn't sure about the latest fad, Picasso.

When the Federal Reserve Bank of New York put out an edict declaring that it would not cover loans to banks that released money to their customers for the sole purpose of speculation, William considered that the first nail had been driven into the speculators' coffin. He immediately reviewed the bank's lending programme, and estimated that Kane and Cabot had more than $26 million outstanding on such commitments. At the next board meeting he advised the board to call in these loans as quickly as possible, certain that, with such a government regulation in place, stock prices must inevitably fall in the long term.

'William, you're far too cautious for your own good,' said Simmons. 'Don't you see that we can't afford to jump off this bandwagon and let every Tom, Dick and Harry and Cabot make a profit?'

'And don't you see that the market is fuelled by loans that at some time will have to be repaid, and that's when the wheels come off the bandwagon, it will come crashing to a halt and we'll end up taking heavy losses.'

'No, I can't—' began Simmons, his voice rising.

'Gentlemen, gentlemen,' interrupted Alan Lloyd. 'This is a boardroom, not a boxing ring. I suggest that we take a vote. Those in favour . . .'

William lost the vote by 12 to 2.

26

By THE END of the year, Abel had invited four employees from the Plaza to join him in Chicago. They had three things in common: they were young, ambitious and honest. Within six months, only 37 of the original 110 employees were still working at the Richmond.

At the end of the financial year, Abel cracked open a large bottle of champagne with Davis Leroy to celebrate the annual figures for the Chicago Richmond. They had declared a profit of $3,468; small, but the first profit the hotel had ever shown in its thirty years' existence. Abel was projecting a profit of more than $25,000 in 1929.

Davis Leroy raised his glass. 'Once you've got this place in shape, Abel, perhaps you should turn your attention to the rest of the group.'

'I'm not moving until I've found the right man to take my place.'

'Whatever you say,' said Davis as Abel refilled his glass.

◄◇►

Davis began to visit Chicago more regularly, and he and Abel often went to baseball games and the races together. On one occasion, when Davis had lost $700 on the first six races, he threw his arms round Abel and said, 'Why do I bother with horses? You're the only gamble I've ever made.'

Whenever Melanie Leroy dined at the hotel with her father Abel couldn't take his eyes off her, although she never gave him a second look. And on the rare occasions when they spoke, she didn't suggest that he might substitute 'Melanie' for 'Miss Leroy'. That was, until she discovered he was the holder of an economics degree from Columbia, and had read Kafka as well as Fitzgerald. She softened a little more when he became manager of the Chicago Richmond, and from time to time dined with him in the hotel, when she would discuss the work she was doing for her liberal arts degree at the University of Chicago. Emboldened, he invited her to a concert, and then a fortnight later to the theatre. He even began to feel a proprietorial jealousy whenever she brought other men to dine at the hotel, though she never came with the same escort twice.

So greatly had the cuisine improved under Abel's new regime that people who had lived in Chicago for thirty years and scarcely realized the hotel existed were now making regular dinner reservations every Saturday evening.

During his second year Abel had the whole hotel redecorated – for the first time in twenty years – and dressed the staff in smart new green-and-gold uniforms. One guest who had stayed at the Richmond for a week every year for the past decade actually turned around and went back out of the front door, thinking he had walked into the wrong establishment. When Al Capone booked a dinner party for sixteen in a private room to celebrate his thirtieth birthday, Abel knew he had arrived.

◀◎▶

Abel's personal wealth also multiplied during this period, as the stock market flourished. He had left the Plaza with $8,000 eighteen months before, and his brokerage account now stood at over $30,000. He felt confident that the market would continue to rise, so he always reinvested his profits. His personal requirements were still modest. He had acquired three new suits and two pairs of brown patent leather shoes. His accommodation and food were provided by the hotel, and he had few out-of-pocket expenses.

The Continental Trust Bank had handled the Richmond account for more than thirty years, so Abel had transferred his own account to them when he first arrived in Chicago. Every morning he would go to the bank and deposit the hotel's previous day's takings. One morning, after he'd completed this task, the teller asked if he could spare a moment to see the manager. Abel didn't hide his surprise. He knew his personal account was never overdrawn, so he assumed the meeting must have something to do with the Richmond. But the bank could hardly complain that the hotel's account was in the black for the first time in years. The teller guided Abel through a tangle of corridors until they reached a closed wooden door. A gentle knock, and he was ushered in.

'Good morning, Mr Rosnovski. My name is Curtis Fenton,' said the manager. He shook hands with Abel before motioning him to a green leather button chair on the other side of the desk. The manager was a short, rotund man who wore half-moon spectacles and an impeccable white collar and black tie to go with his three-piece banker's suit.

'Thank you,' said Abel nervously. He retained, from his days in Russia, a natural fear of the unknown.

'I would have invited you to lunch, Mr Rosnovski . . .'

Abel's heartbeat steadied a little. He was reasonably confident that bank managers did not dispense free meals when they had unpleasant messages to deliver.

'. . . but something has arisen that requires my immediate attention, so I hope you won't mind if I discuss the problem with you without delay.' Abel said nothing, something else the Russians had taught him. Fenton went on, 'I'll come straight to the point, Mr Rosnovski. One of my most respected customers, an elderly lady, Miss Amy Leroy' – the name made Abel sit up instantly – 'is in possession of twenty-five per cent of the Richmond Group stock. She has offered this holding to her brother, Mr Davis Leroy, several times in the past, but he has always reluctantly turned her down. I can understand Mr Leroy's reasoning. He already owns seventy-five per cent of the company and I daresay he feels he has no need to worry about the other twenty-five per cent, which, incidentally, was a legacy from their late father. However, Miss Leroy still wishes to dispose of her stock, as it has never paid a dividend.'

Abel was not surprised to hear that.

'Mr Leroy has indicated that he has no objection to her selling the stock to a third party, as she feels that at her age she would like to have a little cash to spend. I thought I would apprise you of the situation, Mr Rosnovski, in case you know of someone who might wish to purchase my client's shares.'

'How much is Miss Leroy hoping to realize for her stock?' asked Abel.

'Oh, I believe she'd be willing to let it go for as little as sixty-five thousand dollars.'

'Sixty-five thousand dollars is rather high for a stock that has never paid a dividend,' said Abel. 'And has no prospect of doing so for some years,' he added.

'Ah,' said Curtis Fenton, 'but you must remember that the value of the eleven hotels should also be taken into consideration.'

'But control of the company would still remain in the hands of Mr Leroy, which makes Miss Leroy's twenty-five per cent holding nothing but pieces of paper.'

'Come, come, Mr Rosnovski, twenty-five per cent of eleven hotels would be a very valuable asset in return for a mere sixty-five thousand dollars.'

'Not while Mr Leroy has overall control. Offer Miss Leroy forty thousand dollars, Mr Fenton, and I may be able to find you someone who is interested.'

'You don't think that person might consider going a little higher, do you?' Mr Fenton's eyebrow raised on the word *higher*.

'Not a penny more, Mr Fenton.'

The bank manager brought his fingertips delicately together, well aware of how much Abel had deposited with the bank.

'In the circumstances, I can only ask Miss Leroy what her response would be to such an offer. I will contact you again as soon as she has instructed me.'

After he left Curtis Fenton's office, Abel hurried back to the hotel to double-check his personal holdings. His brokerage account stood at $33,112 and his personal checking account at $3,008. He found it difficult to concentrate on his daily responsibilities, wondering how Miss Leroy would react to his bid and daydreaming about what he would do if he held a 25 per cent interest in the Richmond Group.

He thought for some time about informing Davis Leroy, fearful that the genial Texan might view him as a threat. But after a couple of days he decided the fairest thing would be to call his boss and tell him exactly what he had in mind.

'I want you to know why I am doing this, Davis. I believe the Richmond Group has a great future, and you can be sure that I'll work even harder if I know my own money is involved.' He paused. 'But if you want to take up that twenty-five per cent yourself, I shall naturally withdraw my bid.'

To his surprise, the escape ladder was not grasped.

'Well, see here, Abel, if you have that much confidence in the group, go ahead, son, and buy Amy out. I'd be proud to have you for a partner. You've earned it. By the way, I'll be up next week for the Reds–Cubs game. Care to join me?'

'Sure would,' said Abel. 'And thank you, Davis – you'll never have cause to regret your decision.'

'I'm sure I won't, partner.'

Abel returned to the bank a week later. This time it was he who asked to see the manager. Once again he sat in the green leather button chair and waited impatiently for Curtis Fenton to speak.

'I am surprised to find,' began Fenton, not looking at all surprised, 'that Miss Leroy will accept a bid of forty thousand dollars for her twenty-five per cent holding in the Richmond Group. As I have now secured her agreement, I must ask if you are in a position to disclose your buyer.'

'Yes,' said Abel confidently. 'I will be the principal.'

'I see, Mr Rosnovski' – again not showing any surprise. 'May I ask how you propose to pay the forty thousand dollars?'

'I shall liquidate my stock holdings and release any spare cash in my personal account, which will leave a shortfall of about four thousand dollars. I hope the bank will be willing to loan me that sum, since you are so confident that the Richmond Group stock is undervalued. In any case, four thousand dollars probably represents nothing more than the bank's commission on the deal.'

Curtis Fenton blinked, and tried not to frown. Gentlemen did not usually make that sort of comment in his office; it stung all the more because Abel had the sum exactly right. 'Will you give me a little time to consider your proposal, Mr Rosnovski?'

'If you wait long enough, I won't need a loan,' said Abel. 'The way the market's climbing at the moment, my other investments will soon be worth the full forty thousand.'

Abel had to wait a further week before he was informed that Continental Trust was willing to back him. He immediately cleared both his accounts, and borrowed a little under $4,000 to make up the shortfall on the forty thousand.

Within six months he had paid off the $4,000 loan by careful buying and selling of stock between March and August 1929, some of the most bullish days the stock market had ever experienced. By September 1929 both his accounts were back in credit, and he even had enough spare cash to buy a new Buick to go with his 25 per cent of the Richmond Group. His holding in Davis Leroy's empire also gave him the confidence to pursue his daughter and the other 75 per cent.

A week later, he invited Melanie to a Mozart concert at the Chicago Symphony Hall. Donning his latest suit, which reminded him that he was gaining a little weight, and wearing his first silk tie, he felt confident as he glanced in the mirror that the evening would be a success. After the concert, Abel avoided the Richmond, excellent though its food had become, and escorted Melanie to the Loop for dinner. He was particularly careful to allow her to talk about subjects she felt at ease with: her upcoming degree, and her father, although she also seemed fascinated by the recent success of the hotel. Emboldened, he asked her to join him in his room for a drink. It was the first time she had seen it, and she appeared surprised by how many books were on the shelves, and how many pictures hung on the walls.

Abel poured the Coca-Cola she requested, dropped two cubes of ice into it and felt a new confidence from the smile that rewarded him when he handed her the glass. He couldn't help staring briefly at her slim, crossed legs. He poured himself a

bourbon and put on the Chicago Symphony Orchestra's performance of *Eine kleine Nachtmusik*.

Abel sat down beside her and reflectively swirled the drink in
his glass. 'For many years I heard no music. When I did, Mozart
spoke to my heart as no other composer has done.'

'How very European you sound sometimes, Abel.' She pulled
free the edge of her silk dress, which Abel was sitting on. 'Who
would have thought a hotel manager would have even heard of
Mozart?'

'One of my ancestors, the second Baron Rosnovski,' said Abel,
'once met the maestro, and became a close friend of the Mozart
family, so I have always felt he was part of my life.'

Melanie's smile was unfathomable. Abel leaned sideways and
kissed her cheek below the ear, where her fair curls were drawn
back from her face. 'Frederick Stock captured the mood of the
third movement to perfection, don't you think?' he said.

Abel tried a second kiss. This time she turned her face towards
him and allowed herself to be kissed on the lips. Then she drew
away.

'I think I ought to be getting back to the university.'

'But you've only just arrived,' said Abel.

'Yes, I know, but I have to be up in time for an early morning
class.'

Abel kissed her again. She fell back on the couch as he tried
to move his hand onto her breast. She broke away quickly.

'I must be going, Abel,' she insisted.

'Oh, come on,' he said, 'you don't have to go yet.' Once again
he pulled her towards him.

This time she pushed him away more firmly. 'Abel, what do
you think you're doing? Just because you take me to a concert
and buy me an occasional meal doesn't mean you have the right
to maul me.'

'But we've been going out for months,' said Abel. 'I didn't
think you'd mind.'

'We have not been going out for months, Abel. I dine with
you occasionally in my father's hotel, but you shouldn't construe
that to mean there's anything between us.'

'I'm sorry,' said Abel. 'The last thing I wanted you to think was that I was going too far. I simply wanted you to know how I feel.'

'I would never consider starting a relationship with a man,' she said, 'who I wasn't going to marry.'

'But I do want to marry you,' said Abel quietly.

Melanie burst out laughing.

'What's so funny about that?' he asked, sitting bolt upright.

'Don't be silly, Abel, I could never marry you.'

'Why not?' demanded Abel, shocked by the finality of her statement.

'A southern lady would never consider marrying a first-generation Polish immigrant,' she replied, pushing her silk dress back into place.

'But I am a baron,' said Abel, a little haughtily.

Melanie burst out laughing again. 'You don't think anybody believes that, do you, Abel? Don't you realize the whole staff laughs behind your back whenever you mention your title?'

Abel was stunned, his face draining of all colour. 'They laugh at me behind my back?' he repeated. His normally slight accent had become pronounced.

'Yes,' she said. 'Surely you know that your nickname in the hotel is the Chicago Baron.'

Abel was speechless.

'Now, don't be silly and get all self-conscious about it, Abel. I think you've done a wonderful job for Daddy, and I know he admires you, but I could never marry you.'

'*You could never marry me,*' Abel said quietly.

'Of course not. Daddy likes you, but he wouldn't want a Polack as a son-in-law.'

'I'm sorry to have offended you,' said Abel, rising from the sofa.

'You haven't, Abel. I'm flattered. Let's forget you ever raised the subject. Perhaps you would be kind enough to take me back to the university?'

Somehow he managed to walk across and help Melanie on with her cloak. He became more conscious of his limp as he escorted her down the corridor. They went down in the elevator, and neither spoke as he drove her to the university. He parked the car and accompanied her to the front lodge, where he kissed her hand.

'I do hope this doesn't mean we can't still be friends,' said Melanie.

'Of course not,' he managed.

'Thank you for taking me to the concert, Abel. I'm sure you'll have no trouble in finding a nice Polish girl to marry you. Good night.'

'Goodbye,' said Abel.

-<o>-

On March 21, 1929, Blair and Company announced its merger with the Bank of America, the third in a series of bank consolidations that seemed to point to a brighter tomorrow. On March 25, Tony Simmons sent William a note pointing out that the market had broken another all-time record, and proceeded to invest even more of the bank's money into stocks. By then William had sold seventy-five per cent of his stock, a move that had already cost him more than $2 million – and one that clearly worried Alan Lloyd.

'I hope to goodness you know what you're doing, William.'

'Alan, I've been beating the stock market since I was fourteen, and I've always done it by bucking the trend.'

But as the market continued to climb through the summer of 1929, even William stopped selling, and began to wonder if Tony Simmons's judgement had been right all along.

As the time for Alan Lloyd's retirement drew nearer, Simmons's undisguised ambition to succeed him as chairman began to take on the look of a *fait accompli*. The prospect troubled William, who considered Simmons's thinking far too conventional. He was always a yard behind the rest of the market, which is fine during boom years when investments are going well, but can be disastrous in lean times, more complicated times. A shrewd investor, in William's opinion, did not just run with the herd, thundering or otherwise, but worked out in advance the direction in which that herd would be turning next. William still felt that the stock market looked risky, while Simmons was convinced that America was entering a golden era.

William's other problem was that Tony Simmons was only forty-three, and if he was appointed chairman of Kane and Cabot, William could not hope to succeed him for at least another twenty years. That hardly fitted in with what Harvard described as 'one's career pattern'.

Despite these distractions, the image of Katherine Brookes continually interrupted his thoughts. He wrote to her as often as he could about the sale of her stocks and bonds: formal typewritten letters that elicited no more than formal handwritten responses. She must have thought he was the most conscientious banker on Wall Street. Then, early in the fall, she wrote to tell him that she had found a buyer for the Florida estate. William wrote requesting that she allow him to negotiate the terms of the sale on the bank's behalf. She agreed by return of post.

William took the train to Florida a week later. During the journey he had begun to wonder if his image of Mrs Brookes would turn out to be an illusion, and he stepped off the train with some apprehension, only to be overwhelmed by how much more beautiful she appeared in person than in his recollection. The slight wind blew her black dress against her body as she stood waiting on the platform, revealing a silhouette that ensured that every man except William would look at her a second time. William's eyes never left her.

She was still in mourning, and her manner towards him was so reserved and correct that William initially despaired of making any impression. He spun out the negotiations with the farmer who was purchasing Buckhurst Park for as long as he could, and persuaded Katherine to retain one-third of the sale price while the bank took the other two-thirds. Finally, after the legal papers were signed, he could find no more excuses for not returning to Boston. He invited her to dinner at his hotel on the final evening, determined to reveal something of his feelings for her. Not for the first time, she took him by surprise. Before he had broached the subject she asked him, twirling her glass to avoid looking at him, if he would like to stay at Buckhurst Park for the weekend.

'A chance for us to talk about something other than finance,' she suggested. William remained silent.

Finally she found the courage to continue. 'The strange thing is that I seem to have enjoyed the last few days more than any time I can remember.' She blushed again. 'I've expressed that badly, and you'll think the worst of me.'

William's pulse quickened. 'Katherine, I've wanted to say something like that for the past eight months.'

'Then you'll stay for a few days?'

'You bet I will,' said William, taking her hand.

That night she installed him in a guest bedroom at Buckhurst Park. William would always look back on those days as a golden interlude in his life. He rode with Katherine, and she outjumped him. He swam with her, and she out-distanced him. He walked with her, and always needed to turn back first. Finally he resorted to playing poker with her, and won $3.5 million over the weekend.

'Will you take a cheque?' she said grandly.

'You forget, I know what you're worth, Mrs Brookes. But I'll make a deal with you. You have to go on playing until you've won it all back.'

'That may take some time.'

'That's fine by me,' said William.

He found himself telling Kate of long-forgotten incidents from his past, things he had never discussed even with Matthew – his respect for his father, his love for his mother, his blind hatred of Henry Osborne, his ambitions for Kane and Cabot. She in turn told him of her childhood in Boston, her school days in Virginia and her early marriage to Max Brookes.

When they said goodbye at the station, he kissed her for the first time.

'Kate, I'm going to say something very presumptuous. I hope one day you'll feel the same about me as you did about Max.'

'I already do,' she said quietly.

William touched her cheek. 'Don't stay out of my life for another eight months.'

'I can't – you've sold my house.'

—◦—

On the journey back to Boston, feeling happier and more settled than at any time since his father's death, William drafted a report on the sale of Buckhurst Park, his mind returning continually to Kate and the past few days. Just before the train drew into South Station, he scribbled a quick note in his illegible handwriting.

Kate,

I find I'm missing you already, and it's only been a few hours. Please write and let me know when you'll be coming to Boston. Meanwhile I'll be getting back to work, and may be able to put you out of my mind for quite long periods of time (i.e. 10+/- 5 minutes) at a stretch.

Love,

William

P.S. You still owe me $17.5 million dollars.

He had just dropped the envelope into the mailbox on Charles Street when all thoughts of Kate were driven from his mind by the cry of a newsboy.

'Wall Street Collapse!'

William seized a copy of the paper and rapidly skimmed the front page. The market had plummeted overnight. Some financiers were saying it was nothing more than a readjustment; William saw it as the beginning of the landslide he had been predicting for months. He hurried to the bank, and almost ran to the chairman's office.

'I'm confident that the market will recover during the next few weeks,' Alan Lloyd said soothingly.

'No it won't,' said William. 'The market is stretched to its limit. Overloaded with small investors who thought they would make a quick buck and are now going to have to run for cover. Can't you see the balloon is about to burst? I'm going to sell every stock in my possession. By the end of the year the bottom will have dropped out of the market. I did warn the board in February, Alan.'

'I still don't agree with you, William, but I'll call a full board meeting immediately, so we can discuss your views in greater detail.'

'Thank you,' said William. He returned to his office, and immediately picked up the telephone on his desk.

'I forgot to tell you, Alan. I've met the woman I'm going to marry.'

'Does she know yet?'

'No.'

'I see,' said Alan. 'Then your marriage will closely resemble your banking career. Anyone directly involved will be informed after you've made your decision.'

William laughed, picked up the other phone and put in a sell order on the rest of his stock. Tony Simmons was standing in the doorway when he put the telephone down. From the expression on his face, it appeared that he thought William had gone quite mad.

'You could lose your shirt if you dump all your stocks with the market in its present state.'

'I'll lose a lot more than my shirt if I hold onto them,' replied William.

The loss he suffered during the following week was over $1 million, which would have buried a less confident man. William reinvested his capital in any material that had a sharp edge: gold, silver, nickel and tin.

At a board meeting the following day, he also lost – by 8 votes to 6 – his proposal to immediately liquidate the bank's stocks. Tony Simmons convinced the board that it would be irresponsible not to hold out a little longer. The only small victory William notched up was persuading his fellow directors that the bank should not buy any more shares.

The market rose a few points the following day, which gave William the opportunity to sell most of what was left of his own stock. By the end of the week, when the index had risen steadily for four days in a row, William was even beginning to wonder if he had been over-reacting, but all his past experience and instinct told him he had made the right decision. Alan Lloyd said nothing; the money William was losing was not his business, and in any case, he was looking forward to a quiet retirement.

On October 22, the market suffered further heavy losses and William again begged Alan to get out while he still had a chance. This time Alan listened, and allowed William to place a sell order on some of the bank's major stocks. The following day the market collapsed in an avalanche of selling, and it didn't matter what the bank tried to dispose of, because there were no longer any buyers in the market. During the next week the dumping of stock turned into a stampede as every small investor in America put in a sell order as they tried to get out as quickly as possible. Such was the panic that the ticker tape machine could not keep pace with the transactions. Only when the Exchange opened the next morning, after the clerks had worked all through the night, did traders know how much the market had lost.

William had sold off nearly all the stock in his trust, and his personal loss was proportionately far smaller than the bank's. After losing more than $3 million in four days, even Tony Simmons had taken to acting on William's advice.

On October 29, Black Tuesday, as it came to be known, the market started to fall again. 16,610,030 shares were traded. The truth, though few would admit it, was that every financial establishment in America was insolvent. If every one of their customers had demanded cash – or if they in turn had tried to call in all their loans – the whole banking system would have collapsed overnight.

A board meeting held on November 9th opened with one minute's silence in memory of John J. Riordan, president of the County Trust and a director of Kane and Cabot, who had shot himself the day before. It was the eleventh suicide in Boston banking circles in two weeks, and the dead man had been a close personal friend of Alan Lloyd's. Alan went on to announce that Kane and Cabot had now lost nearly $4 million. Almost all the bank's small investors had gone under, and most of the larger ones were having impossible cash flow problems.

Angry mobs had begun to gather outside banks in Wall Street, and the elderly guards had to be replaced by Pinkerton agents.

'Another week of this,' said Alan, 'and every one of us will be wiped out.' He offered his resignation, but the directors would not hear of it. His position was no different from that of any other chairman of any major American bank. Tony Simmons also offered his resignation, but once again his fellow directors didn't even call for a vote. As Simmons no longer appeared to be the obvious candidate to succeed Alan Lloyd, William kept a magnanimous silence.

As a compromise, Simmons was dispatched to London to take overall charge of the bank's operations in Europe. Out of harm's way, thought William, after the board had appointed him as the new Investment Director. He immediately invited Matthew Lester to join him as his deputy. This time Alan Lloyd didn't even raise an eyebrow, which made William wonder if he should have insisted that Matthew also be invited to join the board; but the moment had passed.

Matthew wasn't able to join the bank until early in the spring, which was the earliest his father felt able to release him. Lester's hadn't been without its own troubles.

The winter of 1929 could not have been worse, and William tried to remain dispassionate as he watched small and large firms alike, run by Bostonians he had known all his life, go under. He even began to wonder if Kane and Cabot could survive.

At Christmas he spent a glorious week in Florida with Kate, helping her pack her belongings in trunks and tea chests – 'The ones Kane and Cabot let me keep,' she teased – for her return to Boston. William's Christmas presents filled another tea chest, making her feel quite guilty about his generosity.

'What can a penniless widow hope to give you in return?' she mocked.

William returned to Boston in high spirits, hoping his time with Kate heralded the start of a better year.

27

ABEL STROLLED INTO the dining room of the hotel and was surprised to find Melanie sitting at her father's table. She wasn't looking her usual well-groomed self, and appeared tired and apprehensive. He nearly walked over to ask her if everything was all right but, remembering their last meeting, decided against it. On the way back to his office he found Davis Leroy standing by the reception desk. He had on the checked jacket he had been wearing the first time Abel had seen him at the Plaza.

'Is Melanie in the dining room?' Davis asked.

'Yes, she is,' said Abel. 'I didn't realize you were coming into town today, Davis. I'll get the Presidential Suite ready for you immediately.'

'Only for one night, Abel, and I'd like to have a private word with you later.'

'Of course.'

Abel didn't like the sound of 'private', wondering if Melanie had complained to her father about him. Was that why he had found it impossible to talk to Davis during the past few days?

Leroy hurried past him into the dining room, while Abel went over to the reception desk to check whether the Presidential Suite was available. Half the rooms in the hotel were unoccupied, so it came as no surprise that it was free. He booked Davis in, and then waited by the reception desk for over an hour. He saw Melanie leave the dining room, her face red, as if she'd been crying. Her father came out a few minutes later.

'Get yourself a bottle of bourbon, Abel – don't tell me we don't have one – and then join me in my suite.'

Abel picked up a couple of bottles from his safe and joined Leroy on the seventeenth floor, still wondering if Melanie had complained about him.

'Open the bottle and pour me a very large one, Abel,' Leroy instructed.

Once again Abel felt the fear of the unknown. His palms began to sweat. Surely he was not going to be fired for wanting to marry the boss's daughter? He and Leroy had been friends for over a year now, close friends, he thought.

'And you'd better fill your glass as well, Abel.'

Abel carried out his boss's instructions, but only toyed with his drink while he waited for Leroy to speak.

'Abel, I'm wiped out.' Leroy paused, took a gulp and then poured himself another drink.

Abel didn't speak, partly because he couldn't think what to say. After taking a swig of bourbon, he managed, 'But you still own eleven hotels.'

'Used to own,' said Davis Leroy. 'Have to put it in the past tense now, Abel. I no longer own any of them; the bank took possession last Thursday.'

'But they belong to you – they've been in your family for two generations,' said Abel.

'That's true, but they aren't any longer. Now they belong to a bank. There's no reason why you shouldn't know the whole truth, Abel; after all, the same thing's happening to almost everyone in America right now, big or small. About ten years ago I borrowed two million dollars from the bank, using the hotels as collateral. I invested the money right across the board in stocks and bonds, fairly conservatively and in well-established companies. I built the capital up to nearly five million, which was one of the reasons the hotel losses never bothered me too much – they were tax deductible against the profits I was making in the market. Today I couldn't give them shares away. We may as well use them as toilet paper in the hotels. For the last three weeks I've been selling as fast as I can, but there are no buyers out there. The bank foreclosed on my loan last Thursday. Most people who are affected by the crash only have pieces of paper to cover their losses, but in my case, the bank that backed me held the deeds of the hotels as security against the original loan. So when the bottom dropped out of the market, they immediately took possession of the properties. The bastards are going to sell them just as soon as they can find a buyer.'

'That's madness,' said Abel. 'They'll get nothing for them right now, but if they got behind us, we could show them a worthwhile return on their investment.'

'I know *you* could, Abel, but they've got my past record to throw back in my face. I went up to their head office in Boston and told them about you. I assured them I'd devote all my time to the group if they would just support us in the short term, but they weren't interested. They fobbed me off with some smooth young puppy who had all the textbook answers about cash flows, no capital base and credit restrictions.' Leroy paused to take a swig of bourbon. 'Right now, the best thing we can do is get ourselves drunk, because I am finished, penniless, bankrupt.'

'Then so am I,' said Abel quietly.

'No, you have a great future ahead of you, son. Whoever takes over this group can't make a move without you.'

'You forget that I own twenty-five per cent of the group.'

Davis Leroy stared at him.

'Oh my God, Abel. I hope you didn't put *all* your money into me.' His voice was becoming thick.

'Every last cent,' said Abel. 'But I don't regret it, Davis. Better to lose with a wise man than win with a fool.' He poured himself another drink.

Tears were filling Leroy's eyes. 'You know, Abel, you're the best friend I've ever had. You knock my hotel into shape, you invest your own money, I make you penniless, and you don't even complain. And then for good measure my daughter refuses to marry you.'

'You didn't mind me asking her?' said Abel, more confident than he would have been before his third bourbon.

'Silly, stuck up snob doesn't know a good thing when she sees it. She wants to marry some horse-breeding gentleman from the South with at least a couple of Confederate generals in his family tree, or if she marries a northerner, his great-great-great grand-father will have come over on the *Mayflower*. If everyone who claims they had a relative on that boat were ever on board together, the damn thing would have sunk long before it left England. Too bad I don't have another daughter for you, Abel. I sure would have been proud to have you as a son-in-law. You and I would have made a great team, but I still reckon you can beat them all by yourself. You're young – you still have everything ahead of you.'

At twenty-four, Abel suddenly felt very old.

'Thank you for your confidence, Davis,' he said. 'Who gives a damn for the stock market anyway? You know you're the best friend I ever had.'

Abel poured himself another bourbon, and swallowed it in one gulp. Between them they finished both bottles by the early morning. When Davis fell asleep in his chair, Abel managed to stagger down to his room on the tenth floor, undress and collapse onto his bed.

He was awakened from a deep sleep by a loud banging on the door. His head was going round and round, but the banging went on and on, louder and louder. Somehow he managed to grope his way to the door. It was a bellboy.

'Come quickly, Mr Rosnovski, come quickly,' the boy said as he ran down the hall.

Abel threw on a dressing gown and slippers and staggered down the corridor to join the bellboy, who was holding the elevator door open for him.

'Quickly, Mr Rosnovski,' the boy repeated.

'What's the hurry?' demanded Abel, his head still throbbing as the elevator moved slowly down.

'Someone has jumped out the window.'

Abel sobered up immediately. 'A guest?'

'Yes, I think so,' said the bellboy, 'but I'm not sure.'

The elevator came to a stop on the ground floor. Abel thrust back the iron gates and ran out into the street. Police cars were already surrounding the hotel, headlights on, sirens wailing. He wouldn't have recognized the broken body lying on the sidewalk if it had not been for the checked jacket. A policeman was taking down details. A man in plainclothes walked across to join Abel.

'You the manager?'

'Yes, I am.'

'Do you have any idea who this man might be?'

'Yes,' said Abel, slurring the word. 'His name is Davis Leroy.'

'Do you know where he's from, or how we can contact his next of kin?'

Abel averted his eyes from Davis's body and answered automatically.

'He's from Dallas. Miss Melanie Leroy is his next of kin, his daughter. She's a student living on the university campus.'

'We'll get someone right over to her.'

'No, don't do that. I'll go and see her myself,' said Abel.

'Thank you, sir. It's always better if they don't hear the news from a stranger.'

'What a terrible, unnecessary thing,' said Abel, his eyes drawn back to the body of his friend.

'He's the seventh one in Chicago today,' said the officer flatly as he closed his little black notebook. 'We'll need to check his room later. Don't rent it again until we give you an all-clear.' The policeman strolled towards an ambulance as it screeched to a halt.

Abel watched the stretcher-bearers remove what was left of Davis Leroy from the sidewalk. He suddenly felt cold, sank to his knees and was violently sick in the gutter. Once again he had lost his closest friend. Perhaps if I'd drunk less and thought more, I might have been able to save him. He picked himself up, returned to his room, took a long, cold shower and somehow managed to get dressed. He ordered some black coffee and then reluctantly returned to the Presidential Suite. Other than a couple of empty bourbon bottles, there seemed to be no sign of the drama that had taken place only a few minutes earlier. Then he saw the letters on the side table by a bed that had not been slept in. The first was addressed to Melanie, the second to a lawyer in Dallas and the third to Abel Rosnovski. He tore it open, his hands shaking almost uncontrollably.

Dear Abel,

    I'm taking the only way out after the bank's decision. There's nothing left for me to live for, and I'm too old to start over. I want you to know I believe you're the one person who might make something out of this terrible mess.

    I've made a new will in which I've left you my 75 per cent of the stock in the Richmond Group. I realize it's worthless, but it will at least secure your position as the legal owner of the group. As you had the guts to buy 25 per cent with your own money, you deserve the right to see if you can make some deal with the bank. I've left everything else to Melanie. Please be the one who tells her.

    I would have been proud to have you as a son-in-law, partner.

    Your friend,
        Davis

Abel read the letter again before placing it in his wallet.

He drove slowly over to the university campus soon after first light. He broke the news as gently as he could to Melanie. He sat nervously on the couch, not knowing what he could add to the stark message of death. She took it surprisingly well, almost as if she had known it might happen, although she was obviously moved. But there were no tears in front of Abel – perhaps later, when he wasn't there. He felt sorry for her for the first time in his life.

28

ON JANUARY 4, 1930, Abel Rosnovski boarded a train for Boston. He took a taxi from the station to Kane and Cabot, and arrived at the bank a few minutes early. He sat in a reception room that was larger and more ornate than any bedroom in the Chicago Richmond. He started reading *The Wall Street Journal*, which was trying to assure its readers that 1930 was going to be a better year. He doubted it. A prim middle-aged woman entered the room.

'Mr Kane will see you now, Mr Rosnovski.'

Abel rose and followed her down a long corridor into a small oak-panelled room. Behind a large leather-topped desk sat a tall, good-looking man who must, Abel thought, have been about the same age as himself. His eyes were as blue as Abel's but that was the only similarity. There was a picture on the wall behind him of an older man, whom the young man behind the desk greatly resembled. I'll bet that's Dad, Abel thought bitterly. You can be sure he'll survive the collapse; banks always seem to win, whatever happens.

'My name is William Kane,' said the man, rising and extending his hand. 'Please have a seat, Mr Rosnovski.'

'Thank you,' said Abel coolly, shaking his hand.

'Perhaps you will allow me to apprise you of the current situation as I see it,' said William.

'Of course.'

'Mr Leroy's tragic and premature death . . .' William began, hating the pomposity of his words.

Caused by your callous attitude, thought Abel.

'. . . appears to have left you with the immediate responsibility of running the Richmond Group until the bank is in a position to find a buyer. Although all of the shares in the group are now in your name, the property, in the form of eleven hotels, which was held as collateral for the late Mr Leroy's loan of two million dollars, is legally in our possession. If you wish to disassociate yourself from the whole process, we will understand.'

An insulting suggestion, thought William, but it had to be said.

The sort of thing a banker would expect a man to do, walk away the moment a problem arose, thought Abel.

William continued. 'Until the two-million-dollar debt to the bank is cleared, I'm afraid we must consider the estate of the late Mr Leroy insolvent. We at the bank appreciate your personal involvement with the group, and we have done nothing about disposing of the hotels until we had the opportunity to speak to you in person. We thought it possible you might know of some party interested in the purchase of the property, as the buildings, the land and the business are obviously a valuable asset.'

'But not valuable enough for the bank to consider backing me,' said Abel. He ran his hand wearily through his thick, dark hair. William didn't respond. 'How long will you give me to find a buyer?'

William hesitated for a moment when he saw the silver band around Abel Rosnovski's wrist. He had seen that band somewhere before, but he couldn't recall where.

'Thirty days. You must understand that the bank is carrying the day-to-day losses on ten of the eleven hotels. Only the Chicago Richmond is currently showing a small profit.'

'If you would give me enough time, Mr Kane, I could turn all the hotels into profitable concerns. I know I could. Just give me the chance to prove I can do it, sir.' Abel felt the last word sticking in his throat.

'Mr Leroy assured the bank that you were worth backing when he came to visit our last fall,' said William. 'But these are hard times. There's no telling if the hotel trade will pick up, and we are not hoteliers, Mr Rosnovski, we're bankers.'

Abel was beginning to lose his temper with this smoothly dressed 'young puppy'. 'They'll be even harder times for my hotel staff,' he said. 'What will they do if you sell off the roof from over their heads? What do you imagine will happen to them?'

'I'm afraid they are not our responsibility, Mr Rosnovski. I must act in the bank's best interests.'

'Don't you mean in *your* best interests, Mr Kane?' said Abel sharply.

The banker flushed. 'That was an unjust remark, Mr Rosnovski, and I would greatly resent it if I did not understand what you are going through.'

'Too bad you didn't show some understanding for Mr Leroy,' said Abel. 'You killed him, Mr Kane, just as surely as if you pushed him out of that window yourself. You and your "wash your hands" colleagues, sitting here in your smart offices while we sweat our guts out so you can rake it in when times are good, and rub our faces in the dirt when times are bad.'

William, too, was becoming angry, but unlike Abel he did not show it. 'This line of discussion is getting us nowhere, Mr Rosnovski. I must warn you that if you are unable to find a buyer for the group within thirty days, I shall have no choice but to put the hotels up for auction on the open market.'

'You'll be advising me to ask another bank for a loan next,' said Abel sarcastically. 'You *know* my record and you won't back me, so why should anyone else take the risk?'

'What you choose to do now is entirely up to you, Mr Rosnovski. My board's instructions are simply to dispose of the assets and wind up the account as quickly as possible, and that is what I intend to do. Perhaps you would be kind enough to contact me no later than' – he glanced at his diary – 'February fourth to let me know whether you have had any success in finding a buyer. Good day, Mr Rosnovski.'

William rose from behind the desk, and again offered his hand. This time Abel ignored it.

He walked to the door, but paused before leaving the office. 'I thought after the death of Davis Leroy, Mr Kane, you might feel embarrassed enough to offer a helping hand. I was wrong.

Your only interest is the bottom line, but when you go to bed at night, Mr Kane, be sure to think about me. When you wake up in the morning, think about me again, because I'll never stop thinking about my plans for you.'

William stood frowning at the closed door. That silver band bothered him – where had he seen it before?

His secretary entered the room. 'What a dreadful little man,' she said.

'No, not really,' said William. 'He thinks we were responsible for the death of his business partner, and that we're now dissolving his company without any thought for his employees, not to mention himself, when he has actually proved to be rather good at his job. Mr Rosnovski was remarkably polite given the circumstances. I'm sorry the board didn't take my advice and back him.' William sat down in his chair, suddenly feeling exhausted.

29

ABEL ARRIVED back in Chicago later that evening, still furious with his treatment at the hands of William Kane. He didn't catch exactly what the boy was shouting at the corner newsstand as he hailed a cab and climbed into the back seat.

'The Richmond Hotel, please.'

'Are you from the newspapers?' asked the driver as he moved out onto State Street.

'No. Why do you ask?'

'Oh, only because you asked for the Richmond and the place is swarming with journalists.'

Abel couldn't remember any functions scheduled for the Richmond which might attract the press.

The driver continued: 'If you're not a newspaperman, maybe I should take you to another hotel.'

'Why?' asked Abel, even more puzzled.

'Well, you won't have a very good night's sleep if you're booked in there.'

'Why not?' demanded Abel.

'Because the Richmond has been burned to the ground.'

They turned the corner of Drake Street, and Abel was faced head on with the smouldering shell of the Chicago Richmond Hotel. There were police cars, fire engines, charred wood and water flooding the street, while onlookers craned their necks from behind a barrier. Abel stared at the scorched remains of Davis Leroy's flagship.

'That'll be two dollars,' said the taxi driver.

The Pole is wise when the damage is done, thought Abel as he clenched his fist and started banging on his lame leg. He felt no pain – there was nothing left to feel.

'You bastards!' he shouted aloud. 'I've been lower than this before, and I'll still beat every one of you. Germans, Russians, Turks, that bastard Kane, and now this. Everyone. I'll beat you all. Nobody kills Abel Rosnovski.'

The assistant manager saw Abel gesticulating by the cab and ran over to him. Abel forced himself to be calm.

'Did everybody get out safely?' were Abel's first words.

'Yes, thank God. The hotel was nearly empty, and luckily the fire started in the middle of the afternoon, so getting everybody out wasn't a great problem. There were one or two minor injuries and burns – three people were taken to Chicago General – but there's nothing for you to worry about on that count.'

'Good, that's a relief. Thank God the hotel was well insured – over a million, if I remember. We may yet be able to turn this disaster to our advantage.'

'Not if what they're suggesting in today's papers is true.'

'What do you mean?' asked Abel.

'I'd rather you read it for yourself, boss.'

Abel walked over to the nearby newsstand and paid the boy two cents for the latest edition of the *Chicago Tribune*.

The banner headline told it all: RICHMOND HOTEL BLAZE – ARSON SUSPECTED.

Abel shook his head incredulously. 'Can anything else go wrong?' he muttered.

'Got yourself a problem?' the newsboy asked.

'A little one,' said Abel, and returned to his assistant manager. 'Who's in charge of the police inquiry?'

'That officer over there, leaning on the patrol car,' said the assistant manager, pointing to a prematurely balding man with deep sunken eyes. 'His name's Lieutenant O'Malley.'

'It would be,' said Abel. 'Tell the staff I'll see them all in the annexe at ten o'clock tomorrow morning. If anybody wants me before then, I'll be staying at the Stevens.'

'Will do, boss.'

Abel walked over to Lieutenant O'Malley and introduced himself.

The policeman stooped slightly and shook hands with him. 'Ah, the long-lost ex-manager has returned to his charred remains.'

'I don't find that funny, officer,' said Abel.

'I'm sorry, sir,' he said. 'It isn't funny. It's been a long night. Let's go and have a drink.'

He took Abel by the elbow and guided him across Michigan Avenue to a corner diner, where he ordered two milk shakes.

Abel laughed when the white, frothy mixture was put in front of him. Since he had never had a childhood, it was his first milk shake.

'I know. It's funny, everybody in this city is secretly drinking bourbon and beer,' said the policeman, 'so someone has to play it straight. In any case, Prohibition isn't going to last forever, and then my troubles will really begin, because the mobsters are going to discover that I really do like milk shakes.'

Abel laughed for a second time.

'Now to your problems, Mr Rosnovski. First, I have to tell you I don't think you have a snowball's chance in hell of picking up the insurance money on your hotel. The fire experts have gone over the remains of the building, and found the place was soaked in kerosene. No attempt to even disguise it. There were traces of the stuff all over the basement. One match and it would have gone up like a Roman candle.'

'Do you have any idea who's responsible?' asked Abel.

'Let me ask the questions. Do you know anyone who might bear a grudge against the hotel, or against you personally?'

Abel grunted. 'About fifty people, Lieutenant. I cleared out a real nest of vipers when I first arrived here. I can give you a list, if you think it might help.'

'It might, but the way people are talking out there, I may not need it. If you pick up any definite information, let me know, Mr Rosnovski, because I warn you, you have enemies.'

'Anyone in particular?' asked Abel.

'Somebody is suggesting that you did it because you lost everything in the crash, and needed the insurance money.'

Abel leaped off his stool.

'Calm down, calm down. I know you've been in Boston all day, and more important, you have a reputation in Chicago for building hotels up, not burning them down. But someone did set fire to the Richmond and you can bet your ass I'm going to find out who. Let's leave it at that for the moment.' He swivelled off his own stool. 'The milk shake's on me, Mr Rosnovski. I may call in a favour from you at some time in the future.'

As the two men walked towards the door, the policeman smiled at the girl who took his fifty cents, admiring her ankles and cursing the new fashion for long skirts. 'Keep the change, honey,' he said.

'A big thank you,' the girl replied.

'Nobody appreciates me,' said the lieutenant.

Abel laughed for a third time, which he would not have thought possible half an hour before.

'By the way,' O'Malley added as they reached the door. 'The insurance people are looking for you. I can't remember the name of the guy, but I guess he'll find you soon enough. Don't get angry with him if he suggests you were involved. Who can blame him? Keep in touch, Mr Rosnovski – I'll be wanting to talk to you again, when the milk shakes will be on you.'

Abel watched as the lieutenant vanished into the crowd of spectators, then walked slowly to the Stevens Hotel and booked himself in for the night. The desk clerk, who had already checked in most of the Richmond's guests, couldn't suppress a smile at booking the manager in as well.

Once he was alone in his room, Abel sat down and wrote a long letter to Mr William Kane, giving him whatever details about the fire he could supply, and telling him that he intended to use his unexpected freedom to make a tour of the other hotels in the group. He saw no point in hanging around in Chicago warming himself on the Richmond's embers in the vain hope that someone would come along and bail him out.

After a first-class breakfast at the Stevens the next morning –
it always made Abel feel good to be in a well-run hotel – he
withdrew $5,000 in cash from the hotel account and gave every
member of his staff two weeks' wages, telling them they could
stay on at the annexe for at least a month, or until they had found
new jobs. He then walked over to the Continental Trust to apprise
Curtis Fenton of Kane and Cabot's attitude – or to be more
accurate, of William Kane's attitude. He added, without a great
deal of hope, that he was looking for a buyer for the Richmond
Group at $2 million.

'That fire isn't going to help us, but I'll see what I can do,'
said Fenton, sounding far more positive than Abel had expected.
'At the time you bought the twenty-five per cent from Miss Leroy,
I told you I thought the hotels were a valuable asset. Despite the
crash I see no reason to change my mind about that, Mr
Rosnovski. I've watched you running your hotel for nearly two
years now, and I'd back you if the decision were left to me
personally, but I fear the bank would never agree to support the
Richmond Group. We've been aware of the financial shenanigans
for far too long to have any faith in the group's future, and that
fire was the last straw. Nevertheless, I do have some outside
contacts, and I'll see if they can do anything to help. You may
have more admirers in this city than you realize, Mr Rosnovski.'

30

ABEL DROVE SOUTH in the Buick he'd bought just before the market crashed. He'd decided to begin his tour of the group with the St Louis Richmond.

The trip to all the hotels in the group took nearly four weeks, and although most of them were run-down and, without exception, losing money, none of them was, in Abel's view, a hopeless case. They all had good locations; some were even the best-placed hotel in the city. Old man Leroy must have been a shrewder man than his son, thought Abel. He checked every hotel's insurance policy carefully; no problems there. When he finally reached the Dallas Richmond, the last stop on his itinerary, he was certain that anyone who managed to buy the group for $2 million would be making a sound investment and, if they decided to employ him, he knew exactly what needed to be done to make the group profitable.

On his return to Chicago he once again checked into the Stevens. There were several messages awaiting him. Lieutenant O'Malley wanted him to contact him soonest. So did William Kane, Curtis Fenton, and finally a Mr Henry Osborne. He began with the law, and arranged to meet O'Malley at the diner on Michigan Avenue.

Abel sat on a stool with his back to the counter, staring across the street at the charred remains of the Richmond Hotel while he waited for the lieutenant. O'Malley was a few minutes late, and didn't bother to apologize as he took the next stool and swivelled round to face Abel.

273

'You owe me a favour,' said the lieutenant, 'and nobody in Chicago gets away with owing O'Malley a milk shake.'

Abel ordered two, one giant, one regular.

'What did you find out?' asked Abel as he passed the detective two red-and-white-striped straws.

'The boys from the fire department were right – it was arson. We've arrested a guy called Desmond Pacey, who turns out to be the old manager of the Richmond. That was in your time, right?'

'I'm afraid it was,' said Abel.

'Why do you say that?' asked the lieutenant.

'I sacked Pacey for embezzling. He said he'd get even with me if it was the last thing he did. I didn't pay any attention – I've faced too many threats in my life, Lieutenant, to take any of them seriously, especially from a creep like Pacey.'

'Well, I have to tell you we've taken him seriously, and so have the insurance people, because they won't be paying out one cent until it's proved there was no collusion between you and Pacey.'

'That's all I need at the moment,' said Abel. 'But how can you be so sure it was Pacey?'

'He showed up at the casualty ward of the nearest hospital, the same day as the fire, with severe burns on his hands and chest. He came clean pretty quick, but I couldn't be sure what his motive was until now. So that just about wraps the case up, Mr Rosnovski.'

The lieutenant sucked on his straw until a loud gurgle convinced him he had drained the last drop.

'Another shake?' asked Abel.

'No, I'd better not. I promised my wife I'd cut down.' He stood up. 'Good luck, Mr Rosnovski. If you can prove to the insurance boys that you had no involvement with Pacey, you'll get your money. I'll do everything I can to help if the case ever gets to court. Keep in touch.'

Abel watched the detective disappear through the door. He gave the waitress a dollar. Once he was back on the sidewalk, Abel stood and stared into space, a space where the Richmond

Hotel had been less than a month ago. He turned and walked back to the Stevens.

There was another message from Henry Osborne, still giving no clue as to who he was. There was only one way to find out. Abel called the number, and was put through to the claims inspector of the Great Western Casualty Insurance Company. He made an appointment to see Osborne at noon. He then called William Kane in Boston and gave him a report on all the hotels in the group.

'And may I say again, Mr Kane, that I could turn those hotels' losses into profits if your bank would just give me the chance. What I did in Chicago, I know I can do for the rest of the group.'

'Possibly you could, Mr Rosnovski, but I'm afraid it won't be with Kane and Cabot's money. May I remind you that you have only a few days left in which to find a backer? Good day, sir.'

'Ivy League snob,' said Abel after the line had gone dead. 'I'm not classy enough for your money, am I? Some day, you bastard . . .'

—◦—

The next item on Abel's agenda was the insurance man.

Henry Osborne turned out to be tall and good-looking, with dark eyes and a mop of dark hair turning grey around the temples, and an easy, congenial manner. He had little to add to what Lieutenant O'Malley had told Abel. The Great Western Casualty Insurance Company had no intention of paying any part of the claim while the police were pressing for a charge of arson against Desmond Pacey, and until it was proved that Abel himself was in no way involved. Despite the blunt statement, Osborne seemed to be very understanding about the whole problem.

'Has the Richmond Group enough money to rebuild the hotel?' he asked.

'Not a red cent,' said Abel. 'The rest of the group is mortgaged up to the hilt, and the bank is pressing me to sell.'

'Why your bank, Osborne?'

Abel explained how he had come to own the group's shares without actually owning the hotels.

'Surely the bank can see for themselves how well you ran this hotel? Every businessman in Chicago knows that you were the first manager ever to make a profit for Davis Leroy. I realize the banks are going through hard times, but even they ought to know when to make an exception, especially when it's in their own interest.'

'Not this bank.'

'Continental Trust?' said Osborne. 'I've always found old Curtis Fenton a bit starchy, but amenable enough.'

'It's not Continental any more. The hotels are now owned by a Boston outfit called Kane and Cabot.'

Henry Osborne went white and sank back in his chair.

'Are you okay?' asked Abel.

'Yes, I'm fine.'

'Have you had dealings with Kane and Cabot in the past?'

'Off the record?' said Henry Osborne.

'Sure.'

'Yes, my company came up against them once before, and we ended up losing every penny.'

'How come?'

'I can't reveal the details. A messy business – let's just say one of the directors took advantage of a carefully worded contract.'

'Which one?' asked Abel.

'Which one have you been dealing with?'

'William Kane.'

Osborne didn't regain his colour. 'Be careful,' he said. 'He's the world's meanest son of a bitch. I could give you the lowdown on him, but it would have to be in the strictest confidence because he's not a man to cross.'

'I intend to cross him,' said Abel, 'so I may well be in touch. I have a score to settle with Mr Kane.'

'Well, you can count on me to help in any way I can if William Kane is involved,' said Osborne, rising from behind his desk, 'but that must be strictly between us. And if the court finds that Desmond Pacey set fire to the Richmond and no one else was involved, the company will pay your claim in full the same day.'

He opened the door for Abel. 'Then perhaps we can do some additional business with your other hotels.'

'Perhaps,' said Abel.

Abel walked back to the Stevens, to find another message awaiting him. A Mr David Maxton wondered if he was free to join him for lunch at one.

'David Maxton,' he said out loud, and the receptionist looked up. 'Why do I know that name?'

'He owns this hotel, Mr Rosnovski.'

'Ah, yes, of course. Please let Mr Maxton know that I shall be delighted to have lunch with him.' Abel glanced at his watch. 'And would you tell him that I may be a few minutes late?'

'Certainly, sir,' said the receptionist.

Abel went up to his room and changed into a new white shirt, wondering what David Maxton could possibly want.

The dining room was already packed when he walked in. The headwaiter showed him to a private table in an alcove where the owner of the Stevens was sitting alone. He rose to greet his guest.

'Abel Rosnovski, sir.'

'Yes, I know you,' said Maxton. 'Or, to be more accurate, I know you by reputation. Do sit down, and let's eat.'

Abel was compelled to admire the Stevens. The food and the service were every bit as good as the Plaza. If he was to run the best hotel in Chicago, this would be the one he'd be measured against.

The headwaiter reappeared with menus. Abel studied his carefully, politely declined a first course and selected the beef, the quickest way to tell if a restaurant is dealing with the right butcher. David Maxton did not look at his menu, but simply ordered the salmon.

'You must be wondering why I invited you to join me for lunch, Mr Rosnovski,' said Maxton.

'I assumed,' said Abel, laughing, 'you were going to ask me to take over the Stevens.'

'You're absolutely right, Mr Rosnovski.'

Abel was speechless. It was Maxton's turn to laugh. Even the arrival of the waiter wheeling a trolley of the finest beef did not help. The carver sharpened his knife. Maxton squeezed a slice of lemon over his salmon and continued.

'My manager is due to retire in five months, after twenty-two years of loyal service, and the assistant manager will also be leaving soon afterwards, so I'm looking for a new broom.'

'Place looks pretty clean to me,' said Abel.

'That doesn't mean it can't be improved, Mr Rosnovski. Never be satisfied with standing still,' added Maxton. 'I've been watching your activities carefully for the past two years. It wasn't until you took the Richmond over that it could even be classified as a hotel. It was a huge motel before that. In another two or three years it would have been a rival to the Stevens if some idiot hadn't burned the place down.'

'Potatoes, sir?'

Abel looked up at an attractive junior waitress. She smiled at him.

'No, thank you. Well, I'm very flattered, Mr Maxton, both by your comments and by the offer.'

'I think you'd be happy here, Mr Rosnovski. The Stevens is a well-run hotel, and I would be willing to start you off at fifty dollars a week and two per cent of the profits. And you could begin as soon as it suited you.'

'I'll need a few days to think it over, Mr Maxton,' said Abel, 'although I confess I'm tempted. But I still have a few problems to deal with at the Richmond.'

'Peas or cabbage, sir?' The same waitress, the same smile.

The face looked familiar. Abel felt sure he had seen her somewhere before. Perhaps she had once worked at the Richmond.

'Cabbage, please.'

He watched her walk away. There was definitely something familiar about her.

'Why don't you stay on at the hotel as my guest for a few days,' Maxton said, 'and see how we run the place? It may help you come to a decision.'

'That won't be necessary, Mr Maxton. After only one day as a guest I knew how well the hotel is run. My problem is that I own the Richmond Group.'

David Maxton's face registered surprise. 'I had no idea,' he said. 'I assumed old Davis Leroy's daughter would have inherited his stock.'

'It's a long story,' said Abel, and he spent the next twenty minutes explaining to Maxton how he had come into the owner-ship of the group's stock, and the position in which he now found himself. 'What I really want to do is raise the two million dollars myself and build the group up into something worthwhile, so I could give the Stevens a good run for its money.'

'I see,' said Maxton as a waiter removed his empty plate.

A waitress arrived with their coffee. The same waitress. The same familiar look. It was beginning to bother Abel.

'And you say Curtis Fenton of Continental Trust is looking for a buyer on your behalf?'

'He has been for almost a month,' said Abel. 'In fact, I'll know later this afternoon if they've had any success, but I'm not optimistic.'

'Well, that's all most interesting. I had no idea the Richmond Group was looking for a buyer. Will you please keep me informed either way?'

'Certainly,' said Abel.

'How much time is the bank giving you to find the two million?'

'Only a few more days, so it shouldn't be long before I can let you know my decision.'

'Thank you,' said Maxton, rising from his place. 'It's been a pleasure to meet you, Mr Rosnovski. I'm sure I'd enjoy working with you.' He shook Abel's hand warmly.

The waitress smiled at Abel again as he passed her on his way out of the dining room. When he reached the headwaiter, he stopped and asked what her name was.

'I'm sorry, sir, we're not allowed to give the names of any of the staff to our customers — it's strictly against company policy. If you have a complaint, perhaps you'd be kind enough to make it to me, sir.'

'No complaint,' said Abel. 'On the contrary, an excellent lunch.'

With a job offer under his belt, Abel felt more confident about facing Curtis Fenton. He was certain the banker would not have found a buyer, but nonetheless he strolled over to the Continental Trust with a spring in his heels. He liked the idea of being the manager of the best hotel in Chicago. Perhaps he could turn it into the best hotel in America. As soon as he arrived at the bank he was ushered into Curtis Fenton's office. The tall, thin banker – did he wear the same suit every day or did he have three identical ones? – offered Abel a seat, a large smile appearing across his usually solemn face.

'Mr Rosnovski, how good to see you again. If you'd come this morning, I would have had no news for you, but only a few moments ago I received a call from an interested party.'

Abel's heart leaped with surprise and pleasure. 'Can you tell me who it is?'

'I'm afraid not. The party concerned has given me strict instructions that he must remain anonymous, as the transaction would be a private investment which would be in potential conflict with his own business.'

'David Maxton,' Abel murmured. 'God bless him.'

'As I said, Mr Rosnovski, I'm not in a position—'

'Quite, quite,' mimicked Abel. 'How long do you think it will be before you're in a position to let me know the gentleman's decision one way or the other?'

'I may have more news for you by Monday,' said Fenton, 'so if you happen to be passing by—'

'Happen to be passing by?' said Abel. 'You're talking about my whole future.'

'Then perhaps we should make a firm appointment for ten o'clock on Monday morning.'

Abel whistled 'Stardust' as he walked down Michigan Avenue on his way back to the Stevens. He took the elevator up to his room and called William Kane to ask for an extension until the following Monday, telling him he might have found a buyer. Kane agreed without comment.

'You win either way, don't you?' Abel said as he put the receiver back on its cradle.

Abel sat on the bed, his fingers tapping the footboard, and wondered how he could pass the time until Monday. He wandered down into the hotel lobby. There she was again, the waitress who had served him at lunch, now on tea duty in the Tropical Garden. Abel's curiosity got the better of him. He walked over and took a seat at the far end of the room.

'Good afternoon, sir,' she said. 'Would you like some tea?' The same familiar smile again.

'We know each other, don't we?'

'Yes, we do, Wladek.'

Abel cringed at the sound of the name, and reddened slightly, remembering how the short, fair hair had once been long and curly, and the lips so inviting. 'Zaphia. We came to America together on the *Black Arrow*. Of course, you went to Chicago. What are you doing here?'

'I work here, as you can see. Would you like some tea, sir?' Her Polish accent warmed him.

'Have dinner with me tonight.'

'I can't, Wladek. We're not allowed to go out with the customers. If we do, we automatically lose our jobs.'

'I'm not a customer,' said Abel. 'I'm an old friend.'

'An old friend who was going to come and visit me in Chicago as soon as he had settled down in New York,' said Zaphia. 'And when he finally did come, he didn't even remember I was here.'

'I know, I know. Forgive me. Zaphia, please have dinner with me tonight. Just this once.'

'Just this once,' she repeated.

'Meet me at Brundage's at seven o'clock. Would that suit you?'

Zaphia flushed at the name. It was the classiest restaurant in town, and she would have been out of her depth there as a waitress, let alone as a customer.

'No, let's go somewhere less grand, Wladek.'

'Where?'

'Do you know the Sausage, on the corner of Forty-Third?'

'No, but I'll find it. Seven o'clock.'

'Seven o'clock, Wladek. By the way, do you want any tea?'

'No, I think I'll skip it.'

She smiled and walked away. She was much prettier than he remembered. Perhaps killing time until Monday wasn't going to be quite so difficult after all.

—◇—

The Sausage brought back all of Abel's worst memories of his first days in America. He sipped a cold ginger beer while he waited for Zaphia and watched with professional disapproval as the waiters went about their work. He was unable to decide which was worse – the service or the food.

Abel swivelled round and saw Zaphia standing in the doorway looking nervous and unsure. She was wearing a long yellow dress that looked as if it had recently been let down a few inches to conform to the latest fashion, but still revealed how shapely her figure was. She searched the tables for a moment, and her cheeks reddened as she became aware that the eyes of several men suggested that she wasn't a customer but looking for a customer.

She walked quickly over to Abel. 'Good evening, Wladek,' she said in Polish as she took the seat beside him.

'I'm so glad you could make it,' Abel said in English.

'I'm sorry I'm late,' she replied in English after a moment's hesitation.

'It's not important. Would you like something to drink, Zaphia?'

'Just a coke, please.'

Neither of them spoke for a moment, then they both started to talk at once.

'I'd forgotten how pretty . . .' said Abel.

'How have you . . . ?' said Zaphia.

She smiled shyly. Abel found himself wanting to touch her. He remembered experiencing the same feeling the first time he had seen her, more than eight years ago.

'How's George?' she asked.

'I haven't seen him for a couple of years,' admitted Abel,

feeling guilty. 'I've been working at a hotel here in Chicago, and then—'

'I know,' said Zaphia. 'Somebody burned it down.'

'Why didn't you ever come over and say hello?'

'I didn't think you'd remember, Wladek. And I was right.'

'How did you recognize me?' said Abel. 'I've put on so much weight.'

'The silver band,' she said simply.

Abel looked down at his wrist and laughed. 'I already have a lot to thank this band for, and now I can add that it's brought us together again.'

She avoided his eyes. 'What are you doing now you no longer have a hotel to run?'

'I'm looking for a job,' said Abel, not wanting to intimidate her with the possibility that he might be her boss in a few weeks' time.

'There's a big job coming up at the Stevens. My boyfriend told me.'

'Your boyfriend?' said Abel, repeating the unwelcome word.

'Yes. The hotel will soon be looking for a new assistant manager. Why don't you apply for it? I'm sure you'd have a good chance of getting it, Wladek. I always knew you would be a success in America.'

'I might,' Abel said. 'It was kind of you to let me know. Will your boyfriend be applying?'

'Oh, no, he's far too junior to be considered – he's only a waiter in the dining room.'

Abel smiled. 'Shall we have dinner?' he said.

'I'm not used to eating out,' Zaphia admitted, gazing helplessly at the menu. Abel wondered if she still couldn't read English, and ordered for both of them.

She ate everything put in front of her, and kept saying thank you, even when a waiter spilled gravy on her dress. Abel found her uncritical enthusiasm a tonic after Melanie's bored sophistication. They exchanged stories of what had happened to them since they arrived in America. Zaphia had found a job in domestic service and progressed to being a waitress at the Stevens, where she had been working for the past six years. Abel continued to talk of his own experiences, until finally she glanced at her watch.

'Look at the time, Wladek. It's past eleven, and I'm on first breakfast call at six tomorrow.'

Abel had not noticed the hours slip by. He would happily have sat there talking to Zaphia for the rest of the night, soothed by her admiration, which she expressed so artlessly.

'Can we see each other again, Zaphia?' he asked as they walked back to the Stevens arm in arm.

'If you'd like to, Wladek.'

They stopped at the servants' entrance at the back of the hotel.

'This is where I have to leave you,' she said. 'If you were to become the assistant manager, Wladek, you'd be allowed to go in by the front entrance.'

'Would you mind calling me Abel?' he asked her.

'Abel?' she said as if she were trying the name on like a new glove. 'But your name is Wladek.'

'It was, but it isn't any longer. My name is Abel Rosnovski.'

'Abel,' she repeated, and seemed to hesitate. 'I can't remember if it was Abel who killed Cain, or Cain who killed Abel.'

Abel could remember.

'Thank you for dinner. It was lovely to see you again. Good night . . . Abel.'

'Good night, Zaphia,' he said, and she was gone.

Abel walked slowly around the block and into the hotel by the front entrance.

He spent the weekend thinking about Zaphia and the memories associated with her – the stench of the steerage quarters, the confused queues of immigrants on Ellis Island and, above all, their brief but passionate encounter in the lifeboat. He began to take all his meals in the hotel dining room to be near her while keeping an eye on the boyfriend, who, he concluded, must be the young, pimply one. He thought he had pimples. He hoped he had pimples. Yes, he did have pimples. He was also, Abel had to admit the best looking of all the waiters, with or without pimples.

Abel asked Zaphia to come out with him again on Saturday night, but she was working the evening shift. However, he managed to accompany her to church on Sunday morning, and listened with mingled nostalgia and exasperation to the Polish priest intoning the unforgettable words of the Mass and delivering a sermon on chastity. It was the first time Abel had been in a church since his days at the castle. At that time he had yet to experience the cruelty that now made it impossible for him to believe in a benevolent deity. His reward for attending church came when Zaphia allowed him to hold her hand as they walked back to the hotel.

'Have you thought any more about the position at the Stevens?' she asked.

'I have a meeting that will decide things tomorrow.'

'Oh, I'm so glad, Abel. I'm sure you'd make a very good assistant manager.'

'Thank you,' said Abel, realizing they had been talking about different things.

'Would you like to have supper with me and my cousins tonight?' Zaphia asked. 'I always spend Sunday evening with them.'

'Yes, I'd like that very much.'

Zaphia's cousins lived in the heart of the Polish community. They were very impressed when she arrived accompanied by a friend who drove a new Buick. The family, as Zaphia called them, consisted of two sisters, Katya and Janina, and Katya's husband, Janek. Abel presented the sisters with a bunch of roses, and answered all their questions about his future prospects in fluent Polish. Zaphia was obviously embarrassed, but Abel knew the same would be required of any young man who visited a Polish-American household for the first time. Aware of the envy in Janek's eyes, he made an effort to play down his progress since his early days at the meat packers'. Katya served a simple Polish meal of *pierogi* and *bigos*, which Abel would have eaten with a good deal more relish fifteen years ago. He ignored Janek, and concentrated on the sisters. Perhaps they approved of the pimply youth.

On their way back to the Stevens Zaphia asked, with a flash of the coquettishness he remembered, if it was considered safe to drive a motor car and hold a lady's hand at the same time. Abel laughed and put his hand back on the steering wheel.

'Will you have time to see me tomorrow?' he asked.

'I hope so, Abel,' she said. 'Perhaps by then you'll be my boss.'

He smiled to himself as he watched her go through the back door, wondering how Zaphia would feel if she knew the real consequences of tomorrow's meeting. He did not move until she had disappeared through the service entrance.

'Assistant manager,' he mused, laughing out loud as he climbed into bed and threw his pillow on the floor.

—◁◦▷—

Abel woke a few minutes before five the following morning. It was still dark outside when he called for an early edition of the *Tribune*. He went through the motions of reading the financial section before getting dressed, and strolled into the breakfast room when it opened at seven o'clock. Zaphia was not on duty that morning, but the pimply boyfriend was, which Abel took to be a bad omen. After breakfast he returned to his room and paced around as he waited for the minutes to pass. He checked his tie in the mirror for the twentieth time, and once again looked at his watch. He estimated that if he walked very slowly, he would arrive at the bank as its doors were opening. In fact he was five minutes early, and had to walk once around the block, looking pointlessly into store windows at expensive jewellery, radios and hand-tailored suits. Would he ever be able to afford a hand-tailored suit, he wondered. He arrived back at the bank at four minutes past ten.

'Mr Fenton is taking a long distance call at the moment,' the secretary informed Abel. 'Can you come back in half an hour, or would you prefer to wait?'

'I'll come back,' said Abel, not wishing to appear overanxious.

It was the longest thirty minutes he could remember since he'd boarded the train to Moscow. He studied every shop window on La Salle Street, even the women's clothes, which only made him think of Zaphia.

On his return to the Continental Trust the secretary quickly ushered him into Fenton's office. He didn't want to shake hands with the manager because his own hands were sweating.

'Good morning, Mr Rosnovski. Do have a seat.'

Curtis Fenton took a file out of his desk drawer. Abel could see the word 'Confidential' written across the cover.

'Now,' Fenton began, 'I hope you'll find my news agreeable. The principal concerned is willing to go ahead with the purchase of the hotels.'

'I don't believe it,' said Abel.

'You haven't heard the terms yet.' Fenton looked at Abel and smiled. 'But I think you'll find them favourable. The principal will put up the full two million dollars required to clear Mr Leroy's debt, and at the same time he will form a new company in which the shares will be split sixty per cent to him, and forty per cent to you. Your forty per cent is therefore valued at eight hundred thousand dollars, which will be treated as a loan by the new company, that will be made for a term not to exceed ten years, at four per cent interest, which can be paid off from the company profits. That is to say, if the company makes a profit of one hundred thousand dollars in any given year, forty thousand dollars of that profit would be set against your eight hundred thousand debt, plus the four per cent interest. If you clear the loan in under ten years, you'll be given a one-time option of buying the remaining sixty per cent of the company for a further three million dollars. That would give my client a first-class return on his investment, and you the opportunity to own the Richmond Group outright.'

Abel wanted to leap out of his chair, but sat still, allowing Mr Fenton to continue. 'In addition to this, you will receive a salary of five thousand dollars per annum, and your position as president of the group will give you complete day-to-day control of the company. You will be asked to refer to me only on matters concerning finance. I have been entrusted with the task of reporting directly to your principal, and he has asked me to represent his interests on the board of the new Richmond Group. I am happy to comply with this only if it is acceptable to you. My client wishes to stress that he does not wish to be personally involved. As I have mentioned, there might be a conflict of interests for him if his colleagues were to become aware of his involvement, which I am sure you will understand. He also insists that you will at no time make any attempt to discover his identity. He will give you fourteen days to consider his terms, on which there can be no negotiation, as he considers – and I must say I agree with him – that his terms are fair.'

Abel could not speak.

'Pray do say something, Mr Rosnovski.'

'I don't need fourteen days to make a decision,' Abel finally managed to say. 'I accept your client's terms without discussion. Please thank him, and tell him I will of course respect his request for anonymity and am delighted that you will be representing him on the board.'

'That's splendid,' said Fenton, permitting himself a rare smile. 'Now, a few minor points. The bank accounts for all the hotels in the group will be lodged with Continental Trust affiliates, and the main account will remain in this office under my direct control. I will receive one thousand dollars a year as a director of the new company.'

'I'm glad you're going to get something out of the deal,' said Abel, with a grin.

'I beg your pardon?'

'I'm pleased to be working with you, Mr Fenton.'

'Your principal has also placed two hundred and fifty thousand dollars on deposit with the bank, to be used for the day-to-day expenses of the hotels over the next few months. This will also be regarded as a loan at four per cent. You are to advise me if this amount turns out to be insufficient. However, I believe it would enhance your standing with my client if you found the two hundred and fifty thousand to be enough.'

'It's more than enough,' said Abel.

'Excellent,' said Fenton as he opened a desk drawer and produced a large Cuban cigar.

'Do you smoke?'

'Yes,' said Abel, who had never smoked a cigar before in his life.

Abel coughed himself down La Salle Street all the way back to the Stevens. David Maxton was standing proprietorially in the foyer when he arrived. Abel stubbed out his half-finished cigar with some relief and walked over to him.

'Mr Rosnovski, you look a happy man this morning.'

'I am, sir, and I'm only sorry to have to tell you that I won't be working for you as the manager of this hotel.'

'I'm sorry to hear that, Mr Rosnovski, but frankly that news doesn't surprise me.'

'Thank you for everything,' said Abel, injecting as much feeling as he could into the words and the handshake that accompanied them.

He went into the dining room in search of Zaphia, but she hadn't come on duty yet. He took the elevator to his room, relit the cigar, took a cautious puff and waited a moment before calling Kane and Cabot. A secretary put him through to William Kane.

'Mr Kane, I have found it possible to raise the money required to take over the Richmond Group. A Mr Curtis Fenton of Continental Trust will be in touch with you later today to provide you with the details. There will therefore be no necessity to place the hotels for sale on the open market.'

There was a short pause, during which Abel thought with satisfaction how galling this news must be to William Kane.

'Thank you for informing me, Mr Rosnovski. May I say how delighted I am that you've found someone to back you. I wish you every success for the future.'

'Which is more than I wish you, Mr Kane.'

Abel put the phone down, lay on his bed and thought about that future.

'One day,' he promised the ceiling, 'I am going to make you want to jump out of a hotel bedroom on the seventeenth floor.' He picked up the phone again and asked the girl on the switchboard to get him Mr Henry Osborne at Great Western Casualty.

31

WILLIAM WAS more amused than annoyed by Rosnovski's belligerent attitude. He was sorry he had been unable to persuade the bank to support the proud Pole who believed so strongly that he could turn the Richmond Group around. He fulfilled his remaining responsibilities by informing the Finance Committee that Abel Rosnovski had found a backer and preparing the legal documents for the takeover of the hotels, before closing the bank's file on the Richmond Group.

A few days later Matthew Lester arrived in Boston to take up his position as manager of the bank's investment portfolio. His father had made no secret of the fact that he felt any experience gained in a rival establishment would be a valuable part of Matthew's long-term preparation to be chairman of Lester's. William's workload was instantly halved when Matthew joined him, although his time became even more fully occupied. He found himself dragged, protesting in mock horror, onto tennis courts and into swimming pools at every available free moment; only Matthew's suggestion of a ski trip to Vermont brought a determined 'No' from William, but the increased activity at least served to distract him from his impatience to see Kate again.

Matthew was frankly incredulous. 'I must meet the woman who can make William Kane daydream at a board meeting that's discussing whether the bank should buy more gold.'

'Wait till you see her, Matthew. I think you'll agree she's pure gold.'

'I believe you. I just don't want to be the one to tell my sister. She still thinks you're waiting for her.'

William laughed. He'd quite forgotten about Susan Lester.

The little pile of letters from Kate, which had been growing weekly, lay in a locked drawer of William's bureau in the Red House. He read them over again and again, until he knew them virtually by heart. At last the one he had been waiting for arrived, appropriately dated.

> *Buckhurst Park*
> *14 February 1930*
>
> *Dearest William,*
>
> *Finally I have packed up, sold off, given away or otherwise disposed of everything left here, and I shall be coming up to Boston on the nineteenth. I am almost frightened at the thought of seeing you again. What if this whole marvelous enchantment bursts like a bubble in the cold winter of the Eastern Seaboard? Dear God, I hope not. I can't be sure how I would have gotten through these lonely months without your support.*
>
> *Looking forward to seeing you,*
> *Love,*
> *Kate*

The night before she was due to arrive, William promised himself that he would not rush her into anything that either of them might later regret. As he told Matthew, it was impossible to assess the extent to which her feelings for him might have been due to her emotional vulnerability after her husband's death.

'I've never heard such rubbish,' said Matthew. 'You're in love, and that's an end of it.'

―◦―

The moment William spotted Kate getting off the train from Miami and saw the infectious smile that lit up her face, he abandoned his cautious intentions. He pushed through the throng of travellers and took her in his arms.

'Welcome home, Kate.'

He was about to kiss her when, to his surprise, she drew back.

'William, I don't think you've met my parents.'

That night William dined with the Higginson family, and discovered how beautiful Kate would be when she was an old woman. They grabbed every moment they could together, whenever William could escape from the bank's business and Matthew's tennis racquet. When Matthew met her for the first time, he offered William all his gold shares in exchange for one Kate.

'I never undersell,' replied William. 'And unlike you, Matthew, I have never been interested in quantity – only quality.'

'Then I insist you tell me,' demanded Matthew, 'where will I find such a rare commodity?'

'In the liquidation department,' replied William.

'Turn her into a personal asset, William, and quickly, because if you don't, you can be sure someone else will.'

◄○►

Abel stubbed out the Corona for a second time, swearing that he would not light another cigar until he had cleared the $2 million that he needed for complete control of the Richmond Group. This was no time for Cuban cigars, while the Dow Jones Index was at its lowest point in history and long soup lines were forming in every city in America. He gazed at the ceiling and considered his priorities. First, he needed to salvage the best staff from the Chicago Richmond.

He climbed off the bed, put on his jacket and walked across to the Richmond annexe, where most of those who had not found employment since the fire were still living. Abel gave everyone he trusted, and who was willing to leave Chicago, a job in one of the other ten hotels. He made it clear that in these difficult times their jobs were secure only if the group started to show a profit. He was aware that all the other hotels were being run as dishonestly as the old Chicago Richmond had been. That, he assured them, would change, and change quickly. He put his three former assistant managers in charge of the Dallas Richmond, the Miami Richmond and the St Louis Richmond, and appointed new assistant managers for the remaining seven hotels – in Houston, Mobile, Charleston, Atlanta, Memphis, New Orleans and Louisville.

Abel set up his headquarters in the Chicago Richmond annexe, and decided to open a small restaurant on the ground floor. It made sense to be based near his backer and his banker rather than to settle in one of the hotels in the South. And, just as important, Zaphia was in Chicago, and Abel was beginning to feel confident that, given time, he could replace the pimply youth.

By the time he was ready to travel to New York to recruit more staff, Zaphia assured him she no longer had any interest in the pimply boyfriend. The night before his departure they made love for the second time. After their first experience in the lifeboat, his attentive care and gentle expertise took her by surprise.

'How many girls have there been since the *Black Arrow?*' she teased.

'None that I really cared for,' he replied.

'Enough of them for you to forget *me.*'

'I never forgot you,' he said untruthfully. He leant over and kissed her again, as it wasn't a conversation he wished to continue.

◄○►

Kane and Cabot's net loss in 1929 ended up at over $7 million, which turned out to be about par for a bank its size. Many smaller establishments had gone under, and William found himself conducting a sustained holding operation that kept him under constant pressure.

When Franklin D. Roosevelt was elected President of the United States on a ticket of relief, recovery and reform, William feared that the New Deal would have little to offer Kane and Cabot. Business picked up slowly, and William found himself planning tentatively for expansion.

Meanwhile, Tony Simmons completed several successful takeovers in London, and made a better than expected profit for Kane and Cabot during his first two years. His achievements looked all the more impressive when measured against those of William, who had barely been able to break even during the recession.

In the autumn Alan Lloyd called Simmons back to Boston to make a full report to the board on the bank's activities in London. At that meeting Simmons was able to announce that the year's figures for the London office would show a profit of over a million dollars for the first time. He also let it be known that he intended to put his name forward for the chairmanship when Alan retired. William was completely taken by surprise, as he had dismissed Simmons's chances when he had disappeared across the Atlantic under a small cloud. It seemed inexplicable that that cloud had been blown away, not by Simmons's acuity, but simply because the British economy had been less paralysed than America's. The abruptness of Tony Simmons's return to favour left William with little time in which to persuade the board that they should support him before his opponent's momentum for the chairmanship became unstoppable.

Kate listened sympathetically to William's problems, often offering a shrewd observation, and only occasionally admonishing him for being too gloomy. Matthew, acting as William's eyes and ears, reported that the board was split between those who considered William too young to hold such a responsible position, and those who blamed Simmons for the extent of the bank's losses in 1929. It seemed that most of the non-executive members of the board, who had not worked directly with William, were more influenced by the age difference between the two contenders than by any other factor. Again and again Matthew heard the words, 'William's time will come.' Once, tentatively, he played the role of devil's advocate.

'With your holdings in the bank, William, you could appoint three more members of the board and get yourself comfortably elected.'

William dismissed the idea as unworthy of consideration. He wanted to become chairman solely on merit. That, after all, was how his father had gained the position, and he knew that it was nothing less than Kate would expect of him.

In January 1932, Alan Lloyd circulated to every board member notice of a meeting that would be held on his sixty-fifth birthday. Its sole purpose, he informed them, was to elect his successor. As the day for the crucial meeting drew nearer, Matthew found himself carrying the investment department almost single-handedly, while William devoted himself to his campaign to capture the chairmanship.

—◦—

When Abel arrived in New York, the first thing he did was to look up George Novak. He was not surprised to find him out of work and living in a garret on East Third Street. Abel had forgotten what the houses in this neighbourhood, some shared by twenty families, were like. The smell of stale food permeated every room, toilets didn't flush and beds were slept in by at least three different people every twenty-four hours. The bakery had been closed down, and George's uncle was now employed in a large mill on the outskirts of New York. The mill couldn't afford to take on George as well. When Abel offered him a job, George leapt at the chance to join his old friend at the Richmond Group – in any capacity.

Abel recruited several other Poles who George assured him would work any hours, and despite their personal difficulties were scrupulously honest, among them a pastry chef, a desk clerk and a headwaiter. Most hotels on the East Coast had cut their staff to a bare minimum, which had made it easy for him to pick up experienced people, three of whom had worked with him at the Plaza.

The following week, Abel and George set out on a tour of all the hotels in the group. Abel asked Zaphia to join them, even offering her the chance to work in any hotel she chose, but she refused to leave Chicago, the only place in America where she felt at home. As a compromise, she moved across to Abel's rooms at the Richmond annexe whenever he was in Chicago. George, who had acquired middle-class morals along with his American citizenship, pressed the advantages of matrimony on Abel, although he didn't seem to have heeded the advice himself.

It came as no surprise to Abel that the other hotels in the

group were still being incompetently, and in most cases dishonestly, run, but most of the staff, fearful for their jobs in a time of widespread unemployment, welcomed him as the potential saviour of the group's fortunes. He did not find it necessary to fire staff in the grand manner he had adopted when he had first arrived in Chicago. In some cases Abel found that simply moving personnel from one hotel to another stopped the rot. Most of those who knew of his reputation and feared the reprisals had already departed. But some heads still had to roll, and they were invariably attached to the necks of employees who had worked for the group for years and who could not, or would not, change their ways simply because Davis Leroy was no longer in charge.

-◦-

All seventeen members of the board were present to celebrate Alan Lloyd's sixty-fifth birthday. The meeting was opened by the chairman, who delivered a farewell speech lasting only fourteen minutes, which William thought would never come to an end. Tony Simmons was nervously tapping a yellow legal pad with his pen, occasionally glancing across at William. Neither was listening to Alan's words. At last Alan sat down, to loud applause, or as loud as is appropriate for sixteen Boston bankers. When the clapping had died away, Alan rose for the last time as chairman of Kane and Cabot.

'And now, gentlemen, we must elect my successor. The board is presented with two outstanding candidates, the chairman of our overseas division, Mr Tony Simmons, and the director of the American investment department, Mr William Kane. They are both well known to you, gentlemen, and I have no intention of speaking at length on their respective merits. Instead I have invited each candidate to address the board on his plans for the future of Kane and Cabot were he to be elected chairman.'

William rose first, as had been decided the previous day by the toss of a coin. He spoke for twenty minutes, explaining in detail that it would be his intention to broaden the bank's base by moving into fields where Kane and Cabot had not previously ventured. He also wanted to forge stronger links with New York, and mentioned the possibility of opening a holding company that specialized in commercial banking. Some of the older board members shook their heads, making no attempt to hide their disapproval. He finished by saying that he wanted the bank to expand, challenging the new generation of financiers now leading America. He hoped that Kane and Cabot would enter the second half of the twentieth century as one of the largest financial institutions in the country. When he sat down he was buoyed by the murmurs of approbation, and he leaned back to listen to his rival's speech.

When Tony Simmons rose, he took a far more conservative line, and emphasized his age and experience, which William accepted was his trump card. The bank should consolidate its position for the next few years, he said, moving only into carefully selected investments, and sticking to the traditional modes of banking that had earned the bank the reputation it currently enjoyed. He had learned his lesson during the crash of '29, and his main concern, he added – to laughter – was to be certain that Kane and Cabot entered the second half of the twentieth century. When Simmons sat down, William had no way of knowing in whose favour the board might swing, though he believed the majority would be more inclined to opt for expansion than standing still.

Alan Lloyd informed the directors that neither he nor the two contestants would be voting. The other fourteen members were passed ballot papers, which they duly filled in and handed back to Alan, who began to count them slowly. William found he could not look up from his doodle-covered pad, which also bore the imprint of his sweating hand. When Alan had completed the task of counting, a hush came over the boardroom.

He announced six votes for Kane and six votes for Simmons, with two abstentions. A babble of conversation broke out around the table, and Alan called for order. William took a deep breath in the silence that followed, not knowing what the chairman would do next.

Alan Lloyd paused before saying, 'I feel that the appropriate course of action, given the circumstances, is to take a second vote.

If either of the members who abstained on the first ballot now finds himself able to support a candidate, that might give one of the contestants an overall majority.'

The little slips were passed out again. William could not bear even to watch this time, although he could not avoid hearing the steel-nibbed pens as they scratched their votes. Once again the ballots were returned to Alan Lloyd. Once again he opened them slowly one by one, but this time he called out the votes.

'William Kane. Tony Simmons. Tony Simmons. Tony Simmons.'

Three votes to one for Simmons.

'William Kane. William Kane. Tony Simmons. William Kane. William Kane. William Kane.'

Six votes to four in favour of William.

'Tony Simmons. Tony Simmons. William Kane.'

Seven votes to six in favour of William. It seemed to William that Alan took a lifetime to open the final voting slip.

'Tony Simmons. The vote is seven each, gentlemen.'

Although Alan had never told anyone whom he supported for the chair, everyone in the room knew that he would now have to cast the deciding vote.

'As the voting has twice resulted in a dead heat, and since I assume that no member of the board is likely to change his mind, I must cast my vote for the candidate I feel is best qualified to succeed me as chairman of Kane and Cabot. That candidate is Tony Simmons.'

William could not believe what he'd heard, and Simmons looked almost as shocked. He rose from his seat to a round of applause, changed places with Alan Lloyd at the head of the table, and addressed the board of Kane and Cabot for the first time as the bank's chairman. He thanked the board for their support, and praised William for not taking advantage of his strong shareholding and family history with the bank to try to influence the vote. He invited William to be deputy chairman, and suggested that Matthew Lester should take Alan Lloyd's place on the board; both proposals received unanimous support.

William's only thought was that if he had insisted that

Matthew be appointed to the board when he first joined the bank, he would now be chairman.

—◦—

By the end of his first year as president, the Richmond Group was operating with only half the staff it had employed in 1929, but still showed a net loss of a little over $100,000. Few employees left voluntarily, and not just because they feared they wouldn't find another job, but because they now believed in the future of the Group.

Abel set himself the target of breaking even in 1932. He felt that the only way he could achieve this was to let every manager in the group take the responsibility for his own hotel, offering them a share in the profits, much as Davis Leroy had done when Abel had first come to the Chicago Richmond.

For several months he spent his time travelling from hotel to hotel, never staying in any of them for more than a few days. He did not allow anyone, other than the faithful George, his surrogate eyes and ears in Chicago, to know which hotel he might turn up at next. He broke this exhausting routine only to spend the occasional night with Zaphia, or to visit Curtis Fenton at the bank.

After a full assessment of the group's financial position, Abel had to make some more unpleasant decisions. The most drastic was to close the hotels, in Mobile and Charleston, that were losing so much money that he feared they would become an insurmountable drain on the rest of the group's finances. The staff at the other hotels watched the axe fall, and worked even harder. Every time he arrived back at his little office in Chicago there was a clutch of memos demanding immediate attention – burst pipes in washrooms, cockroaches in bedrooms, flashes of temper in kitchens, and the inevitable dissatisfied customer threatening a lawsuit.

—⊞—

Henry Osborne re-entered Abel's life with a welcome cheque for $750,000 from Great Western Casualty Insurance, once they'd established that there was no evidence to implicate him with any involvement in the fire at the Chicago Richmond. Lieutenant O'Malley's evidence had proved conclusive, especially when he added that he would be happy to repeat his findings in court. Abel realized he owed the detective more than a milk shake, and was happy to settle with Great Western at what he considered a fair price. Henry Osborne, however, suggested that he hold out for a larger amount, and share a percentage of the difference with him. Abel refused, and lost any respect he had for Osborne. If he was willing to be disloyal to his own company, there wasn't much doubt that he would have no qualms about working behind Abel's back when it suited him.

—◇—

In the spring of 1932 Abel was surprised to receive a letter from Melanie Leroy, more cordial in tone than she had ever been in person. He was flattered, even excited, and called her to make a date for dinner at the Stevens, a choice he regretted the moment they entered the dining room and he saw Zaphia was on duty, looking a little jaded as she came to the end of her shift. Melanie, in contrast, looked ravishing in an orange dress that revealed quite clearly what her body would be like if the peel were removed. He should have taken her to a different restaurant. What had made him choose the Stevens? How could he be so adroit when it came to business matters, and so clumsy in his personal life?

'It's wonderful to see you looking so well, Abel,' Melanie remarked as she took her seat. 'Of course everybody knows how well you're doing with the Richmond Group.'

'The Baron Group,' said Abel.

Melanie flushed slightly. 'I didn't realize you'd changed the name.'

'Yes, I changed it quite recently,' lied Abel. He had in fact decided at that very moment that every hotel in the group would be known in future as a Baron hotel. He wondered why he'd never thought of it before.

'An appropriate name,' said Melanie, smiling.

Abel was aware that Zaphia was staring at them from the other side of the room, but it was too late to do anything about it.

'You're not working?' he enquired as he scribbled the words 'Baron Group' on the back of his menu.

'No, not at the moment. A woman with a liberal arts degree in this city has to sit around and wait for every man to be employed before she can hope for a job.'

'If you ever want to work for the Baron Group,' said Abel, emphasizing the name slightly, 'you only have to let me know.'

'No, no,' said Melanie. 'I'm just fine.' She quickly changed the subject to music and the theatre. Talking to her was an unaccustomed and pleasant challenge for Abel; she still teased him, but with intelligence, making him feel more confident in her company than he ever had in the past. They didn't have coffee until well after eleven, by which time Zaphia had gone off duty. He drove Melanie home to her apartment, and was surprised when she invited him in for a drink. He sat on the sofa while she poured him a prohibited whiskey and put a record on the phonograph.

'I can't stay long,' he said. 'Busy day tomorrow.'

'That's what *I'm* supposed to say,' said Melanie. 'Please don't rush away. This evening has been such fun – quite like old times.'

She sat down beside him, her dress rising above her knees. Not quite like old times, Abel thought. He made no attempt to resist when she edged towards him. In a few moments he was kissing her – or was she kissing him? His hands wandered onto those legs and then to her breasts, and this time she seemed to respond willingly. It was she who eventually led him by the hand to her bedroom, threw back the coverlet, turned around and asked him to unzip her. Abel obliged in nervous disbelief, and switched out the light. Melanie certainly wasn't lacking in experience, and she didn't leave him in any doubt how much she was enjoying herself. After they'd made love, Abel lay awake while Melanie fell asleep in his arms.

In the morning they made love a second time.

'I shall watch the Baron Group with renewed interest,' she told him as he began to dress. 'Not that anyone doubts that it's going to be a huge success.'

'Thank you,' said Abel.

'Perhaps we might see each other again.'

'Why not?' said Abel.

She kissed him on the cheek as a wife might when seeing her husband off to work.

'I wonder what kind of woman you'll end up marrying,' she said innocently as she helped him on with his overcoat.

He looked at her and smiled sweetly. 'When I make that decision, Melanie, you can be certain I won't forget your excellent advice.'

'What do you mean?' asked Melanie coyly.

'I'll make sure to find myself a nice Polish girl.'

<o>

Abel and Zaphia were married a month later at Holy Trinity Polish Mission. Zaphia's brother-in-law Janek gave her away, and George was the best man. The reception was held at the Stevens, and the drinking and dancing went on late into the night. George never stopped moving as he battled around the room photographing the guests in every possible permutation and combination. By tradition, each man paid a token sum to dance with Zaphia, and it wasn't until after a midnight supper of *barszcz*, *pierogi* and *bigos* downed with wine, brandy and Danzig vodka, that Abel and Zaphia were allowed to retire to the bridal suite.

Abel was pleasantly surprised when Curtis Fenton told him the following morning that the reception at the Stevens had been paid for by Mr Maxton, and was to be considered a wedding gift. Abel used the money he had put aside for the reception as the down payment on a little house on Rigg Street.

For the first time in his life Abel owned a home of his own.

PART FOUR

1932-1941

32

WILLIAM DECIDED to take a month's vacation in England before making any firm decision about his future. He briefly considered resigning from Kane and Cabot, but Matthew convinced him that it would serve no purpose and, in any case, his father would not have approved.

Matthew appeared to take his friend's defeat even harder than William. Twice in the following week he arrived at the bank with the obvious signs of a hangover, and left early, with important work unfinished. William let the incidents pass without comment, and on the Friday he invited Matthew to join him and Kate for dinner. Matthew declined, claiming that he had a backlog of work to catch up on. William wouldn't have given it another thought if he hadn't seen Matthew dining at the Ritz-Carlton that evening with an attractive woman who William could have sworn was married to one of Kane and Cabot's departmental managers. Kate didn't comment, other than to say that Matthew didn't look very well.

William only hoped that Matthew would be able to cope with two desks while he was away. That was the moment he decided he couldn't face a whole month in England without Kate, and suggested she join him for the trip.

'A month abroad with a strange man?' she said, placing a hand coyly over her lips. 'What would your grandmothers have thought?'

'That you are nothing more than a wanton hussy.'

William and Kate sailed on the *Mauretania*, sleeping in separate cabins. Once they had settled into the Savoy, in separate rooms, in fact on separate floors, William reported to the London branch of Kane and Cabot in Lombard Street, and fulfilled the ostensible purpose of his trip by making a thorough review of the bank's European activities. Morale was high, and he discovered that Tony Simmons had been well liked and admired by the London staff, so there was little left for William to do but murmur his approval.

He and Kate spent a glorious month in London, attending the opera, the Old Vic and the Albert Hall by night, while by day he showed her the Tower of London, Fortnum's and the Royal Academy, where he bought a painting by William Sickert.

Kate had her photograph taken standing next to a guard outside Buckingham Palace. Although William didn't try to distract them this time, they still didn't blink. It brought back memories of his mother. William and Kate then walked hand in hand down Whitehall and had their photograph taken standing outside Number Ten, Downing Street.

'Now we've done everything that's expected of a self-respecting American,' suggested William.

'Except visit Oxford,' said Kate. 'My father was a Rhodes scholar and I'd love to visit his old college.'

The following morning William hired a Bullnose Morris, and set off through the winding roads and country lanes that led to the University city. William parked the car outside the Radcliffe and they spent the rest of the morning wandering around the colleges – Magdalen, superb by the river, Christ Church, grandiose but cloisterless, Balliol, where Kate's father had spent a couple of idle years and Merton, where they just sat on the grass and dreamed.

'Can't sit on the grass, sir,' said the voice of a college porter.

They laughed, jumped up and walked hand in hand like a couple of undergraduates beside the Isis, where they watched eight Matthews straining to propel their boat along as swiftly as possible.

After a late lunch they started back for London, stopping at

Henley-on-Thames for tea at the Bell Inn overlooking the river. After scones and a large pot of strong English tea, Kate suggested that perhaps they should be leaving if they still hoped to be back at the Savoy before nightfall. But when William inserted the crank into the Bullnose Morris, despite several attempts, he couldn't get the engine to turn over. Finally he gave up and, as it was getting dark, decided that they would have to spend the night in Henley. He returned to the front desk of the Bell and requested two rooms.

'Sorry, sir, I only have one double room available,' said the receptionist.

William hesitated for a moment and then said, 'We'll take it.'

Kate tried to hide her surprise, but said nothing; the receptionist looked at them suspiciously.

'Mr and Mrs . . . ?'

'Mr and Mrs William Kane,' said William firmly. 'We'll be back later.'

'Shall I put your cases in the room, sir?' the hall porter asked.

'We don't have any,' William replied, smiling.

'I see, sir,' an eyebrow rising.

William led a bewildered Kate up Henley's High Street until he turned down a path that led to the parish church.

'May I ask what we're doing, William?'

'Something I should have done a long time ago, my darling.'

In the Norman vestry, William found a church warden piling up some hymnals.

'Where can I find the vicar?' William asked.

The church warden straightened himself to his full height and regarded William pityingly.

'In the vicarage, I dare say.'

'Where's the vicarage?'

'You're an American gentleman, aren't you, sir?'

'Yes,' said William, trying not to sound impatient.

'The vicarage will be next door to the church, won't it?' said the church warden.

'I suppose it will,' said William. 'Can you stay here for the next ten minutes?'

'Why should I want to do that, sir?'

William extracted a large, white £5 note from his inside pocket and unfolded it. 'Make it fifteen minutes to be on the safe side, please.'

The church warden studied the banknote carefully before placing it in the collection box. 'Americans,' he muttered.

William quickly guided Kate out of the church. As they passed the notice board in the porch, he read, 'The Very Reverend Simon Tukesbury, MA (Cantab), Vicar of this Parish', and next to that pronouncement, hanging by a nail, was an appeal for a new church roof. 'Every penny towards the necessary £500 will help', it declared, not very boldly. William hastened up the path to the vicarage, with Kate following a few steps behind. A smiling, pink-cheeked, plump woman answered his sharp rap on the door.

'Mrs Tukesbury?'

'Yes?' she smiled.

'May I speak to your husband?'

'He's having his tea at the moment. Would it be possible for you to come back a little later?'

'I'm afraid it's rather urgent,' William insisted.

Kate still said nothing.

'Well, in that case I suppose you'd better come in.'

The vicarage was early sixteenth century, and the small beamed front room was warmed by a welcoming log fire. The vicar, a tall, spare man, was eating wafer-thin cucumber sandwiches. He rose to greet them.

'Good afternoon, Mr . . . ?'

'Kane, sir, William Kane.'

'What can I do for you, Mr Kane?'

'Kate and I,' said William, 'want to get married.'

Kate's mouth was open, but no words came out.

'Oh, how delightful,' said Mrs Tukesbury.

'Yes, indeed,' said the vicar. 'Are you a member of this parish? I don't seem to remember . . .'

'No, sir, I'm an American. I worship at St Paul's in Boston.'

'Massachusetts, I presume, not Lincolnshire,' said the Very Reverend Tukesbury.

'That's right,' said William, realizing for the first time there was a Boston in England.

'Splendid,' said the vicar, his hands raised as if he were about to give a blessing. 'And when did you have in mind for this union of souls?'

'Today, sir.'

'Today?' said the vicar.

'Today?' repeated Kate.

'I am not familiar with the traditions in the United States that surround the solemn, holy and binding institution of marriage, Mr Kane,' said the startled vicar, 'although one reads of some very strange happenings involving some of your countrymen from the State of Nevada. I can, however, inform you that those customs have not yet found their way to Henley-on-Thames. In England you must reside for a full calendar month in a parish before you can be married in its church, and the banns have to be posted on three separate occasions, unless there are very special and extenuating circumstances. Even if such circumstances exist, I would still have to seek the bishop's dispensation, and I couldn't do that in less than three days.'

Kate spoke for the first time. 'How much do you still need to raise for the church's new roof?'

'Ah, the roof. Now there is a sad story, but I won't embark upon it at this moment – early eleventh century, you know—'

'How much do you need?' asked William, tightening his grasp on Kate's hand.

'We are hoping to raise five hundred pounds. We've done commendably well so far; we've reached twenty-seven pounds four shillings and four pence in only seven weeks.'

'No, no, dear,' said Mrs Tukesbury. 'You haven't remembered the one pound eleven shillings and two pence I made from my Bring and Buy sale last week.'

'Indeed I haven't, my dear. How inconsiderate of me to overlook your personal contribution. That will make altogether . . .' began the Reverend Tukesbury as he tried to add the figures in his head, raising his eyes towards Heaven for inspiration.

William took his wallet from an inside pocket, wrote out a

cheque for £500 and without another word handed it to the Very Reverend Tukesbury.

'I – ah, I see there are special circumstances, Mr Kane,' said the vicar. His tone changed. 'Have either of you ever been married before?'

'Yes,' said Kate. 'My husband was killed in a plane crash four years ago.'

'Oh, how distressing for you,' said Mrs Tukesbury. 'I am so sorry, I didn't—'

'Shush, my dear,' said the man of God, now more interested in the church roof than in his wife's sentiments. 'And you, sir?'

'I have never been married,' said William.

'I shall have to telephone the bishop.' Clutching William's cheque, the Very Reverend Mr Tukesbury disappeared into his study.

Mrs Tukesbury invited Kate and William to sit down, and offered them some cucumber sandwiches and a cup of tea. She chatted on, but William and Kate did not hear her words as they sat gazing at each other.

The vicar returned three cucumber sandwiches later.

'It's highly irregular, highly irregular, but the bishop has agreed, on condition, Mr Kane, that you confirm that the marriage has taken place with the American embassy tomorrow morning, and then with your own bishop at St Paul's in Boston – Massachusetts, who must give a church blessing when you return home.'

He was still clutching the £500 cheque.

'All we need now are two witnesses,' the vicar continued. 'My wife can act as one, and we must hope that the church warden is still on duty, so he can be the other.'

'He is still on duty,' said William.

'How can you be so sure, Mr Kane?'

'He cost me one per cent.'

'One per cent?' said the Very Reverend Mr Tukesbury, baffled.

'A down payment on the church roof,' explained Kate.

The vicar ushered William, Kate and his wife out of the house and down the little path to the church, where the church warden was waiting. 'Indeed, I perceive that Mr Sprogget has remained on duty . . . He has never done so for me; you obviously have a way with you, Mr Kane.'

Simon Tukesbury put on his vestments and a surplice while the church warden looked on in disbelief.

William turned to Kate and kissed her gently. 'I know it's a damn silly question in the circumstances my darling, but will you marry me?'

'Good God,' said the Very Reverend Mr Tukesbury, who had never blasphemed in the previous fifty-seven years of his mortal existence. 'You mean you haven't even proposed?'

⭑

Twenty minutes later, Mr and Mrs William Kane left the parish church of Henley-on-Thames, Oxfordshire. At the last moment Mrs Tukesbury had to supply the ring, which she removed from a curtain rail in the vestry. It was a perfect fit. The Very Reverend Mr Tukesbury had a new roof, Mr Sprogget had a yarn to tell them down at the Green Man, while Mrs Tukesbury decided, after consulting her husband, that she would not inform the Mothers' Union of how the money for the new roof had been raised.

Outside the vestry door the vicar handed William a piece of paper. 'Two shillings and sixpence, please.'

'What for?' asked William.

'Your marriage certificate, Mr Kane.'

'You should have taken up banking, sir,' said William, handing Mr Tukesbury half a crown.

William and his bride walked in blissful silence back down the High Street to the Bell Inn. They had a quiet dinner in the fifteenth-century oak-beamed dining room, and retired to their suite a few minutes after the grandfather clock in the hall had struck nine times. As they disappeared up the creaky wooden staircase to their room, the receptionist turned to the hall porter and winked. 'If those two are married, I'm the King of England.'

William started to hum 'God Save the King'.

⭑

The following morning Mr and Mrs Kane had a leisurely breakfast while the car was being repaired at a local garage. A young waiter poured them coffee.

'Do you like it black, or shall I add some milk?' asked William innocently.

An elderly couple at the next table smiled benignly at them.

'With milk, please,' said Kate, reaching across and touching William's hand gently.

He smiled at her, aware the whole room was now staring at them.

They returned to London with the car's hood down so they could enjoy the cool spring air as they drove through Henley, over the Thames, on through Beaconsfield and into London.

'Did you notice the look the porter gave you this morning, darling?' asked William.

'Yes. Perhaps we should have shown him our marriage certificate.'

'No, no, you'd have spoiled his whole image of the wanton American hussy. The last thing he wants to tell his wife when he gets home tonight is that we really were married.'

They arrived back at the Savoy in time for lunch, and the desk manager was surprised to be asked to cancel Kate's room. He was heard to comment later, 'Young Mr Kane appeared to be such a gentleman. His late and distinguished father would never have behaved in such a manner.'

William and Kate took the *Aquitania* back to New York, but not before calling in at the American embassy in Grosvenor Gardens to inform the Ambassador of their new marital status. The senior consul gave them a long form to fill out, charged them one pound and kept them waiting for well over an hour. The embassy, it seemed, was not in need of a new roof. William wanted to visit Cartier in Bond Street and buy Kate a gold wedding ring, but she would not hear of it – nothing was going to make her part with the brass curtain ring.

33

WITH AMERICA STILL in the grip of the Depression, Abel was becoming more than a little apprehensive about the future of the Baron Group. Two thousand banks had closed during the past couple of years, and more were shutting their doors every week. Nine million people were unemployed, which at least meant that Abel had no difficulty in finding experienced staff for all his hotels. Despite this, the Baron Group lost $72,000 in 1932, the year in which Abel had predicted they would break even. He began to wonder if his backer's purse and patience would hold out long enough to allow him the chance to turn things around.

Recently Abel had begun to take an active interest in politics, sparked by Anton Cermak's successful campaign to become Mayor of Chicago. Cermak had pressed Abel to join the Democratic Party, which had launched a virulent campaign against Prohibition. Abel had thrown his support wholeheartedly behind the candidate, because Prohibition had proved so damaging to the hotel trade. The fact that Cermak was an immigrant from Czechoslovakia had created an immediate bond between the two men, and Abel had been delighted when he was chosen as a delegate to the Democratic National Convention held in Chicago in 1932, where Cermak had brought a packed audience to its feet with the words: 'It's true I didn't come over on the *Mayflower*, but I came over as soon as I could.'

At the convention Cermak introduced Abel to Franklin D. Roosevelt, who had made a lasting impression on him. Later that year FDR went on to win the Presidential election casily, sweeping Democratic candidates into office all over the country. One of the newly elected aldermen at Chicago City Hall was Henry Osborne.

—<o>—

In 1933 the Baron Group cut its losses to $23,000, and one of the hotels, the St Louis Baron, actually declared a profit. When President Roosevelt broadcast his first fireside chat over the airwaves on March 12, exhorting his countrymen 'to once again believe in America', Abel's confidence soared, and he decided to reopen the two hotels he had closed in 1929.

Zaphia was beginning to comment on his long absences in Charleston and Mobile while he took the two hotels out of mothballs. She had never wanted him to be anything more than the deputy manager of the Stevens. With every month that passed she became more aware that she was not keeping pace with her husband's ambitions, and she even feared he was beginning to lose interest in her.

She was also becoming anxious that she had not borne Abel a child, although the doctor assured her that there was nothing to prevent her from becoming pregnant. He offered the suggestion that perhaps her husband should also be examined, but Zaphia didn't tell Abel, knowing he would regard this as a slur on his manhood. Finally, when she had almost given up hope, and after the subject had become so charged that it was difficult for them to discuss it at all, Zaphia missed her period.

She waited hopefully for another month before saying anything to Abel or seeing the doctor. A month later, he confirmed that she was pregnant.

Zaphia gave birth to a daughter on New Year's Day 1934. They named her Florentyna, after Abel's sister. Abel was besotted with the child from the moment he set eyes on her, and Zaphia knew at once that she would no longer be the first love of his life.

George and a cousin of Zaphia's became the child's *Kums*, and Abel threw a traditional ten-course Polish dinner on the evening of the christening. Numerous gifts were presented to the child, including a beautiful antique ring from Abel's unknown backer. He returned the gift in kind when the Baron Group made a profit of $63,000 at the end of the year. Only the Mobile Baron was still losing money.

After Florentyna's birth Abel spent more and more time at home, and he decided that the moment had come to build a new Baron in the Windy City. He intended to make his new hotel the flagship of the group in memory of Davis Leroy. The company still owned the site on Michigan Avenue, and although Abel had received several offers for the land, he had always held out, hoping that one day he would be in a strong enough financial position to rebuild the Old Richmond. The project required capital, and Abel was glad he hadn't touched the $750,000 insurance payout from Great Western Casualty.

He told Curtis Fenton of his intention at their monthly board meeting, adding the sole proviso that if David Maxton did not want a rival to the Stevens, Abel would drop the whole project. A few days later, Curtis Fenton assured Abel that his backer had no objection to the idea of a Chicago Baron.

It took Abel fifteen months to build the new hotel, with a helping hand from Alderman Henry Osborne, who hurried through the permits required by City Hall in the shortest possible time. The Chicago Baron was opened in May 1936 by the mayor, Edward J. Kelly, who after the assassination of Anton Cermak had become the leader of the Democratic Party in Illinois. In memory of Davis Leroy, the hotel had no seventeenth floor – a tradition Abel continued in every new Baron he built.

The Chicago Baron was praised by the press both for its design and for the speed of its construction. Abel eventually spent well over a million dollars on the new hotel, and it looked as though every penny had been put to good use. The public rooms were large and sumptuous, with high stucco ceilings and decorations in pastel shades of green, pleasant and relaxing; the carpets were thick and luxurious. The dark green embossed 'B' was discreet but ubiquitous, adorning everything from the flag that fluttered above the entrance of the forty-two-storey building to the neat lapel of the most junior bellhop. Both Illinois senators were in attendance to address the two thousand assembled guests at the official opening. Mr Maxton took his place among the guests, puzzled as to why he was seated on the top table.

'This hotel already bears the hallmark of success,' said J. Hamilton Lewis, the senior senator, 'because, my friends, it is the man, not the building, who will always be known as "The Chicago Baron".' Abel beamed with undisguised pleasure as the two thousand guests roared their approval.

When Abel rose from his place to reply, he began by thanking the Mayor, the senators and a dozen congressmen for attending the opening. He ended his speech with the popular catchphrase, 'You ain't seen nothin' yet.'

George had been briefed to lead a standing ovation. He didn't need to, as everyone was already on their feet when Abel sat down. He smiled. He was beginning to feel at ease among big-businessmen and senior politicians, who treated him as an equal. Zaphia hovered uncertainly in the background during the lavish celebration: the occasion was a little too much for her, and she felt uneasy with Abel's new friends. She neither understood nor cared for success on her husband's scale; and even though she could now afford the most expensive wardrobe, she still managed to look unfashionable and out of place, and was only too aware that this annoyed Abel. She stood to one side while he chatted to Alderman Henry Osborne.

'This must be the high point of your life,' said Osborne as he slapped Abel on the back.

'High point? I've only just turned thirty,' said Abel.

A camera flashed as he placed an arm around the Alderman's shoulder. Abel beamed, realizing for the first time how exciting it was to be treated as a public figure. 'I'm going to put Baron hotels across the globe,' he said, just loud enough for the eavesdropping reporter to hear. 'I intend to be to America what César Ritz was to Europe. Whenever an American is travelling, he must think of the Baron as his second home.'

34

WILLIAM FOUND IT difficult to settle down at Kane and Cabot under his new chairman. The promises of FDR's New Deal were passing into law with unprecedented rapidity, and William and Tony Simmons found it impossible to agree on whether the implications for investment were good or bad. But expansion – on one front at least – became inevitable when Kate announced soon after their return from England that she was pregnant, news that brought her parents and her husband great joy. William tried to modify his working hours to suit his new role as a married man, but to begin with he found himself chained to his desk throughout the hot summer evenings. Kate, cool and happy in her flowered maternity smock, supervised the decoration of the nursery at the Red House while William found for the first time in his working life that he no longer minded not being the last to leave the office in the evenings.

◄○►

While Kate and the baby, which was due at Christmas, brought William great happiness at home, Matthew was making him increasingly uneasy at work.

He had taken to drinking with companions William did not know, and coming to the office late without explanation. As the months passed, William found he could no longer rely on his friend's judgement. At first he said nothing, hoping it was no more than a reaction to the repeal of Prohibition. But it soon became clear that it wasn't, as the problem went from bad to worse.

The final straw came when Matthew arrived at the office two hours late one morning, obviously suffering from a hangover. He then made a simple, avoidable mistake, selling off an important investment which resulted in a small loss for a client who had been hoping to make a handsome profit. William knew the time had finally come for an unpleasant, but necessary, head-on confrontation.

When William had finished his pep talk, Matthew admitted his error and apologized profusely. William was thankful to have the row out of the way, and was about to suggest they go to lunch together when his secretary rushed into his office.

'It's your wife, sir, she's been taken to the hospital.'

'Why? What's wrong?' asked William.

'I think it's the baby,' said his secretary.

'But it's not due for at least another six weeks,' said William.

'I know, sir, but Dr MacKenzie sounded anxious, and wanted you to come to the hospital as quickly as possible.'

Matthew, who a moment before had seemed a broken reed, immediately took over and drove William to the hospital. Memories of William's mother's death and her stillborn daughter came flooding back to them both as Matthew drew into the hospital parking lot.

William did not need to be guided to the Richard Kane maternity wing, which Kate had officially opened only a few months before. He found a nurse standing outside the delivery room; she informed him that Dr MacKenzie was with his wife, and that she had lost a lot of blood. William paced up and down the corridor helplessly, numbly waiting, exactly as he had done years before. How unimportant being chairman of the bank now seemed, compared with the thought of losing Kate. When had he last said to her, 'I love you'?

Matthew sat with William, paced with William, stood with William, but said nothing. There was nothing to be said. Occasionally a nurse ran in or out of the delivery room. Seconds turned into minutes, and minutes into hours. Finally, Dr MacKenzie appeared, a surgical mask covering his nose and mouth, his forehead shining with little beads of sweat. William could not see the expression on the doctor's face until he removed the white mask, to reveal a huge smile.

'Congratulations, William. You have a son, and Kate is just fine.'

'Thank God,' breathed William, clinging onto Matthew.

'Much as I respect the power of the Almighty,' said Dr MacKenzie, 'I feel I had a little to do with this particular birth myself.'

William laughed. 'Can I see Kate?'

'No, not right now. I've given her a sedative, and she's sleeping. She lost rather more blood than was good for her, but she'll be fine after a night's rest. A little weak, perhaps, but ready to see you first thing in the morning. But there's nothing to stop you seeing your son. Don't be surprised by his size; remember, he's quite premature.'

Dr MacKenzie guided William and Matthew down the corridor to a room in which they peered through a pane of glass at a row of six little pink heads in cribs.

'That one,' said Dr MacKenzie, pointing to the infant on the end.

William stared at the wrinkled little face, his vision of a fine, upstanding son destined to be the next chairman of the bank rapidly receding.

'Well, I'll say one thing for the little devil,' said Dr MacKenzie cheerfully. 'He's better-looking than you were at that age.'

William laughed with relief.

'What are you going to call him?'

'Richard Higginson Kane.'

The doctor patted him affectionately on the shoulder. 'I hope I live long enough to deliver Richard's firstborn.'

That same afternoon William wired the rector of St Paul's, who registered the boy for a place in September 1945. Having planted the first step in Richard's career the new father and Matthew got thoroughly drunk, overslept and were late arriving at the hospital the next morning to see Kate. William took Matthew for another look at young Richard.

'Ugly little brute,' said Matthew. 'Not at all like his beautiful mother.'

'That's what I thought,' said William.

'Spitting image of you, though.'

William returned to Kate's flower-filled room.

'Do you like your son?' Kate asked her husband. 'He's so like you.'

'I'll hit the next person who says that,' William said with a grin. 'He's the ugliest little brute I've ever seen.'

'Oh, no!' said Kate in mock indignation. 'He's beautiful!'

'A face only a mother could love,' said William, as he hugged her.

She clung to him, and said, 'What would Grandmother Kane have said about our firstborn entering the world after less than eight months of marriage?'

'I don't want to seem uncharitable,' said William, mimicking his grandmother, 'but anyone born after less than fifteen months must be considered of dubious parentage. Less than nine months is definitely unacceptable in society, and they should be packed off abroad ... By the way, I forgot to tell you something before they rushed you into the hospital.'

'What's that?'

'I love you.'

Kate and young Richard had to stay in hospital for nearly three weeks, and it wasn't until just before Christmas that she was fully recovered. William became the first male Kane to change a nappy and push a perambulator. He told Matthew it was high time he found himself a good woman and settled down.

Matthew laughed defensively. 'You're getting positively middle-aged. I'll be looking for grey hairs next.'

One or two had already appeared during the chairmanship battle but Matthew hadn't commented.

<o>

William was not able to put a finger on exactly when his relationship with Tony Simmons began to deteriorate. Simmons started to veto his policy suggestions, and his negative attitude to any proposals he made caused William to seriously consider resigning as a member of the board.

Matthew was not helping matters by returning to his former habits. The period of reform had not lasted more than a few weeks, and if anything he was now drinking more heavily than before, and arriving at the bank later each morning. William wasn't sure how to handle the situation, and found himself continually covering for his friend. At the end of each day he would double-check Matthew's mail, and return any unanswered telephone calls.

By the summer of 1934, with President Roosevelt's New Deal being implemented, investors began to regain some confidence and took their money from under their beds and began to deposit it in banks. Some literally appeared carrying suitcases full of cash. William felt that perhaps the time had come to step tentatively back into the stock market and even began to expand his own portfolio, but Simmons vetoed the suggestion that the bank should follow his lead in an offhand memorandum to the Financial Committee. William stormed into Simmons's office without knocking, and asked if he wanted his resignation.

'Certainly not, William. As you know, it has always been my policy to run this bank in a conservative manner. I am not willing to charge headlong back into the market and risk our investors' money.'

'But we're losing business hand over fist to other banks while we sit on the sidelines. Banks we wouldn't even have considered as rivals a few years ago will soon be overtaking us.'

'Overtaking us in what, William? Not in reputation. Quick profits perhaps, but not reputation.'

'But we have to be interested in profits as well,' said William. 'It's a bank's duty to make good returns for its investors, not to mark time in a gentlemanly fashion.'

'I would rather stand still than lose the reputation this bank built up under your grandfather and father over the better part of half a century.'

'Yes, but both of them were always open to new ideas to expand the bank's activities.'

'In good times,' said Simmons.

'And in bad.'

'Why are you so upset, William? You still have a free hand in the running of your own department.'

'Like hell I do. You block anything that even suggests enterprise.'

'Let's start being honest with each other, William. One of the reasons I have had to be particularly cautious lately is that Matthew's judgement is no longer reliable.'

'Leave Matthew out of this. It's me you're blocking. I am head of the department.'

'I can't leave Matthew out of it. I only wish I could. The overall responsibility to the board for anyone's actions is mine, and he is the number two in our most important department.'

'Therefore he's my responsibility, because I'm the number one in that department.'

'No, William, it cannot remain your responsibility alone that Matthew comes into the office drunk at eleven o'clock in the morning – no matter how long and close your friendship has been.'

'Don't exaggerate.'

'I'm not exaggerating, William. For over a year now this bank has been carrying Matthew, and the only thing that's stopped me from mentioning it to you before is your close personal relationship with him and his family. I wouldn't be sorry to see him hand in his resignation. A bigger man would have done so long ago, and a close friend would have told him so.'

'Never,' said William. 'If he goes, I go.'

'So be it, William. My first responsibility is to our investors, not to your old school chums.'

'You'll live to regret that, Tony,' said William. He stormed out of the chairman's office and returned to his own room in a furious temper.

'Where is Mr Lester?' he demanded as he passed his secretary.

'He's not in yet, sir.'

William looked at his watch, exasperated. 'Tell him I'd like a word the moment he arrives.'

'Yes, sir.'

William paced up and down his office, cursing. Everything Simmons had said about Matthew was true, which only made matters worse. He began to think back to when Matthew's drinking bouts had begun, searching for an explanation. His thoughts were interrupted by his secretary.

'Mr Lester has just arrived, sir.'

Matthew entered the room looking rather sheepish, displaying all the signs of another hangover. He had aged badly in the past year, and his skin had lost its fine, athletic glow. William hardly recognized him as the man who had been his closest friend for nearly twenty years.

'Matthew, where the hell have you been?'

'I overslept,' Matthew replied off-handedly, scratching at his face. 'Rather a late night, I'm afraid.'

'You mean you drank too much.'

'No, I didn't have that much. It was a new girlfriend who kept me awake all night. She was insatiable.'

'When will you stop, Matthew? You've slept with nearly every single woman in Boston.'

'Don't exaggerate, William. There must be one or two left – at least I hope so. And don't forget all the thousands of married ones.'

'It's not funny, Matthew.'

'Oh, come on, William. Give me a break.'

'Give you a break? I've just had Simmons on my back complaining about you, and what's more, he's right. Your judgement has gone to pieces. You'll sleep with anything wearing a skirt, and worse, you're drinking yourself to death. Why, Matthew? Tell me why. There must be some explanation. Up until a year ago you were one of the most reliable men I'd ever met in my life. What is it, Matthew? What am I supposed to tell Simmons?'

'Tell him to go to hell and mind his own business.'

William was unable to hide his anger. 'Matthew, be fair, it *is* his business. We're running a bank, not a bordello, and you came here as a director on my personal recommendation.

'And now I'm not measuring up to your high standards, is that what you're saying?'

'No, I'm not saying that.'

'Then what the hell are you saying?'

'Buckle down and do some work for a few weeks. In no time everyone will have forgotten all about it.'

'Is that what you want?'

'Yes.'

'I shall do as you command, O Master,' said Matthew, and he clicked his heels and walked out of the room.

'Oh, hell,' said William as he sank back into his chair.

That afternoon William needed to go over a client's portfolio with Matthew, but nobody was able to find him. He had not returned to the office after lunch, and was not seen again that day.

Even the pleasure of putting young Richard to bed that evening could not distract William from his anxiety about Matthew. William was trying to teach him to count, but having little success.

'If you can't count, Richard, how can you ever hope to be a banker,' William was saying as Kate entered the nursery.

'Perhaps he'll end up doing something worthwhile,' said Kate.

'What's more worthwhile than banking?'

'Well, he might be a musician, or a baseball player, or even President of the United States.'

'Of those three I'd prefer him to be a ball player – it's the only one that pays a decent salary,' said William as he tucked Richard up.

'You look exhausted, darling. I hope you haven't forgotten that we're having drinks with Andrew MacKenzie this evening.'

'Oh hell, it had totally slipped my mind. When's he expecting us?'

'In about an hour.'

'Well, first I'm going to take a long, hot bath.'

'I thought that was a woman's privilege,' said Kate.

'Tonight I need a little pampering. I've had a nerve-racking day.'

'Tony Simmons causing trouble again?'

'Yes, but I'm afraid this time he's right. He's been complaining about Matthew's drinking. I was only thankful he didn't mention the womanizing. It's become impossible to take Matthew anywhere nowadays unless the drink and the eldest daughter – not to mention the occasional wife – have been safely locked up before his arrival.'

William soaked in the tub for more than half an hour, and Kate had to drag him out before he fell asleep. Despite her prompting, they arrived at the MacKenzies' twenty-five minutes late, to find that Matthew was already well on the way to being inebriated and was trying to pick up a congressman's wife. William wanted to intervene, but Kate prevented him.

'Don't say anything,' she said.

'I can't stand here and watch my closest friend going to pieces in front of my eyes,' said William. 'I have to do something.'

But in the end he took Kate's advice, and spent an unhappy evening watching Matthew become progressively more drunk. From the other side of the room Tony Simmons was glancing pointedly at William, who was relieved when Matthew left early, even if it was in the company of the only unattached woman at the party. Once Matthew had gone, William started to relax for the first time that day.

'How is little Richard?' Dr MacKenzie asked.

'He can't count yet,' said William.

'That's good news. He might end up doing something worthwhile after all.'

'Exactly what I said,' said Kate. 'What a good idea, William, he can be a doctor.'

'He should be able to manage that,' said MacKenzie. 'I don't know many doctors who can count.'

'Except when they send their bills,' said William.

MacKenzie laughed. 'Will you have another drink, Kate?'

'No thank you, Andrew. It's time we went home. If we stay any longer, only Tony Simmons and William will be left, and we'd have to listen to them talk banking for the rest of the evening.'

'Thanks for the party, Andrew,' said William. 'By the way, I must apologize for Matthew's behaviour.'

'Why?' said Dr MacKenzie.

'Oh, come on, Andrew, not only was he drunk, but there wasn't a woman in the room he didn't proposition.'

'I might well do the same if I were in his predicament,' said Dr MacKenzie.

'What makes you say that?' said William. 'You can't approve of his conduct just because he's single.'

'No I don't, but I try to understand, and realize I might be a little irresponsible faced with the same problem.'

'What do you mean?' said William.

'Oh, my God,' said Dr MacKenzie. 'You're his closest friend, and he hasn't told you?'

'Told us what?' said Kate and William together.

Dr MacKenzie looked at them with disbelief in his eyes.

'You'd better come to my study. Both of you.'

William and Kate followed him into a small room, lined almost floor to ceiling with medical books interspersed with occasional photographs of Dr MacKenzie's student days at Cornell and the odd framed certificate.

'Please sit down,' he said. 'William, I make no apologies for what I'm about to say, because I assumed you knew that Matthew was gravely ill, suffering from Hodgkin's disease. He's known about his condition for over a year.'

William fell back in his chair, for a moment unable to speak. 'Hodgkin's disease?'

'An almost invariably fatal inflammation and enlargement of the lymph nodes,' said the doctor rather formally.

William shook his head incredulously. 'But why didn't he tell me?'

'My guess is he's too proud to burden anyone else with his problems. He'd rather die in his own way than let anyone know what he's going through. I've begged him for the last six months to tell his father, and I've certainly broken my professional promise to him by letting you know, but I can't allow you to go on blaming him for his behaviour without knowing the truth.'

'Thank you, Andrew,' said William. 'How can I have been so blind and so stupid?'

'Don't blame yourself,' said Dr MacKenzie. 'There's no way you could have known.'

'Is there really no hope?' asked Kate.

'None. It's only the length of time I can't be sure about.'

'Are there no clinics, no specialists? Money wouldn't be a problem.'

'Money can't buy everything, William. I've already consulted the three best surgeons in America, and even one in Switzerland. I'm afraid they all agree with my diagnosis. Medical science hasn't yet discovered a cure for Hodgkin's disease.'

'How long does he have to live?' asked Kate in a whisper.

'Six months at the outside would be my bet, but more likely three.'

'And I thought I had problems,' said William. He held tightly onto Kate's hand. 'We must be going, Andrew. Thank you for telling us.'

'Do what you can for him,' said the doctor, 'but for God's sake, be understanding. Let him do what he wants to do. These are Matthew's last few months, not yours. And don't ever let him know I told you.'

William and Kate drove home in silence. As soon as they reached the Red House, William phoned the woman Matthew had left the party with.

'Would it be possible to speak to Matthew Lester?'

'He's not here,' said a rather irritated voice. 'He dragged me off to the Revue Club, and after a couple of drinks he left with another woman.' She hung up.

The Revue Club. William looked it up in the phone book, then drove over to the north side of town and, after questioning a taxi driver, eventually found the club. He knocked on the door. A hatch slid open.

'Are you a member?'

'No,' said William firmly, and passed a ten-dollar bill through the grille.

The hatch slid shut and the door opened. William walked across the middle of the dance floor, looking slightly incongruous in his three-piece banker's suit. The dancers twined around each other and swayed incuriously away from him. William's eyes searched the smoke-filled room for Matthew, but he wasn't there. Finally he thought he recognized one of Matthew's more recent girlfriends, sitting in a corner with a sailor. William went over to her.

'Excuse me, miss.'

She looked up, but clearly didn't recognize William.

'The lady's with me. Beat it,' said the sailor.

'Have you seen Matthew Lester?'

'Matthew who?' said the girl.

'I told you to get lost,' said the sailor, rising to his feet.

'One more word out of you and you'll be back on deck,' said William.

The sailor had seen anger like that in a man's eyes once before in his life, and had nearly lost an eye for his trouble. He sat back down.

'Where's Matthew?'

'I don't know a Matthew, honey.' Now she sounded frightened.

'Six feet two, blond hair, dressed like me and probably drunk.'

'Oh, you mean Martin. He calls himself Martin here, not Matthew.' She began to relax. 'Now let me see, who did he go off with tonight?' She turned her head towards the bar and shouted at the bartender. 'Terry, who did Martin leave with?'

The bartender removed a dead cigarette butt from the corner of his mouth. 'Jenny,' he said, and put the unlit cigarette back in place.

'Jenny, that's right,' said the girl. 'Now, let me see, she's short sessions. Never gives a man more than half an hour, so they should be back soon.'

'Thank you,' said William.

He took a seat at the bar and a scotch with a lot of water, feeling more and more out of place by the minute. Finally the bartender, the unlit cigarette still in his mouth, nodded in the direction of a girl who was coming through the door.

'That's Jenny, if you still want her,' he said. Matthew was nowhere to be seen.

The bartender waved for Jenny to join them. A slim, short, dark, not unattractive girl winked at William and walked towards him, her hips swinging.

'Looking for me, darling? Well, I'm available, but it's ten dollars for half an hour.'

'No, I don't want you,' said William.

'Charming,' said Jenny.

'I'm looking for the man who you were with. Matthew – I mean Martin.'

'Martin, he was too drunk to get it up with the help of a crane, but he paid his ten dollars – he always does. A real gentleman.'

'Where is he now?' asked William impaticntly.

'I don't know. He said he was going to walk home.'

William drove slowly through the rain covered streets, following the route towards Matthew's apartment, looking carefully at every man he passed. Some hurried on when they saw him staring at them, while others tried to engage him in conversation. He had stopped at a traffic light outside an all-night diner when he caught sight of Matthew through the steamy window, weaving his way through the tables with a cup in his hand. William parked the car, walked into the diner and took the seat opposite him. Matthew was slumped on the table next to a cup of untouched coffee.

'Matthew, it's me,' said William, looking at his crumpled friend. Tears started to run down his cheeks.

Matthew looked up and spilled some of his coffee. 'You're crying, old fellow. Lost your girl, have you?'

'No, I've lost my closest friend.'

'Ah, they're much harder to come by.'

'I know,' said William.

'I have a good friend,' said Matthew, slurring his words. 'He's always stood by me until we quarrelled for the first time the other day. My fault though. You see, I've let him down rather badly.'

'No, you haven't,' said William.

'How can you know?' said Matthew angrily. 'You're not even fit to know him.'

'Let's go home, Matthew.'

'My name is Martin,' said Matthew.

'I'm sorry, Martin, let's go home.'

'No, I want to stay here. There's this girl who may come by later. I think I'm ready for her now.'

'I have some fine old malt whiskey at my place,' said William. 'Why don't you join me?'

'Any women at your place?'

'Yes, plenty of them.'

'You're on, I'll come.'

William hoisted Matthew up and guided him slowly towards the door. As they passed two policemen sitting at the counter, William heard one of them say, 'Goddamn fairies.'

He helped Matthew into the car and drove him to Beacon Hill. Kate was waiting up for them.

'You should have gone to bed, darling.'

'I couldn't sleep,' she said.

'I'm afraid he's nearly incoherent.'

'Is this the girl you promised me?' asked Matthew.

'Yes, she'll take care of you,' said William, as he and Kate helped him up to the guest room and put him on the bed. Kate started to undress him.

'You must undress as well, darling,' he said. 'I've already paid my ten dollars.'

'When you're in bed,' said Kate gently.

'Why are you looking so sad, beautiful lady?' said Matthew.

'Because I love you,' said Kate, tears beginning to form in her eyes.

'Don't cry,' said Matthew. 'There's nothing to cry about. I'll manage it this time, you'll see.'

When they had undressed him, William covered him with a sheet and a blanket. Kate turned out the light.

'You promised you'd come to bed with me,' Matthew said drowsily.

She closed the door quietly.

William slept on a chair outside Matthew's room for fear he might wake up in the night and try to leave. Kate woke him in the morning, before taking in some breakfast to Matthew.

'What am I doing here, Kate?' were his first words as she pulled open the curtains and he blinked in the morning light.

'You came back with us after Andrew MacKenzie's party last night,' Kate replied rather feebly.

'No, I didn't. I went to the Revue Club with that awful girl, Patricia something or other, but luckily Jenny was there, not that she had to do much to earn her ten dollars. God, I feel lousy. Can I have a tomato juice? I don't want to be unsociable, but the last thing I need is breakfast.'

'Of course, Matthew,' said Kate, removing the tray.

William came in. He and Matthew stared at each other in silence.

'You know, don't you?' said Matthew finally.

'Yes,' said William. 'I've been a fool, and I hope you'll forgive me.'

'Don't cry, William. I haven't seen you do that since you were twelve when Covington was beating you up and I had to drag him off you. Remember? I wonder what Covington's up to now? Probably running a brothel in Tijuana; it's about all he was fit for. Mind you, if Covington is running it, the place will be damned efficient, so lead me to it. Don't cry, William. Grown men don't cry. Nothing can be done. I've seen all the specialists from New York to Los Angeles to Zürich, and there's nothing they can do. Do you mind if I skip the office this morning? I still feel bloody awful. Kate can wake me up if I stay too long, or if I'm too much trouble, and I'll find my own way home.'

'This is your home now,' said William.

Matthew's voice changed. 'Will you tell my father, William? I can't face him. You're an only son – you understand the problem.'

'Yes,' said William. 'I'll go down to New York tomorrow and let him know, if you'll promise to stay here. I won't stop you from getting drunk if that's what you want to do, or from having as many women as you like, but you must stay here.'

'Best offer I've had in weeks, William. Now I think I'll sleep some more. I get so tired nowadays.'

William watched Matthew fall into a deep sleep, and removed the half-empty glass from his hand. A tomato juice stain was forming on the sheets.

'Don't die,' he said quietly. 'Please don't die, Matthew. Have you forgotten that you and I are going to run the biggest bank in America?'

—◦—

William went to New York the following morning to see Charles Lester. The great man shrank into his seat and seemed to age visibly at William's news.

'Thank you for coming, William, and telling me personally. I knew something had to be wrong when Matthew stopped visiting me, without warning. I'll come up to Boston every weekend. I'm so glad he's with you and Kate, and I'll try not to make it too obvious how hard I took the news. God knows what he's done to deserve this. Since his mother died, I've built everything for him, and now there's no one to leave it to.'

'Come to Boston whenever you want to, sir – you'll always be most welcome.'

'Thank you, William, for everything you're doing for my son.' The old man looked up at him. 'I wish your father were alive to see how worthy his son is of the name Kane. If only I could change places with my son, and let him live . . .'

'I ought to be getting back to him soon, sir.'

'Yes, of course. Tell him I love him; tell him I took the news stoically. Don't tell him anything different.'

'Yes, sir.'

William travelled back to Boston that night to find that Matthew had stayed at home with Kate and was sitting on the veranda reading America's latest bestseller, *Gone With The Wind*. He looked up as William came in.

'How did the old man take it?' were his first words when William entered the room.

'He cried,' said William.

'The chairman of Lester's Bank cried?' said Matthew. 'I hope no one tells the shareholders.'

Matthew stopped drinking, returned to work and worked as hard as he could right up until the last few days. William was amazed by his determination, and continually tried to make him slow down. But Matthew kept well on top of his work, and would tease William by checking *his* mail at the end of each day. In the evenings, before the theatre or dinner, Matthew would play tennis with Kate, or row against William on the Charles.

'I'll know I'm dead when I can't beat you,' he mocked.

Matthew never entered hospital, preferring to stay at the Red House. For William, the weeks went so slowly and yet so quickly, waking each morning and wondering if Matthew would still be alive.

Matthew died on a Thursday, forty pages still to read of *Gone With The Wind*.

—◦—

Matthew's funeral was held at St Patrick's Cathedral in New York, and William and Kate stayed with Charles Lester. In the past few months he had become an old man, and as he stood by the graves of his wife and his only son, he told William he no longer saw any purpose in life. William said nothing; no words of his could help the grieving father.

William and Kate returned to Boston the following day. The Red House seemed strangely empty without Matthew. The past months had been at once the happiest and the unhappiest period in William's life. Matthew's illness had brought William closer to both him and Kate than normal life would ever have allowed.

When William returned to the bank he found it difficult to get back into any sort of normal routine. He would get up and start to head towards Matthew's office for advice or a laugh, but Matthew was no longer there. It was weeks before William could accept that the room was empty.

Tony Simmons could not have been more understanding, but it didn't help. William lost all interest in banking, even in Kane and Cabot, as he went through months of remorse over Matthew's death. He had always taken it for granted that he and Matthew shared a common destiny, that they would grow old together. No one commented that William's work was not up to its usual high standard, although Kate grew worried by the hours William would spend alone.

Then one morning she woke to find him sitting on the edge of the bed, staring at her. She blinked at him. 'Is something wrong, darling?'

'No. I'm just looking at my greatest asset, and making sure I never take it for granted.'

35

AT BREAKFAST the following morning, Kate pointed to a small item on page 17 of the *Globe*, reporting the opening of the Chicago Baron.

William smiled as he read the article. Kane and Cabot had been foolish not to listen when he had advised them to back the Richmond Group. It pleased him that his own judgement on Rosnovski had turned out to be right, even though the bank had missed out on the deal. His smile broadened as he read the nickname 'The Chicago Baron'. Then, suddenly, he felt sick. He examined the photograph accompanying the article more closely, but there was no mistake, and the caption confirmed his worst fear: 'Abel Rosnovski, the chairman of the Baron Group, talking with Mieczyslaw Szymczak, a governor of the Federal Reserve Board, and Alderman Henry Osborne.'

William dropped the paper onto the breakfast table and didn't finish his coffee. He left the house without another word. As soon as he arrived at his office, he called Thomas Cohen at Cohen, Cohen and Yablons.

'It's been a long time, Mr Kane,' were Cohen's first words. 'I was very sorry to learn of the death of your friend, Mr Lester. How are your wife and your son – Richard – isn't that his name?'

William always admired Cohen's instant recall of names and relationships.

'They're both well, thank you, Mr Cohen. And how is Thaddeus?'

'He's just become a partner of the firm, and recently made

me a grandfather. So what can I do for you, Mr Kane?' Thomas Cohen also recalled that William could only manage about one sentence of small talk.

'I want to employ, through you, the services of a reliable private investigator. I do not wish my name to be associated with the inquiry, but I need a full update on Henry Osborne, who, it seems, is now an alderman in Chicago. I want to know everything he's done since he left Boston, and in particular whether there is any personal or professional connection between him and Abel Rosnovski, the president of the Baron Group.'

There was a pause before the lawyer said, 'I understand.'

'Can you report to me in one week?'

'Two please, Mr Kane, two,' said Cohen.

-◦-

Thomas Cohen was as reliable as ever, and a full report appeared on William's desk by the fifteenth morning. He read the dossier several times, underlining certain passages. There appeared to be no formal business relationship between Abel Rosnovski and Henry Osborne. Rosnovski, it seemed, found Osborne useful as a political fixer, but nothing more. Osborne had drifted from job to job since leaving Boston, ending up in the claims office of the Great Western Casualty Insurance Company. That was probably how he had come into contact with Rosnovski, as the old Chicago Richmond had been insured by Great Western. When the hotel was burned to the ground, the insurance company had originally refused to pay the claim. A certain Desmond Pacey, the former manager, had been sent to prison for ten years after pleading guilty to arson, and there had initially been some suspicion that Rosnovski might have been involved. But nothing was proved, and the insurance company settled for three-quarters of a million dollars. Osborne, the report went on, was now an alderman and a full-time politician at City Hall. It was common knowledge that he hoped to become the next congressman for Illinois. He had recently married a Miss Marie Axton, the daughter of a wealthy drug manufacturer, and as yet they had no children.

William went over the report once again to be sure he had

not missed anything, however inconsequential. Although there did not seem to be a great deal to connect the two men, he couldn't help feeling that the association between Abel Rosnovski and Henry Osborne, both of whom detested him, for totally different reasons, was potentially dangerous. He mailed a cheque to Thomas Cohen and requested that he update the file every quarter. But as the months passed, and the quarterly reports revealed nothing new, he began to stop worrying, thinking that perhaps he had overreacted to the photograph in the *Boston Globe*.

‑‹o›‑

Kate presented William with a daughter in the spring of 1936; they christened her Virginia. William started changing diapers again, and such was his fascination with 'the little lady' that Kate had to rescue the child each night for fear *she* would never get any sleep. Richard, now three years old, didn't care too much for the new arrival to begin with, but time and a new electric train set helped to allay his jealousy.

By the end of the year William's department at Kane and Cabot had made a handsome profit for the bank. He had emerged from the lethargy that had overcome him following Matthew's death, and was fast regaining his reputation as a shrewd investor in the stock market, not least when 'Sell'em Short Smith' admitted he had only perfected a technique developed by William Kane of Boston. Even Tony Simmons's direction had become less irksome. Nevertheless, William was secretly frustrated by the knowledge that he could not hope to become chairman of Kane and Cabot until Simmons retired in fifteen years' time, but he wasn't sure what he could do about it.

36

CHARLES LESTER had grown very old in the three years since Matthew's death, and it was rumoured in financial circles that he had lost all interest in his work, and was rarely seen at the bank. So it didn't come entirely as a surprise when William read of the old man's death in the *New York Times*.

The Kanes travelled down to New York for the funeral. Everyone seemed to be there, including John Nance Garner, the Vice President of the United States. After the funeral, William and Kate took the train back to Boston, numbly conscious that they had lost their last close link with the Lester family.

Three months later, William received a letter from Sullivan and Cromwell, the distinguished New York lawyers, asking him if he would be kind enough to attend the reading of the will of the late Charles Lester at their offices on Wall Street.

William decided to attend the reading, more out of loyalty to the Lester family than from any desire to find out what Charles Lester had left him. He hoped for a small memento that would remind him of Matthew and would join the 'Harvard Oar' that hung on the wall of his study at the Red House. He also looked forward to the opportunity to renew his acquaintance with so many members of the Lester family whom he had come to know during his school and college vacations.

He drove down to New York in his newly acquired Daimler the night before the reading and stayed at the Harvard Club. The will was to be read at ten o'clock the following morning, and he was surprised to find on his arrival at the offices of Sullivan and Cromwell that more than fifty people were already present. Many of them glanced up at him as he entered the room, and he greeted several of Matthew's cousins and aunts, who looked rather older than he remembered them; he could only conclude they must be thinking the same about him. He searched the room for Matthew's sister Susan, but couldn't see her. He assumed that by now she must be married and have a brood of young children.

As ten o'clock struck, Mr Arthur Cromwell entered the room, accompanied by an assistant carrying a brown leather folder. Everyone fell silent in hopeful expectation. The lawyer began by explaining that the contents of the will had not been disclosed until now, three months after Charles Lester's death, at Mr Lester's specific instruction. Having no son to whom to leave his fortune, he had wanted the dust to settle following his death before his final intentions were made clear.

William looked around the room and studied the faces, many of which were clearly intent on every syllable coming from the lawyer's mouth. Arthur Cromwell took nearly an hour to read the handwritten will. After reciting the usual bequests to family retainers, charities and a rather large donation to Harvard University, he went on to reveal that Charles Lester had divided the remainder of his fortune among his relations, treating them more or less according to their degree of kinship. His daughter Susan received the largest share of the estate, while his five nephews and three nieces each received an equal portion of the remainder. All their money and stock were to be held in trust by the bank until they were thirty. Several other cousins, aunts and distant relations were to receive cash payments.

William was surprised when Mr Cromwell announced, 'That disposes of all the known assets of the late Charles Lester.'

People began to shuffle around in their seats, and a murmur of nervous conversation broke out.

'It is not, however, the end of Mr Lester's Last Will and Testament,' said the imperturbable lawyer. Everyone stopped fidgeting, fearful of some late and unwelcome thunderbolt.

Mr Cromwell went on. 'I shall now continue in Mr Lester's

own words: "I have always considered that a bank and its reputation are only as good as the people who serve it. It was well known that I had hoped my son Matthew would succeed me as chairman of Lester's, but his tragic and untimely death sadly intervened. Until now, I have never divulged my choice of a successor. I therefore wish it be known that I desire William Lowell Kane, son of one of my dearest friends, the late Richard Lowell Kane, and at present the deputy chairman of Kane and Cabot, to be appointed chairman of Lester's Bank and Trust Company following the next full board meeting."'

There was an immediate uproar. Everyone looked around the room in search of the mysterious William Lowell Kane, of whom few but the immediate Lester family had ever heard.

'I have not yet finished,' said Arthur Cromwell quietly.

Silence fell once more. Some of the would-be beneficiaries were now looking apprehensive.

The lawyer continued: 'All the above grants and divisions of stock in Lester and Company are expressly conditional upon the beneficiaries voting for Mr Kane at the next annual general meeting, and continuing to do so for at least the following five years, unless Mr Kane himself indicates that he does not wish to accept the chairmanship.'

Uproar again replaced the quiet murmurings. William wished he were a million miles away, not sure whether to be deliriously happy or to concede that he was the most detested person in the room.

'That concludes the Last Will and Testament of the late Charles Lester,' said Mr Cromwell, but only the front row heard his words. William looked up to see Susan Lester walking towards him. The puppy fat had disappeared, but the attractive freckles remained. He smiled, but she walked straight past him without acknowledging his presence.

As William made his way to the door, a tall, grey-haired man wearing a pin-striped suit and a silver tie caught up with him.

'You are William Kane, are you not, sir?'

'Yes, I am,' said William nervously.

'My name is Peter Parfitt,' said the stranger.

'One of the bank's vice chairmen,' said William.

'Correct, sir. I do not know you, but I know something of your reputation, and I count myself lucky to have been acquainted with your distinguished father. If Charles Lester thought you were the right man to be chairman of his bank, that's good enough for me.'

William had never been so relieved in his life.

'Where are you staying in New York?' asked Parfitt.

'At the Harvard Club.'

'Splendid. May I ask if you are free for dinner tonight, by any chance?'

'I had intended to return to Boston this evening,' said William, 'but now I expect I'll have to stay in New York for a few more days.'

'Good. Why don't you join me and my wife for dinner at my home, say eight o'clock?'

The banker handed William his card, with an address embossed in copperplate script. 'I shall enjoy the opportunity of chatting with you in more convivial surroundings, and learning what plans you might have for the future of the bank.'

'Thank you, sir,' said William, pocketing the card as other people crowded around him. Some stared at him with hostility; others wanted to offer their congratulations.

When William eventually managed to make his escape and return to the Harvard Club, the first thing he did was to phone Kate to tell her the news.

She said very quietly, 'How happy Matthew would be for you, darling.'

William didn't respond, aware that Matthew should have been the next chairman.

'When are you coming home?'

'Heaven knows. I'm dining tonight with a Mr Peter Parfitt, a vice chairman of Lester's. He's welcomed my appointment, which could make life much easier. I'll spend the night here at the club and call you sometime tomorrow to let you know how things are panning out.'

'All right, darling.'

'All quiet on the Eastern Seaboard?'

'Well, Virginia has cut a tooth and seems to think she deserves special attention, Richard was sent to bed early last night for being rude to Nanny, and we all miss you.'

William laughed. 'Makes my problems look fairly mundane. I'll call you tomorrow, my darling.'

'Yes, please do. By the way, many congratulations. I approve of Charles Lester's judgement, even if we are going to have to move to New York.'

―◦―

William arrived at Peter Parfitt's home on East Sixty-Fourth Street just after eight o'clock that evening, and was taken by surprise to find that his host had dressed for dinner. William felt slightly ill at ease in his dark banker's suit, and explained to his hostess that he had originally intended to return to Boston that evening. Diana Parfitt, who turned out to be Peter's second wife, could not have been more charming, and seemed as delighted as her husband that William was to be the next chairman of Lester's. During an excellent dinner, William could not resist asking Parfitt how he thought the rest of the board would react to Charles Lester's bombshell.

'They'll all fall in line,' said Parfitt. 'I've spoken to most of them already. There's a full board meeting on Monday morning to confirm your appointment, and I can only see one small cloud on the horizon.'

'What's that?' asked William, trying not to sound anxious.

'Well, between you and me, the other vice chairman, Ted Leach, was rather expecting to be appointed chairman himself. In fact, I think I would go as far as saying he assumed he was the natural successor. We'd all been informed that no nominations could be considered until after the will had been read, but Charles's wishes must have come as rather a shock to Ted.'

'Will he put up a fight?' asked William.

'I'm afraid he might, but there's nothing for you to worry about.'

'I don't mind admitting,' said Diana Parfitt as she studied the rather flat soufflé in front of her, 'that Ted Leach has never been my favourite man.'

'Now, dear,' said Parfitt reprovingly, 'we mustn't say anything behind Ted's back before William has had a chance to judge for himself. There's no doubt in my mind that the board will confirm William's appointment at the meeting on Monday, and there's even the possibility that Ted will resign.'

'I don't want anyone to feel he has to resign because of me,' said William.

'A very creditable attitude,' said Parfitt. 'But don't bother yourself about a puff of wind. I'm confident that the whole matter is well under control. You return to Boston, and I'll keep you informed on the lie of the land.'

'Perhaps it might be wise if I dropped in to the bank tomorrow. Wouldn't your colleagues find it a little curious if I make no attempt to meet any of them?'

'No, I don't think that would be advisable given the circumstances. In fact, it might be wiser for you to stay out of the way until the board has confirmed your appointment. They won't want to seem any less independent than they can help, and some of them may already feel like glorified rubber stamps. Take my advice, Bill, you go back to Boston. I'll call you with the good news around noon on Monday.'

William reluctantly agreed, and went on to spend a pleasant evening discussing with the Parfitts where he and Kate might stay in New York while they were looking for a permanent home. He was somewhat surprised that Peter Parfitt seemed to have no desire to discuss his own views on the direction the bank should be taking, but assumed it was because his wife was present. The evening ended with a little too much brandy, and William did not arrive back at the Harvard Club until after one o'clock.

The first thing he did on returning to Boston was to let Tony Simmons know what had transpired in New York; he did not want him to hear about the appointment from anyone else. Simmons turned out to be apprehensive when he heard the news.

'I'm sorry that you'll be leaving us, William. Lester's may well be two or three times the size of Kane and Cabot, but it will be very hard to replace you. I hope you'll consider very carefully before accepting the offer.'

William was surprised by Tony's response.

'Frankly, Tony, I would have thought you'd be only too happy to see the back of me.'

'William, when will you accept that my first interest has always been the bank? There has never been any doubt in my mind that you are one of the shrewdest investment advisors in America today. If you leave Kane and Cabot now, many of the bank's most important clients will want to follow you.'

'I wouldn't even transfer my own trust funds to Lester's,' said William, 'let alone expect any of the bank's clients to move their accounts because I'd left.'

'Of course you wouldn't solicit them to join you, William, that's not your style, but some of them will want you to continue managing their portfolios. Like your father and Charles Lester, they believe quite rightly that banking is about people and reputations.'

William and Kate spent a tense weekend awaiting a call from Peter Parfitt following the result of the board meeting in New York. William sat nervously in his office the whole of Monday morning, answering every telephone call personally, but he had still heard nothing as the morning dragged into the afternoon. He didn't even leave the office for lunch. Parfitt finally called a little after five.

'I'm afraid there's been an unexpected development, Bill,' were his opening words.

William's heart sank.

'Nothing for you to worry about, but the board wants the right to oppose your nomination and put up their own candidate. One of them has produced legal opinions suggesting that the relevant clause in the will has no validity. I've been given the unpleasant task of asking if you would be willing to fight an election against the board's candidate.'

'Who would be the board's candidate?' asked William.

'No names have been mentioned yet, but I imagine it will be

Ted Leach. No one else has shown any interest in running against you.'

'I'd like a little time to think about it,' William replied. 'When will the next board meeting be?'

'A week from today. But don't go and get yourself all worked up about Ted Leach; I'm still confident you'll win easily. I'll keep you informed of any further developments.'

'Do you want me to come down to New York, Peter?'

'No, not for the moment. I don't think that would help matters.'

William thanked him and put the phone down, then packed his old leather briefcase and left the office, feeling more than a little depressed. Tony Simmons, lugging a suitcase, caught up with him in the directors' parking lot.

'I didn't know you were going out of town, Tony.'

'It's only one of those monthly bankers' dinners in New York. I'll be back by tomorrow afternoon. I think I can safely leave Kane and Cabot for twenty-four hours in the capable hands of the next chairman of Lester's.'

William laughed. 'I may already be the ex-chairman,' he said, and explained the latest development. Once again he was surprised by Simmons's reaction.

'It's true that Ted Leach has always hoped to be the next chairman of Lester's,' he said. 'That's common knowledge in financial circles. But he's a loyal servant of the bank, and I can't believe he would oppose Charles Lester's express wishes.'

'I didn't realize you knew him,' said William.

'I don't know him all that well,' said Tony. 'He was a class ahead of me at Yale, and I occasionally come across him at these infernal dinners, which you'll have to attend once you're a chairman. He's bound to be there tonight. I'll have a word with him if you like.'

'Yes, please do, but do be careful, won't you?' said William.

'My dear William, you've spent the past ten years of your life telling me I'm far too careful.'

'I'm sorry, Tony. Funny how one's judgement is influenced

when facing a personal problem, however sound it might be considered when dealing with other people's. I'll put myself in your hands, and do whatever you advise.'

'Good. Leave it to me. I'll see what Leach has to say for himself, and call you first thing in the morning.'

◄○►

Tony Simmons called from New York a few minutes after midnight, waking William from a fitful sleep.

'Have I woken you, William?'

'Yes, but it doesn't matter, Tony.'

William switched on the light by the bed and looked at his alarm clock. 'Well, you did say you'd call first thing in the morning.'

Simmons laughed. 'I'm afraid what I have to tell you won't seem quite as amusing. The man opposing you for the chairmanship of Lester's is Peter Parfitt.'

'*What?*' said William, suddenly wide awake.

'He's been trying to steamroller the board into supporting him behind your back. Ted Leach, as I expected, is in favour of your appointment as chairman. However, the board is split down the middle.'

'Damn. First, thank you, Tony, and second, what the hell do I do?'

'If you want to be the next chairman of Lester's, you'd better get yourself down here pretty fast. Some of the members of the board are asking why you've been hiding away in Boston.'

'Hiding away?'

'That's what Parfitt's been telling them for the past few days.'

'The bastard.'

'Now that you mention the subject, I'm unable to vouch for his parentage,' said Simmons.

William laughed.

'Come and stay at the Yale Club. We can talk the whole thing over first thing in the morning.'

'I'll get there as quickly as I can.'

He put the phone down and looked across at the sleeping

Kate, blissfully unaware of his latest problem. How he wished he could manage that. A curtain only had to flutter in the breeze and he would wake up. She would probably sleep through the Second Coming. He scribbled a few lines of explanation and put the note on her bedside table; then he dressed, packed – this time including a dinner jacket – and set off for New York.

The roads were clear at one in the morning, and the run in the Daimler seemed the quickest he had ever managed. He arrived in New York accompanied by cleaners, mailmen, news-boys and the morning sun, and checked in at the Yale Club as the hall clock chimed once. It was six-fifteen. He unpacked and decided to rest for an hour before waking Tony Simmons, but the next thing he heard was an insistent tapping on his door. Sleepily, he got up to open it, to find Simmons standing in the corridor.

'Nice dressing gown, William,' he said, grinning.

'I must have fallen asleep. If you can wait a minute I'll be right with you,' said William.

'No, no, I have to catch a train back to Boston. Someone has to run the office. You take a shower and get dressed while we talk.'

William went into the bathroom and left the door open.

'Now your main problem—' started Simmons.

William put his head around the bathroom door. 'I can't hear you while the water's running.'

Simmons waited for it to stop. 'Peter Parfitt is your main problem. He assumed he was going to be the next chairman, and that his would be the name that was read out in Charles Lester's will. Since then he's been playing boardroom politics and trying to turn the directors against you. Ted Leach would like you to join him for lunch today at the Metropolitan Club when he'll fill you in on the finer points. He may bring two or three other board members with him on whom you can rely. The board, by the way, still seems to be split right down the middle.'

William nicked himself with his razor. 'Damn. Which club did you say?'

'The Metropolitan, just off Fifth Avenue on East Sixtieth Street.'

'Why there, and not somewhere on Wall Street?'

'William, when you're dealing with the Peter Parfitts of this world, you don't telegraph your intentions. Keep your wits about you, and play the whole thing very coolly. From what Leach tells me, he thinks you can still win.'

William came back into the bedroom with a towel around his waist. 'I'll try,' he said. 'To be cool, that is.'

Simmons smiled. 'Now I must get back to Boston. My train leaves Grand Central in ten minutes.' He looked at his watch. 'Damn, six minutes.' He paused at the bedroom door. 'You know, your father never trusted Peter Parfitt. A little too smooth, he always used to say. Never anything more, just "a little too smooth". Good luck, William.'

'How can I begin to thank you, Tony?'

'You can't. Just put it down to my trying to atone for the lousy way I treated Matthew. But frankly, for Kane and Cabot's sake, I hope you lose.'

William smiled as he watched the door close. As he put in his collar stud, he reflected on how curious it was that he had spent years working closely with Tony Simmons without ever really getting to know him, but that after a few days of personal crisis he found himself liking and trusting the man. He went down to the dining room and had a typical club breakfast: a hard boiled egg, one piece of burnt toast, butter and English marmalade from someone else's table. The porter handed him a copy of *The Wall Street Journal*, which hinted on an inside page that everything was not running smoothly at Lester's following the nomination of William Kane as its next chairman. At least the *Journal* didn't seem to know who his rival was.

William returned to his room and asked the operator for a number in Boston. He was kept waiting for a few minutes before he was put through.

'I do apologize, Mr Kane. I had no idea it was you on the line. May I congratulate you on your appointment as chairman of Lester's. I hope this means our New York office will be seeing a lot more of you in the future.'

'That may well depend on you, Mr Cohen.'

'I'm not sure I understand,' the lawyer replied.

William explained what had happened over the past few days, and read out the relevant clause of Charles Lester's will. 'Do you think his wishes would stand up in court?' he asked finally.

'Who knows? I can't think of a precedent for such a situation. A nineteenth-century Member of Parliament once bequeathed his constituency in a will and no one objected, and the beneficiary went on to become Prime Minister. But that was over a hundred years ago – and in England. Now, in this case, if the board decided to contest Mr Lester's will and you took them to court, I wouldn't care to predict which way the judge might jump. Lord Melbourne didn't have to contend with a surrogate of New York County. Nevertheless, a nice legal conundrum, Mr Kane.'

'What do you advise?'

'I am a Jew, Mr Kane. I came to this country on a ship from Germany at the turn of the century, and I've always had to fight for anything I've wanted. How badly do you want to be chairman of Lester's?'

'Very badly, Mr Cohen.'

'Then you should listen to an old man who has, over the years, come to view you with great respect and, if I may say so, with some affection. I'll tell you exactly what I'd do if I were faced with your predicament.'

An hour later William put the phone down and, having some time to kill, strolled up Park Avenue thinking about Cohen's sage advice. On the way to the Metropolitan Club he passed a site on which a huge building was under construction. A large billboard announced: 'The next Baron hotel will be in New York. When the Baron has been your host, you'll never want to stay anywhere else.' He smiled, and walked with a lighter step towards his lunch appointment.

Ted Leach, a short, dapper man with dark brown hair and a lighter moustache, was standing in the foyer waiting for him, and shook him warmly by the hand. William admired the Renaissance style of the club, which Leach told him had been built by Otto

Kuhn and Stanford White in 1891. J. P. Morgan had founded it when one of his closest friends was blackballed at the Union League, Leach told him as they strolled into the bar.

'An extravagant gesture even for a very close friend,' William suggested, trying to make conversation.

'Indeed,' said Leach. 'Now, what will you have to drink, Mr Kane?'

'A dry sherry, please,' said William.

A boy in a smart blue uniform returned a few moments later with a dry sherry and a scotch and water; he hadn't needed to ask Mr Leach for his order.

'To the next chairman of Lester's,' said Leach, raising his glass.

William hesitated.

'Don't drink, Mr Kane. As you know, you should never drink to yourself.'

William laughed, unsure of what to say.

A few moments later two older men came into the bar and walked across to join them, both tall and assured in their bankers' uniform of grey three-piece suits, stiff collars and dark, unpatterned ties. Had they been strolling down Wall Street, William would not have given them a second glance. In the Metropolitan Club he studied them carefully as Leach introduced them.

'Mr Alfred Rodgers and Mr Winthrop Davies. Both board members.'

William's smile was reserved, now uncertain whose side any-one was on. The two newcomers studied him with interest. No one spoke for a moment.

'Where do we start?' asked Rodgers, a monocle falling from his eye as he spoke.

'By going up to lunch,' said Leach.

The three of them turned, obviously knowing exactly where they were going. William followed. The dining room on the second floor was vast, with another magnificent high ceiling. The maître d' placed them in a window seat, overlooking Central Park, where no one could overhear their conversation.

'Let's order and then talk,' said Leach.

Through the window William could see the Plaza Hotel. Memories of his celebration with the grandmothers and Matthew came flooding back to him – and there was something else he was trying to recall about that tea at the Plaza . . .

'Mr Kane, let's put our cards on the table,' said Leach. 'Charles Lester's decision to appoint you as chairman of the bank came as a surprise to all of us, not to put too fine a point on it. But if the board were to ignore his wishes, the bank could be plunged into chaos, and none of us want that. He was a shrewd old buzzard, and he will have had his reasons for wanting you to be chairman. That's good enough for me.'

William had heard those sentiments before – from Peter Parfitt.

'All three of us,' said Davies, taking over, 'owe everything we have to Charles Lester, and we will carry out his wishes if it's the last thing we do as members of the board.'

'It may turn out to be just that,' said Leach, 'if Parfitt succeeds in becoming chairman.'

'I'm sorry, gentlemen,' said William, 'to have caused you so much consternation. If my appointment as chairman came as a surprise to you, it was nothing less than a bolt from the blue for me. When I attended the reading of the will, I imagined I'd receive some minor personal memento in memory of Mr Lester's son, not the opportunity to run his bank.'

Leach smiled when he heard the word 'opportunity'. 'We understand the position you've been placed in, Mr Kane, and you must trust us when we say we're on your side. We are aware you may find that difficult to accept, after the treatment you've received from Peter Parfitt.'

'I have to believe you, Mr Leach, because I have no choice but to place myself in your hands. How would you summarize the current situation?'

'The situation is clear,' said Leach. 'Parfitt's campaign is well organized, and he now feels he's acting from a position of strength. I am assuming, Mr Kane, that you have the stomach for a fight.'

'I wouldn't be here if I didn't, Mr Leach. And now that you've summed up the position so succinctly, perhaps you'll allow me to suggest how we should go about defeating Mr Parfitt.'

'Certainly,' said Leach.

The eyes of all three bankers were fixed on William.

'You are undoubtedly right in suggesting that Parfitt feels he's in a strong position, because until now he's always been the one on the attack, knowing what's going to happen next. The time has come for us to go on the attack, where and when he least expects it – in his own boardroom.'

'How do you propose we go about that, Mr Kane?' asked Davies.

'I'll explain if you'll first permit me to ask you two questions. How many directors have a vote?'

'Sixteen,' said Leach instantly.

'And with whom does their allegiance lie at this moment?'

'Not the easiest question to answer, Mr Kane,' Davies chipped in. He took a crumpled envelope from his inside pocket and studied the back of it before he continued. 'I estimate that we can count on six certain votes, and Parfitt can be sure of five. But it came as a shock to me to discover this morning that Rupert Cork-Smith – he was Charles Lester's oldest friend – is unwilling to support you. It's very odd, because I know he doesn't care for Parfitt. That would make it six apiece.'

'So we have until Thursday,' said Leach, 'to make sure of three more votes.'

'Why Thursday?' asked William.

'That's the day of the next board meeting,' answered Leach, stroking his moustache. 'And Item One on the agenda is the election of a new chairman.'

'I was told the next board meeting wasn't until Monday,' said William in astonishment.

'By whom?' Davies asked.

'Peter Parfitt,' said William.

'His tactics,' Leach commented, 'have hardly been those of a gentleman.'

'I've learned enough about that gentleman,' William said,

placing an ironic stress on the word, 'to make me realize I'll have to take the battle to him.'

'Easier said than done, Mr Kane. He's very much in the driving seat at this moment,' said Davies, 'and I'm not sure how we go about removing him from it.'

'Let's switch the traffic lights to red,' replied William. All three men looked puzzled, but didn't comment. 'Who has the authority to call a board meeting?' he continued.

'While the board is without a chairman, either vice chairman,' said Ted Leach, 'which means Parfitt or me.'

'How many board members form a quorum?'

'Nine,' said Davies.

'And who is the company secretary?'

'I am,' said Alfred Rodgers, who until that moment had hardly opened his mouth – one of the many qualities William always looked for in a company secretary.

'How much notice do you have to give to call an emergency board meeting, Mr Rodgers?'

'Every director must be informed at least twenty-four hours beforehand, although it has never actually happened since the crash of twenty-nine. Charles Lester always tried to give at least six days' notice.'

'But the bank's rules do allow for an emergency meeting to be held at twenty-four hours' notice?' said William.

'Yes, they do, Mr Kane,' Rodgers affirmed, his monocle now firmly in place and focused on William.

'Excellent. Then let's call our own board meeting.'

The three bankers stared at him as if they had not quite heard him clearly.

'Think about it, gentlemen,' William continued. 'Mr Leach, as vice chairman, calls a board meeting, and Mr Rodgers, as company secretary, immediately informs all the directors.'

'When would you want this board meeting to take place?' asked Leach.

'Three o'clock tomorrow afternoon.'

'Good God, that's cutting it a bit fine,' said Rodgers. 'I'm not sure—'

'It's only cutting it a bit fine for Parfitt, wouldn't you say?' said William.

'Fair point,' said Leach. 'And what do you have planned for this meeting?'

'Leave that to me. Just be sure that it's legally convened, and that every director is given at least twenty-four hours' notice.'

'I wonder how Parfitt will react?' said Leach.

'I don't give a damn,' said William. 'That's the mistake we've been making all along. Let him start worrying about us for a change. As long as he's given the full twenty-four hours' notice and he's the last director informed, we have nothing to fear. We don't want him to have any more time than necessary to stage a counterattack. And gentlemen, don't be surprised by anything I do or say tomorrow. Trust my judgement; just make sure you're there to support me.'

'You don't feel we ought to know what you have in mind?'

'No, Mr Leach. You must appear to be uninvolved, and doing no more than carrying out your duty as directors of the bank. However, it will be important for Mr Rodgers to be fully prepared to conduct an election without looking as if he was aware it was coming.'

It was beginning to dawn on Ted Leach and his two colleagues why Charles Lester had chosen William Kane to be their next chairman. They left the Metropolitan Club a few minutes later, more confident than when they had arrived, despite being totally in the dark about what Kane had planned for the board meeting they were about to call. William, on the other hand, having carried out the first part of Thomas Cohen's instructions to his satisfaction, was actually looking forward to the more difficult second part.

He spent most of the afternoon and evening in his room at the Yale Club, making copious notes and going over his tactics for the next day's meeting. At six o'clock, he took a short break to call Kate.

'Where are you, darling?' she said. 'Stealing away in the middle of the night to I know not where.'

'To my New York mistress,' said William.

'Poor girl,' said Kate. 'What's her advice on the devious Mr Parfitt?'

'Haven't had time to ask her, we've been so busy doing other things. While I have you on the phone, what's your advice?'

'Do nothing Charles Lester or your father wouldn't have approved of,' said Kate, suddenly serious.

'They're probably playing golf together on the eighteenth cloud and taking a side bet, while keeping an eye on me the whole time.'

'Whatever you do, William, you won't go far wrong if you remember they're watching you.'

37

WHEN DAWN BROKE William was already awake, having managed to sleep only fitfully. He rose a little after six, had a cold shower, went for a long walk through Central Park to clear his head and returned to the Yale Club for a light breakfast. There was a message waiting for him in the front hall from his wife. He read it, and laughed out loud. 'If you're not too busy, could you remember to buy a New York Yankees baseball cap for Richard?'

He picked up a copy of *The Wall Street Journal*, which was still running the story of friction in Lester's boardroom over the selection of a new chairman. It now had Parfitt's version of events, hinting that his appointment would be confirmed at Thursday's board meeting. William wondered whose version would be reported in tomorrow's paper. How he would have liked to read Friday's *Journal* now.

After another call to Thomas Cohen, he spent the morning double-checking the articles of incorporation and the bylaws of Lester's Bank. He skipped lunch in favour of F.A.O. Schwarz, where he bought a baseball cap for his son.

At two-thirty he took a cab to Lester's Bank in Wall Street, and arrived outside the front door a few minutes before three. The young doorman asked him who he had an appointment with.

'I'm William Kane.'

'Yes, sir. You'll want the boardroom.'

Good Heavens, thought William, I don't even know where it is.

The doorman noticed his embarrassment. 'Take the corridor on the left, sir, and it's the second door on the right.'

'Thank you,' said William, and walked slowly down the long corridor. Until that moment, he had always thought the expression 'butterflies in the stomach' a stupid one. He felt that his heartbeat must be louder than the ticking of the clock in the hall; he would not have been surprised to hear himself chiming three o'clock.

Ted Leach was standing at the entrance to the boardroom. 'There's going to be trouble,' were his opening words.

'That's hardly a surprise,' said William. 'But that's the way Charles Lester would have liked it, because he always faced trouble head on.'

William strode into the impressive oak-panelled room, where a number of men were standing in groups of two or three, deep in conversation. He did not need to count heads to know that every director was present. This was not going to be one of those board meetings a director could afford to miss. The buzz of talk ceased the moment William entered the room. He took the chairman's place at the head of the long mahogany table before Peter Parfitt could realize what was happening.

'Gentlemen, please be seated,' he said, hoping his voice sounded authoritative.

Ted Leach and some of the other directors took their seats immediately; others seemed more reluctant.

'Before anyone says anything,' began William, 'I would, if you will allow me, like to make a brief opening statement, and then you can decide how you wish to proceed. I feel that's the least we can do to comply with the wishes of the late Charles Lester.'

One or two reluctant board members took their seats. Every eye in the room was fixed on William.

'Thank you, gentlemen. To start with, I would like to make it clear to all of you that I have absolutely no desire to be the chairman of this bank' – he paused for effect – 'unless it is the wish of the majority of its directors. I am, gentlemen, at present deputy chairman of Kane and Cabot, and own fifty-one per cent of that bank's stock. Kane and Cabot was founded by my grandfather, and I think it compares favourably in reputation, if not in size, with Lester's. Were I required to leave Boston and move to New York to become the next chairman of this bank, in compliance with Charles Lester's wishes, it would not be easy for myself or for my family. However, as it was Charles Lester's desire that I should do just that – and he was not a man to make such a proposition lightly – I am bound to take his wishes seriously. I would also like to add that his son, Matthew Lester, was my closest friend for over fifteen years, and I consider it a tragedy that it is me, and not him, who is addressing you today as your prospective chairman.'

Some of the directors nodded their approval.

'Gentlemen, if I were fortunate enough to secure your support today, I would be willing to sacrifice everything I have in Boston in order to serve you. I hope it is unnecessary for me to give you a detailed account of my banking experience. I shall assume that you will have taken the trouble to find out why Charles Lester thought I was the right man to succeed him. My own chairman, Tony Simmons, whom many of you know, has asked me to stay on at Kane and Cabot, and to ignore Mr Lester's wishes.

'I had intended to inform Mr Parfitt yesterday of my decision – had he taken the trouble to call me. I had the pleasure of dining with Mr and Mrs Parfitt last week at their home, and on that occasion Mr Parfitt informed me that he had no interest in becoming the next chairman of this bank. My only rival, in his opinion, was Mr Leach, your other vice chairman. I have since consulted Mr Leach, and he informs me that I have always had his support for the chair. I assumed, therefore, that both vice chairmen were backing me. But after reading this morning's *Wall Street Journal*, not that I have relied upon its predictions since I was eight years old' – a little laughter – 'I felt I should attend today's meeting to assure myself that I had not lost the support of both vice chairmen, and that the *Journal*'s account was inaccurate. Mr Leach called this board meeting, and I must now ask him if he still backs me to succeed Charles Lester as the bank's next chairman.'

William looked across at Leach, whose head was bowed. The wait for his verdict seemed interminable, although it was only a few seconds. A thumbs down from him would mean the Parfitt-lians would slaughter the Christian.

Leach raised his head slowly and said, 'Gentlemen, I support Mr Kane unreservedly.'

William looked directly at Peter Parfitt for the first time that day. He was sweating profusely, and when he spoke he did not raise his eyes from the yellow pad in front of him.

'Some members of the board,' he began, 'felt I should throw my hat into the ring—'

'And all this has happened since we spoke last week, when you told me you would be happy to go along with Charles Lester's wishes?' interrupted William, allowing a small note of surprise to enter his voice.

Parfitt raised his head a little. 'The situation is not quite that simple, Mr Kane.'

'Oh, yes it is, Mr Parfitt. Have you changed your mind since I dined in your home, or do you still support me?'

'I've been assured that it is the wish of several directors that I should stand against you.'

'Despite your telling me only a week ago you had no interest in being chairman?'

'I would like to be able to state my own position,' said Parfitt, 'before you assume too much. This is not your boardroom yet, Mr Kane.'

'Please do so, Mr Parfitt.'

So far the meeting had gone exactly as William had planned. His own speech had been carefully prepared, and Parfitt now laboured under the disadvantage of having lost the initiative, to say nothing of having been publicly denounced as duplicitous at best.

'Gentlemen,' he began, as if searching for words. 'Well . . .'

All eyes were now on Parfitt, giving William the chance to relax a little and study the faces of the other directors.

'Several members of the board approached me privately after I had dinner with Mr Kane,' said Parfitt, 'and I felt that it was no more than my duty to respect their wishes and offer myself for election. I have never at any time wanted to oppose the wishes of

Mr Lester, whom I greatly admired and respected. Naturally, I would have informed Mr Kane of my intention before Thursday's scheduled board meeting, but I confess to having been taken somewhat by surprise by today's events.'

He drew a deep breath. 'I have served Lester's for twenty-two years, six of them as your vice chairman. I feel, therefore, that I have the right to be considered for the chair. I would be delighted if Mr Kane were to join the board as deputy chairman, but I now find myself unable to back his appointment as chairman. I hope my fellow directors will support a man who has worked for this bank for over twenty years, rather than an unknown outsider chosen on the whim of a man distraught over the death of his only son. Thank you, gentlemen.'

Given the circumstances, William was rather impressed by the speech, but Parfitt did not have the benefit of Mr Cohen's advice on the power of the last word in a close contest. William rose again.

'Gentlemen, Mr Parfitt has pointed out that I am personally unknown to you. I therefore want none of you to be in any doubt about the type of man I am. As I have said, I am the grandson and the son of bankers. I've been a banker all my life, and it would be less than honest of me to pretend I would not be honoured to serve as the next chairman of Lester's. If, on the other hand, after all you have heard today, you decide to back Mr Parfitt, so be it. I will return to Boston and continue to serve my own bank quite happily. I will, moreover, announce publicly that I have no interest in being chairman of Lester's, so nobody will be able to accuse you of having failed in your duty to carry out the provisions of Charles Lester's will. I do not wish to become chairman by default, but by acclamation.

'There are, however, no conditions under which I would be willing to serve on your board under Mr Parfitt. I stand before you, gentlemen, at the grave disadvantage of being, in Mr Parfitt's words, "an unknown outsider". I have, however, the advantage of being supported by a man who cannot be present today; a man whom all of you respected and admired, a man not known for yielding to whims or making hasty decisions. I therefore suggest that the board waste no more time in deciding whom they wish to serve as the next chairman of Lester's. If any of you has any doubts about my ability to run this bank, then vote for Mr Parfitt. I shall not vote myself, gentlemen, and I assume Mr Parfitt will not do so either.'

'You *cannot* vote,' said Parfitt sharply. 'You are not a member of this board. I am, and I shall exercise my privilege and vote.'

'So be it, Mr Parfitt. No one will ever be able to say you did not take every possible opportunity to gain an advantage.'

William waited for his words to sink in. A director who was unknown to William looked as if he was about to speak, so he quickly continued, 'I will ask Mr Rodgers, as company secretary, to carry out the electoral procedure. When you have cast your votes, gentlemen, perhaps you could pass the ballot papers back to him.'

Alfred Rodgers' monocle had been popping in and out periodically throughout the meeting. Nervously, he passed voting slips to his fellow directors. When each had written down the name of the candidate he supported, the slips were returned to him.

'Perhaps it might be prudent, given the circumstances, Mr Rodgers, if the votes were counted aloud, thus making sure no inadvertent error is made that might lead to the necessity of a second ballot.'

'Certainly, Mr Kane.'

'Does that meet with your approval, Mr Parfitt?'

Parfitt nodded his agreement without looking up.

'Thank you. Perhaps you would be kind enough to read the votes out, Mr Rodgers.'

The company secretary opened the first voting slip.

'Parfitt.'

And then the second.

'Parfitt.'

The decision was now out of William's hands. The fate of the prize he had told Charles Lester at the age of twelve would be his, would be decided in the next few seconds.

'Kane. Parfitt. Kane.'

Three votes to two against him. Was he going to meet the same fate as he had in his contest with Tony Simmons?

'Kane. Kane. Parfitt.'

Four votes each. Parfitt was still sweating profusely, and he didn't exactly feel relaxed himself.

'Parfitt.'

No expression crossed William's face. Parfitt allowed himself a smile. Five votes to four.

'Kane. Kane. Kane.'

Parfitt's smile disappeared.

Just two more, two more, pleaded William, almost out loud.

'Parfitt. Parfitt.'

Rodgers took a long time opening a voting slip which someone had folded and refolded.

'Kane.'

Eight votes to seven in William's favour.

The last piece of paper was now being opened. William watched Alfred Rodgers's lips. The company secretary looked up; for that one moment he was the most important person in the room.

'Kane.'

Parfitt's head sank into his hands.

'Gentlemen,' declared the company secretary, 'the tally is nine votes for Mr Kane, seven votes for Mr Parfitt. I therefore declare Mr William Kane to be the duly elected chairman of Lester's Bank.'

A silence fell over the room as every head except Parfitt's turned towards William and waited for the new chairman's first words.

William exhaled a great rush of air, and stood once again, this time to face his board.

'Thank you, gentlemen, for the confidence you have placed in me. It was Charles Lester's desire that I should be your next chairman, and I am delighted you have confirmed his wishes with your vote. I promise that I will serve this bank to the best of my ability, but I will be unable to do so without the wholehearted support of the board. If Mr Parfitt would be kind enough . . .'

Parfitt looked up hopefully.

'. . . to join me in the chairman's office in a few minutes' time, I would be much obliged. After I have seen Mr Parfitt, I would then like to see Mr Leach. I hope, gentlemen, that during the next few days I will have the opportunity of meeting each of you individually. The next board meeting will be the scheduled monthly one. This meeting is now adjourned.'

The directors began to rise, talking among themselves. William walked quickly into the corridor, avoiding Peter Parfitt's stare. Ted Leach caught up with him and guided him to the chairman's office.

'That was some risk you took,' said Leach, 'and you only just pulled it off. What would you have done if you'd lost the vote?'

'Driven back to Boston and got on with my job,' said William, trying to sound unperturbed.

Leach opened the door to the chairman's office. The room was almost exactly as William remembered it; perhaps it had seemed a little larger when, as a prep school boy, he had told Charles Lester that one day he would run his bank. He glanced up at the portrait behind the desk and winked at the late chairman, then sat in the big red leather chair and put his elbows on the mahogany desk. He removed a small leather-bound book from his jacket pocket, placed it on the desk in front of him and waited. A moment later there was a knock on the door. An old man entered, leaning heavily on a black stick with a silver handle. Ted Leach left them alone.

'My name is Rupert Cork-Smith,' the man said, with a hint of an English accent.

William rose to greet him. He was the oldest member of the board. His long grey sideburns and heavy gold watch came from a past era, but his reputation for probity was legendary in banking circles. No man needed to sign a contract with Rupert Cork-Smith his word had always been his bond. He looked William firmly in the eye.

'I voted against you, sir, and naturally you can expect my resignation to be on your desk within the hour.'

'Will you have a seat, sir?' William said gently.

'Thank you, sir.'

'I think you knew my father and grandfather.'

'I had that privilege. Your grandfather and I were at Harvard together, and I remember your father's untimely death with considerable sadness.'

'And Charles Lester?' said William.

'Was my closest friend. The provision in his will has preyed upon my conscience. It was no secret that my first choice as chairman would not have been Peter Parfitt. I would have supported Ted Leach for the job, but I have never abstained from anything in my life, so I felt I had to support whichever candidate stood against you, as I found myself unable to vote for a man I had never met.'

'I'm grateful for your honesty, Mr Cork-Smith, but now I have a bank to run. I need you at this moment far more than you need me, so I beg you not to resign.'

The old man looked deeply into William's eyes. 'I'm not sure if it would work, young man. I can't change my attitudes over-night,' said Cork-Smith, both hands resting on his cane.

'Give me six months, sir, and if you still feel the same way, I won't put up a fight.'

There was a long silence before Cork-Smith spoke again: 'Charles Lester was right: you are the son of Richard Kane.'

'Will you continue to serve this bank, sir?'

'I will, young man. There's no fool like an old fool, don't you know.'

Rupert Cork-Smith rose slowly with the aid of his stick. William jumped up to help him, but was waved away.

'Good luck, my boy. You can rely on my total support.'

'Thank you, sir.'

When he opened the door, William saw Peter Parfitt waiting in the corridor. As Cork-Smith left, the two men did not speak.

Parfitt blustered in. 'Well, I tried, and I lost. A man can't do more,' he said, laughing. 'No hard feelings, Bill?' He extended his hand.

'There are no hard feelings, Mr Parfitt,' said William, not offering him a seat. 'As you rightly say, you tried, and you lost. You will now resign as a director of this bank.'

'I'll do what?' said Parfitt incredulously.

'Resign,' said William.

'That's a bit rough, isn't it, Bill? My action wasn't personal. I simply felt—'

'I don't want you in my bank, Mr Parfitt. You'll leave tonight and never set foot on the premises again.'

'And if I say I won't go? I own a good many shares in the bank and I still have a lot of support on the board. What's more, I could take you to court.'

'I would recommend that you read the bank's bylaws, Mr Parfitt.' William picked up the small leather-bound book that was lying on the desk and turned over a few pages. Having found a paragraph he had marked that morning, he read aloud. '"The chairman has the right to remove any office holder in whom he has lost confidence." I have lost confidence in you, Mr Parfitt, and you will therefore resign. You will receive two years' pay, and any other benefits to which you are entitled. If, on the other hand, you force me to remove you, you will leave the bank with nothing other than your stock and your reputation, whatever that is worth. The choice is yours.'

'Won't you give me a second chance?'

'I gave you a chance last week when you invited me to dinner, and you lied and dissembled. Those are not traits I am looking for in my deputy chairman. Will it be resignation, or do I have to throw you out, Mr Parfitt?'

'Damn you, Kane. I'll resign.'

'Good. Then you'll sit down and write the letter now.'

'No. I'll let you have it in the morning, in my own good time.'

'Now – or I'll fire you,' said William.

Parfitt hesitated, then sank heavily into a chair. William

handed him a sheet of the bank's headed paper and proffered a pen. Parfitt took out his own pen and started writing. When the letter was finished, William picked it up and read it through carefully.

'Good day, Mr Parfitt.'

Parfitt left without another word. William allowed himself a smile as Ted Leach entered the room.

'You asked to see me, Mr Chairman?'

'Yes,' said William. 'I want to appoint you as the bank's new deputy chairman. Mr Parfitt felt he had to resign.'

'Oh, I'm surprised to hear that. I would have thought . . .'

William passed him the letter. Leach read it and then looked back at William.

'I shall be delighted to be deputy chairman. Thank you for your confidence in me.'

'Good. I'd be obliged if you would arrange for me to meet every director during the next few days. I'll be at my desk at eight o'clock tomorrow morning.'

'Yes, Mr Chairman.'

'Perhaps you will also be kind enough to give Mr Parfitt's letter of resignation to the company secretary?'

'As you wish, Mr Chairman.'

'My name is William – that was another mistake Mr Parfitt made.'

Leach smiled tentatively. 'I'll see you tomorrow morning' – he hesitated – 'William.'

After he'd left, William sat in Charles Lester's chair and whirled himself around in an uncharacteristic burst of sheer glee until he was dizzy. He then looked out of the window onto Wall Street, elated by the bustling crowds and the sight of the leading banks and brokerage houses of America. This was where he'd wanted to be all his life.

'And who, pray, are you?' demanded a female voice from behind him.

He swivelled around to find a primly dressed middle-aged woman looking at him irately.

'I might ask you the same question,' said William.

'I am the chairman's secretary,' the woman said stiffly.

'And I,' said William, 'am the chairman.'

◄o►

William moved to New York the following Monday, but it was some weeks before Kate and the family were able to join him. First he had to find a house suitable for the new chairman of Lester's Bank, and more importantly a school that could guarantee Richard a place first at St Paul's, and later at Harvard.

For the next three months, as William tried to extricate himself from Boston as well as carrying out his job in New York, he wished that every day had forty-eight hours. He found the umbilical cord was harder to sever than he'd anticipated. Tony Simmons was fully supportive, and William began to appreciate why Alan Lloyd had backed him to be chairman of Kane and Cabot. For the first time he was even willing to admit that Alan might have been right.

Kate's life in New York was soon fully occupied. Virginia could almost toddle across a room and find her way into William's study before Kate could catch up with her, and all Richard wanted was a new Windbreaker so he would be like every other boy in New York. As the wife of the chairman of a New York bank Kate was expected to give cocktail parties and private dinners regularly, subtly making sure that directors and major clients always had a chance to have a private word with William, so they could seek his advice or voice their opinions. She handled these occasions with great charm and diplomacy, and William was eternally grateful to the liquidation department of Kane and Cabot for supplying him with his greatest asset.

When Kate informed him that she was going to have another baby, all he could ask was, 'When did I find the time?' Virginia was thrilled by the news, not fully understanding why Mummy was getting so fat, and Richard refused to discuss it.

◄o►

When William faced his first AGM a month later, his position as chairman was unanimously confirmed. William tried not to smile when Mr Cohen reminded him that several of the shareholders wouldn't inherit a dime if they failed to vote for him. William was surprised to see Peter Parfitt seated in the back row, arms folded, and even more surprised to see Susan Lester seated next to him. When it came to the vote their arms remained folded.

◄○►

Kate gave birth to their third child at the end of William's first year as chairman of Lester's, a second girl, whom they named Lucy. William taught Virginia how to rock Lucy's cradle; while Richard, now ready to enter the first grade at the Buckley School, used the new arrival as the opportunity to talk his father into buying him a new baseball bat. Lucy, unable to make any articulate demands, nevertheless became the third woman who could twist William around her little finger.

In William's first year as chairman of Lester's the bank's profits were slightly up, and he assured the shareholders who attended his second AGM that he could see no reason why there shouldn't be an even greater improvement next year.

38

ON SEPTEMBER 1, 1939, German troops marched into Poland.

One of William's first reactions was to think of Abel Rosnovski. The new Baron hotel on Park Avenue was already becoming the toast of New York, and the quarterly reports from Thomas Cohen showed that Rosnovski was going from strength to strength. But his latest ideas for expansion into Europe might now have to be put on hold for some time. Cohen could still find no direct association between Rosnovski and Henry Osborne.

William had never thought that America would involve herself in another European war, but he kept the London branch of Lester's open to indicate which side he was on, and never for one moment considered selling off his twelve thousand acres in Hampshire and Lincolnshire. Tony Simmons, on the other hand, informed William that he intended to close Kane and Cabot's London branch.

The two chairmen now met regularly, on relaxed and friendly terms since they no longer had any reason to see themselves as rivals. Each had come to use the other as a sounding board for new ideas. As Tony had predicted, Kane and Cabot had lost some of its more important clients when William became the chairman of Lester's, but William always kept Tony fully informed whenever an old client expressed a desire to move his account, and he never solicited anyone to join him. When they sat down at a corner table of Locke Ober's for their monthly lunch, Tony lost no time in repeating his intention to close the London branch of Kane and Cabot.

'But why?' asked William.

'My first reason is simple,' said Tony as he sipped his imported Burgundy, not giving a moment's thought to the likelihood that German boots were about to trample on the grapes in most of the vineyards of France. 'I think the bank will lose money if we don't cut our losses and get out of England.'

'Of course you might lose a little money,' said William, 'but we must be seen to be supporting the British.'

'Why?' asked Tony. 'We're a bank, not a supporters' club.'

'Britain's not a baseball team, Tony; it's a nation of people to whom we owe our entire heritage . . .'

'You should take up politics,' said Tony. 'I'm beginning to think your talents are wasted in banking. Nevertheless, there's another, far more important reason why we should close the branch. If the Germans were to march into Britain the way they have into Poland and France – and in Joe Kennedy's opinion, that is exactly what they plan to do – the bank will be taken over and we would lose every penny we have in London.'

'Over my dead body,' said William. 'If Hitler puts so much as a foot on British soil, America will enter the war the same day, whatever our ambassador in London says.'

'Never,' said Tony. 'FDR has said again and again, "All aid short of war." And in any case, the America Firsters would raise an almighty hue and cry.'

'Never listen to a politician who says never,' said William. 'Especially Roosevelt. When he says "never", that only means not today, or at least not this morning. You only have to remember that Woodrow Wilson never stopped saying "never" in 1916.'

Tony laughed. 'When are you going to run for the Senate, William?'

'Never,' said William with a smile.

'I respect your feelings, William, but I want out.'

'You're the chairman,' replied William. 'If the board backs you, you can close the London branch tomorrow. I would never use my position to act against a majority decision, as you well know.'

'Until you merge Kane and Cabot with Lester's. Then it would become your decision.'

'I've told you before, Tony, I'd never attempt to do that while you're chairman.'

'But I think we *ought* to merge.'

'What?' said William, spilling some Burgundy on the table-cloth, unable to believe what he'd just heard. 'Good heavens, Tony, I'll say one thing for you, you're never predictable.'

'I have the best interests of the bank at heart, as always, William. Think about the present situation for a moment. New York is now, more than ever, the centre of US finance, and when England is invaded by Hitler, it will become the centre of world finance. In fact, I'd go further and say that given those circumstances the dollar will replace the pound as the world's leading currency. That's where Kane and Cabot needs to be. And if we merged we'd create a more broadly based institution, because our specialties are complementary. Kane and Cabot has always done a great deal of ship and heavy-industry financing, while Lester's does very little. Conversely, you do a lot of underwriting, and we hardly touch it. Not to mention the fact that in several European cities we're unnecessarily duplicating offices.'

'Tony, I agree with everything you've said, but I still want to keep a presence in Britain.'

'Exactly proving my point. Kane and Cabot's London branch might close, but we'd still have Lester's. Then if London goes through a rough patch, it wouldn't matter as much, because we'd be consolidated, and therefore stronger.'

'But Roosevelt's restrictions on merchant banks would mean we could only work out of one state. So a merger could only succeed if we ran the entire operation from New York, leaving Boston as nothing more than a branch office.'

'I'd still back you,' said Tony. 'You might even consider taking Lester's into commercial banking, which would solve the whole problem.'

'No, Tony. FDR's made it impossible for an honest man to do both. In any case, my father taught me that you can serve either a small group of rich people or a large group of poor people, but not both, so Lester's will remain in traditional merchant banking as long as I'm chairman. But if we did decide to merge the banks, don't you foresee other problems?'

'Very few we couldn't overcome, given goodwill on both sides. But you'd have to consider the implications carefully, William, because after a merger you'd become a minority shareholder, and would lose overall control of the new bank. That would leave you vulnerable to a takeover bid.'

'I'll take that risk, if it means I'd become chairman of one of the largest financial institutions in America.'

—◦—

William returned to New York that evening, and immediately called a board meeting of Lester's to outline Tony Simmons's proposal. Once he found that the board approved of a merger in principle, he instructed each of the bank's vice presidents to consider the full implications in greater detail.

The departmental heads took three months before they reported back to the board, and to a man they came to the same conclusion: a merger was no more than common sense, not least because the two banks were complementary in so many ways. Moreover, William's shareholdings ensured that Lester's would own 51 per cent of Kane and Cabot, making the merger simply a marriage of convenience. Some of the directors could not understand why William hadn't thought of the idea before. Ted Leach was of the opinion that Charles Lester must have had it in his mind when he nominated William as his successor.

The details of the merger took over a year to complete as teams of lawyers were kept at work into the small hours preparing the necessary paperwork. In the exchange of shares, William ended up as the largest stockholder with 8 per cent of the new company, and was appointed the new bank's president and chairman. Tony Simmons remained in Boston as one deputy chairman, with Ted Leach in New York as the other. The new merchant bank was renamed Lester, Kane and Company, but continued to be referred to as Lester's.

William arranged a press conference in New York to announce the successful merger, and he chose Monday, December 8, 1941, to brief the financial world of his vision for the future. The press conference was cancelled when, hours before, the Japanese launched their attack on Pearl Harbor.

An embargoed press release had been sent to the newspapers some days before, but the news that America had declared war on Japan meant that the Tuesday-morning financial pages allocated the announcement of the merger only a few column inches. This lack of coverage, however, was not foremost in William's mind.

He couldn't work out how or when he was going to tell Kate that it was his intention to join up.

PART FIVE

1941–1948

39

ABEL STUDIED the news item on the merger of Lester, Kane and Company in the financial section of the *Chicago Tribune*.

With all the space devoted to America entering the war, he would have missed the brief announcement had it not been accompanied by a small photograph of William Kane, so out of date that it looked as if he hadn't changed since his meeting with Abel in Boston more than ten years before. Certainly he appeared too young to fit the journal's description of him as the brilliant and incisive chairman of the newly formed Lester, Kane and Company. The article went on to predict: 'The new company, a joining together of two old established family banks, could well become one of the most prestigious financial institutions in America.' The *Trib* concluded that the stock would be divided between about twenty shareholders who were related to, or closely associated with the Lester and the Kane families. The largest shareholders would be Mr Kane with eight per cent, and the late Mr Lester's daughter with six per cent.

Abel was delighted by this particular piece of information, realizing that it meant Kane must have sacrificed overall control of the bank to become chairman of a far larger institution. He read the item again, and couldn't deny that William Kane had risen far higher in the world since they had crossed swords, but then so had he. And he still had an old score to settle with the newly designated chairman of Lester, Kane and Company.

So handsomely had the Baron Group's fortunes prospered over the past decade that Abel had been able to repay all the

377

loans to his backer within the stipulated ten-year period, securing him 100 per cent of the company.

Not only had he paid off the loan by the last quarter of 1939, but the profits for 1940 had passed the half-million mark. This milestone coincided with the opening of two new Barons, in Washington and San Francisco.

Although Abel had become a less attentive husband during this period, as much a result of Zaphia's unwillingness to keep pace with his ambitions as anything else, he could not have been a more doting father. Zaphia, longing for a second child, finally goaded him into seeing his doctor. When he learned that because of a low sperm count, probably caused by sickness and malnutrition in his days as a prisoner of the Germans and the Russians, Florentyna would almost certainly be his only child, he gave up all hope of a son, and proceeded to lavish everything on his daughter.

Abel's reputation as a hotelier was quickly spreading across America, and the press had taken to referring to him as 'The Chicago Baron'. He no longer cared about the jokes behind his back. Wladek Koskiewicz had arrived and, more importantly, he was here to stay. The profits from his fourteen hotels for the last fiscal year were just short of a million dollars, and with this new surplus of capital, he decided the time had come for even further expansion.

Then the Japanese attacked Pearl Harbor.

Since that dreadful day of September 1, 1939, when the Nazis had marched into Poland, later to meet the Russians at Brest-Litovsk and once again divide his homeland between them, Abel had been sending large sums of money to the British Red Cross for the relief of his countrymen. He had waged a fierce battle, both within the Democratic Party and in the press, to push an unwilling America into the war, even if it meant being on the side of the Russians. His efforts so far had been fruitless, but on that Sunday in December, with every radio station across the country blaring out the details of the Japanese attack to an incredulous nation, Abel knew that America could no longer sit on the fence.

The following day he listened to President Roosevelt inform

the nation that America was at war with Japan, and three days later, on December 11th, Hitler told the world that Germany and Italy had declared war on the United States.

Abel had every intention of assisting the Allied effort, but first he had a private declaration of war he wished to make, and to that end he placed a call to Curtis Fenton at the Continental Trust Bank. Over the years Abel had grown to trust Fenton's judgement, and he had kept him on the board of the Baron Group long after he gained overall control, as he wished to retain a close link with the Continental Trust.

Fenton came on the line, with his usual formal but cautious manner.

'How much spare cash am I holding in the group's reserve account?' asked Abel.

Fenton extracted the file marked 'Number 6 Account', recalling the days when he could have put all Mr Rosnovski's affairs into one small file. He scanned some figures.

'A little under two million dollars.'

'Good,' said Abel. 'I want you to start taking an interest in a bank called Lester, Kane and Company. Find out the name of every shareholder, what percentage they hold, and if there are any conditions under which they'd be willing to sell. All this must be done without the knowledge of the bank's chairman, Mr William Kane, and without any mention of my name.'

Fenton took a deep breath, but said nothing. He was glad that Abel could not see the look of anguish on his face. Why would he want to put money into anything to do with William Kane? Fenton had also read in *The Wall Street Journal* about the merging of the two famous family banks, although what with Pearl Harbor and his wife's birthday, he had nearly missed the announcement. Rosnovski's request jogged his memory – he must send a congratulatory wire to William Kane. He pencilled a note on the bottom of the Baron Group file while listening to Abel's instructions.

'When you have it all broken down, I want to be briefed in person, nothing on paper.'

'Yes, Mr Rosnovski.'

'I'd also like you to add to your quarterly reports the details of every official statement issued by Lester's, and to find out which companies they do business with.'

'Certainly, Mr Rosnovski.'

'Thank you, Mr Fenton. By the way, my market research team is advising me to open a new Baron in Montreal.'

'The war doesn't worry you, Mr Rosnovski?'

'Good God, no. If the Germans reach Montreal we can all close down, Continental Trust included. In any case, we beat the bastards last time, and we'll beat them again. The only difference is that this time I intend to be part of the action. Good day, Mr Fenton.'

Will I ever understand what goes on in the mind of Abel Rosnovski? Curtis Fenton wondered as he hung up the phone. His thoughts switched back to Mr Rosnovski's other request, for the details on Lester's stock. This worried him even more than his attitude to the Germans, as clearly he considered both as the enemy. Although William Kane no longer had any connection with Rosnovski, Fenton feared where it might end if Rosnovski obtained a substantial holding in the new bank. He decided against expressing his fears to Rosnovski for the time being, supposing the day would come when one of them would explain what they were up to.

Abel had wondered if he should tell Fenton why he wanted to buy stock in Lester's, but came to the conclusion that the fewer people who knew, the better.

He put William Kane temporarily out of his mind and asked his secretary to find George, who he'd recently appointed a vice president of the Baron Group in charge of new acquisitions. George had progressed under Abel's wing, and was now his most trusted lieutenant. Sitting in his office on the 42nd floor of the Chicago Baron, Abel looked down on Lake Michigan, but his thoughts were on Poland. He knew he could never live in his homeland again, but he still wanted his castle restored to him. He feared that he would never see the castle again, now that it was well inside Russian territory and under Stalin's control. The idea of the Germans or the Russians once again occupying his magnificent castle made him want to— His thoughts were interrupted by George.

'You wanted to see me, Abel?'

George was the only member of the group who called the Chicago Baron by his first name.

'Yes, George. Do you think you could keep the hotels ticking over for a few months if I were to take a leave of absence?'

'Sure can,' said George. 'Does this mean you're finally going to take that vacation?'

'No. I'm going to war.'

'What?' said George. 'Who with?'

'I'm flying to New York tomorrow morning to enlist in the army.'

'You're crazy – you could get yourself killed.'

'That isn't what I had in mind,' replied Abel. 'Killing some Germans is what I plan to do. The bastards didn't get me the first time around, and I have no intention of letting them get me now.'

George continued to protest that America could win the war without Abel's help. Zaphia protested too; she hated the very thought of war. Florentyna, almost eight years old, wasn't quite sure what war meant, but she did understand that Daddy would have to go away for a very long time. She burst into tears.

Despite their combined protests, Abel took the first flight to New York the following day. All America seemed to be travelling in different directions, and he found the city full of young men in khaki or navy blue bidding farewell to parents, sweethearts and wives, assuring them – but not always believing – that now America had joined the war, it would be over in a few weeks.

He arrived at the New York Baron in time for dinner. The dining room was packed, with girls clinging desperately to soldiers, sailors and airmen, while Frank Sinatra crooned to the rhythms of Tommy Dorsey's big band. As Abel watched the young people on the dance floor, he wondered how many of them would ever have a chance to enjoy an evening like this again. He couldn't help remembering Sammy's explanation of how he had become maître d' at the Plaza. The three men senior to him had returned from the western front with one leg between them. None of the kids dancing tonight could begin to know what war was really like. He couldn't join in the celebration – if that's what it was. He went up to his room instead.

In the morning he dressed in a plain dark double-breasted suit and reported to the recruiting office in Times Square. Abel signed in as Wladek Koskiewicz, painfully aware that if they knew it was the Chicago Baron who was trying to enlist he would end up in a swivel chair with gold braid on his sleeve.

The recruiting office was even more crowded than the hotel dance floor had been the night before, but here no one was clinging on to anyone. Abel couldn't help noticing that the other recruits appeared to be a great deal younger and fitter than him. The entire morning had passed before he was handed and had filled out one form – a task he estimated would have taken his secretary ten minutes. He then stood in line for two more hours, waiting to be interviewed by a recruiting sergeant, who asked him what he did for a living.

'Hotel management,' said Abel, and went on to tell the officer of his experiences during the first war. The sergeant stared in silent disbelief at the five foot seven, 190-pound man standing in front of him.

'You'll have to take a full physical tomorrow morning,' the recruiting sergeant said when Abel's monologue had come to an end, adding, as if it was no less than his duty, 'Thank you for volunteering, Mr Koskiewicz.'

The next day Abel had to wait several more hours for his physical examination. The doctor in charge was fairly blunt about his general condition. He had been protected from such comments for several years by his position and success, and it came as a rude awakening when he was classified as 4F.

'You're overweight, your eyes aren't too good and you have a limp. Frankly, Koskiewicz, you're plain unfit. We can't take soldiers into battle who are likely to have a heart attack even before they find the enemy. That doesn't mean we can't use your talents; there's a lot of admin work to be done in this war, if you're interested.'

'No, thank you – sir. I want to fight the Germans, not send them letters.'

He returned to his hotel that evening depressed, but decided he wasn't licked yet. The next day he tried another recruiting office, but he slumped back to the Baron after the same result. The second doctor had been a little more polite, but he was every bit as firm about Abel's condition, and once again he ended up with a 4F classification. It was obvious to Abel that he was not going to be allowed to fight anybody in his present state of health.

At seven o'clock the next morning he enrolled in a gymnasium on West Fifty-Seventh Street, where he engaged a private instructor to do something about his physical condition. For three months he worked every day on reducing his weight and improving his general fitness. He boxed, wrestled, ran, jumped, skipped, pressed weights and starved. When he was down to 155 pounds, the instructor told him he was never going to be much fitter or thinner. Abel returned to the first recruiting office and filled in the same form, once again signing it Wladek Koskiewicz. Another recruiting sergeant was a lot more responsive this time, and the medical officer put him on the reserve list.

'But I want to go to war now,' said Abel. 'Before it's all over.'

'We'll be in touch with you, Koskiewicz,' said the sergeant. 'Just keep yourself fit. There's no telling when we'll need you.'

Abel left, furious, as younger, leaner men were signed up without question for active service. As he barged through the door he walked straight into a tall, gangling man wearing a uniform adorned with medals and stars on its shoulders.

'I'm sorry, sir,' said Abel.

'Young man . . .' said the general.

Abel walked on, not thinking that the general could possibly be addressing him, as no one had called him young man for – he didn't want to think how long, even though he was still only thirty-five.

The general tried again. 'Young man,' he said a little louder.

This time Abel turned around. 'Me, sir?'

'Yes, you, sir. Will you come to my office please, Mr Rosnovski?'

Damn, thought Abel. Now nobody's going to let me join in this war.

The general's temporary office turned out to be at the back of the building, a small room with a desk, two wooden chairs, peeling green paint and no door. Abel would not have allowed the most junior member of his staff at a Baron to work in such conditions.

'Mr Rosnovski,' the general began, 'my name is Mark Clark and I command the US Fifth Army. I'm here on an inspection tour, so literally bumping into you was a pleasant surprise. I've been an admirer of yours for a long time. Your story is one to inspire any American. So tell me what you are doing in a recruiting office.'

'What do you think?' said Abel, not thinking. 'I'm sorry, sir,' he corrected himself quickly. 'I didn't mean to be rude, it's just that no one wants to let me take part in this damn war.'

'What do you want to do in this damn war?'

'Sign up and fight the Germans.'

'As a foot soldier?' asked the general incredulously.

'Yes, sir. Don't you need every man you can get?'

'We most certainly do,' said General Clark, 'but I can put your particular talents to far better use than as a foot soldier.'

'I'll do anything,' said Abel. 'Anything.'

'Will you, now? Anything? If I asked you to place your hotel at my disposal as our army headquarters in New York, how would you react to that? Because frankly, Mr Rosnovski, that would be far more use to me than if you personally managed to kill a dozen Germans.'

'The Baron is yours. Now will you let me go to war?'

'You know you're mad, don't you?' said General Clark.

'I'm Polish,' said Abel, and they both laughed. 'You must understand,' Abel continued, his tone once again serious, 'I was born in Poland. I saw my home taken by the Germans, my sister raped by the Russians. I escaped from a Russian labour camp, and was lucky enough to reach the safety of these shores. I'm not mad. This is the only country on earth where you can arrive with nothing and make something of yourself through hard work, regardless of your background. Now those same bastards who tried to stop me the first time round want another war. Well, I'm going to make sure they lose it.'

'Well, if you're so eager to join up, Mr Rosnovski, I could use you, but not in the way you imagine. General Deniers needs someone to take overall responsibility as quartermaster for the Fifth Army while they're fighting in the front line. Napoleon was right when he said an army marches on its stomach, so you could play a vital role. The job carries the rank of major. That's one way in which you could unquestionably help America to win the war. What do you say?'

'I'll do it, General.'

'Thank you, Major Rosnovski.'

◄○►

Abel spent the weekend in Chicago with Zaphia and Florentyna. Zaphia asked him what he wanted her to do with his fifteen suits.

'Hold onto them,' he replied. 'I'm not going to war to get killed.'

'I'm pretty confident you won't be killed in a Baron hotel,' she said. 'That wasn't what I meant. It's just that your suits are now all three sizes too large for you.'

Abel laughed, and took all his old clothes to the Polish refugee centre. He then flew back to New York, cancelled any advance reservations for the Baron, and twelve days later handed the building over to the American Fifth Army. The press hailed this act as 'the selfless gesture of a man who had been a refugee during the First World War'.

For the next eight months Abel organized the smooth running of the New York Baron for General Clark and only after continual grumbling was he finally called up for active duty. He reported to Fort Benning to complete an officers' training programme. When he finally received his orders to join General Deniers of the Fifth Army, his destination turned out to be somewhere in North Africa. He began to wonder if he would ever set foot on German soil.

The day before Abel left to go overseas, he drew up a will, instructing his executors to offer the Baron Group to David Maxton on favourable terms should he not return. He divided the rest of his estate between Zaphia and Florentyna. It was the first time in two decades that he had thought about death – not that he was sure how he could get himself killed in a regimental canteen.

As his troop ship sailed out of New York harbour, Abel looked across at the Statue of Liberty, remembering how he had felt on seeing the statue for the first time nearly twenty years before. Once the ship had passed the Lady he did not look at her again, but said out loud, 'Next time I look you in the eye, ma'am, America will have won this war.'

◄◦►

Abel crossed the Atlantic with two of his top chefs and five kitchen staff who had recently enlisted. The ship docked in Algiers in May 1942. Abel immediately commandeered the only half-decent hotel in Algiers, and turned it into a headquarters for General Clark. He spent almost a year in the heat and the dust and the sand of the desert, making sure that every member of the division was as well fed as possible.

'We eat badly, but my bet is that we eat a damn sight better than the Germans,' was General Clark's comment.

Although he knew he was playing a valuable role in the war, Abel still itched to get into a real fight, but a quartermaster-major in charge of catering is rarely sent to the front line other than to fill empty billycans.

He wrote regularly to Zaphia and George, and watched by photograph as his beloved Florentyna grew up. He received the occasional letter from Curtis Fenton, reporting that the Baron Group was making steady progress, as every hotel on the Eastern Seaboard was packed because of the continual movement of troops and civilians. Abel was sad not to have been at the opening of the Montreal Baron, where George had represented him. It was the first time he had missed the launch of a new hotel, but it made him realize just how much he had achieved in America, and how much more he wanted to return to the land he now felt was his home – but not before the war was over.

Abel soon became bored with Africa and its mess kits, baked beans, blankets and fly swatters. There had been one or two spirited skirmishes out in the western desert, or so the men returning from the front assured him, but he never saw any action himself. He even drove one of the supply trucks to the front so that he could hear the firing, but it only made him even more frustrated.

One day, to his delight, orders came through that the Fifth Army was to be posted to Italy. Abel hoped this might eventually lead to a chance to see his homeland once again.

The Fifth Army, led by General Clark, landed in amphibious craft on the southern Italian coast, with aircraft giving tactical cover. They met considerable resistance, first at Anzio and then at Monte Cassino, but the action never involved Abel. His chest was now covered in medals that showed where he'd been, not what he'd done. He began to dread the end of a war in which he'd seen no combat, and would end up decorated for serving a million meals. But he could never come up with a plan that would get him to the front line. His chances were not improved when he was promoted to Lieutenant Colonel and sent to London to await further orders.

—◦—

After D-Day in June 1944, the great thrust across the English Channel and into Europe began. Abel was transferred to the First Army under General Omar N. Bradley, and detailed to the Ninth Armored Division. The Allies liberated Paris on August 25, and Abel paraded with the American and Free French soldiers down the Champs Elysées to a heroes' reception, even if he was some way behind General de Gaulle. He studied the unbombed magnificent city, and decided on the site where he would build the first Baron hotel in Europe.

The Allies moved on through France and crossed the German border in the final push towards Berlin. Local provisions were almost non-existent, because the countryside through which the

Allies marched had been ravaged by the retreating German army. Whenever Abel arrived in a new town, he would commandeer the largest hotel and the remaining food supplies before any other American quartermaster had worked out where to start looking. British and American officers were always happy to dine with the Ninth Armored Division, and wondered how it managed to requisition such fresh provisions. On one occasion when General George S. Patton joined General Bradley for dinner, Abel was introduced to the fighting general, who always led his troops into battle brandishing an ivory-handled revolver.

'The best meal I've had in the whole damn war,' declared Patton.

─◦─

By February 1945 Abel had been in uniform for nearly three years, and he realized the war in Europe would be over in a matter of months. General Bradley kept sending him congratulatory notes and meaningless decorations to adorn his ever-expanding uniform, but they didn't help. Abel begged to be allowed to fight in just one battle, but Bradley continued to turn a deaf ear.

Although it was the responsibility of a junior officer to lead the supply trucks up to the front lines and supervise food for the troops, Abel often carried out that duty himself. And as he did in the running of his hotels, he never allowed any of his staff to know when or where he would next appear.

It was the continual flow of blanket-covered soldiers on stretchers into camp that March morning that made Abel decide to take a look for himself. He could no longer bear the one-way traffic of limbless bodies. He rounded up a lieutenant, a sergeant, two corporals and twenty-eight privates, and headed for the front.

The twenty-mile drive was excruciatingly slow that morning. Abel took the wheel of the leading truck – it made him feel a little like General Patton – as his convoy inched its way through heavy rain and thick mud; he had to pull off the road several times to allow ambulance details the right of way as they returned from the front. Wounded bodies took precedence over empty stomachs. Abel prayed that most were no more than wounded, but only an occasional nod or wave suggested any sign of life. It became more obvious to Abel with each mud-clogged mile that something big was going on near Remagen, and he could feel the beat of his heart quicken.

When he finally reached the command post he could hear enemy fire in the near distance. He pounded his leg in anger as he watched stretcher-bearers bringing back yet more dead and wounded comrades. He was sick of learning about the war at second hand. He suspected that any reader of *The New York Times* was better informed than he was.

Abel brought his convoy to a halt by the side of the field kitchen and jumped out of the truck, shielding himself from the heavy rain, feeling ashamed that others only a few miles away were shielding themselves from bullets. He supervised the unloading of 100 gallons of soup, a ton of corned beef, 200 chickens, half a ton of butter, 3 tons of potatoes and 100 ten-pound cans of baked beans – plus boxes of the inevitable K rations – in readiness for those going to, or returning from, the battlefield. He left his cooks to prepare the meal and the orderlies to peel the potatoes, while he went straight to the tent of the commanding officer, Brigadier General John Leonard, passing yet more dead and wounded soldiers on the way.

As he was about to enter the tent, General Leonard, accompanied by his aide, came rushing out. He conducted a conversation with Abel while on the move.

'What can I do for you, Colonel?' Leonard asked.

'I've started preparing the food for your battalion, sir, as requested in overnight orders.'

'You needn't bother with the food for now, Colonel. At first light this morning Lieutenant Burrows of the Ninth discovered an undamaged railroad bridge north of Remagen – the Ludendorff Bridge – and I gave orders that it should be crossed immediately and a bridgehead established on the far side of the river. Up to now, the Germans have blown up every bridge across the Rhine long before we got there, so we can't hang around waiting for lunch before they demolish this one.'

'Did the Ninth get across?' asked Abel.

'Sure did,' replied the general, 'but they encountered heavy resistance from a forest on the far side. The first platoons were ambushed, and God knows how many men we lost. So you'd better hold that food, Colonel, because my only interest now is in seeing how many of my men I can get back alive so they can join you for dinner.'

'Is there anything I can do to help?' asked Abel.

Leonard stopped walking for a moment, and studied the overweight colonel who had clearly seen no action.

'How many men do you have under your direct command?'

'One lieutenant, one sergeant, two corporals and twenty-eight privates. Thirty-three in all, including myself, sir.'

'Good. Report to the field hospital with your men. Turn them into stretcher-bearers, and bring back as many wounded as you can.'

'Yes, sir.' Abel ran all the way back to the field kitchen, where he found most of his men sitting in a corner of the tent, smoking.

'Get up, you lazy bastards. We've got real work to do for a change.'

Thirty-two men snapped to attention.

'Follow me!' shouted Abel. 'On the double!'

He turned and started running again, this time towards the field hospital. A young doctor was briefing sixteen medical corpsmen when Abel and his out-of-breath, unfit, untrained unit appeared at the entrance of the tent.

'Can I help you, sir?' asked the doctor.

'No, but I hope I can help you. I have thirty-two men who've been detailed by General Leonard to join your group.' It was the first his men had heard of it.

The doctor stared in amazement at the colonel. 'Yes, sir.'

'Don't call me sir,' said Abel. 'We're here to assist you.'

'Yes, sir,' the doctor repeated.

He handed Abel a carton of Red Cross armbands, which the cooks, kitchen orderlies and potato peelers put on as the doctor briefed them on what was taking place in the forest on the other side of the Ludendorff Bridge.

'The Ninth has sustained heavy casualties. Those of you with medical expertise will remain in the battle zone, while the rest will bring back as many of the wounded as possible.'

Abel was delighted to be taking an active part in the war at last. The doctor, now in command of forty-nine men, allocated eighteen stretchers, and each soldier received a full medical pack. He then led his motley band through the mud and rain towards the Ludendorff Bridge, with Abel only a yard behind. When they reached the Rhine they saw row upon row of blankets, covering lifeless bodies. They marched silently across the bridge in single file, passing the remnants of the German explosion that had failed to destroy the foundations of the bridge.

On up towards the forest they marched, the sound of gunfire growing in intensity. Abel found himself simultaneously exhilarated by being so close to the enemy, and horrified by the evidence of what modern weaponry was capable of inflicting on his fellow man. From everywhere came cries of anguish from his comrades who until that day had wistfully thought the end of the war was near. For many of them, it was over.

The young doctor stopped again and again, doing the best he could for each man he came across. Sometimes he would mercifully put an end to a wounded man's suffering with a single shot of his pistol. Abel guided the walking wounded back towards the Ludendorff Bridge, and organized the stretcher-bearers to assist those unable to help themselves. By the time they reached the edge of the forest, only the doctor, one of the potato peelers and Abel were left of the original party; all the others were assisting the wounded back to the field hospital.

As the three of them entered the forest, they could hear enemy guns roaring ahead of them. Abel saw the outline of a big German gun, hidden in undergrowth and still pointing towards the bridge, but damaged beyond repair. Then he heard a volley of bullets that sounded so loud he realized the enemy must only be a few hundred yards away.

He dropped to one knee, his senses heightened to screaming point. Suddenly there was another burst of fire in front of him. Abel got to his feet and ran forward, reluctantly followed by the doctor and the potato peeler. They ran on for a hundred yards, until they came to a lush green meadow covered with white crocuses and littered with bodies.

'It's a massacre!' screamed Abel, as he heard the retreating fire. The doctor made no comment; he had screamed three years before.

'Don't worry about the dead,' was all the doctor said. 'Just see if you can find anyone who has half a chance of surviving.'

'Over here,' shouted Abel, kneeling beside a sergeant lying in the German mud. He couldn't see Abel – both his eyes were missing. Abel placed little bits of gauze in the sockets and waited impatiently.

'He's dead, Colonel,' said the doctor, not giving the man a second glance. Abel ran on to another body and then another, but it was always the same, and only the sight of a severed head standing upright in the mud stopped him in his tracks. He found himself reciting words he had learned at the feet of the Baron: 'Blood and destruction shall be so in use and dreadful objects so familiar that mothers shall but smile when they behold their infants quartered by the hands of war.'

'Does nothing change?' he asked.

'Only the battlefield,' replied the doctor.

When Abel had checked thirty – or was it forty? – men, he once again turned to the doctor, who was trying to save the life of a captain whose head, but for a closed eye and his mouth, was swathed in blood-soaked bandages.

Abel stood over the doctor, watching helplessly, studying the captain's shoulder patch – the Ninth Armored. He recalled General Leonard's words, 'God knows how many men we've lost'.

'Fucking Germans,' said Abel.

'Yes, sir,' said the doctor.

'Is he dead?' asked Abel.

'Might as well be,' the doctor replied mechanically. 'He's losing so much blood it can only be a matter of time.' He looked up. 'There's nothing left for you to do here, Colonel. Why don't you try to get this one back to the field hospital. He just might have a chance. And let the base commander know that I intend to go forward, and I need every man he can spare.'

Abel helped the doctor carefully lift the captain onto a stretcher, then he and the potato peeler tramped slowly through the forest and back across the bridge, the doctor having warned him that any sudden movement to the stretcher could result in a fatal loss of blood. Abel didn't allow the potato peeler to rest for a moment during the two-mile trek to the field hospital. He wanted to give the captain every chance to live. Afterwards he would return to assist the doctor in the forest.

When they finally reached the field hospital both men were exhausted. As they passed the stretcher over to a medical team, Abel felt certain the captain was already dead.

As the captain was wheeled slowly away he opened his unbandaged eye, which focused on Abel. He tried to raise an arm. Abel could have leapt with joy at the sight of the open eye and the moving hand. He saluted, and prayed the man would live.

He limped out of the hospital, eager to return to the forest, but was stopped by the duty officer.

'Colonel,' he said, 'I've been looking for you everywhere. There are over three hundred men who need feeding. Christ, man, where have you been?'

'Doing something worthwhile for a change.'

Abel thought about the young captain as he slowly headed back to the field kitchen.

For both of them the war was over.

40

THE CAPTAIN was taken into the tent and laid gently on an operating table.

William could see a nurse looking down at him, but was unable to hear what she was saying. He wasn't sure if it was because his head was swathed in bandages, or because he'd lost his hearing. He shut his eye, and thought. He thought a lot about the past; he thought a little about the future; he thought quickly in case he died. If he lived, there would be plenty of time for thinking. His mind turned to Kate. The nurse saw a tear trickling out of the corner of his one eye.

Kate hadn't understood his determination to enlist. He had accepted that she would never understand, and that he would not be able to justify his reasons to her, so he had stopped trying. The memory of her desperate face when they parted still haunted him. He had never really thought about death – no young man ever does – but now he wanted desperately to live and return to his family.

William had left Lester's under the joint control of Ted Leach and Tony Simmons until he returned. Until he returned . . . He had given no instructions for them in case he did not return. Both of them had begged him not to go. Two others who didn't understand. When he had finally signed up, he couldn't face the children. Richard, aged nine, had held back the tears until his father told him that he could not come with him to fight the Germans. Virginia and Lucy, thank God, were too young to understand.

They sent William first to Officers' Candidate School in Vermont. The last time he had visited Vermont was to go skiing with Matthew, slowly up the hills and quickly down; Matthew always in front of him both on the way up and on the way down. One thing was certain. Had Matthew lived, he would surely have signed up. The course lasted for three months, and made him fitter than he'd been since he left Harvard.

His first assignment was in a London full of Yanks, where he acted as a liaison officer between the Americans and the British. He was billeted at the Dorchester, which the British War Office had seconded for use by the American High Command. William read somewhere that Abel Rosnovski had offered the Baron in New York for the same purpose, and silently applauded his magnanimity. The blackouts, the doodlebugs and the air raid sirens all made him realize that he was involved in a war, but he felt strangely detached from what was going on only a hundred miles south-east of Hyde Park Corner. Throughout his life he had always taken the initiative; never been an onlooker. Moving between Eisenhower's staff headquarters in St James's and Churchill's War Operations room in Storey's Gate wasn't William's idea of initiative. It didn't look as if he was going to meet a German face-to-face for the entire duration of the war, unless Hitler marched down Whitehall and into Trafalgar Square, when surely even Nelson would climb down from his column and join in the fighting.

When a division of the US First Army was posted to Scotland for training exercises with the Black Watch, William was sent along as an observer. During the long, slow rail journey north he began to realize that he was no more than a glorified messenger boy, and wondered why he'd ever signed up. But once he was in Scotland, everything changed. There the air was filled with the noise of battle, as soldiers prepared themselves to face the enemy. When he returned to London he put in a request for an immediate transfer to the First Army. His commanding officer, who never believed in keeping a man who wanted to see action behind a desk, released him.

Once they considered William Kane was fit enough to die, he

returned to Scotland and joined his new regiment at Inveraray, preparing for the invasion they all knew had to come soon. Training was hard and intense. Nights spent in the Scottish hills fighting mock battles with the Black Watch were a marked contrast to evenings at the Dorchester writing reports, scurrying down to the safety of the basement whenever an air raid siren was heard.

Three months later Captain William Kane was parachuted into northern France to join General Bradley's army as it advanced across Europe. The scent of victory was in the air, and William wanted to be the first Allied soldier in Berlin.

The First Army advanced towards the Rhine, determined to cross any bridge they could find. Captain Kane received orders that morning, that his division was to cross the Ludendorff Bridge and engage the enemy a mile north-east of Remagen, in a forest on the far side of the river. From the crest of a hill he watched the Ninth Armored cross the bridge, expecting it to be blown sky high at any moment.

Captain Kane followed with 120 men under his command, most of them, like himself, going into action for the first time. No more exercises with wily Scots pretending to kill each other with blank cartridges – followed by a meal together in the mess. These were real Germans, with real bullets, real death – and certainly few would be dining together afterwards.

When William reached the edge of the forest, he and his men met with no resistance, so they decided to press on. He was beginning to think the Ninth must have done such a thorough job that his platoon would only have to follow them through, when from nowhere there was a sudden hail of bullets and mortars. Everything seemed to be coming at them at once. The men went down, trying to find a tree to protect them, but over half the platoon was lost in a matter of seconds. The battle, if that's how it could be described, had lasted for less than a minute, and William hadn't even seen a German. As he crouched behind a tree in the wet undergrowth he saw, to his horror, the next wave of the Ninth Division coming through the forest. Without a thought, he ran from his shelter out into the open to warn them of the ambush.

The first bullet hit him in the side of the head, and as he sank to his knees he continued to wave and to shout a frantic warning to his advancing comrades. The second bullet hit him in the neck, and a third in the chest. He lay still in the German mud and waited to die, never having even seen the enemy – a dirty, unheroic death.

The next thing William remembered was being carried on a stretcher, but he couldn't hear or see anything, and wondered whether it was night, or he was blind. It seemed a long journey, and then his eye opened and focused on a colonel who saluted before limping out of the tent. There was something familiar about the man, but he couldn't think what. The medical orderlies took him into the tent and placed him on an operating table. He tried to fight off sleep, for fear it might be death.

He was conscious that two people were trying to move him. They turned him over as gently as they could, and then one of them stuck a needle into him. He sank into a deep sleep, and dreamed of Kate, his mother, and then of Matthew playing football with his son Richard. He slept.

He woke. They must have moved him to another bed; a glimmer of hope replaced the thought of inevitable death. He lay motionless, his one eye fixed on the canvas roof of the tent, unable to move his head. A nurse came over to study a chart, and then him. He slept.

He woke. How much time had passed? Another nurse. This time he could see a little more, and he could now move his head, if only with great pain. He lay awake as long as he possibly could; he wanted to live. He slept.

He woke. Four doctors were studying him. Deciding what? He could not hear them speak, so he learned nothing. He was moved once again, this time to an ambulance. The doors closed behind him, the engine revved up and the ambulance began to move over rough ground while a new nurse sat by his side holding him steady. The journey felt like an hour, but he could no longer be certain of time. The ambulance reached smoother ground, and finally came to a halt. Once again he was moved, this time across a flat surface and then up a slope into a dark room. After another wait the room began to move, another ambulance perhaps. The room took off. A nurse stuck another needle into him, and he remembered nothing until he felt the plane landing and taxiing to a halt. They moved him once again. Another ambulance, another nurse, another smell, another city. New York. There's no smell like New York. The latest ambulance drove him over a smoother surface, continually stopping and starting until it finally arrived at its destination.

They carried him out once again, up some more steps and into a small, white-walled room, where they placed him in a comfortable bed. He felt his head touch a soft pillow, and when he next woke he thought he was alone. But then his eye focused and he saw Kate standing beside him. He tried to lift his hand and touch her, to speak, but no words came. She smiled, but he knew she could not see his smile, and when he woke again she was still there, but wearing a different dress. How many times had she come and gone? She smiled again. He tried to move his head a little, and saw his son Richard. He had grown so tall, so good-looking. He wanted to see his daughters, but couldn't turn his head any further. They moved into his line of vision. Virginia – she couldn't be that old, surely? And Lucy – it wasn't possible. Where had the years gone? He slept.

He woke. He could now move his head from side to side; some bandages had been removed, and he could see more clearly. He tried to say something, but no words came. Kate was watching him, her fair hair shorter now, no longer falling to her shoulders, her soft brown eyes and unforgettable smile, looking beautiful, so beautiful. He said her name. She smiled. He slept.

He woke. Fewer bandages than before. This time his son spoke.

'Hello, Daddy.' His voice had broken.

He heard him and replied, 'Hello, Richard,' but didn't recognize the sound of his own voice. A nurse helped him to sit up. He thanked her. A doctor touched his shoulder.

'The worst is over, Mr Kane. It won't be long now before you're able to go home.'

He smiled as Kate came into the room, followed by Virginia and Lucy. So many questions to ask them. Where should he begin? There were gaps in his memory that demanded filling. Kate told him he had nearly died. He knew that, but had not realized that over a year had passed since his division had been ambushed in the forest at Remagen.

Where had the months of unawareness gone, life lost, resembling death? Richard was now twelve, already preparing for St Paul's. Virginia was nine and Lucy nearly seven. He would have to get to know them all over again.

Kate was somehow even more beautiful than he remembered her. She told him how she had never accepted the possibility that he would die, how well Richard was doing at school, and how Virginia and Lucy were quite a handful. She braced herself to tell him about the scars on his face and chest; they would take time to heal. She thanked God that the doctors were confident there was nothing wrong with his mind, and that, given time, his sight would be fully restored. All she wanted to do was to assist that recovery. When he could finally speak, his first question was, 'Who won the war?'

—◦—

Each member of the family played a part in the recovery process. Richard helped his father to walk until he no longer needed crutches. Lucy helped him with his food until he could once again hold a knife and fork. Virginia read Mark Twain to him – William wasn't sure if the reading was for her benefit or his, they both enjoyed it so much. Kate stayed awake at night when he could not sleep. And then, at last, the doctors allowed him to return home for Christmas.

Once William was back in East Sixty-Eighth Street, his recovery accelerated, and the doctors were predicting that he would be able to return to work within six months. A little scarred, but very much alive, he was finally allowed to see visitors.

The first was Ted Leach, somewhat taken aback by William's

appearance – something he hadn't been prepared for. William learned from him that Lester's had flourished in his absence, and that his colleagues looked forward to welcoming him back to work. He also told him that Rupert Cork-Smith had passed away. His next visitor, Tony Simmons, also had sad news: Alan Lloyd too was dead. William would miss their prudent wisdom. Thomas Cohen called by to say how glad he was to learn of William's recovery, and to confirm, as if it were necessary, that time had marched on by informing him that he was now semi-retired, and had turned over most of his clients to his son Thaddeus, who had opened an office in New York. William remarked on both the Cohens being named after apostles.

'By the way, I have one piece of information you ought to be aware of.'

William listened to the old lawyer in silence, and became angry, very angry.

41

GENERAL ALFRED JODL signed Germany's unconditional surrender at Rheims on May 7, 1945. The war in Europe was over. Three months later Abel arrived back in a New York preparing for victory celebrations to mark the end of the war.

Once again the streets were filled with young people in uniform, but this time their faces showed relieved elation, not forced gaiety. Abel was saddened by the sight of so many men with one leg, one arm, blind or badly scarred. For them the war would never be over, no matter what pieces of paper had been signed on the other side of the world.

He walked into the Baron in his colonel's uniform, but no one recognized him. When they had last seen him in civilian clothes more than three years ago, there had been no lines on his then youthful face. He now looked older than his thirty-nine years, and the deep furrows on his forehead showed that the war had left its mark. He took the elevator to his 42nd floor office, where a security guard told him firmly that he was on the wrong floor.

'Where's George Novak?' asked Abel.

'He's in Chicago, Colonel,' the guard replied.

'Then get him on the phone.'

'Who shall I say is calling him?'

'Abel Rosnovski.'

The guard moved quickly.

George's familiar voice crackled down the line. Abel immediately realized just how good it was to be back – and how much he now wanted to go home.

He decided not to stay a moment longer in New York, but to fly the eight hundred miles to Chicago. He took George's latest reports with him to study on the plane. He read every detail of the Baron Group's progress during the war years, and it was obvious that George had managed to keep the group on an even keel during his absence. But if they were to move forward Abel realized that he would have to start employing new staff immediately, before his rivals picked up the best of those returning from the front.

When Abel arrived at Midway Airport, George was standing by the gate waiting to greet him. He had hardly changed – he'd put on a little weight, and lost a little hair perhaps – and after an hour of swapping stories and bringing each other up to date on the past three years, it was almost as though Abel had never been away. Abel would always be thankful to the *Black Arrow* for introducing him to his senior vice president.

George commented on Abel's limp, which seemed more pronounced than when he had gone away. 'The Hopalong Cassidy of the hotel business,' he said mockingly. 'Soon you won't have a leg to stand on.'

'Only a Pole would make such a dumb crack,' replied Abel.

George grinned at him, looking like a puppy that had been scolded by its master.

'Thank God I had a dumb Polack to take care of everything while I was away searching for Germans,' said Abel.

'Did you find any?'

'No. The moment they heard I was coming, they ran away.'

'They must have sampled your cooking,' suggested George.

Abel couldn't resist walking once around the Chicago Baron before he drove home. The veneer of luxury had worn rather thin because of wartime shortages. He could see several things that needed renovation if not replacement, but that would have to wait; right now all he wanted to do was see his wife and daughter. But when he arrived home the first shock came. In George there had been little change in three years, but Florentyna was now eleven, and had blossomed into a beautiful young girl, while

Zaphia, although only thirty-eight, had grown plump, dowdy and prematurely middle-aged.

To begin with, she and Abel were not quite sure how to treat each other, and after only a few weeks Abel began to realize that their relationship could never be the same again. Zaphia made little effort to make him feel she had missed him, and appeared to take no pride in his achievements. Her lack of interest saddened him, and when he tried to get her involved in his life and work, she simply didn't respond, but seemed content to remain at home and have as little involvement with the Baron Group as possible. He began to wonder how long he could remain faithful. On the rare occasions when they made love, he found himself thinking of other women. Soon he began to find any excuse to flee Chicago and Zaphia's silently accusing face.

He spent much of the first six months following his return to America visiting every hotel in the Baron Group in the same way he had when he had first taken over the Richmond Group after Davis Leroy's death. If a trip fell during the school vacation, Florentyna would often accompany him. Within a year, all the hotels were back to the high standards he expected of them, and Abel was ready to move forward again. He informed Curtis Fenton at the group's quarterly meeting that his market research team was now advising him to build a hotel in Mexico and another in Brazil, while looking for other new sites.

'The Mexico City Baron and the Rio de Janeiro Baron,' said Abel. Who would have believed it?

'Well, you have adequate funds to cover the building costs,' said Fenton. 'The cash has certainly been accumulating in your absence. In fact, you could build a Baron almost anywhere you choose. Heaven knows where you'll stop, Mr Rosnovski.'

'One day, Mr Fenton, I'll build a Baron in Warsaw. Only then will I think about stopping. I might have played a small part in licking the Germans, but I still have a little score to settle with the Russians.'

Fenton laughed. That evening, when he repeated the story to his wife, she said, 'Then why not the Moscow Baron?'

'So what's my position with Lester's bank?' demanded Abel.

The sudden change in tone bothered Fenton. It worried him that Abel still clearly held William Kane responsible for Davis Leroy's premature death. He opened an unmarked file and started to read from it.

'Lester, Kane and Company's stock is divided among fourteen members of the Lester family and six past and present employees. Mr William Kane is the largest stockholder, with eight per cent in his family trust.'

'Are any of the Lester family willing to sell their stock?' asked Abel.

'Perhaps, if we were to offer the right price. Miss Susan Lester, the late Charles Lester's daughter, has given us reason to believe she might consider parting with her stock, and Mr Peter Parfitt, a former vice chairman of Lester's, has also shown some interest.'

'What percentages do they hold?'

'Susan Lester holds six per cent. Parfitt has two per cent.'

'How much do they want?'

While Fenton checked his file, Abel glanced at Lester's latest annual report. His eyes came to a halt at Article Seven, which had been underlined. He smiled.

'Miss Lester wants two million dollars for her six per cent, and Mr Parfitt one million dollars for his two per cent.'

'Mr Parfitt is greedy,' said Abel. 'We'll wait until he's hungry. Buy Susan Lester's stock immediately, without revealing who you represent, and keep me briefed on any change of heart by Parfitt.'

Curtis Fenton coughed.

'Is something bothering you, Mr Fenton?'

Fenton hesitated. 'No, nothing,' he said unconvincingly.

'Good, because I'm putting someone else in overall charge of that particular account whom you may know. Henry Osborne.'

'Congressman Osborne?'

'Yes – do you know him?'

'Only by reputation,' said Fenton, with a faint note of disapproval.

Abel ignored the implied comment. He was only too aware of Osborne's reputation, but he had the ability to cut through bureaucracy and take quick political decisions, making him in Abel's opinion a worthwhile risk. And they had something else in common. They both loathed William Kane.

'I shall also be inviting Mr Osborne to become a director of the Baron Group.'

'As you wish,' said Fenton unhappily, wondering if he should express his personal misgivings about Osborne.

'Let me know as soon as you've closed the deal with Miss Lester.'

'Yes, Mr Rosnovski,' said Fenton, closing the file.

Abel returned to the Baron to find Henry Osborne waiting in the lobby.

'Congressman,' said Abel as they shook hands. 'Why don't you join me for lunch?'

'Thank you, Baron,' said Osborne. They laughed, and went arm in arm into the dining room, where they sat at a corner table. Abel chastised a waiter when he noticed that a button was missing from his tunic.

'How's your wife, Abel?'

'Swell. And yours, Henry?'

'Just great.' They both knew they were both lying.

'Anything of interest to report?'

'That concession you needed in Seattle has been taken care of,' said Henry in hushed tones. 'The documents will be pushed through the local council some time in the next few days. You should be able to start building the new Seattle Baron next month.'

'We're not doing anything too illegal, are we?'

'Nothing your competitors aren't up to,' Henry assured him. 'That I can promise you.'

'I'm glad to hear it, Henry. I don't want any trouble with the law.'

'No, no,' said Osborne. 'Only you and I know exactly what's going on.'

'Good. You've made yourself very useful to me over the years, Henry, and I have a little reward for your past services. How would you like to become a director of the Baron Group?'

'I'd be flattered, Abel,' replied the Congressman.

'Don't overdo it, Henry. After all, you've been angling for it for some time.' Both men laughed. 'But to be fair, you've been invaluable with those state and city building permits. I'm far too busy to deal with politicians and bureaucrats. In any case, Henry, they prefer to deal with a Harvard man – even if he doesn't so much open doors as kick them down.'

'You've been very generous in return, Abel.'

'It's no more than you've earned. Now, I want you to take on a rather trickier problem. It concerns our mutual friend from Boston.'

42

THE LETTER lay on a table by William's chair in the living room. He picked it up and read it for the third time, trying to figure out why Abel Rosnovski would want to buy so heavily into Lester's, and why he had appointed Henry Osborne as a director of the Baron Group. He dialled a number he didn't need to look up.

When Thaddeus Cohen arrived at East Sixty-Eighth Street, he had no need to introduce himself. He was the spitting image of his father; his hair was beginning to go grey and thin in exactly the same places, and the tall, spare frame was encased in a similar suit. Perhaps it was even the same suit.

'You don't remember me, Mr Kane,' said the lawyer.

'Of course I do,' said William as he rose to shake hands. 'The great debate at Harvard. Nineteen twenty . . .'

'Eight. You won the debate, but sacrificed your membership of the Porcellian.'

William burst out laughing. 'Maybe we'll do better if we're on the same team. Assuming your brand of socialism will allow you to act for an unashamed capitalist.'

For a moment they might both have been undergraduates again.

William smiled. 'You never did get that drink at the Porcellian. What would you like?'

Thaddeus Cohen declined the offer. 'I don't drink,' he said, blinking in the same disarming way that William recalled so well. 'And I'm afraid I'm now an unashamed capitalist, as well.'

He also turned out to have his father's head on his shoulders. Clearly he'd been fully briefed on the Rosnovski-Osborne file, and was able to answer all of William's questions. William explained exactly what he now required.

'An immediate report and a further update every three months. Secrecy is of paramount importance. I need to find out why Abel Rosnovski is buying Lester's stock. Does he still feel I'm responsible for Davis Leroy's death? Is he continuing his battle with Kane and Cabot even now that it's part of Lester's? What role is Henry Osborne playing in all this? Would a meeting between myself and Rosnovski help, especially if I told him it was the bank, and not me, who refused to support the Richmond Group?'

Thaddeus Cohen's pen was scratching away as furiously as his father's had before him.

'All these questions must be answered as quickly as possible so I can decide if it's necessary to inform my board.'

Thaddeus Cohen gave his father's shy smile as he shut his briefcase. 'I'm sorry that you should be troubled in this way while you're still convalescing. I'll report back to you as soon as I can ascertain the facts.' He paused at the door. 'I greatly admire what you did at Remagen.'

—◦—

On May 7, 1946, Abel travelled to New York to celebrate the first anniversary of VE Day. He had laid on a dinner for more than a thousand Polish-American veterans to be held at the Baron hotel, and had invited General Kazimierz Sosnkowski, commander in chief of the Polish Forces in France, to be the guest of honour. He had looked forward to the event for weeks, and invited Florentyna to accompany him to New York, as Zaphia made it clear that she didn't want to come.

On the night of the celebration, the banquet room of the New York Baron was magnificently adorned. Each of the 120 tables was decorated with the stars and stripes of America as well as the white and red of the Polish national flag. Huge photographs of Eisenhower, Patton, Bradley, Clark, Paderewski and Sikorsky adorned the walls. Abel sat at the centre of the head table with the general on his right and Florentyna on his left.

After a seven-course meal, General Sosnkowski rose to address the gathering. He announced that Colonel Rosnovski had been made a Life President of the Polish Veterans' Society, in acknowledgement of the personal sacrifices he had made for the Polish-American cause, and in particular his generous gift of the New York Baron to the US Army throughout the entire duration of the war. Someone who had drunk a little too much shouted from the back of the room, 'Those of us who survived the Germans somehow managed to survive Abel's cooking as well.'

The thousand veterans laughed, cheered and toasted Abel in Danzig vodka. But they fell silent when the general spoke movingly of the plight of post-war Poland, now in the grip of Stalinist Russia, and urged his fellow expatriates to be tireless in their campaign to secure sovereignty for their native land. Abel, like everyone else in the room, wanted to believe that Poland could one day be free again. He also dreamed of seeing his castle restored to him, but doubted if that would ever be possible following Stalin's coup at Yalta.

The general went on to remind the guests that Polish-Americans had, per capita, sacrificed more lives to the war than any other ethnic group in the United States. 'How many Americans know that Poland lost six million of her people while Czechoslovakia lost one hundred thousand? Some have said we were stupid not to surrender when we must have known we were beaten. How could a nation that staged a cavalry charge against the might of the Nazi tanks ever believe it was beaten? And, my friends, I tell you, we'll never be defeated.'

The general ended by telling his intent audience the story of how Abel had led a band of men to rescue wounded troops at the battle of Remagen. When he had finished, the veterans stood and cheered the two men resoundingly. Florentyna's smile revealed how proud she was of her father.

Abel was surprised when his experiences on the battlefield at Remagen hit the papers the next morning, because Polish achievements were rarely reported in any medium other than *Dziennik Zwiazkowy*. He basked in his newfound glory as an unsung American hero, and spent most of the day posing for photographers and giving interviews.

By the evening, when the sun had finally disappeared, Abel felt a sense of anticlimax. The general had flown to Los Angeles for another function, Florentyna had returned to school at Lake Forest, George was in Chicago and Henry Osborne in Washington. The New York Baron suddenly seemed large and empty, but Abel felt no desire to return to Chicago, and Zaphia.

He decided to have an early dinner, and to go over the weekly reports from the other hotels in the group before retiring to the penthouse. He seldom ate alone in his private suite, preferring to eat in one of the dining rooms – which was a sure way of keeping in constant contact with hotel operations. The more hotels he acquired and built, the more he feared losing touch with his staff on the ground.

He took the elevator downstairs and stopped at the reception desk to ask how many guests were booked for the night, but was distracted by a striking woman signing a registration form. He could have sworn he knew her, but he was unable to get a good look at her face. When she had finished writing, she turned and smiled at him.

'Abel,' she said. 'How marvellous to see you.'

'Good God, Melanie. I hardly recognized you.'

'No one could fail to recognize you, Abel.'

'I didn't even know you were in New York.'

'Only overnight. I'm here on business for my magazine.'

'You're a journalist?' asked Abel.

'No, I'm the economic advisor to a group of magazines with headquarters in Dallas. I'm here on a market research project.'

'Very impressive.'

'I can assure you it isn't. But it keeps me out of mischief.'

'Are you free for dinner by any chance?'

'What a nice idea, Abel. But I need a bath and a change of clothes, if you don't mind waiting.'

'Sure, I can wait. I'll meet you in the dining room. Why don't you join me in about an hour.'

She smiled a second time, and followed a bellhop to the

elevator. Abel became aware of her perfume as she walked away.

He checked the dining room to be sure his table had fresh flowers, then went to the kitchen to select the dishes he thought she'd most enjoy. Finally he sat down at the corner table and waited impatiently. He found himself glancing at his watch every few minutes, and looking at the entrance hoping Melanie would appear. She took a little over an hour, but when the maître d' ushered her to his table it turned out to be worth the wait. She was wearing a long, clinging dress that shimmered and sparkled under the dining room lights in an unmistakably expensive way. She looked ravishing. Abel rose to greet her as a waiter opened a bottle of vintage Krug.

'Welcome, Melanie,' he said, raising his glass. 'It's good to see you still stay at the Baron.'

'It's good to see the Baron in person,' she replied. 'Especially on his day of triumph.'

'What do you mean?'

'I read all about last night's dinner in the *New York Post*, and how you risked your life to save the wounded at Remagen. They made you sound like a cross between Audie Murphy and the Unknown Soldier.'

'It's all rather exaggerated,' said Abel.

'I've never known you to be modest about anything, Abel, so I can only assume every word must be true.'

'The truth is, I've always been a little frightened of you, Melanie.'

'The Baron is frightened of someone? I don't believe it.'

'Well, I'm no southern gentleman, as you once made only too clear.'

'And you never stop reminding me.' She smiled, teasingly. 'Did you marry your nice Polish girl?'

He poured her a second glass of champagne.

'Yes, I did.'

'How did that work out?'

'Not so well. We've drifted apart, and in truth I'm to blame. Too many late nights.'

'With other women?'

'No. Other hotels.'

Melanie laughed, and gave him a warm smile.

'And did you find yourself a husband?'

'I sure did. I married a real southern gentleman with all the right credentials.'

'Many congratulations.'

'I divorced him last year – after accepting a large settlement.'

'Oh, I'm sorry,' said Abel, sounding pleased. 'More champagne?'

'Are you by any chance trying to seduce me, Abel?'

'Not before you've finished your soup, Melanie. Even first-generation Polish immigrants have some standards, although I admit it's my turn to do the seducing.'

'Then I must warn you, Abel, I haven't slept with another man since my divorce came through. No lack of offers, but no one's been quite right. Too many groping hands and not enough affection.'

Over smoked salmon, young lamb, crème brulée and a pre-war Mouton Rothschild, they reviewed their lives since their last meeting.

'Coffee in the penthouse, Melanie?'

'Do I have any choice, after such an excellent meal?'

Abel laughed and escorted her out of the dining room. She was teetering very slightly on her high heels as she entered the elevator. Abel touched the button marked '42'. Melanie looked up at the numbers as they ticked by. 'Why no seventeenth floor?' she asked innocently. Abel couldn't find the words to tell her.

'The last time I had coffee in your room . . .' Melanie tried again.

'Don't remind me,' said Abel. They stepped out of the elevator on the 42nd floor, and the bellhop held open the door to his suite.

'Good God,' said Melanie as her eyes swept around the penthouse. 'I must say, Abel, you've certainly learned how to adjust to the style of a multimillionaire. I've never seen anything more sumptuous in my life.'

A knock at the door stopped Abel as he was about to reach out for her. A young waiter appeared with a pot of coffee and a bottle of Remy Martin.

'Thank you, Mike,' said Abel. 'That will be all for tonight.'

'Will it?' Melanie said, smiling.

The waiter left quickly.

Abel poured some coffee and brandy. Melanie sipped slowly, sitting cross-legged on the floor. Abel sat down beside her. She stroked his hair, and tentatively he began to move his hand up her leg. God, how well he remembered those legs. As they kissed for the first time, Melanie kicked a shoe off and knocked her coffee all over the Persian rug.

'Oh, hell!' she said. 'Your beautiful rug.'

'It's not important,' said Abel as he pulled her back into his arms and started to unzip her dress. Melanie unbuttoned his shirt, and Abel tried to take it off while still kissing her, but his cufflinks got in the way, so he helped her out of her dress instead. Her figure was exactly as he remembered it, except that it was enticingly fuller. Those firm breasts and long, graceful legs. He gave up the one-handed battle with the cufflinks and released her from his grasp to quickly undress, aware what a physical contrast he offered to her beautiful body and hoping that all he had read about women being fascinated by powerful men was true. Gently, he caressed her breasts and began to part her legs. The soft Persian rug was proving better than any bed. It was her turn to try to undress completely while they were kissing. She too gave up, and finally freed herself to take off everything except for – at Abel's request – her suspender belt and nylon stockings.

When he heard her moan, he was aware of how long it had been since he had experienced such ecstasy, and then of how quickly the sensation passed. Neither of them spoke for several moments, both breathing heavily.

Then Abel chuckled.

'What are you laughing at?' Melanie asked.

'I was just recalling Dr Johnson's observation about the position being ridiculous and the pleasure momentary.'

Melanie laughed and rested her head on his shoulder. Abel

was surprised to find that he no longer found her irresistible. He was wondering how quickly he could be rid of her without actually being rude, when she said, 'I'm afraid I can't stay all night, Abel. I have a breakfast appointment across at the Stevens. I don't want to look as if I spent the night on your Persian rug.'

'Must you go?' said Abel, sounding desperate, but not too desperate.

'I'm sorry, darling, yes.' She stood up and walked to the bathroom.

Abel watched her dress, and helped her with the zipper. How much easier it was to fasten at leisure than it had been to unfasten in haste. He kissed her gallantly on the hand as she left.

'I hope we'll see each other again soon,' he said, lying.

'I hope so, too,' she said, aware that she didn't mean it.

He closed the door behind her and walked over to the phone by his bed. 'Which room is Miss Melanie Leroy booked into?' he asked.

There was a moment's pause; he tapped impatiently on the table, listening to the flicking of the registration cards.

'There's no one registered under that name, sir,' came the eventual reply. 'We have a Mrs Melanie Seaton from Dallas, Texas, who arrived this evening and checks out in the morning.'

'Yes, that will be the lady. See that her bill is charged to me.'

'Yes, sir.'

Abel replaced the phone and took a long cold shower before going to bed. He was about to turn off the lamp that had illuminated his first adulterous act, when he noticed the large coffee stain in the middle of the Persian rug.

'Clumsy bitch,' he said as he switched off the light.

◄○►

William recovered his vigour and sense of well-being rapidly over the following months, and the scars on his face and chest began to fade. At night Kate would still sit up with him until he fell asleep. The terrible headaches and periods of amnesia were now things of the past, and the strength had finally returned to his right arm.

Kate did not allow him to return to work until they had taken a long cruise in the Caribbean, on which William was able to relax more than at any time since his and Kate's month together in England. Kate revelled in the fact that there were no banks on board for him to do business with, although she feared that if the cruise lasted another week he would acquire the ship on behalf of Lester's, reorganizing the crew, routes and timings. By the time they docked in New York harbour, she could not dissuade him from returning to the bank the following morning.

—◦—

Several more coffee stains appeared on Abel's Persian rug during the next few months, some caused by compliant waitresses, others by non-paying hotel guests, as he and Zaphia grew further apart.

What he hadn't anticipated was that his wife would hire a private detective to check on him, and would then sue for divorce. Divorce was almost unknown in Abel's circle of Polish friends. He tried to talk her out of continuing with the action, aware that it would only harm his standing in the Polish community, but worse, it would be a setback to any social or political ambitions he had started to nurture. But Zaphia was determined to carry on with the proceedings. Abel was surprised to find that the woman who had been so unsophisticated in his triumph was, to use George's words, a little vixen in her revenge.

When Abel consulted his lawyer, he found out just how many waitresses and non-paying guests he had entertained during the past year. He gave in. The only thing he fought for was custody of Florentyna, now almost thirteen, and the most important person in his life.

After a long struggle, Zaphia agreed to his demands, accepting a settlement of $500,000, the deeds to the house in Chicago and the right to see Florentyna on the last weekend of every month.

Abel moved his headquarters and permanent home to New York. George dubbed him 'The Baron-in-Exile' as he roamed America north and south building new hotels, only returning to Chicago when he needed to consult Curtis Fenton.

—◦—

When the first report came in from Thaddeus Cohen, William was left in no doubt that Rosnovski was actively looking for stock in Lester's Bank; he had approached all the other beneficiaries of Charles Lester's will, but only one transaction had been concluded. Susan Lester had refused to see Cohen, so he was unable to find out why she had sold her 6 per cent. All he could ascertain was that she had had no financial reason to do so.

The report was admirably comprehensive. Henry Osborne, it seemed, had been appointed a director of the Baron Group in May 1946, with special responsibility for securing Lester shares. Susan's stock had been acquired in such a way that it was impossible to trace the acquisition back through either Rosnovski or Osborne. Cohen was certain that Rosnovski was willing to pay at least $750,000 to secure Peter Parfitt's 2 per cent. William didn't need to be reminded of the havoc Rosnovski could create once he was in possession of 8 per cent of Lester's stock, and could invoke Article Seven. One problem for William was that Lester's growth compared unfavourably with that of the Baron Group, which was already catching up with its main rivals, the Hilton and Sheraton groups.

He wondered again if he should brief his board of directors on this latest information, and even whether he ought to contact Rosnovski direct. After several sleepless nights, he turned to Kate for advice.

'Do nothing,' she said, 'until you can be absolutely certain his intentions are as disruptive as you fear. The whole affair may turn out to be a storm in a teacup.'

'With Henry Osborne involved, you can be certain the storm will spill over into the saucer and I can't afford to sit around and wait to find out what he's planning to do next.'

'He might have mellowed, William. It's more than twenty years since you've had any personal dealings with the man.'

William relaxed for a few days, until he read Thaddeus Cohen's next report.

PART SIX

1948–1952

43

PRESIDENT TRUMAN won a surprise victory for a second term
in the White House, despite headlines in the *Chicago Tribune*
informing the world that Thomas E. Dewey was the next President of the United States. William knew very little about the
haberdasher from Missouri, except what he read in the newspapers, and as a staunch Republican, he hoped that his party
would find the right man to lead them into the 1952 campaign.

The Baron Group profited greatly from the post-war explosion
in the American economy. Not since the twenties had it been so
easy to make so much money so quickly – and by the early fifties,
people were beginning to believe that this time it was going to last.

Abel was not content with financial success alone; as he grew
older, he began to worry about Poland's future, and to feel that
he could no longer remain an onlooker. What had Pawel Zaleski,
the Polish Consul in Turkey, said? 'Perhaps in your lifetime you
will see Poland rise again.'

Abel felt, as he watched one puppet communist government after another come into power, that he had risked his life
at Remagen for nothing. He began to do everything he could
to persuade the United States Congress to take a more militant
attitude towards Russian control of its Eastern European satel-
lites. He lobbied politicians, briefed journalists and organized
dinners in Chicago, New York and other centres of the Polish-
American community, until the Polish cause itself became
synonymous with 'The Chicago Baron'.

Dr Teodor Szymanowski, formerly professor of history at the

419

University of Cracow, wrote a glowing editorial about Abel's role in Poland's 'Fight to Be Recognized' in the journal *Freedom*, which prompted Abel to get in contact with him. Aware only of the vigour of the professor's opinions, when he was ushered into his study at Princeton Abel was surprised by his physical frailty.

Szymanowski greeted Abel warmly, and poured him a Danzig vodka without asking what he would like. 'Baron Rosnovski,' he said, handing him the glass. 'I have long admired you, and your work for our cause. Although we make such little headway, you never seem to lose faith.'

'Why should I? I've always believed anything is possible in America.'

'But I fear, Baron, that the very men you are now trying to influence are the same ones who have allowed these atrocities to take place, and they will not admit that in the cold light of day.'

'I don't understand what you mean, Professor. Why won't they assist us? After all, in the long run it must be in their interests.'

The professor leaned back in his chair. 'You are surely aware, Baron, that the American armies were given specific orders in 1944 to slow down their eastward advance and allow the Russians to take control of as much of central Europe as they could lay their hands on. Patton could have marched into Berlin long before the Russians, but Eisenhower ordered him to hold back. It was our leaders in Washington – the same men you are trying to persuade to put American guns and troops back in Europe – who gave Eisenhower those orders.'

'But they couldn't have known how large an empire the USSR would become,' said Abel. 'The Russians had been our allies. I accept that we were too conciliatory towards them at the end of the war, but it surely can't have been the Americans who betrayed the Polish people.'

Before Szymanowski spoke, he closed his eyes wearily.

'I wish you could have known my brother, Baron. I heard only last week that he died six months ago in a Soviet camp not unlike the one from which you escaped.'

Abel was about to offer his sympathy, but Szymanowski raised a hand.

'No, don't say anything. You have known the camps yourself. You would be the first to realize that sympathy is not a solution. We must try to change the world while others sleep.' Szymanowski paused. 'My brother was sent to Russia by the Americans.'

Abel stared at him in disbelief.

'By the Americans? How is that possible? If he was captured in Poland by Russian troops—'

'My brother was not taken prisoner in Poland. He was liberated from a German prisoner of war camp near Frankfurt. The Americans kept him in a DP camp for a month and then handed him over to the Russians.'

'Why would they do that?'

'The Russians wanted all Slavs repatriated. Repatriated so they could then be exterminated or enslaved. The ones Hitler didn't kill, Stalin did. And I can prove that my brother was in the American Sector for over a month.'

'But,' said Abel, 'was he an exception, or were there others like him?'

'There were hundreds of thousands,' said Szymanowski without apparent emotion. 'Perhaps as many as a million. I doubt if we will ever know the true figure. The whole evil affair was known as Operation Kee Chanl.'

'But surely if people knew that the Americans had been sending liberated prisoners back to die in Russia, they'd be horrified.'

'There is no proof, no official documentation. Mark Clark, like Nelson, turned a blind eye, allowing a few of the prisoners warned by sympathetic GIs to escape before the Americans could send them to the camps. One of the lucky ones was with my brother.' The professor paused. 'Anyway, it's too late to do anything now.'

'But the American people should be told. I'll form a committee, print pamphlets, make speeches. Surely Congress will listen to us if the evidence is overwhelming.'

'Baron Rosnovski, I think this one is too big even for you. You must understand the mentality of world leaders. The Americans agreed to hand over those poor devils because Stalin demanded it as part of an overall package. I am sure they never thought there would be trials, labour camps and executions to follow. And no one is going to admit to being indirectly responsible for the extermination of thousands of innocent people. I had rather hoped the conclusion you might come to was that you must play a more direct role in politics.'

'I have no desire to stand for election,' said Abel. 'For that job you need to be a cross between Babe Ruth and Henry Fonda, and I'm more like Hopalong Cassidy. But that won't stop me from making my voice heard, and I think I know exactly the right man to contact because he hates the communists even more than I do.'

The moment Abel was back in New York, he went straight to his office, picked up a telephone and asked his secretary to locate a man who was beginning to make a name for himself for not being afraid to sit in judgement on anybody.

Joseph McCarthy's secretary came on the line and asked who wanted to speak to the senator. 'I'll see if he's free,' she said when she learned who it was.

'Mr Rosenevski,' said the unmistakable voice of the senator. Abel wondered if McCarthy had mangled his name on purpose, or if it was just a bad connection. 'What is this matter of grave importance you wanted to discuss with me?' Abel hesitated. 'Your secrets are safe with me,' he heard the senator say.

'Of course,' said Abel, collecting his thoughts. 'You, Senator, have been a forthright spokesman for those of us who would like to see the Eastern European nations freed from the yoke of communism.'

'I'm glad you appreciate my efforts, Rosenevski.'

This time Abel was sure McCarthy had mispronounced his name on purpose, but decided not to comment on it.

'You do realize,' the senator continued, 'that only after the traitors have been driven from within our own government can any real action be taken to free your captive people.'

'That's exactly what I want to speak to you about, Senator. You've had brilliant success in exposing treachery within our own government. But to date, one of the communists' greatest crimes has gone unnoticed.'

'Just what great crime did you have in mind, Mr Rosenevski? I've come across so many since I arrived in Washington.'

'I am referring' Abel drew himself up a little straighter in his chair – 'to the forced repatriation of thousands of displaced Polish citizens by the American authorities after the war in Europe ended. Innocent enemies of communism were sent back to Poland and then transported to Russian camps, to be enslaved and often exterminated.' He waited for a response, but none was forthcoming. He heard a click, and wondered if someone else had been listening to their conversation.

'How can you be so ill informed, Rosenevski?' said Senator McCarthy, his tone suddenly aggressive. 'You dare to telephone me to say that Americans – loyal United States soldiers – sent thousands of your people to Russia and nobody heard a word about it? Even a Polack couldn't be that dumb. I have to wonder what kind of person accepts a lie like that without demanding proof. Do you expect me to believe that American soldiers are disloyal? Is that what you want? Tell me, Rosenevski, what is it with you people? Are you too blind to recognize communist propaganda even when it hits you right in the face? Do you have to waste the time of an overworked United States senator because of a rumour cooked up by the *Pravda*'s Red slime simply to create unrest in America's immigrant communities?'

Abel sat motionless, stunned by the outburst. He was glad McCarthy couldn't see his startled face.

'Senator, I'm sorry to have wasted your time,' he said quietly. 'I hadn't thought of it in quite that way before.'

'Well, it just goes to show you how tricky these Commie bastards can be,' said McCarthy, his tone softening. 'You have to keep an eye on them all the time. Anyway, I hope you're more alert now to the real dangers the American people face.'

'I am indeed, Senator. Thank you for taking the trouble to speak to me. Goodbye, Senator.'

'Goodbye, Mr Rosenevski.'

The click of the phone sounded not unlike another slamming door.

44

WILLIAM BECAME aware that he was getting older when Kate teased him about his greying hair. If that wasn't bad enough, Richard started to bring young ladies home for tea.

William almost always approved of Richard's choices, perhaps because they were all so similar to Kate, although in his opinion she was more beautiful in middle age than any of them. Virginia and Lucy, now also teenagers, as the press was starting to describe their generation, brought him great happiness as they grew up in the image of their mother.

Virginia was developing into a talented artist, and the walls of the kitchen and the children's bedrooms were covered in her latest works of genius, as Richard mockingly described them. Virginia's revenge came the day Richard started taking cello lessons, when even the servants murmured uncharitable comments whenever the bow came into contact with the strings. Lucy adored them both, and considered Virginia, with uncritical prejudice, to be the next Edward Hopper, and Richard a future Casals.

In Kate's eyes, all three of her children were just perfect. Richard soon improved enough at the cello to join the St Paul's school orchestra, while one of Virginia's paintings could be found hanging in the drawing room. But it became clear to all of them that Lucy was going to be the beauty of the family when, at the age of thirteen, she started receiving phone calls from boys who until then had only shown an interest in baseball and go-karts.

In 1951 Richard was offered a place at Harvard, and although he did not win the top mathematics scholarship, Kate was quick to point out to William that he had played both hockey and the cello for St Paul's, neither of which her husband had managed. William was secretly proud of Richard's achievements, but mumbled something about not knowing many bankers who specialized in either hockey or the cello.

Banking was now moving into an expansionist period, as Americans began to believe in a lasting peace. William found himself working hours that weren't on the clock, and for a short time the threat of Abel Rosnovski, and the problems associated with him, faded into the background. Until . . .

◄o►

In 1951 the Federal Aviation Administration granted a new airline company called Interstate Airways, a franchise for flights between the east and west coasts. The airline approached Lester's Bank to help them raise the necessary $30 million on the Stock Exchange to comply with government regulations.

William believed the burgeoning airline industry was well worth supporting, and spent a considerable amount of his time setting up a public offering to raise the funds for Interstate. The bank put its full financial muscle behind the new company, and William realized that his personal reputation was at stake when he went to the market for the $30 million. The details of the offering were announced in July, and the stock was snapped up in a matter of days. William received lavish praise from all quarters for the way he had carried the project through to such a successful conclusion. He could not have been happier about the outcome, until he read in Thaddeus Cohen's latest report that 10 per cent of the airline's stock had been purchased by one of Abel Rosnovski's satellite corporations.

William knew that the time had come to acquaint Ted Leach and Tony Simmons with his fears. He asked Tony to fly up to New York, where he told both vice chairmen the saga of Abel Rosnovski and Henry Osborne.

'Why didn't you tell us about all this before?' Simmons asked.

'I dealt with over a hundred companies the size of the Richmond Group when I was at Kane and Cabot, Tony, and many of them threatened me with some form of revenge, which I never took seriously. I only became convinced Rosnovski still harboured a grudge when he purchased six per cent of the bank's shares from Susan Lester.'

'Why would she be willing to dispose of her shares?' asked Simmons.

William ignored the question. 'I didn't bother either of you at the time but when he picked up ten per cent of Interstate I felt—'

'It's possible you may be overreacting,' said Leach. 'And if that's the case, it would be unwise to inform the rest of the board of your suspicions. The last thing we want a few days after launching a new company is to encourage everyone to dump their stock.'

'I agree with Ted,' said Simmons. 'Perhaps the time has come for you to make a personal approach to Rosnovski, and see if you can sort out your differences?'

'Nothing would give him more pleasure,' snapped William. 'That way, he'd be left in no doubt that the bank feels under siege.'

'Don't you think his attitude might change if he learned how hard you tried to talk the bank into backing the Richmond Group? Not forgetting that—'

'I'm not convinced that would make any difference.'

'So what do you think the bank should do?' asked Leach. 'We can't prevent Rosnovski from buying Lester stock if he can find a willing seller. If we went in for buying our own shares, far from stopping him, we'd be playing right into his hands by pushing up the price and raising the value of his holding.'

'And don't forget,' interjected Simmons, 'that there's nothing the Democrats would enjoy more than a banking scandal, with an election just a few months away.'

'I hear what you say, gentlemen,' said William, 'but I had to let you know what Rosnovski was up to in case he springs another surprise.'

'I suppose there's an outside chance,' said Simmons, 'that the whole thing is innocent, and he simply thought Interstate was a good investment.'

'That's just not credible, Tony. Don't forget that my stepfather is also involved. Why do you think Rosnovski employed Henry Osborne in the first place?'

'Now you can't afford to let yourself become paranoid, William. I feel sure we'll find—'

'Don't become paranoid?' barked William. 'Try not to forget the power our Articles of Incorporation gives any shareholder who gets his hands on eight per cent of the bank's stock – an article I originally inserted to protect myself from being removed from the board. Rosnovski already owns *six* per cent, and if that's not bad enough, he could wipe out Interstate Airways overnight simply by placing all his stock on the market without warning.'

'But he'd gain nothing from that,' said Ted Leach. 'On the contrary, he'd stand to lose a great deal of money.'

'Yes, of course he'd lose money if he dumped his Interstate stock, but that wouldn't bother him – his hotels are making record profits and he can claim against tax. As bankers, our credibility depends on the fickle confidence of the public, which Rosnovski can now shatter as and when it suits him.'

'Calm down, William,' said Simmons. 'It hasn't come to that yet. Now that we know what Rosnovski's up to, we can keep a close eye on him. The first thing we have to do is make sure that no one else sells their stock in Lester's without first offering it to the bank.'

'Agreed,' said Leach. 'And I still think you should speak to Rosnovski personally. At least that way we'd find out what his intentions are and we could prepare ourselves accordingly.'

'Is that also your opinion, Tony?'

'Yes, I agree with Ted. I think you should contact Rosnovski directly, and have it out with him.'

William sat in silence for a few moments. 'If you both feel that way, I'll give it a try,' he eventually said. 'I don't agree with you, but I may be too personally involved to make a dispassionate judgement. Give me a few days to think about how I should go about it.'

◄○►

Four days later, William gave his secretary instructions that he was not to be interrupted under any circumstances. He knew that Abel Rosnovski was sitting at his desk in the New York Baron: he'd had a man posted in the lobby of the hotel all morning, whose task was to report the moment Rosnovski turned up. Rosnovski had arrived at the hotel at 7.27 a.m., gone straight up to his office on the 42nd floor and had not been seen since. William picked up his telephone and dialled the number himself.

'New York Baron, how may I help you?'

'Mr Rosnovski, please,' said William nervously. He was put through to a secretary.

'Mr Rosnovski, please,' he repeated. This time his voice was a little steadier.

'May I ask who is calling?' the secretary said.

'My name is William Kane.'

There was a long silence – or did it simply seem long to William?

'I'll just check to see if he's in, Mr Kane.'

Another long silence.

'Mr Kane?'

'Mr Rosnovski?'

'What can I do for you, Mr Kane?' asked a very calm, lightly accented voice.

William looked down at the written notes on the pad in front of him. He could hear his heart beating.

'I'm a little concerned about your holdings in Lester's Bank, Mr Rosnovski,' he said, 'and also about the strong position you've taken in one of the companies we represent. I thought perhaps the time had come for us to meet and discuss your intentions. There is also a personal matter I should like to make known to you,' Word period.

Another long silence. Had he been cut off?

'There are no conditions on which I'd agree to hold a meeting with you Kane. I know enough about you already without wanting to hear your excuses for the way you treated Davis Leroy. My advice to you is to keep your eyes open night and day; that way you'll discover soon enough what my intentions are, and they differ greatly from those you'll find in the Book of Genesis. One day you're going to want to jump out of the seventeenth-floor window of your bank, because you'll be in so much trouble with your own board. Don't ever forget, Kane, that I only need two per cent more of the bank's stock to invoke Article Seven, and we both know the consequences of that, don't we?'

William didn't respond.

'Perhaps then you'll finally appreciate how Davis Leroy felt, wondering what the bank might do about his future. Now you can sit and wonder what I'm going to do with yours once I'm in possession of eight per cent of Lester's stock.'

Rosnovski's words chilled William, but he forced himself to respond calmly. 'I can understand how you feel, Mr Rosnovski, but I still think it might be worthwhile for us to get together and talk about our differences. There are one or two things you clearly aren't aware of.'

'Like the way you swindled Henry Osborne out of five hundred thousand dollars, Mr Kane?'

William was momentarily speechless, but once again he managed to control his temper.

'No, Mr Rosnovski. What I wanted to discuss with you has nothing to do with Mr Osborne. It's a personal matter, and involves only you. However, I can assure you that I have never swindled Henry Osborne out of one red cent.'

'That's not what he tells me. He says you were responsible for the death of your own mother, just so you wouldn't have to honour your debt to him. After your treatment of Davis Leroy, I find that only too easy to believe.'

William had never had to fight harder to control his emotions – who the hell did this man think he was? – and it took him several seconds to manage a reply. 'May I suggest we clear this whole misunderstanding up by meeting at a neutral place of your choice, where no one would recognize us?'

'There's only one place where no one would recognize you, Mr Kane.'

'Where's that?'

'Heaven,' said Abel, and placed the phone back on the hook.

45

'GET ME Henry Osborne at once,' Abel said to his secretary.

He drummed his fingers on the desk while the girl took nearly fifteen minutes to find Congressman Osborne, who it turned out had been showing some of his constituents around the Capitol building.

'What can I do for you, Abel?'

'I thought you'd want to be the first to hear that Kane knows everything. So now the battle is out in the open.'

'What do you mean, knows everything? Does he know I'm involved?' Osborne asked anxiously.

'He sure does. He also knows about my holdings in Lester's Bank and Interstate Airways.'

'How could he possibly know that? Only you and I know about it.'

'You and I and Curtis Fenton,' said Abel, interrupting him.

'Right. But he'd never tell Kane.'

'He must have. There's no other way he could have found out. Don't forget that Kane dealt directly with Fenton when I bought the Richmond Group from his bank. They must have maintained some sort of contact.'

'Oh hell!'

'You sound worried, Henry.'

'If Kane knows everything, it's a different ball game. I'm warning you, Abel, he's not in the habit of losing.'

'Nor am I,' said Abel. 'William Kane doesn't frighten me, not while I have all the aces in my hand. So where do we stand with Parfitt?'

'He's come down to $600,000 so I could close the deal now, if you wanted me to.'

'No, I can wait,' said Abel. 'There's no hurry. Parfitt and Kane aren't exactly bosom pals so he won't be selling his two per cent to him. For the time being, we'll allow Kane to wonder what we're up to. After my phone conversation with him this morning, I can assure you that, to use a gentleman's expression, he's perspiring. But I'll let you in on a secret, Henry: I'm not sweating, because I have no intention of making a move until I'm good and ready.'

'Fine,' said Osborne. 'I'll let you know if anything comes up that we should be worried about.'

'You must get it into your head, Henry, that there's nothing for *us* to worry about. We have your friend Mr Kane by the balls, and I now intend to squeeze them very slowly.'

'I'll enjoy watching that,' said Osborne, sounding a little happier.

'Sometimes I think you hate Kane more than I do.'

Osborne laughed nervously. 'Have a good trip to Europe.'

Abel put the phone back on the hook and sat staring into space as he considered his next move, his fingers still tapping noisily on the desk. Then he picked up the phone again.

'Get Mr Curtis Fenton at Continental Trust Bank.' His fingers continued to tap. A few moments later the phone rang.

'Fenton?'

'Good morning, Mr Rosnovski. How are you?'

'I want to close all my accounts with your bank.'

There was no reply.

'Did you hear me, Fenton?'

'Yes,' said the stupefied banker. 'May I ask why, Mr Rosnovski?'

'Because Judas never was my favourite apostle, Fenton, that's why. As of this moment, you are no longer on the board of the Baron Group. You will shortly receive written confirmation of this conversation, and instructions about which bank my accounts should be transferred to.'

'But I don't understand, Mr Rosnovski. What have I done?'

Abel hung up as his daughter walked into the office.

'That didn't sound very pleasant, Daddy.'

'It wasn't meant to be, but it's nothing to concern yourself with, darling,' said Abel, his tone changing immediately. 'Did you manage to find all the clothes you'll need for the trip?'

'Yes, thank you, Daddy, but I'm not sure what they're wearing in London and Paris. I just hope I've got it right. I don't want to stick out like a sore thumb.'

'You'll stick out, all right, my darling – anyone would with your style. You'll be the most beautiful thing Europe's seen in years. They'll know your clothes didn't come out of a ration book. Those young men will be falling over themselves to get at you, but they'll find me standing in their way.' Florentyna laughed. 'Now, let's go and have some lunch and discuss what we're going to do while we're in London.'

Ten days later, after Florentyna had spent a long weekend with her mother in Chicago, father and daughter flew from Idlewild to Heathrow. The flight took nearly fourteen hours, and when they arrived at Claridge's, the only thing they wanted to do was have a long sleep.

Abel was making the trip for three reasons: first, to confirm the sites of new Baron hotels in London, Paris and possibly Rome; second, to accompany Florentyna on her first visit to Europe before she went to Radcliffe to study modern languages; and third, and most important, to visit his castle in Poland and find out if there was even an outside chance of proving his ownership.

London turned out to be a success for both of them. Abel's advisors had found a site on Hyde Park Corner, and he instructed his solicitors to begin negotiations immediately for the land and the permits that would be needed before England's capital could boast a Baron.

Florentyna found the austerity of post-war London somewhat forbidding compared to the freedom of her own life, but Londoners seemed to be undaunted by their war-damaged city, still believing themselves to be a world power. She was invited to lunches, dinners and balls, and her father was proved right about the effect she would have on the gentlemen of England. She returned each night with sparkling eyes and stories of new conquests – most forgotten by the following morning, but not all: she couldn't make up her mind between an Etonian lieutenant serving with the Grenadier Guards, or a member of the House of Lords who was in-waiting to the King. She wasn't quite sure what 'in-waiting' meant, but he certainly didn't hang about whenever she appeared.

In Paris the pace didn't slacken. They both spoke excellent French, and got along as well with the Parisians as they had with the Londoners. Abel and Florentyna walked down the Champs Elysées hand in hand, which reminded him of when he marched down the centre of the road with the free French. He tried to think why Paris looked so different from London. It was Florentyna who pointed out that the Germans hadn't bombed the city.

Abel was normally bored by the end of the second week of any vacation, and would start counting the days until he could get back to work. But not while he had Florentyna as his companion. She had become the centre of his life as well as the heir to his fortune.

When the time came to leave Paris, neither of them wanted to go. They stayed on a few extra days, using the excuse that Abel was negotiating to buy a famous, but somewhat run-down, hotel on the Boulevard Raspail. He did not inform the owner, a M. Neuffe, who looked, if it were possible, even more run-down than the hotel, that he planned to demolish the building and start again from scratch. No sooner had M. Neuffe signed the papers than Abel ordered the building to be razed to the ground. With no more excuses for remaining in Paris, he and Florentyna reluctantly departed for Rome.

After the confidence of the English and the gaiety of the French, the sullen and dilapidated Eternal City dampened their spirits. The Romans felt they had nothing to celebrate, many feeling they had backed the wrong side, while others refused to admit defeat. In Rome, Abel found only an overpowering sense of financial instability, and decided to shelve his plans to build a Baron there. Florentyna sensed his growing impatience to see his castle in Poland once again, so she suggested they leave Rome a few days early.

Abel had found it more difficult to obtain a visa for Florentyna and himself to cross the border into an Iron Curtain country than a permit to build a new 500-room hotel in London. A less persistent man would have given up, but with the appropriate visas firmly stamped in their passports, Abel hired a car and the two of them set off for Slonim. Once they reached the border they were kept waiting for several hours, helped only by the fact that Abel was fluent in the language. Had the guards known why his Polish was so good, they would doubtless have thought twice about allowing him to cross the border. He changed $500 into zlotys – that at least seemed to please the Poles – and drove on. With every mile, Florentyna became more aware of how much the journey meant to her father.

'Daddy, I can't remember you ever being so excited about anything.'

'This is where I was born,' Abel explained. 'After such a long time in America, where things change every day, it's almost unreal to be back in a place where it looks as if nothing's changed in thirty years.'

As they drew nearer to Slonim, Abel's senses heightened in anticipation of seeing his birthplace once again. Across nearly forty years he heard his childish voice ask the Baron whether the hour of the submerged peoples of Europe had arrived, and if he would be able to play his part. Tears came to his eyes at the thought of how short that hour had been, and what an insignificant part he had played.

At last they rounded the final bend before the long approach to the Baron's estate. When Abel saw the great iron gates that led to the castle, he laughed aloud in excitement and brought the car to a halt.

'It's all just as I remember it,' he declared. 'Nothing's changed. Let's go and see the cottage where I spent the first five years of my life – I don't expect anyone's living there now. Then we'll go and visit my castle.'

Florentyna followed as he marched confidently down a small

track into a forest of moss-covered birches and oaks that hadn't changed in a hundred years. After about twenty minutes they came to a small clearing, and there in front of them was the trapper's cottage. Abel stood and stared. He had forgotten how tiny his first home was; could nine people really have lived there? The thatched roof was now in disrepair, the stone walls dilapidated and the windows broken. The once tidy vegetable garden had disappeared in the matted undergrowth. Was the cottage still occupied?

Florentyna took her father by the arm and led him slowly to the front door. He stood there, unable to move, so she knocked. They waited in silence. She knocked again, this time a little louder, and they heard someone moving inside.

'All right, all right,' said a querulous voice in Polish, and a few moments later the door inched open, revealing an old woman, bent and thin, dressed entirely in black. Wisps of untidy snow-white hair escaped from her headscarf, and her tired grey eyes looked vacantly at the visitors.

'It's not possible,' Abel said softly in English.

'What do you want?' asked the old woman suspiciously. She had no teeth, and the line of her nose, mouth and chin formed a perfect concave arc.

Abel answered in Polish, 'May we come in and talk to you?'

Her eyes looked fearfully from one to the other. 'Old Helena hasn't done anything wrong,' she said in a whine.

'I know,' said Abel gently. 'I have brought good news for you.'

With some reluctance she pulled open the door and allowed them to enter the bare, cold room, but she didn't offer them a seat. The room hadn't changed – two chairs, one table and a reminder that until he had left the cottage Abel hadn't known what a carpet was. Florentyna shivered.

'I can't get the fire going,' wheezed the old woman, prodding the faintly glowing log in the grate with her stick. She scrabbled ineffectually in her pocket. 'I need paper.' She looked at Abel, showing a spark of interest for the first time. 'Do you have any paper?'

Abel looked at her steadily. 'Don't you remember me?' he asked.

'I don't know you.'

'You do, Helena. My name is – Wladek.'

'You knew my little Wladek?'

'I am Wladek.'

'Oh, no,' she said with sad and distant finality. 'He was too good for me – the mark of God was upon him. The Baron took him away to be an angel. Yes, he took away Matka's littlest one . . .'

Her old voice cracked and died away. She sat down, but the ancient, lined hands were fidgeting in her lap.

'I have returned,' said Abel, kneeling in front of her. The old woman paid him no attention, simply muttering on as though she were quite alone in the room.

'They killed my husband, my Jasio, and all my lovely children were taken to the camps except little Sophia. I hid her and they went away.' Her voice was even and resigned.

'What happened to little Sophia?' asked Abel.

'The Russians stole her in the next war,' she said dully. Abel shuddered. The old woman roused herself from her memories. 'What do you want?' she demanded. 'Why are you asking me these questions?'

'I wanted you to meet my daughter, Florentyna.'

'I had a daughter called Florentyna once, but now there's only me.'

'But I . . .' began Abel, starting to unbutton his shirt.

Florentyna stopped him. 'We know,' she said, smiling at the old woman.

'How can you possibly know? It was all long before you were even born.'

'They told us in the village,' said Florentyna.

'Have you any paper with you?' the old woman asked. 'I need paper for the fire.'

Abel looked at his foster mother helplessly. 'No,' he replied. 'I'm sorry, we didn't bring any with us.'

'Then what do you want?' repeated the old woman, once again hostile.

'Nothing,' said Abel, now resigned to the impossibility that she would remember him. 'We just wanted to say hello.' He took out his wallet, removed all the zloty notes he had obtained at the border and handed them to her.

'Thank you, thank you,' she said as she took each note, her old eyes watering with pleasure.

Abel bent over to kiss her, but she backed away.

Florentyna took her father's arm, and led him out of the cottage and back down the forest track in the direction of their car.

The old woman watched from the window until she was sure they were out of sight. Then she took the banknotes, crumpled each one into a little ball and laid them carefully in the grate. They kindled immediately. She placed twigs and small logs on top of the blazing zlotys and sat down by her fire, the best in weeks, rubbing her hands together, enjoying the warmth.

Abel did not speak again until the iron gates came into sight. Then he promised Florentyna, trying his best to forget the little cottage and the women who had made it possible for him to live, 'You are about to see the most beautiful castle in the world.'

'You must stop exaggerating, Daddy.'

'In the world,' he repeated quietly.

Florentyna laughed. 'I'll let you know how it compares with Versailles.'

They climbed back into the car and Abel drove through the gates, remembering the first vehicle he'd ever ridden in when he was being escorted the other way. As they bumped slowly up the winding, potholed drive, more memories came flooding back: happy days as a child with the Baron and Leon, unhappy days in the dungeon under the Germans, and the worst day of his life when he was taken away from his beloved castle by the Russians, thinking he would never see his home again. But now he, Wladek Koskiewicz, was returning – returning to claim what was rightfully his.

When they rounded the final bend, Florentyna saw her father's birthright for the first time. Abel brought the car to a halt and gazed at his castle. Neither of them spoke. What was there to say? They stared in shock and disbelief at the remains of the bombed-out shell of his dream.

They climbed slowly out of the car. Still neither spoke. Florentyna held her father's hand very, very tightly as the tears rolled down his cheeks. Only one wall remained precariously standing in a semblance of its former glory; the rest was nothing more than a pile of rubble. He could not bear to tell her of the great halls, the sprawling wings, the vast kitchens and the luxurious bedrooms.

Abel walked across to three mounds, now smooth with thick green moss, that marked the graves of the Baron, his friend Leon and his other beloved Florentyna. He paused at each one, thinking that Leon and Florentyna should still be alive today. He knelt by their side, the dreadful visions of their final moments vividly returning to him. His daughter stood beside him, her hand resting on his shoulder, saying nothing.

A long time passed before Abel rose to his feet. They tramped over the ruins together, hand in hand, broken slabs of stone marking the places where once magnificent staterooms had been filled with laughter. Abel still said nothing. When they clambered down into the dungeons Abel sat on the floor of the damp little room under the grille, or the half of the grille that was still left. He twisted the silver band around and around his wrist.

'This is where your father spent four years of his life.'

'It can't be possible,' said Florentyna.

'It's better now than it was then. At least now there's fresh air, birds singing, the sun shining and a feeling of freedom. Then there was only darkness, death, the stench of death, and worst of all, the hope of death.'

'Come on, Daddy, let's get out of here. Staying can only bring back more unhappy memories.'

Florentyna led her reluctant father back to the car, and drove slowly down the long drive. Abel didn't once look back towards his ruined castle as he passed through its iron gates for the last time.

On the journey to Warsaw, Abel hardly spoke, and Florentyna abandoned any attempt to cheer him up.

When he finally said, 'There is now only one thing left that I must achieve in this life,' she wondered what he could possibly mean, but she did not press him to explain. She did, however, manage to coax him into spending another weekend in London on their return journey, which she hoped would help him forget his demented old foster mother and what was left of his inheritance.

–◦–

They flew to London the next day. Once they had booked into Claridge's, Florentyna went off to see old friends and make new ones. Abel went through the newspapers that had been accumulating at the hotel since they had last been there. He did not like knowing that things didn't stop while he was away; it reminded him only too clearly that the world would keep turning without him. A report on an inside page of the previous day's *Times* caught his attention. Something *had* happened while he was away. An Interstate Airways Vickers Viscount had crashed immediately after take-off from Mexico airport on its way to Panama City. The seventeen passengers and crew had all been killed. The Mexican authorities were placing the blame firmly on Interstate's bad servicing of its aircraft, while Interstate blamed the Mexican mechanics. Abel picked up the phone and asked the switchboard operator for an overseas line.

Saturday. He's probably in Chicago, thought Abel. He thumbed through his little address book to check the home number.

'There'll be a delay of about thirty minutes,' said a precise English voice.

'Thank you,' said Abel, and lay down on the bed to wait impatiently. The phone rang twenty minutes later.

'Your overseas call is on the line, sir,' said the same precise voice.

'Abel, is that you? Where are you?'

'Sure is, Henry. I'm in London.'

'Are you through?' said the girl, who was back on the line.

'I haven't even started,' said Abel.

'I'm sorry, sir, I mean are you speaking to America?'

'Oh yes, sure. Thank you. Jesus, Henry, they speak a different language over here.'

Osborne laughed.

'Now listen. Did you hear about that Interstate plane that crashed at Mexico City?'

'Yes, I did. But there's nothing for you to worry about. The plane was properly insured, so the company's incurred no loss, and the stock has only dropped a few cents.'

'The insurance is the last thing I'm interested in,' said Abel. 'This could be an ideal opportunity to find out just how strong Mr Kane's constitution is.'

'I don't understand, Abel. What are you getting at?'

'Listen carefully, and I'll explain exactly what I want you to do when the Stock Exchange opens on Monday morning. I'll be back in New York by Tuesday to conduct the final movement myself.'

Osborne listened attentively to Abel's instructions. Twenty minutes later, Abel replaced the phone on its hook.

He was through.

46

WILLIAM REALIZED that he could expect more trouble from Abel Rosnovski when Curtis Fenton phoned to let him know that the Chicago Baron was closing all the group's bank accounts with Continental Trust, and accusing Fenton of disloyalty and unethical conduct.

'I thought I did the correct thing in writing to you about Mr Rosnovski's acquisitions in Lester's,' said the banker unhappily, 'and it's ended with my losing one of my most important customers. I don't know how my board of directors will react.'

William calmed Fenton down a little by promising him he would speak to his superiors at Continental Trust. He was, however, more concerned about what Rosnovski's next move would be.

It was another month before he found out. William was checking over the morning mail when a call came through from his broker, who told him that someone had placed a million dollars' worth of Interstate Airways stock on the market. William told him that his trust would pick up the shares, and the broker issued an immediate buy order. At two o'clock that afternoon another million dollars' worth was put on the market. Before William had a chance to pick them up, the price started to fall. By the time the New York Stock Exchange closed at three o'clock, the share price of Interstate Airways had fallen by a third.

At ten minutes past ten the next morning, William received a call from his now agitated broker. Another million dollars' worth of Interstate stock had been placed on the market at the opening bell. The broker reported that the latest dumping had caused an avalanche of sellers. Brokers with Interstate sell orders were rushing onto the floor from every quarter, and the stock was now trading at only a few cents a share. Only twenty-four hours previously, Interstate had been quoted at four and a half dollars.

William instructed Alfred Rodgers, the company secretary, to call a board meeting for the following Monday. Before then he needed to confirm who was responsible for dumping the stock. Not that he was in much doubt. By Wednesday afternoon he had to abandon any attempt at shoring up Interstate by buying all the shares as they came on the market. At the close of business that day, the Securities and Exchange Commission announced that it would be conducting an inquiry into all Interstate transactions. William knew that the Lester's board would now have to decide whether to support the airline for the three to six months it would take the SEC to complete its investigation, or whether to let the company go under. Either alternative looked extremely damaging, both to William's pocket and to the bank's reputation.

It came as no surprise to William when Thaddeus Cohen rang to confirm that the company that had dumped the three million dollars' worth of Interstate shares was one of those fronting for Abel Rosnovski. On Thursday morning a spokesman for Guaranty Investment Corporation issued a press release explaining their reasons for selling: they had been very concerned about Interstate's future after the Mexican government's 'detailed and considered' statement about its inadequate servicing facilities and procedures.

'"Detailed and considered",' said William, outraged. 'The Mexican government hasn't made a less responsible statement since it claimed Speedy Gonzales would win the one hundred metres at the Helsinki Olympics.'

The media made the most of Guaranty Investment's press release, and on Friday the Federal Aviation Administration grounded all Interstate flights until it had conducted a thorough investigation into the airline's servicing facilities and procedures.

William was confident Interstate had nothing to fear from such an inspection, but being grounded was disastrous for its short-term bookings. No aviation company can afford to leave its aircraft on the ground; they can only make money when they're in the air. To compound William's problems, other major companies represented by the bank were considering their positions. The press had been quick to remind it's readers that Lester's was Interstate Airways' underwriter.

To William's surprise, Interstate's shares began to pick up late on Friday afternoon. It didn't take him long to guess why – a guess that was later confirmed by Thaddeus Cohen. The buyer was Abel Rosnovski. He had sold his Interstate shares at the top of the market, and was now buying them back in small amounts while they were on the floor. William shook his head in grudging admiration. Rosnovski was making a small fortune for himself while bankrupting William both financially and in terms of his reputation on Wall Street. William worked out that although the Baron Group must have risked over $3 million, it could well end up making a huge profit.

When the board met on Monday, William explained the entire history behind his clash with Rosnovski, and offered his resignation. The board did not accept it, nor was a vote taken. However, there were murmurings from some of the younger board members, and William knew that if Rosnovski attacked again, his colleagues might not take the same tolerant attitude a second time.

The board went on to consider whether the bank should continue to support Interstate Airways. Tony Simmons convinced them that the FAA's findings would come out in Interstate's favour, and that in time the bank would recover all its money. He had to admit to William after the meeting that this could only help Rosnovski in the long run, but the bank had no choice if it wished to protect its reputation.

Simmons was proved right on both counts. When the SEC published its findings, it declared Lester's 'beyond reproach', although it had some stern words for Guaranty Investment Corporation. When the market started trading the following day, William was not surprised to find Interstate's stock rising steadily. Within weeks the shares were back to four and a half dollars.

Thaddeus Cohen informed William that the principal purchaser was once again Abel Rosnovski.

'That's all I need at the moment,' said William. 'Not only does he make a large profit on the whole transaction, but now he can repeat the exercise whenever it suits him.'

'In fact,' said Thaddeus Cohen, 'that is exactly what you do need.'

'What do you mean, Thaddeus? I've never known you to speak in riddles.'

'Rosnovski's made his first error of judgement. He's broken the law, so now it's your turn to go after him. He probably doesn't even realize that what he's been involved in is illegal, because he's doing it for all the wrong reasons.'

'I still have no idea what you are talking about?'

'Simple,' said Cohen. 'Because of your obsession with Rosnovski – and his with you – it seems that both of you have overlooked the obvious: if you sell shares with the intention of causing the market to drop, in order to pick up those same shares at the bottom and make a profit, you're breaking Rule 10b-5 of the Securities and Exchange Commission, and you're guilty of fraud. There's no doubt in my mind that making a quick profit wasn't Rosnovski's original intention; in fact, we know very well he only wanted to embarrass you. But who's going to believe him if he says he dumped the stock because he thought Interstate was unreliable, then bought it back when it touched rock bottom? Answer, nobody – and certainly not the SEC. I'll have a full written report sent around for your consideration by tomorrow, explaining the legal implications.'

'Thank you,' said William, feeling relieved for the first time in months.

Thaddeus Cohen's report was on his desk at nine the next morning, and once William had considered its implications, he called an emergency board meeting. The directors agreed the course of action that should be taken, and Thaddeus Cohen was instructed to send a copy of his report to the Fraud Department of the SEC.

'Should we send a copy to the *Wall Street Journal*?' suggested Simmons.

'That won't be necessary,' the company secretary assured the board. 'Within moments of the report landing on the SEC desk you can be sure it will be leaked to the *Journal*. They are not known as the securities and exchange colander without reason.' The board members laughed for the first time that day.

Alfred Rodgers's judgement turned out to be correct, because the *Wall Street Journal* ran a front page article on the Wednesday morning which couldn't have been more helpful if it had been dictated by Thaddeus Cohen.

The story went on to give SEC Rule 10b-5 in full, and a leader commented that this was exactly the sort of test case that President Truman had been looking for. A cartoon below the article showed Truman catching a businessman with his hand in the cookie jar.

William smiled as he read through the item, confident that he had heard the last of Abel Rosnovski.

―◇―

Abel frowned and tapped his fingers on his desk as Henry Osborne read the article a second time.

'The boys in Washington,' said Osborne, 'won't be able to resist setting up a full inquiry, especially if there's some political capital to be made of it.'

'But, Henry, you know very well I didn't sell Interstate to make a quick killing on the market,' said Abel. 'I had absolutely no interest in making a profit.'

'I know that,' said Osborne, 'but you try and convince the Senate Finance Committee that the Chicago Baron wasn't interested in financial gain, that all he really wanted to do was settle a personal grudge against William Kane, and they'll laugh you right out of court – or out of the Senate, to be more exact.'

'Damn,' said Abel. 'What the hell do I do now?'

'Well, first you'll have to lie low until this has had time to blow over. Start praying that some bigger scandal comes along for

Truman to get himself worked up about, or that Washington becomes so preoccupied with the election that it doesn't have time to press for an inquiry. With luck, a new administration may even drop the whole thing. Whatever you do, Abel, don't buy any stocks that are in any way connected with Lester's Bank, or the least you're going to end up with is a very large fine. Let me see what I can swing with the Democrats in Washington.'

'Remind Truman's office that I gave fifty thousand dollars to his campaign fund during the last election, and that I will be doing the same for Stevenson.'

'I've already done that,' said Henry. 'In fact, I'd advise you to give fifty thousand to the Republicans as well.'

'They're making a mountain out of a molehill,' said Abel.

'A molehill that Kane will turn into a mountain if we give him half a chance,' replied Osborne.

Abel's fingers continued to tap on his desk.

PART SEVEN

1952–1963

47

THADDEUS COHEN'S next quarterly report revealed that Abel Rosnovski had stopped buying or selling stock in any of Lester's affiliated companies. It seemed he was now concentrating all his energies on building new hotels in Europe. Cohen's opinion was that Rosnovski was lying low until a decision had been made by the SEC following its Interstate inquiry.

Representatives of the SEC had visited William at the bank on several occasions. He had spoken to them with complete frankness, but they never revealed how their inquiries were progressing, or suggested who was responsible for the share collapse. The SEC finally concluded its investigation and thanked William for his cooperation. He assumed he would have to wait a few months before they published their conclusions.

As the election grew nearer and Truman began to look more and more like a 'lame duck' president, William began to fear that Rosnovski might have got away with it. He couldn't help feeling that Henry Osborne must have been able to pull a few strings in Congress, and remembered that Cohen had once underlined a note about a $50,000 donation from the Baron Group to Truman's campaign fund. He was not surprised to read in Cohen's latest report that Rosnovski had donated a further $50,000 to Adlai Stevenson, the Democrats' candidate for President. But he was shocked when he discovered that he'd also given $50,000 to the Eisenhower campaign fund. Cohen had underlined the second figure.

William had never considered supporting anyone for public

office who didn't run on a Republican ticket. He wanted Eisenhower, the compromise candidate who had emerged on the first ballot at the convention in Chicago, to defeat Stevenson, even though a Republican administration was less likely to press for a share-manipulation inquiry.

When General Dwight D. Eisenhower was elected the 34th President of the United States on November 4, 1952 (it appeared that the nation did 'like Ike'), William assumed that Rosnovski had escaped any charge. He only hoped that the experience would persuade him to leave Lester's affairs well alone in the future.

The one small compensation to come out of the election for William was that Henry Osborne lost his congressional seat to a Republican. The Eisenhower jacket had turned out to have long coattails, and Osborne's rival had clung to them. Thaddeus Cohen was inclined to think that Osborne would no longer exert quite the same influence over Abel Rosnovski now he was no longer in office. The rumour in Chicago was that since Osborne's wealthy second wife had divorced him, he'd started gambling again, and was running up debts all over town. William was feeling more relaxed than he had for some time, and looked forward to the prosperous and peaceful era that Eisenhower promised in his Inauguration speech.

—<o>—

During the first months of the new President's administration, William put Rosnovski's threats to the back of his mind, assuming he'd learned his lesson. He told Thaddeus Cohen that he believed they'd heard the last of Abel Rosnovski. Cohen didn't comment, but then he hadn't been asked to.

William put all his efforts into building Lester's, both in size and reputation, increasingly aware that he was now doing it as much for his son as for himself. Some of the younger board members at the bank had already started referring to him as the 'old man'.

'It had to happen,' said Kate.

'Then why hasn't it happened to you?' he asked gallantly.

Kate smiled. 'Now I know how you've closed so many deals with vain men.'

William laughed. 'And one beautiful woman.'

With Richard's twenty-first birthday only a few months away, William revised the provision of his will. He set aside $5 million for Kate, $2 million for each of the girls, and left the rest of the family fortune to Richard, ruefully noting the bite that would be extracted for inheritance taxes, despite a Republican majority in both houses. He also left $1 million to Harvard.

—◇—

Richard had been making good use of his time at Harvard. By the beginning of his senior year he not only appeared set for a summa cum laude, but he was also playing the cello in the university orchestra and was second pitcher for the baseball team. As Kate liked to ask rhetorically, how many students spend Saturday afternoon playing baseball against Yale, and Sunday evening playing the cello in the Lowell concert hall?

Richard's final year passed all too quickly, and when he left Harvard armed with a Bachelor of Arts degree in mathematics, a cello and a baseball bat, all he required before reporting to the Business School on the other side of the Charles River was a good holiday. He flew off to Barbados with a girl named Mary Bigelow, of whose existence his parents were blissfully unaware. Miss Bigelow had studied music, among other things, at Vassar, and when they returned two months later, Richard took her home to meet his parents. William approved of Miss Bigelow; after all, she was Alan Lloyd's great-niece.

Richard began his graduate course at Harvard Business School on October 1, 1954, after taking up residence in the Red House. The first thing he did was to throw out all his father's cane furniture and to remove the paisley wallpaper that Matthew Lester had once thought so fashionable. His grandfather's winged leather chair survived. He installed a television in the living room, an oak table in the dining room, a dishwasher in the kitchen and, more than occasionally, Miss Bigelow in the bedroom.

48

ABEL CUT SHORT a trip to Europe in November 1952 immediately upon hearing the news of David Maxton's fatal heart attack. He attended the funeral in Chicago with George and Florentyna, and later told Mrs Maxton that she could be a guest at any Baron in the world whenever she pleased for the rest of her life. She could not understand why Mr Rosnovski had made such a generous gesture.

When Abel returned to New York the next day, he was delighted to find on the desk of his 42nd-floor office a report from Henry Osborne indicating that the Eisenhower Administration didn't appear to be interested in pursuing an inquiry into Interstate Airways, possibly because the shares had retained their value for over a year. Eisenhower's Vice President, Richard M. Nixon, seemed more involved in chasing the spectral communists whom Joe McCarthy had missed.

Abel spent the next two years flying back and forth across the Atlantic as he continued to build his overseas empire. He only wished the Europeans could erect new hotels at a pace the New World took for granted.

Florentyna opened the Paris Baron in July 1953 and the London Baron in December 1954. Barons were also at various stages of development in Brussels, Rome, Amsterdam, Geneva, Edinburgh, Cannes and Stockholm, all part of a ten-year expansion programme.

Abel had so many deadlines to cope with that he had little time to think about William Kane. He had not made any further attempt to buy stock in Lester's Bank or its subsidiary companies, although he had held on to six per cent of the bank's shares, in the hope he would still be given the chance to deal Kane another blow from which he would not recover quite so easily. Next time, Abel promised himself, he'd make sure he didn't unwittingly break the law. He would have been the first to admit, if only to George, that Curtis Fenton would never have allowed him to make such a foolish mistake.

Abel had already suggested to Florentyna that she should join the board when she left Radcliffe at the end of the academic year. He had decided that she should take over responsibility for all the shops in his hotels and consolidate their buying, as they were fast becoming an empire in themselves.

Florentyna was excited by the prospect, but insisted that she must get some outside training before joining her father. She did not think that her natural gifts for design, colour coordination and organization were any substitute for experience. Abel suggested that she train in Switzerland under Monsieur Maurice at the famed Ecole Hotelière in Lausanne. Florentyna balked at the idea, explaining that she wanted to work for two years in a New York store before deciding whether or not to take charge of the Baron Group's shops. She was determined to be worth employing, 'And not just as my father's daughter,' she informed him. Abel thoroughly approved.

'A New York store? That's easily arranged,' he said. 'I'll give Walter Hoving a call, and you can start at Tiffany's.'

'That's exactly what I don't want to do,' said Florentyna, showing that she'd inherited her father's streak of stubbornness. 'What's the equivalent of a junior waiter at the Plaza Hotel?'

'A salesgirl at a department store,' said Abel, laughing.

'Then that's the job I'll be applying for.'

Abel stopped laughing. 'Are you serious? With a degree from Radcliffe and all the travelling you've done, you want to be an anonymous salesgirl?'

'Starting out as an anonymous waiter at the Plaza didn't stop you from building up one of the most successful hotel groups in the world,' replied Florentyna.

Abel knew when he was beaten. He had only to look into the steel grey eyes of his beautiful daughter to realize she had made up her mind, and that no amount of persuasion, gentle or otherwise, was going to change it.

‹o›

After Florentyna had graduated from Radcliffe she spent a month in Europe with her father, while he checked progress on the latest Baron hotels. She officially opened the Brussels Baron, where she made a conquest of the handsome young managing director, whom Abel accused of smelling of garlic. She had to give him up three days later when it reached the kissing stage, but she never admitted to her father that garlic had been the reason.

When she and Abel returned to New York, she immediately applied for the vacant position (the words used in the classified advertisement) of 'junior sales assistant' at Bloomingdale's. On the application form she gave her name as Jessie Kovats, well aware that no one would leave her in peace if they thought she was the daughter of the Chicago Baron.

Despite protests from her father, she left her suite in the New York Baron and started looking for somewhere to live. Once again Abel gave in, and presented her with a small but elegant apartment on Fifty-Seventh Street near the East River as a twenty-first birthday present.

Florentyna had long before resolved not to let her friends know that she was going to work at Bloomingdale's. She feared they would all want to visit her at the store and her cover would be blown in days, making it impossible for her to be treated like any other trainee. When her friends did enquire, she told them she was helping to run the shops in her father's hotels. None of them gave her reply a second thought.

After completing the store's training course, Jessie Kovats – it took her some time to get used to the name – started in cosmetics. The shop assistants in Bloomingdale's worked in pairs, and Florentyna immediately turned this to her advantage by choosing to work with the laziest girl in the department. This arrangement suited both girls, as Florentyna's choice, a blonde named Maisie, had only two interests in life: the clock when its hands pointed to 6 p.m., and men. The former happened once a day, the latter all through the day.

The two girls soon became comrades without exactly being friends. Florentyna learned a lot from Maisie about how to avoid work without being spotted by the floor manager, as well as how to get picked up by a man.

The cosmetic counter's profits were well up after the girls' first six months together, even though Maisie had spent most of her time trying out the products rather than selling them. She could take two hours just repainting her fingernails. Florentyna, in contrast, had found that she had a natural gift for selling – and thoroughly enjoyed it. After only a few weeks the floor supervisor considered her as proficient as many employees who had been with the company for years.

When Florentyna was moved to Better Dresses, Maisie went along by mutual consent, and passed much of her time trying on the clothes while Florentyna sold them. Maisie was able to attract men – even those in tow with their wives or sweethearts – simply by looking at them. Once they were ensnared, Florentyna would move in and sell them something. Few escaped with untapped wallets.

The profits for the next six months in Better Dresses were up by 22 per cent, and the floor supervisor concluded that the two girls obviously worked well together. Florentyna said nothing to contradict this impression. While other assistants were always complaining about how little work their partners did, Florentyna continually praised Maisie as the ideal colleague, who had taught her so much about how a big store operated. She didn't mention the useful advice that Maisie also imparted on how to cope with over-amorous male customers.

The greatest compliment an assistant can receive at Bloomingdale's is to be asked to serve on one of the front counters facing Lexington Avenue, and so to be among the first faces seen by the public as they enter the building. It was rare for a girl to be invited to work there until she had been with the store for at least five years. Maisie had been with Bloomingdale's since she was seventeen, a full five years, by the time Florentyna had completed her first. But because their sales record together was so impressive, the manager decided to try them both out in the stationery department on the ground floor. Maisie was unable to derive much personal advantage from the stationery department, for although she didn't care much for reading she cared even less for writing. Florentyna wasn't sure after having spent a year with her that she could read or write. Nevertheless, the new post pleased Maisie greatly because she basked in the added attention it brought her. Florentyna suspected that some of the men who walked in off the street to buy stationery did so for no other reason than to chat up Maisie.

Abel admitted to George that he had once slipped into Bloomingdale's and covertly watched Florentyna at work, and had to confess that she was damned good. Florentyna was unquestionably a chip off a formidable old block, and he had no doubt that she would have few problems taking on the responsibilities he had planned for her.

―◇―

Florentyna spent her last six months at Bloomingdale's on the ground floor in charge of six counters, with the new title of Junior Supervisor. Her duties included stock checking, running the cash tills and supervising eighteen sales clerks. Bloomingdale's had already decided that Jessie Kovats was an ideal candidate to be a future supervisor.

She had not yet informed her fellow employees that she would be leaving at the end of the year to join her father as a vice president of the Baron Group. As her time at the store was drawing to a close, she began to wonder what would happen to poor Maisie after she had left. Maisie assumed that Jessie was at Bloomingdale's for life – wasn't everybody? Florentyna even considered offering her a job at one of the shops in the New York

Baron. As long as it was behind a counter at which men could spend money, Maisie was an asset.

One afternoon when Maisie was waiting on a customer – she was now in gloves, scarves and woolly hats – she pulled Florentyna aside and pointed out a young man who was loitering over the gloves, pretending to try on several pairs.

'What do you think of him?' she asked, giggling.

Florentyna glanced at Maisie's latest target with her customary lack of interest, but on this occasion she had to admit that the man was rather attractive.

'They only want one thing, Maisie,' said Florentyna.

'I know,' she said. 'And he can have it.'

'I'm sure he'd be pleased to hear that,' said Florentyna, laughing as she turned to wait on a customer who was becoming impatient at Maisie's indifference to her presence. Maisie took advantage of Florentyna's move and rushed off to serve the young man. Florentyna watched them out of the corner of her eye. She was amused to see that he kept glancing nervously towards her, no doubt checking that Maisie wasn't being spied on by her supervisor. Maisie giggled away, and the young man departed with a pair of dark blue leather gloves.

'Did he measure up to your hopes?' asked Florentyna, conscious that she felt a little envious of Maisie's latest conquest.

'He didn't even ask me out. But I'm sure he'll be back,' she added with a grin.

Maisie's prediction turned out to be accurate, because the next day the young man returned, and was to be seen trying on another pair of gloves, looking even more uncomfortable than before.

'I suppose you'd better go and wait on him,' said Florentyna.

Maisie obediently hurried away. Florentyna nearly laughed out loud when, a few minutes later, the young man departed with another pair of dark blue gloves.

'Two pairs,' declared Florentyna. 'On behalf of Bloomingdale's, I think I can say he deserves you.'

'But he still didn't ask me out,' said Maisie.

'What?' said Florentyna in mock disbelief. 'He must have a glove fetish.'

'It's very disappointing,' said Maisie, 'because I think he's neat.'

'Yes, he's not bad,' admitted Florentyna.

The next day when the young man arrived, Maisie leaped forward to serve him again, leaving another customer in mid-sentence. Florentyna quickly replaced her, and once again watched out of the corner of her eye. This time customer and salesgirl appeared to be deep in conversation.

'It must be the real thing,' ventured Florentyna, after the young man had departed with yet another pair of dark blue leather gloves.

'Yes, I think it is,' replied Maisie. 'But he still hasn't asked me out on a date. Listen, if he comes in tomorrow, could you serve him? I think he's scared to ask me directly. He might find it easier to arrange a date through you.'

Florentyna laughed. 'A Viola to your Orsino.'

'What?'

'It doesn't matter. A greater challenge will be to see if I can sell him a pair of blue leather gloves.'

◄○►

The young man pushed his way through the doors at exactly the same time the next morning and immediately headed towards the glove counter. Florentyna thought that if he was anything, he was consistent.

Maisie dug her in the ribs. Florentyna decided the time had come to enjoy herself. 'Good morning, sir.'

'Oh, good morning,' said the young man, looking surprised – or was he simply disappointed to have ended up with Florentyna?

'Can I help you?'

'No – I mean yes. I would like a pair of gloves,' he added unconvincingly.

'Yes, sir. Have you considered dark blue? In leather? I'm sure we have your size – unless we're sold out.'

The young man looked at her suspiciously as she handed him

the gloves. He tried them on. They were a little too big. Florentyna offered him another pair: they were a little too tight. He looked towards Maisie. She was almost surrounded by a sea of male customers, but she wasn't sinking because she found time to glance across and grin. He didn't return her smile. Florentyna handed him another pair of gloves. They fitted perfectly.

'I think that's what you're looking for,' she said.

'No, it isn't really,' replied the customer, now visibly embarrassed.

Florentyna decided the time had come to put the poor man out of his misery. Lowering her voice, she said, 'I'll go and rescue Maisie. Why don't you ask her out? I'm sure she'll say yes.'

'Oh, no,' said the young man quickly. 'It's not her I want to take out – it's you.' Florentyna was speechless. The young man seemed to muster his courage. 'Will you have dinner with me tonight?'

She heard herself say yes.

'Shall I pick you up at your home?'

'No,' said Florentyna, firmly. The last thing she wanted was to be met at her apartment, where it would be obvious to anyone that she wasn't a salesgirl. 'Let's meet at a restaurant,' she added quickly.

'Where would you like to go?'

She tried to think quickly of a place that would not be too ostentatious.

'Allen's, on Seventy-Third and Third?' he ventured.

'Yes, fine,' said Florentyna, thinking how much better Maisie would have handled the situation.

'Around eight o'clock suit you?'

'Around eight,' replied Florentyna.

The young man departed with a smile on his face. Maisie pointed out that he'd left without buying a pair of gloves.

—◦—

Florentyna took a long time choosing which dress to wear that evening. She wanted to be certain the outfit didn't scream Bergdorf Goodman. She had acquired a small wardrobe especially for Bloomingdale's, but it was strictly for business use, and she had never worn anything from that selection in the evening. If her date – heavens, she didn't even know his name – thought she was a salesgirl, she mustn't disillusion him. In truth, she was actually looking forward to seeing him again.

Florentyna left her apartment on East Fifty-Seventh Street a little before eight, but it was some time before she managed to hail a taxi.

'Allen's, please,' she said to the taxi driver.

'Sure thing, miss.'

Florentyna arrived at the restaurant a few minutes late. Her eyes began to search for the young man. He was standing at the bar, waving. He had changed into a pair of grey flannel slacks and a blue blazer. Very Ivy League, thought Florentyna, although Maisie's description of him as 'dishy' still fitted just as well.

'I'm sorry to be late,' began Florentyna.

'It's not important. What's important is that you came.'

'You thought I wouldn't?'

'I wasn't sure.' He smiled. 'I'm sorry, I don't know your name.'

'Jessie Kovats. And yours?'

'Richard Kane,' said the young man, thrusting out his hand.

She took it, and he held on a little longer than she had expected.

'And what do you do when you're not buying gloves at Bloomingdale's?' she teased.

'I'm at Harvard Business School.'

'I'm surprised they didn't teach you that most people only have two hands.'

He laughed and smiled in such a relaxed and friendly way that she wished she could start again and tell him she was surprised they'd never met in Cambridge when she was at Radcliffe.

'Shall we sit down?' he said, taking her arm and leading her to a table.

Florentyna looked up at the menu on the blackboard.

'Salisbury steak?' she queried.

'A hamburger by any other name,' said Richard.

They both laughed in the way two people do when they don't

know each other well, but want to. She could see he was surprised that she recognized his out-of-context quote.

Florentyna had rarely enjoyed anyone's company more. Richard chatted about New York, the theatre and music – which was obviously his first love – with such grace and charm that he quickly put her at ease. He might have thought she was a salesgirl, but he treated her as if she'd come from one of the oldest Boston families. When he asked, she told him nothing more than that she was Polish, lived in New York with her parents and that her father worked in a hotel. As the evening progressed she found the deception increasingly difficult. Still, she thought, we're unlikely to see each other again.

When neither of them could drink any more coffee, Richard called for the bill. He asked Florentyna which part of town she lived in.

'East Fifty-Seventh Street,' she said, not thinking.

'Then I'll walk you home,' he said, taking her hand.

They strolled up Fifth Avenue, looking into shop windows, laughing and chatting. When he asked about her plans for the future, she simply replied, 'One day I'd like to work in a shop on Fifth Avenue.' Neither of them noticed the empty taxis as they drifted past.

It took them almost an hour to cover the sixteen blocks, and Florentyna nearly told him the truth about herself. When they reached Fifty-Seventh Street she stopped outside a small old apartment block, a hundred yards from her own building.

'This is where my parents live,' she said.

Richard seemed to hesitate, then let go of her hand.

'I hope we'll see each other again,' he said.

'I'd like that,' replied Florentyna in a polite, dismissive way.

'Tomorrow?' Richard asked diffidently.

'Tomorrow?' repeated Florentyna.

'Why don't we go to the Blue Angel and see Bobby Short?' He took her hand again. 'It's a little more romantic than Allen's.'

Florentyna was momentarily taken aback. Her plans for Rich and had not included any tomorrows.

'Not if you don't want to,' he added before she could recover.

'I'd love to,' she said quietly.

'I'm having dinner with my father, so why don't I pick you up around nine o'clock?'

'No, no,' said Florentyna, 'I'll meet you there. It's only a couple of blocks away.'

'Nine o'clock tomorrow night, then.' He bent forward and kissed her gently on the cheek. 'Good night, Jessie,' he said, and disappeared into the night.

Once he was out of sight, Florentyna walked slowly to her apartment, wishing she hadn't told so many white lies. Still, it might all be over in a few days, even if she hoped it wouldn't be.

◄○►

Florentyna left Bloomingdale's the moment the store closed, the first time in nearly two years that she'd left before Maisie. She had a long bath, put on the prettiest dress she thought she could get away with and strolled to the Blue Angel. When she arrived, Richard was waiting for her outside the cloakroom. He held her hand as they walked into the lounge, where the voice of Bobby Short came floating through the smoke-filled air: '*Are you telling me the truth, or is it just another lie?*'

Short raised a hand to Florentyna in acknowledgement. Florentyna pretended not to notice. He had been a guest performer at the Baron on two or three occasions, and it had never occurred to her that he might remember her. Richard had noticed the gesture, and looked around to see who Short was greeting. When they took their table in the dimly lit room, Florentyna sat with her back to the piano to make sure it couldn't happen again.

Richard ordered a bottle of wine without letting go of her hand, then asked about her day. She didn't want to tell him about her day; she wanted to tell him the truth. 'Richard, there's something I must—'

'Hi, Richard.' A tall, handsome man was standing beside the table.

'Hi, Steve. May I introduce Jessie Kovats – Steve Mellon. Steve and I were at Harvard together.'

Florentyna listened to them chat about the New York

Yankees, Eisenhower's golf handicap and why Yale was going from bad to worse. Steve eventually left with a gracious, 'Nice to have met you, Jessie.'

Florentyna's moment had passed.

Richard began to tell her of his plans once he had left business school. He hoped to come to New York and join his father's bank, Lester's. She'd heard that name somewhere before, but couldn't remember in what connection. For some reason, it worried her.

They spent a long evening together, laughing, eating, talking, and just sitting holding hands while they listened to Bobby Short. When they walked home together, Richard stopped on the corner of Fifty-Seventh and kissed her for the first time. She couldn't recall another occasion when she was so aware of a first kiss. When he left her in the shadows of Fifty-Seventh Street, she realized that this time he had not mentioned tomorrow. She felt slightly wistful about the whole non-affair.

Maisie was delighted when a large bunch of roses was delivered to the store the next morning, but was disappointed to find that the card was addressed to Jessie Kovats, with an invitation to join Richard for dinner. She pretended not to be interested.

Florentyna and Richard spent most of the weekend together: a concert, a film – even the New York Knicks did not escape them. When the weekend was over, Florentyna was uncomfortably aware that she had told so many lies about herself that Richard must surely be puzzled by their many inconsistencies. It was becoming more and more difficult to tell him another entirely different, albeit true, story.

When Richard returned to Harvard on Sunday night to start the new term she persuaded herself that her deception was unimportant, as their relationship had come to a natural end. After all, he'd probably meet a nice Radcliffe girl. But he phoned her every day of the week, and came back to New York to see her that weekend. After another month, Florentyna knew it wasn't going to end quite as easily as she had thought. In fact, she knew she was falling in love with him. Once she had admitted this to herself, she decided it couldn't wait any longer. This weekend she would tell him the truth.

49

RICHARD DAYDREAMED through the morning lecture.

He was so much in love with the girl that he could not even concentrate on the Bretton Woods Agreement. How could he tell his father that he intended to marry a Polish girl who worked behind the scarf, glove and woolly hats counter at Bloomingdale's? He was unable to fathom why Jessie was so unambitious when she was clearly very bright; he was certain that if she'd had the same chances as him, she wouldn't have ended up in Bloomingdale's. Richard decided that his parents would have to learn to live with his decision, because that weekend he was going to ask Jessie to be his wife.

Whenever Richard arrived at his parents' home in New York on a Friday evening, he would always go out and pick up something from Bloomingdale's, normally some unwanted item, simply so that Jessie knew that he was back in town (over the past ten weeks he had given a pair of gloves to every distant relative, some of whom he hadn't seen for years). That Friday he told his mother he was going out to buy some razor blades.

'Don't bother, darling, you can use your father's,' she said.

'No, no, it's all right. I need some of my own. We don't use the same brand, in any case,' he added feebly.

He almost ran the eight blocks to Bloomingdale's, and managed to rush in just as the doors were closing. He knew he would be seeing Jessie at seven-thirty, but he could never resist a chance just to look at her. Steve Mellon had told him that love was for poor suckers, and Richard had written on his steamed-up shaving mirror that morning, 'I must be penniless.'

But this evening Jessie was nowhere to be seen. Maisie was sitting in a corner filing her fingernails, and Richard asked her if Jessie was still around. Maisie looked up as if she had been interrupted in the most important task of her day.

'No, she's already gone home. She only left a few moments ago, so she can't have got that far.'

Richard ran out onto Lexington Avenue. He searched for Jessie among the faces of people hurrying home, and spotted her on the other side of the street, walking towards Fifth Avenue. She obviously wasn't heading back to her apartment. When she reached Scribner's bookstore on Forty-Eighth Street, he stopped and watched her go inside. Richard was puzzled. If she wanted something to read, surely she could have got it at Bloomingdale's. He peered through the window as Jessie chatted to a sales clerk, who left her for a few moments and then returned with two books. He could just make out their titles: *The Great Crash, 1929* by John Kenneth Galbraith and *Behind the Curtain* by John Gunther. Jessie signed for them – which surprised Richard even more: why would a salesgirl have an account at Scribner's? – and as she left he ducked behind a pillar.

'Who *is* she?' he said out loud as he watched her enter Bendel's. The doorman saluted respectfully, giving Richard the distinct impression he knew who she was. Once again Richard peered through the window, while transfixed sales assistants fluttered around her with more than casual respect. An older woman appeared with a package, which Jessie had obviously been expecting. She opened it, to reveal a simple yet stunning evening dress. Jessie smiled and nodded as the saleslady placed the dress in a brown and white box, then mouthed the words 'Thank you' and turned towards the door without even signing for her purchase. Richard was so mesmerized by the scene that he barely managed to avoid colliding with her as she stepped out onto the sidewalk and jumped into a cab.

He grabbed one himself, telling the driver to follow her taxi. When they passed the small apartment house outside which they normally parted, he began to feel sick. No wonder she had never invited him in. Jessie's cab continued for another hundred yards, and stopped in front of a smart modern apartment house complete with a uniformed doorman, who stepped forward, saluted and opened the door for her. Richard was no longer puzzled, he was now angry. He jumped out of his cab and started to march up to the door she had disappeared through.

'That'll be ninety-five cents, fella,' said a voice behind him.

'Oh, sorry,' said Richard, and thrust five dollars at the cab driver, not waiting for his change.

'Thanks, buddy,' said the driver. 'Someone sure is happy today.'

Richard brushed past the protesting doorman and managed to catch up with Florentyna as she stepped into the elevator. She stared blankly at him, unable to speak.

'Who are you?' demanded Richard as the elevator door closed.

'Richard,' she stammered. 'I was going to tell you everything, but I never seemed to find the right opportunity.'

'Like hell you were going to tell me everything,' he said, following her out of the elevator to the door of her apartment. 'Stringing me along with a pack of lies for nearly three months. Well, now the time has come for the truth.'

Florentyna had never seen Richard angry before, and suspected it was very rare. He pushed his way brusquely past her as she opened the door, and looked around the apartment. At the end of the entrance hall there was a large living room with a fine Oriental rug and stylish furniture. A superb grandfather clock stood opposite a side table on which there was a bowl of fresh flowers. The room was beautiful, even by the standards of Richard's own home.

'Nice place you've got yourself for a salesgirl,' he said. 'I wonder which of your lovers pays for it.'

Florentyna swung round to face him and slapped him so hard the palm of her hand stung. 'How dare you!' she said. 'Get out of my home.'

As she heard herself saying the words, she started to cry. She didn't want him to leave – ever. Richard took her in his arms.

'Oh God, I'm sorry,' he said. 'That was a terrible thing to say. Please forgive me. It's just that I love you so much and thought I knew you so well, and now I find I don't know anything about you.'

'Richard, I love you too, and I'm sorry I hit you. I didn't mean to deceive you. There's no one else – I can promise you that.' Her voice cracked.

'I deserved it,' he said, and kissed her on the forehead.

They held onto each other for some time without speaking, then sank onto the couch and remained motionless. Gently, he began to stroke her hair until her tears subsided. She slipped her fingers through the gap between his two top shirt buttons. Richard seemed unwilling to make the next move.

'Do you want to sleep with me?' she asked quietly.

'No,' he replied. 'I want to stay awake with you.'

Without speaking further, they slowly undressed each other and made love for the first time, gently and shyly, afraid to hurt each other, desperately trying to please. Finally, Florentyna's head sank onto his shoulder.

'I love you,' said Richard. 'I have since the first moment I saw you. Will you marry me? I don't give a damn who you are, Jessie, or what you do, but I know I must spend the rest of my life with you.'

'I want to marry you too, Richard, but first I have to tell you the truth.'

She pulled his jacket over their naked bodies and began to tell him all about herself, ending by explaining why she was working at Bloomingdale's. When she had completed her story, he did not speak.

'Have you stopped loving me already?' she said. 'Now that you know who I really am?'

'Darling,' said Richard very quietly, 'I have to tell you something. My father detests your father.'

'What do you mean?'

'The only time I ever heard your father's name mentioned in our home, he flew into a rage, and said Abel Rosnovski's sole purpose in life was to destroy the Kane family.'

'What? But why?' said Florentyna, shocked. 'I've never heard of your father. How do they even know each other? You must be mistaken.'

It was Richard's turn to tell Florentyna everything his mother had told him over the years about the feud between their fathers.

'Oh my God. That must have been the "Judas" my father referred to when he changed banks after twenty-five years,' she said. 'What shall we do?'

'Tell them both the truth,' said Richard. 'That we met by accident, fell in love and are going to be married, and that there's nothing they can do to charge our minds.'

'Let's wait for a few days,' said Florentyna.

'Why?' asked Richard. 'Do you think your father can talk you out of marrying me?'

'Never, my darling,' she said, resting her head back on his shoulder. 'But let's find out if there's anything we can do to break it to them gently, without presenting them with a *fait accompli*. Anyway, perhaps they don't feel as strongly as you imagine. After all, you said the affair with the airline company was several years ago.'

'They feel every bit as strongly, I can promise you that. My father would be livid if he saw us together, let alone thought we were going to be married.'

'All the more reason to leave it for a little while before we break the news to them. That will give us time to decide the best way to go about it.'

He kissed her again. 'I love you, Jessie.'

'Florentyna.'

'That's something else I'm going to have to get used to,' he said. 'I love you, Florentyna.'

◄○►

During the next four weeks, Florentyna and Richard found out as much as they could about their fathers' feud: Florentyna by flying to Chicago to ask her mother, who was surprisingly forthcoming on the subject, and then quizzing her godfather with a set of carefully worded questions that revealed George's despair over what he described as 'your father's obsession'; Richard from his father's filing cabinet and a long talk with his mother, who made it very clear that the hatred was mutual. It became more obvious with each discovery that there was going to be no gentle way to break the news of their love.

Richard went to great lengths to take Florentyna's mind off the problem they knew would eventually have to be faced. They went to the theatre, spent an afternoon skating and on Sundays took long walks through Central Park, always ending up in bed long before it was dark. Florentyna accompanied Richard to a New York Yankees game, which she 'still couldn't fathom', and to a concert by the New York Philharmonic, which she 'adored'. She refused to believe he could play the cello until he gave her a private recital in her apartment. She applauded enthusiastically when he had finished his favourite Bach suite.

'We'll have to tell them soon,' he said, placing his bow on a table and taking her into his arms.

'I know. I just don't want to hurt my father.'

'Me too,' he said.

She avoided his eyes. 'Next Friday, Papa will be back from Memphis.'

'Then it's Friday,' said Richard, holding her so close she could hardly breathe.

Richard returned to Harvard on Monday morning and they spoke to each other on the phone every night, remaining resolute, determined that nothing would stop them now.

◄○►

On Friday, Richard came back to New York earlier than usual and spent the afternoon alone with Florentyna, at her apartment. At the corner of Fifty-Seventh and Park, they stopped at the flashing 'Don't Walk' sign, when Richard turned to Florentyna and asked her once again if she would marry him. He took a small red leather box out of his pocket, opened it and placed a ring on the third finger of her left hand, a sapphire set in a circle of diamonds, so beautiful that tears came to Florentyna's eyes. It was a perfect fit. Passersby looked at them strangely as they stood on the corner, clinging to each other, ignoring the green 'Walk' sign. When eventually they did observe its command, they kissed before parting, and walked in opposite directions to confront their parents. They had agreed to meet at Florentyna's apartment as soon as the ordeal was over.

Florentyna walked purposefully towards the Baron hotel, trying to smile through her tears and occasionally looking at the ring. It felt new and strange on her finger and she imagined that the eyes of all who passed would be drawn to the magnificent sapphire, which looked so beautiful next to the antique ring that used to be her favourite. She touched it and found that it gave her courage, although Florentyna was aware she was walking more and more slowly as she neared the hotel.

When she reached the reception desk, the clerk told her that her father was in the penthouse with George Novak, and called to say she was on her way up. The elevator reached the 42nd floor far too quickly, and Florentyna hesitated before leaving its safety. She stood alone in the corridor for a moment before knocking quietly on the door. Abel opened it immediately.

'Florentyna, what a lovely surprise. Come on in, my darling. I wasn't expecting to see you today.'

George Novak was standing by the window, looking down on Park Avenue. He turned to greet his goddaughter. Florentyna's eyes pleaded with him to leave. If he stayed, she knew she would lose her nerve. Go, go, go, she said in her mind. George sensed her anxiety immediately.

'I must get back to work, Abel. There's a goddamn maharajah checking in tonight.'

'Tell him to park his elephants at the Plaza,' said Abel genially. 'Now that Florentyna's here, stay and have another drink.'

George looked at Florentyna, but the message was clear.

'No, Abel, I have to go. He's taken the whole of the thirty-third floor. The least he'll expect is for the vice president to greet him. See you soon, little Kum,' he said, kissing her on the cheek and briefly clasping her arm, almost as though he knew she needed strength. As soon as he had gone, Florentyna wished he had stayed.

'How's Bloomingdale's?' said Abel, ruffling her hair affectionately. 'Have you told them yet they're going to lose the best junior
supervisor they've had in years? They're sure going to be surprised when they hear that Jessie Kovats's next job will be to open
the Edinburgh Baron.' He laughed out loud.

'I'm going to be married,' said Florentyna, shyly extending her
left hand. She could think of nothing to add, so she simply waited
for his reaction.

'This is a bit sudden, isn't it?' said Abel, sounding more than
a little shocked.

'Not really, Daddy. I've known him for some time.'

'Do I know the boy? Have I ever met him?'

'No, Daddy, you haven't.'

'Where does he come from? What's his background? Is he
Polish? Why have you been so secretive about him, Florentyna?'

'He's not Polish, Daddy. He's the son of a banker.'

Abel went white and picked up his drink, swallowing it in one
gulp. Florentyna knew exactly what must be going through his
mind as he poured himself another drink, so she got the truth out
quickly.

'His name is Richard Kane.'

Abel swung around to face her. 'William Kane's son?' he
demanded.

'Yes.'

'How could you even think about marrying William Kane's
son? Do you know what that man has done to me?'

'I think so.'

'You couldn't begin to know,' shouted Abel, and let forth a
tirade of abuse that seemed to go on forever, and only served to
convince Florentyna that her father had gone mad. In the end
she interrupted him.

'You've said nothing I don't already know.'

'*Nothing*, young lady?' he shouted. 'Did you know that William
Kane was responsible for the death of my closest friend? He
caused Davis Leroy to commit suicide, and, not finished with that,
he tried to bankrupt me. If David Maxton hadn't come to my
rescue, Kane would have taken away my hotels and sold them

without a second thought. Where would I be now if he'd had his way? You'd have been lucky to end up as a shop assistant at Bloomingdale's. Have you thought about that, Florentyna?'

'Yes, Daddy, I've thought of little else for the past few weeks. Richard and I are horrified about the hatred that exists between you and his father. He's facing him now.'

'Well, I can tell you how he'll react,' said Abel. 'He'll go berserk. That man will never allow his precious WASP son to marry you, so you might as well forget the whole crazy idea.' His voice had risen again to a shout.

'I can't forget it, Father,' she said evenly. 'We love each other, and we need your blessing, not your anger.'

'You listen to me, Florentyna,' said Abel, his face now red with fury. 'I forbid you to see that boy ever again. Do you hear me?'

'Yes, I hear you. But I won't be parted from Richard because you hate his father.'

She found herself clutching her ring finger and trembling slightly.

'It will not happen,' said Abel, the colour in his face deepening. 'I will never agree to the marriage. My own daughter deserting me for the son of that bastard Kane. I say you will not marry him.'

'I'm not deserting you. I would have run away with him if that were true, but I could never marry anyone behind your back.' She was aware of the tremble in her voice. 'But I'm over twenty-one, and I will marry Richard. Please, Daddy, won't you meet him? Then you'll begin to understand why I feel the way I do about him.'

'He will never be allowed to enter my home. I do not want to meet any child of William Kane. Never, do you hear me?'

'Then you leave me with no choice but to decide between you.'

'Florentyna, if you marry that boy, I'll cut you off without a penny. Without a penny, do you hear me?' His voice softened. 'Use your common sense, girl – you'll get over him. You're young, and there are lots of other men who'd give their right arm to marry you.'

'I don't want lots of other men,' said Florentyna. 'I've met the man I'm going to marry, and it's not his fault that he's his father's son. Neither of us chose our father.'

'If your own family isn't good enough for you, then go,' roared Abel. 'And I swear I won't have your name mentioned in my presence again.' He turned away and stared out of the window.

'Daddy, we're going to be married. Although we're both past the stage of needing your consent, we do ask for your blessing.'

Abel looked away from the window. 'Are you pregnant? Is that the reason?'

'No, Father.'

'Have you slept with him?'

The question shook Florentyna, but she didn't hesitate. 'Yes,' she replied. 'Many times.'

Abel raised his arm and hit her full across the face. Blood started to trickle down her chin and she nearly fell. She turned, ran out of the room and pressed the elevator button. The door slid open and George stepped out. She had a fleeting glimpse of his shocked expression as she stepped quickly into the lift and jabbed repeatedly at the Close Door button. As George stood and watched her crying, the doors closed slowly and she disappeared from sight.

Florentyna took a cab straight to her apartment. On the way, she dabbed at her cut lip with a tissue. Richard was already there, waiting by the entrance, head bowed and looking miserable.

She jumped out of the cab and ran to him. Once they were upstairs, she unlocked the door and quickly stepped inside, feeling blessedly safe.

'I love you, Richard.'

'I love you, too,' he said as he gently put his arms around her.

'I don't have to ask how your father reacted,' she said, clinging to him desperately.

'I've never seen him so angry,' said Richard. 'He called your father a liar and a crook, nothing more than a jumped-up Polish immigrant. He asked me why I didn't want to marry someone from my own background.'

'What did you say to that?'

'I told him someone as wonderful as you couldn't be replaced by the daughter of some suitable family friend, and he completely lost his temper. He threatened to cut me off without a penny if I married you,' he continued. 'When will they understand we don't give a damn about their money? I tried appealing to my mother for support, but even she couldn't control my father's anger. He ordered her to leave the room. I've never seen him treat my mother that way before. She was weeping, which only made my resolve stronger. I left while he was in mid-sentence. God knows, I hope he doesn't take it out on Virginia and Lucy. What happened when you told your father?'

'He hit me,' said Florentyna very quietly. 'For the first time in my life. I think he'll kill you if he finds us together. Richard, darling, we must get out of here before he discovers where we are, and he's bound to try the apartment first. I'm so frightened.'

'No need to be frightened, Florentyna. We'll leave tonight and go as far away as possible, and to hell with them both.'

'How quickly can you pack?' asked Florentyna.

'I can't. I can never return home now. Once you've packed some things, we'll leave. I've got about a hundred dollars with me and my cello, which is still in your bedroom. How do you feel about marrying a hundred-dollar man, whose next job will be busking on street corners?'

'As much as a salesgirl can hope for, I suppose,' Florentyna said while she rummaged in her bag. 'And to think I dreamed of being a kept woman. No doubt you expected a dowry. Well, I've got two hundred and twelve dollars and an American Express card. You owe me fifty-six dollars, Richard Kane, but I'll consider repayment at a dollar a year.'

Thirty minutes later Florentyna was packed. Then she sat at her desk, scribbled a note and left it on the table by the side of her bed.

Richard hailed a cab. Florentyna was relieved to find how calm he was in a crisis, and it made her feel a little more confident. 'Idlewild,' he said, after placing Florentyna's three suitcases and his cello in the trunk.

At the airport he booked two tickets for San Francisco; they chose the Golden Gate city simply because it looked the most distant point on the map from New York.

At seven-thirty the American Airlines Super Constellation 1049 taxied out onto the runway to start its seven-hour flight. Richard helped Florentyna with her seatbelt. She smiled at him.

'Do you know how much I love you, Mr Kane?'

'Yes, I think so – Mrs Kane,' he replied.

50

ABEL AND GEORGE turned up at Florentyna's apartment a few minutes after she and Richard had left for the airport.

Abel was already regretting the blow he had struck his daughter. He did not care to think about a life without his only child. If he could only reach her before it was too late, he might, with gentle persuasion, still talk her out of marrying the Kane boy. He was willing to offer her anything, *anything*, to prevent the marriage.

George rang the bell twice, but no one answered, so Abel used the key Florentyna had left with him for emergencies. They looked in all the rooms, not expecting to find her.

'She must have left already,' said George as he joined Abel in the bedroom.

'Yes, but where?' said Abel, checking the empty drawers. Then he spotted the envelope on the bedside table, addressed to him. He remembered the last time a letter had been left for him by the side of a bed that had not been slept in. He ripped it open:

Dear Daddy,
Please forgive me for running away, but I love Richard and will not give him up because of your hatred for his father. We are going to be married, and nothing you can do will prevent it. If you ever try to harm him in any way, you will be harming me.
Neither of us intends to return to New York until the senseless feud between our family and the Kanes is ended.

I love you more than you can ever realize, and I will always be thankful for everything you have done for me.

I pray that this isn't the end of our relationship, but until you come to your senses, 'Never seek the wind in the field – it is useless to try and find what is gone.'

Your loving daughter,

Florentyna

Abel collapsed on the bed and passed the letter to George. When George had read it he asked helplessly, 'Is there anything I can do?'

'Yes, George. I want my daughter back, even if it means having to deal with that bastard Kane. There's only one thing I'm certain of: he'll want to stop this marriage whatever sacrifice he has to make. Get him on the phone.'

It took George some time to locate William Kane's unlisted home number. The night security officer at Lester's Bank finally gave it to him when George insisted it was a family emergency. Abel sat on the bed in silence, Florentyna's letter in his hand, reading again the Polish proverb he had taught her as a little girl that she had now quoted to him. When George reached the Kane residence, a formal voice answered the phone.

'May I speak to Mr William Kane?' asked George.

'Who shall I say is calling?'

'Mr Abel Rosnovski,' said George.

'I'll see if he's in, sir.'

'I think that was Kane's butler. He's gone to look for him,' said George as he passed the receiver over to Abel. Abel waited, his fingers tapping on the bedside table.

'William Kane speaking.'

'This is Abel Rosnovski.'

'Indeed?' William's tone was icy. 'And when exactly did you think of setting up your daughter with my son? At the time, no doubt, when you failed so conspicuously to cause the collapse of my bank.'

'Don't be such a damn—' Abel checked himself. 'I want this marriage stopped every bit as much as you do. I only learned of your son's existence today. I love my daughter even more than I hate you, and I don't want to lose her. Can't we get together and work something out between us?'

'No,' said William. 'I asked you that same question once in the past, Mr Rosnovski, and you made it abundantly clear when and where we would next meet.'

'What's the good of raking over the past now, Kane? If you know where they are, perhaps we can stop them. That's what you want too. Or are you so goddamn proud that you'll stand by and watch your son marry my daughter rather than help—'

The telephone clicked as he spoke the word *help*. Abel buried his face in his hands and wept. George took him back to the Baron.

Through that night and the following day, Abel used every shred of influence he had, and every contact he could call on to find Florentyna. He even rang her mother, who took pleasure in letting him know that their daughter had told her all about Richard Kane some time ago.

'He sounded rather nice,' she added.

'Do you know where they are right now?' Abel asked desperately.

'Yes, I do.'

'Where?'

'Find out for yourself.' Another telephone click.

During the next few days Abel placed advertisements in newspapers, and even bought radio time. He tried to get the police involved, but they would only put out a general call, as Florentyna was over twenty-one. Finally he resigned himself to the likelihood that she would be married to the Kane boy by the time he caught up with her.

He reread her letter many times, and resolved that he would never attempt to harm the boy in any way. But the father – that was a different matter. He, Abel Rosnovski, had practically gone down on his knees and pleaded with the man, and he hadn't even listened. As soon as the chance presented itself, he would finish William Kane off once and for all.

George became fearful of the intensity of his old friend's determination. 'Shall I cancel your European trip?' he asked.

Abel had completely forgotten that Florentyna had planned to accompany him to Europe when she had finished her two years with Bloomingdale's at the end of the month. She had been going to open both the Edinburgh and the Cannes Barons.

'I can't cancel,' he replied, although he now didn't care who opened the hotels, or even whether they were opened at all. 'While I'm away, George, keep looking for Florentyna. But if you find her, don't let her know. She mustn't think I'm spying on her; she'd never forgive me if she found out. Your best bet may be Zaphia, but be careful, because you can be sure she'll take every advantage of what has happened.'

'Do you want Osborne to do anything about Lester's stock?'

'No, nothing for the moment. Now is not the appropriate time to finish Kane off. When I do, I want to be certain that he can't recover. Leave Kane alone for the time being. For now, concentrate on finding Florentyna.'

—◦—

Three weeks later, Abel opened the Edinburgh Baron. The hotel looked quite magnificent as it stood on the hill dominating the Athens of the North. Long before Abel opened a new hotel, he would go over everything himself because he knew that it was the little things that annoyed customers. A small electric shock caused by nylon carpets when you touched a light switch, room service that took forty minutes to materialize or rubber pillows that curled around one's ears.

The press had expected Florentyna Rosnovski, the daughter of the Chicago Baron, to perform the opening ceremony, and a gossip columnist on the *Sunday Express* hinted at a family rift and reported that Abel had not been his usual exuberant, bouncy self. Abel denied the suggestion unconvincingly, retorting that he was over fifty — not too old for bouncing, his public relations man had told him to say. The press remained unconvinced, and the following day the *Daily Mail* printed a photograph of a discarded

481

engraved bronze plaque discovered in a dumpster at the back of the hotel, that read:

The Edinburgh Baron
opened by Florentyna Rosnovski
October 17, 1956

Abel flew on to Cannes. Another splendid hotel, this time overlooking the Mediterranean, but it didn't help him get Florentyna out of his mind. Another discarded plaque, this one in French.

Abel was beginning to dread the thought that he might spend the rest of his life without seeing his daughter again. To kill the loneliness, he slept with some very expensive and some rather cheap women. None of them helped. William Kane's son now possessed the only person Abel Rosnovski truly cared for.

France no longer held any excitement for him, and once he had finished his business there, he flew on to Bonn, where he completed negotiations for the site on which he would build the first Baron in Germany. He kept in constant touch with George by phone, but Florentyna had not been found. And there was some disturbing news concerning Henry Osborne.

'He's got himself in heavy debt with the bookmakers again,' said George.

'I warned him last time that I was through bailing him out,' said Abel. 'He's been no damn use to anyone since he lost his seat in Congress. I'll deal with the problem when I get back.'

'He's making threats,' said George.

'What's new about that? I've never let them worry me in the past,' said Abel. 'Tell him whatever it is he wants, it will have to wait until my return.'

'When do you expect to be back?'

'Three weeks, four at the most. I want to look at some sites in Turkey and Egypt. Hilton and Marriott have started building there, and I need to find out why.'

Abel spent more than three weeks looking at sites for hotels in the Arab states. His advisors were legion, most of them claiming the title of Prince and assuring him that they had real influence as a cousin, or a very close personal friend, of the key minister. However, it always turned out to be the wrong minister or too distant a cousin. Abel had no objection to bribery, as long as it ended up in the right hands and in the Middle East *baksheesh* seemed to be accepted as part of the business culture. In America, it was a little more discreet but Henry Osborne had always known which officials needed to be taken care of. The only solid conclusion Abel reached, after twenty-three days in the dust, sand and heat with a glass of soda but no whiskey, was that if his advisors' forecasts about the future importance of the Middle East's oil reserves were accurate, the Gulf States were going to want a lot of hotels, and the Baron Group needed to start planning immediately if it was not going to be left behind.

Abel flew on to Istanbul, where he immediately found the perfect site to build a hotel, overlooking the Bosphorus, only a hundred yards from the old British Consulate. As he stood on the barren ground of his latest acquisition he recalled when he had last been there. He clung onto the silver band that had saved his life. He could hear once again the cries of the mob – it still made him feel frightened and sick although more than thirty years had passed.

Exhausted from his travels, Abel flew home to New York. During the interminable flight he thought of little but Florentyna. As always, George was waiting outside the customs gate to meet him. His expression indicated nothing.

'What news?' asked Abel as he climbed into the back of the Cadillac while the chauffeur put his bags in the trunk.

'Some good, some bad,' said George, touching a button which caused a sheet of glass to glide up between the driver and passenger sections of the car. 'Florentyna has been in touch with Zaphia. She's living in a small house in San Francisco with some old friends from Radcliffe days.'

'Married?' asked Abel.

'Yes.'

Neither spoke for some time.

'And the Kane boy?'

'He's found a job in a bank. It seems a lot of places turned him down, partly because word got around that he didn't complete his course at the Harvard Business School, but mainly because they were afraid that by employing him they'd antagonize his father. He was finally hired as a teller with the Bank of America. Far below what he might have expected with his qualifications.'

'And Florentyna?'

'She's working as the assistant manager in a fashion shop called Wayout Columbus near Golden Gate Park. She's also trying to borrow money from several banks.'

'Why? Is she in any sort of trouble?' asked Abel anxiously.

'No, she's looking for capital to open her own shop.'

'How much has she been asking for?'

'She needs thirty-four thousand dollars for the lease on a small building on Nob Hill.'

Abel thought about George's news, his short fingers tapping on the car window. 'See that she gets the money, George. Make it look as if it's an ordinary bank loan, and be sure it's not traceable back to me.

'Anything you say, Abel.'

'And keep me informed of every move she makes, however insignificant.'

'What about the boy?'

'I'm not interested in him,' said Abel. 'Now, what's the bad news?'

'More trouble with Henry Osborne. It seems he's running up debts all over town. I'm also fairly certain his only source of income is now you. He's still making threats – about letting the authorities know that you condoned bribes in the early days when you first took over the group, and that he fixed an extra payment after the fire at the old Richmond in Chicago. Says he's kept all the details from the day he met you, and he now has a file three inches thick.'

'I'll deal with him in the morning,' said Abel.

George spent the remainder of the drive into Manhattan bringing Abel up to date on the rest of the group's affairs. Everything was satisfactory, except that there had been a takeover of the Lagos Baron after yet another coup. Coups never worried Abel. Revolutionaries quickly discover they aren't hoteliers, and they need visitors if they hope to put any money into their own pockets.

The next morning Henry Osborne called in to see Abel. He looked old and dishevelled, and his once smooth and handsome face was now heavily lined. He made no mention of the three-inch-thick file.

'I need a little help to get me through a tricky period,' said Osborne. 'Been a bit unlucky.'

'Again, Henry? You should know better at your age. You're a born loser with horses and women. How much do you need this time?'

'Ten thousand would see me through,' said Henry.

'Ten thousand!' said Abel, spitting out the words. 'What do you think I am, a gold mine? It was only five thousand last time.'

'Inflation,' said Henry, trying to laugh.

'This is the last time, do you understand me?' said Abel as he took out his cheque book. 'Come begging once more, Henry, and I'll remove you from the board and turn you out without a penny.'

'You're a real friend, Abel. I swear I'll never ask you for another penny. Never again.' He plucked a Romeo y Julieta from the humidor on Abel's desk. 'Thanks, Abel. You'll never regret this.'

Osborne left, puffing away on his cigar. Abel waited for the door to close, then buzzed for George. He appeared moments later.

'How much did he want this time?' asked George.

'Ten thousand,' said Abel, 'but I told him that it was the last time.'

'He'll be back,' said George. 'I'd be willing to bet on that.'

'He'd better not,' said Abel. 'I'm through with him. Whatever he's done for me in the past, it's quits now. Anything new about my girl?'

'She's fine, but it looks as if you were right about Zaphia. She's been making regular trips to the West Coast to see them.'

'Bloody woman,' said Abel.

'Mrs Kane has also been out a couple of times,' added George.

'And Kane?'

'No sign that he's relenting.'

'That's one thing he and I have in common,' said Abel.

'I've set up a facility for Florentyna with the Crocker National Bank of San Francisco,' continued George. 'She has an appointment next Monday with the loan officer. The agreement will look to her like one of the bank's regular loan transactions, with no special favours. In fact, they're charging her half a per cent more than usual, so there'll be no reason for her to become suspicious. She won't be told the loan's covered by your guarantee.'

'Thanks, George, that's perfect. I'll bet you ten dollars she pays it off within two years and never needs to ask for another loan.'

'I'd want odds of five to one on that,' said George. 'Why don't you try Henry; he's more of a sucker.'

Abel laughed. 'Keep me briefed, George, on everything she's up to. Everything.'

51

WILLIAM REMAINED PUZZLED after he'd read Thaddeus Cohen's quarterly report. Why was Rosnovski doing nothing with his holdings in Lester's? With just another 2 per cent of the stock he could invoke Article Seven of Lester's bylaws and demand a place on his board. He shuddered at the thought. It was hard to believe that he was afraid of the SEC regulations, especially as the Eisenhower Administration hadn't shown any interest in pursuing the original inquiry.

William was fascinated to read that Henry Osborne was once again in financial trouble and that Rosnovski kept bailing him out. He could only wonder how much longer that would go on, and what Osborne had on Rosnovski that made it possible for him to keep asking for more. Did Rosnovski have problems of his own? Had his daughter insisted that he drop the feud once and for all, or had he also cut his child off without a penny? Cohen's file also included an update on the affairs of the Baron Group. The London Baron was losing money and the Lagos Baron was out of commission; otherwise, the company continued to grow in strength, while Rosnovski was building eight new hotels around the world. William reread the clipping from the *Sunday Express*, reporting that Florentyna Rosnovski had not opened the Edinburgh Baron, and thought about his son. He closed the report and locked it in his safe.

William regretted his loss of temper with Richard. Although he did not want the Rosnovski girl to be his wife, he wished he had not turned his back so irrevocably on his only son. Kate had pleaded on Richard's behalf, and they'd had a long and bitter argument, and time hadn't helped resolve it. Kate had tried every tactic, from gentle persuasion to tears, but nothing had moved William. Virginia and Lucy didn't need to remind him that they were missing their brother.

'There's no one else who's critical of my paintings,' said Virginia.

'Don't you mean rude?' asked her mother. Virginia tried to smile.

Lucy had taken to locking herself in the bathroom and writing secret letters to Richard, who could never figure out why they always gave the appearance of being damp. Neither of them dared to mention his name in front of their father, and the strain was creating a rift within the family.

William had tried spending more time at the bank, working late into the night in the hope that it might help. It didn't. The bank was once again making heavy demands on his energies at the very time when he most felt like he should be slowing down. He had appointed six new vice presidents in the previous two years, hoping they would take some of the load off his shoulders. The reverse had turned out to be the case. They had created more work, and more decisions for him to make. The brightest of them, Jake Thomas, who'd recently joined him on the board, was already looking like the most likely candidate to take William's place as chairman if Richard didn't give up the Rosnovski girl and come home.

Although the bank's profits continued to rise each year, William found he was no longer interested in making money for money's sake. Perhaps he now faced the same problem Charles Lester had encountered: he had no son to leave his fortune and the chairmanship of the bank to.

—◦—

In the year of their silver wedding anniversary, William decided to take Kate and the girls for a long vacation to Europe in the hope that it might help put Richard out of their minds. They flew to London in a jet for the first time, a Boeing 707, and stayed at the Savoy, which brought back many happy memories of William's first trip to Europe with Kate.

They made a sentimental journey to Oxford, and went to Stratford-on-Avon to see *Richard III* with Laurence Olivier. They might have wished for a king by any other name.

On the return journey from Stratford they stopped at the church in Henley-on-Thames where William and Kate had been married. This time the church needed a new organ. They would have stayed at the Bell Inn, but once again it had only one vacant room. An argument started between William and Kate in the car on the way back to London as to whether it had been the Reverend Tukesbury or the Reverend Dukesbury who had married them. They came to no satisfactory conclusion before reaching the Savoy. On one thing they had been able to agree; the new roof on the parish church had proved a good investment.

William kissed Kate gently as he climbed into bed that night.

'Best five hundred pounds I ever spent,' he said.

They flew to Italy a week later, having seen everything any self-respecting American tourist in England is meant to see, and many they usually miss. In Rome the girls drank a little too much Italian wine on the night of Virginia's birthday and made themselves ill, while William ate too much good pasta and put on seven pounds. All of them would have been much happier if Richard had been with them, and although the girls never mentioned it to their father, they were desperate to meet Florentyna as she must be very special. Virginia cried one night, and Kate tried to comfort her. 'Why doesn't someone tell Daddy that some things are more important than pride?'

When they returned to New York, William was refreshed and eager to plunge back into his work. He lost the seven pounds within weeks.

As the months passed, he felt life was returning to normal, however much he missed his son. Normality disappeared when Virginia, just out of Sweet Briar, announced that she was engaged to be married to a student from the University of Virginia Law School. The news shook William.

'She's not old enough,' he said.

'She's twenty-two,' said Kate. 'She's not a child any longer, William. How do you feel about the prospect of becoming a grandfather?' she added, regretting her words as soon as she had spoken them.

'What do you mean?' said William, horrified. 'She isn't pregnant, is she?'

'Good gracious, no,' said Kate, and then she spoke more softly, as if she had been found out. 'Richard and Florentyna have had a baby.'

'How do you know?'

'Richard wrote to tell me the good news,' replied Kate. 'And Richard has been made a vice-president at the Bank of America. Hasn't the time come for you to forgive him, William?'

'Never,' said William, and left the room without another word.

Kate sighed wearily. He hadn't even asked if his grandchild was a boy or a girl.

—◦—

Virginia's wedding took place in Trinity Church, Boston, on a beautiful spring afternoon in March of the following year. William thoroughly approved of David Telford, the young lawyer with whom she had chosen to spend the rest of her life.

Virginia had wanted Richard to be an usher, and Kate had begged William to invite him to the wedding, but he had steadfastly refused. Although it was meant to be the happiest day of Virginia's life, she would have given back all her presents to have her father and Richard standing together in the family photograph that was taken outside the church. William had wanted to say yes, but he knew that Richard would never agree to coming without the Rosnovski girl.

On the day of the wedding, Richard sent Virginia a present and a telegram. William placed the unopened present in the boot of her car, and would not allow the telegram to be read at the reception.

52

ABEL WAS sitting at his desk in the New York Baron, waiting to see a fund-raiser for the Kennedy campaign. The man was already twenty minutes late. Abel was tapping his fingers impatiently on his desk when his secretary came in.

'Mr Frank Hogan to see you, sir.'

Abel sprang out of his chair. 'Come in, Mr Hogan,' he said, slapping the conservatively dressed young man on the back. 'How are you?'

'Sorry I'm late, Mr Rosnovski,' said the unmistakably Bostonian voice.

'I didn't notice,' said Abel. 'Would you care for a drink?'

'No, thank you, Mr Rosnovski. I try not to drink when I have so many appointments in one day.'

'Absolutely right. I hope you won't mind if I have one,' said Abel. 'I'm not planning on seeing a lot of people today.'

Hogan laughed like a man who knew he was in for a day of listening to other people's jokes.

Abel poured himself a whiskey. 'Now, what can I do for you, Mr Hogan?'

'Well, Mr Rosnovski, we were hoping the Party could count on your support once again.'

'I've always been a Democrat, as you know, Mr Hogan. I supported Franklin D. Roosevelt, Harry Truman and Adlai Stevenson, although I couldn't understand what Stevenson was talking about half the time.' Both men laughed falsely. 'I also helped my old friend Dick Daley in Chicago, and I've been backing young Ed Muskie – the son of a Polish immigrant, you know – since his campaign for Governor of Maine back in fifty-four.'

'You've been a loyal supporter of the Party in the past, there's no denying that, Mr Rosnovski,' said Hogan, in a tone that indicated that the statutory time for small talk was over. 'And we Democrats, not least former Congressman Osborne, have done the odd favour for you in return. I don't think it's necessary for me to go into any details concerning the little incident with Interstate Airways.'

'That's long past,' said Abel, 'and best forgotten.'

'I agree,' said Hogan. 'But although I realize that most self-made multimillionaires wouldn't care to have their affairs looked into too closely, you'll appreciate that we have to be especially careful so near the election. Nixon would love a scandal to get his teeth into at this stage of the race.'

'We understand each other clearly, Mr Hogan. Now that's out of the way, how much were you expecting from me for the campaign?'

'I need every penny I can lay my hands on.' Hogan's words were clipped and confident. 'Nixon's gathering a lot of support across the country, and it's going to be a very close run thing, especially in your home state of Illinois.'

'Well,' said Abel, 'I'll support Kennedy if he supports me. It's as simple as that.'

'He'd be delighted to support you, Mr Rosnovski. We all know you're a pillar of the Polish community, and Senator Kennedy is aware of the brave stand you took on behalf of your countrymen who are in labour camps behind the Iron Curtain, not to mention the service you gave in the war. I've been authorized to let you know that the candidate has already agreed to open your new hotel in Los Angeles on his next campaign trip to California.'

'That's good news,' said Abel.

'The senator is also fully aware of your desire to see Poland granted most favoured nation status in foreign trade with the United States.'

'It's no more than we deserve after our sacrifices in the war,' said Abel. He paused briefly. 'What about the other little matter?'

'Senator Kennedy is canvassing Polish-American opinion on that subject, but we haven't met with any objections so far. Naturally he can't come to a decision before he's elected.'

'Naturally. Would two hundred and fifty thousand dollars help him make that decision?'

Frank Hogan smiled, but didn't reply.

'Two hundred and fifty thousand dollars it is then,' said Abel. 'The money will be in your campaign fund by the end of the week, Mr Hogan.'

The business was over, the bargain struck. Abel rose from behind his desk. 'Please give Senator Kennedy my best wishes, and tell him I'll do everything in my power to make sure he becomes the next President of the United States. I've loathed Richard Nixon since his despicable treatment of Helen Gahagan Douglas, and I have personal reasons for not wanting Henry Cabot Lodge as vice president.'

'I'll be delighted to pass on your message,' said Hogan. 'Thank you for your continued support of the Democratic Party and, in particular, of the candidate.' He thrust out his hand, and Abel grasped it.

'Keep in touch, Mr Hogan. I don't part with that sort of money without expecting a return on my investment.'

'I fully understand.'

Abel accompanied him to the elevator, and returned to his office with a smile on his face. He picked up the phone on his desk.

'Ask Mr Novak to join me.'

George came through from his office on the other side of the corridor a few moments later.

'If Jack Kennedy becomes President, I think it's in the bag, George.'

'Congratulations, Abel, I'm delighted. It will be the fulfilment of one of your greatest dreams. How proud Florentyna will be of you.'

Abel smiled when he heard his daughter's name. 'Do you know what the little minx has been up to?' he said, laughing. 'Did you see last Friday's *Los Angeles Times*?'

George shook his head and Abel passed him a copy of the newspaper. A half-page photograph was circled in red ink. George read the caption aloud: '*Florentyna Kane opens her third Florentyna's shop in LA*. Great photo,' said George.

'She's hoping to open a fourth before the end of the year,' said Abel. 'Florentyna's are fast becoming to California what Balenciaga is to Paris.'

George laughed as he handed back the paper.

'I can't wait for her to open a Florentyna's in New York, probably on Fifth Avenue,' said Abel. 'I'll bet she does it within five years, ten at the most. Do you want to take another bet on that, George?'

'I didn't take the first one, if you remember, Abel. Otherwise I'd already have been out ten dollars.'

Abel looked up, his voice quieter. 'Do you think she'd come and see Senator Kennedy open the new Baron in Los Angeles, George?'

'Not unless her husband is invited as well.'

'Never,' said Abel. 'That boy is nothing. I read your last report. He's left the Bank of America to work with Florentyna; couldn't even hold down a good job.'

'You're becoming a very selective reader, Abel. You know that's not the way it was. Kane's in charge of the company finances, while Florentyna runs the shops. Don't forget that Wells Fargo offered him a job running their acquisitions department, but Florentyna begged him to turn them down and join her. Abel, you'll have to face the fact that their marriage is a success. I know it's hard for you to stomach, but why don't you climb down off your high horse and meet the boy?'

'You're my closest friend, George. No one else in the world would dare to speak to me like that. So no one knows better than you why I can't climb down, not until that bastard William Kane shows he's willing to meet me halfway. I won't crawl again while he's alive to revel in it.'

'What if you were to die first, Abel? You and he are exactly the same age.'

'Then I'd be the loser, and Florentyna would inherit everything.'

'You told me she wasn't going to get a thing. You were going to alter your will in favour of your grandson.'

'I couldn't do it, George. When the time came to sign the document, I just couldn't do it. What the hell – that damned grandson is going to end up with both our fortunes.'

He removed a wallet from his inside pocket, shuffled through several old photos of Florentyna, took out a more recent one and passed it to George.

'Good-looking little boy,' said George.

'Sure is,' said Abel. 'The image of his mother.'

George laughed. 'You never give up, do you, Abel?'

'What do you think they call him?'

'What do you mean?' said George. 'You know very well what his name is.'

'I mean, what do you think they actually call him?'

'How should I know?' said George.

'Find out,' said Abel. 'I care.'

'How am I supposed to do that?' said George. 'Have someone follow them while they're pushing the pram around Golden Gate Park?'

'I'm sure you'll find a way, George,' said Abel. 'Now, have you heard anything recently from Peter Parfitt?'

'Yes, he's been showing a little more interest in parting with his two per cent of Lester's, but I wouldn't trust Henry with the negotiations. With those two working on the sale, everybody will be in on the deal except you, so perhaps I ought to close the transaction on your behalf?'

'Don't do anything for the moment,' said Abel. 'Much as I hate Kane, I don't want any trouble until we know if Kennedy's won the election. If Nixon wins, I'll buy Parfitt's two per cent the same day and go ahead with the plan we discussed. And don't worry about Henry – I've taken him off the Kane case. From now on I'm handling it myself.'

'I do worry,' said George. 'He's in debt to half the bookmakers in Chicago, and I wouldn't be surprised if he turned up in New York on the scrounge any day now.'

'Henry won't be bothering me again. I made it crystal clear when I last saw him that he wasn't going to get another dime out of me. If he does come begging, he'll lose his seat on the board and that's his only source of income.'

'That's exactly why I'm worried,' said George. 'What if he became so desperate that he went to Kane for money.'

'That's impossible, George. Henry hates Kane even more than I do.'

'How can you be so sure of that?'

'Kane's mother was Henry's second wife,' said Abel, 'and when Kane was only sixteen, he threw Henry out of his own home.'

'Good God, how did you come across that piece of information?'

'There's nothing I don't know about William Kane,' said Abel, 'or Henry Osborne, for that matter. Absolutely nothing. And I'd be willing to bet my good leg there's nothing he doesn't know about me. So we just have to be patient for the time being, but there's not a chance of Henry turning stool pigeon. He'd die before he'd admit his real name is Vittorio Togna and he once served a jail sentence for fraud.'

'Does Henry realize you know all this?'

'No. I've kept it to myself for years. If you think a man might threaten you in the future, George, be sure you know everything about his past. I've never trusted Henry since the day he suggested swindling Great Western Casualty while he was still employed by them, although I'd be the first to admit he's been very useful to me over the years. But I'm also confident he isn't going to cause me any trouble in the future. So let's forget Henry and be a little more positive. What's the expected date for the completion of the Los Angeles Baron?'

'Middle of September.'

'Perfect. Just a few weeks before the election. When Kennedy opens the hotel, it will be on every front page in America.'

―◇―

When William returned to New York after a bankers' conference in Washington, he found a message on his desk, requesting that he contact Thaddeus Cohen immediately. The name always made him feel apprehensive, because Cohen was rarely the bearer of good news.

William hadn't spoken to him for some time, because Abel Rosnovski had caused no problems since the abortive telephone conversation on the eve of Richard and Florentyna's marriage, over four years ago. The successive quarterly reports had merely confirmed that Rosnovski wasn't trying to buy or to sell any of the bank's stock. Nevertheless, William rang Cohen on his private line. The lawyer informed him that he had stumbled across a piece of information he did not wish to discuss over the phone. William invited him to come to the bank as soon as it was convenient.

Cohen arrived in William's office forty minutes later. William heard him out in attentive silence.

When Cohen had finished, William said, 'Your father would never have approved of such methods.'

'Neither would yours,' responded Cohen, 'but then they didn't have to deal with the likes of Abel Rosnovski.'

'What makes you think your plan will work?'

'Consider the Sherman Adams case. Only one thousand six hundred and forty-two dollars in hotel bills and a vicuña coat, but it sure embarrassed the hell out of the administration, because Adams was a Presidential assistant. We know Rosnovski is aiming a lot higher than that. So it should be even easier to bring him down.'

'How much is this going to cost me?'

'Twenty-five thousand at the outside, but I may be able to pull it off for less.'

'How will you make sure Rosnovski doesn't realize I'm involved?'

'I'll use a third person as an intermediary, and he won't even know your name.'

'And if your information turns out to be accurate, what would you recommend we do with it?'

'We send all the details to Senator Kennedy's office, then leak it to the press. That should finish off Rosnovski's ambitions once and for all. The moment his credibility has been shattered, he'll be a spent force, and find it impossible to invoke Article Seven of Lester's bylaws, even if he did control eight per cent of the stock.'

'Possibly, but only if Kennedy becomes President,' said William. 'So what happens if Nixon wins? He's way ahead in the opinion polls. And can you really imagine America putting a Roman Catholic in the White House?'

'Who knows?' said Cohen. 'But if they do, for an investment of twenty-five thousand, you'd have a real chance of finishing off Rosnovski once and for all.'

'But only if Kennedy becomes President . . .'

Cohen nodded, but said nothing.

William opened the drawer of his desk, took out a large cheque book marked 'Private Account' and wrote out the figures two, five, zero, zero, zero. It was the first time he'd wanted a Democrat to live in the White House.

—◦—

Abel's prediction that when Kennedy opened the Los Angeles Baron it would be on every front page in America turned out to be a little optimistic, as the candidate had dozens of other events in Los Angeles that day before going head to head with Nixon in a televised debate the following evening. Nevertheless, the opening of the hotel gained wide coverage, and Frank Hogan assured Abel privately that Kennedy had not forgotten the other little matter.

While Kennedy made his speech, heaping praise on the Chicago Baron, Abel's eyes searched the packed audience for his daughter, but he didn't see her.

53

ONCE THE Illinois returns had been verified, John F. Kennedy looked certain to be the thirty-fifth President of the United States. Abel raised his glass to Mayor Daley when he celebrated at the Democratic National Headquarters in Times Square. He didn't get home until nearly five in the morning.

'Hell, I have a lot to celebrate,' he told George. 'I'm going to be the next . . .' He fell asleep before he finished the sentence. George smiled and put him to bed.

⊸o⊱

William watched the election results in the peace of his study on East Sixty-Eighth Street. After the Illinois returns, Walter Cronkite declared it was all over bar the shouting. William picked up his phone and dialled Thaddeus Cohen's home number.

All he said was, 'It looks as if the twenty-five thousand dollars has turned out to be a wise investment, Thaddeus. Now let's be sure there's no honeymoon period for Rosnovski. The best time to make our move would be when he takes his trip to Turkey.'

William placed the phone back on the hook and went to bed. He was disappointed that Nixon had failed to beat Kennedy, and that his cousin Henry Cabot Lodge would not be the vice president. But, he thought, it's an ill wind . . .

⊸o⊱

When Abel received an invitation to be a guest at one of President Kennedy's inaugural balls in Washington, DC, there was only one person he wanted to share the honour with. But after he had talked the idea over with George, he had to accept that Florentyna would never accompany him unless his feud with Richard's father was over. So he would have to go alone.

Abel postponed his trip to Europe and the Middle East. He could not afford to miss the Inauguration, but he could always reschedule the opening of the Istanbul Baron.

He had a new, rather conservative dark blue suit made specially for the occasion, and he took over the Davis Leroy Suite at the Washington Baron for the day of the ceremony. He watched the young President deliver his inaugural speech, full of hope and promise for the future.

'A new generation of Americans, born in this century' – Abel only just qualified – 'tempered by war' – Abel certainly qualified – 'disciplined by a hard and bitter peace' – Abel was over-qualified. 'Ask not what your country can do for you. Ask what you can do for your country.'

The crowd rose to a man, ignoring the snow that had failed to dampen the impact of the new President's brilliant oratory.

Abel returned to the hotel exhilarated. He showered before changing into white tie and tails, also made specially for the occasion. When he studied his ample frame in the mirror, he had to admit that he was not the last word in sartorial elegance. His tailor had done the best he could (he'd made three new and ever expanding evening suits for Abel in the past five years). Florentyna would have castigated him for the extra inches, and for her he would have done something about it. Why did his thoughts always return to Florentyna? He checked his medals. First, the Polish Veterans' Medal, next the decorations for his service in the desert and in Europe, and then his cutlery medals, as he called them, for distinguished service with knives and forks.

In all, seven inaugural balls were held in Washington that evening, and Abel's invitation directed him to the DC Armory. He sat in a corner reserved for Polish Democrats from New York and Chicago. They had a lot to celebrate. Edmund Muskie was in the Senate, and ten more Polish Democrats had been elected to Congress. No one mentioned the two newly elected Polish

Republicans. Abel reminisced happily with some old friends who were among his co-founder members of the Polish-American Congress. They all asked after Florentyna.

Suddenly, everyone in the room leapt to their feet and began cheering and shouting. Abel stood up to find out what all the commotion was about, and saw John F. Kennedy and his glamorous wife enter the ballroom. They stayed for about fifteen minutes, chatted with a few carefully selected guests, and then moved on. Although Abel didn't speak with the President, even though he had left his table and placed himself strategically in his path, he did manage to attract the attention of Frank Hogan as he was leaving with the Kennedy entourage.

'Mr Rosnovski. What a fortuitous meeting.'

Abel would have liked to explain to the boy that with him nothing was fortuitous, but now was neither the time nor the place. Hogan took his arm and guided him quickly behind a large marble pillar.

'I can't say too much at the moment, Mr Rosnovski, as I must stick with the President, but I think you can expect a call from us in the near future. Naturally, the President has rather a lot of appointments to deal with at the moment.'

'Naturally,' said Abel.

'But I'm hoping,' continued Hogan, 'that in your case everything will be confirmed by late March or early April. Allow me to be the first to offer my congratulations, Mr Rosnovski. I'm confident you'll serve the President with distinction.'

Abel watched Hogan literally run off to be sure he caught up with the Kennedy party, which was already climbing into a fleet of open-doored limousines.

'You look pleased with yourself,' said one of Abel's Polish friends as he returned to his table and sat down to attack a tough steak, which would not have been allowed inside a Baron hotel. 'Did Kennedy invite you to be his new Secretary of State?'

They all laughed.

'Not yet,' said Abel, 'But the Secretary of State would be my new boss,' he added under his breath.

He flew back to New York the next morning after visiting the

Polish Chapel of Our Lady of Czestochowa in the National Shrine. It made him think of both Florentynas.

Washington National airport was chaos, and Abel eventually arrived back at the New York Baron three hours later than planned. George joined him for dinner, and knew that all must have gone well when Abel ordered a magnum of Dom Pérignon.

'Tonight we celebrate,' said Abel. 'I saw Hogan at the ball, and my appointment will be confirmed in the next few weeks. The official announcement will probably be made soon after I get back from the Middle East.'

'Congratulations, Abel. There's no one who deserves the honour more.'

'Thank you, George. I can assure you your reward will not be in heaven, because when it's all official, I'm going to appoint you as acting president of the Baron Group during my absence.'

George poured himself a glass of champagne. They were already halfway through the bottle.

'How long do you think you'll be away this time, Abel?'

'Only three weeks. I want to check that I'm not being robbed blind in the Middle East before I go on to Turkey to open the Istanbul Baron. I think I'll take in London and Paris on the way.'

George poured Abel another glass of champagne.

◄○►

Abel spent three more days in England than planned, trying to sort out the problems of the London Baron with a manager who seemed to blame everything that went wrong on the British trade unions. The London Baron had turned out to be one of Abel's few failures, although he could never put his finger on why the hotel continually lost money. He would have considered closing it, but the Baron Group had to have a presence in England's capital, even if it was a loss leader. Once again he fired the manager, made a new appointment and flew off to Paris.

The French capital presented a striking contrast. The Paris Baron on the Boulevard Raspail was one of the most successful in the group, and he'd once admitted to Florentyna, as reluctantly as a parent admits to having a favourite child, that it was his favourite hotel. He found everything as he would have wanted it, and spent only two days there before flying on to the Middle East.

Abel now had sites in five of the Persian Gulf States, but only the Riyadh Baron was under construction. If he'd been a younger man, he would have stayed in the Middle East for a couple of years and sorted things out. But he couldn't abide the sand or the heat, or the difficulty of getting hold of a double whiskey from someone who wouldn't get arrested, so he left matters in the hands of one of his young assistant vice presidents, and flew on to Turkey.

Abel had visited Turkey several times during the past few years keeping an eye on the progress of the Istanbul Baron. For him there would always be something special about Constantinople, as he remembered the ancient city. He was looking forward to opening a Baron in the country from which he had sailed to begin his new life in America.

Before he had even started unpacking his suitcase in yet another Presidential Suite, Abel found fifteen invitations awaiting his reply. It was always the same around the time of a hotel opening: a galaxy of freeloaders hoping to be invited to any opening-night party appeared as if by magic. On this occasion, however, two of the invitations came as agreeable surprises to Abel, as they were both from men who certainly could not be classified as freeloaders, namely the ambassadors of America and Britain. The invitation to the old British Consulate was particularly irresistible, as he had not been inside the building for forty years.

That evening Abel dined as the guest of Sir Bernard Burrows, Her Majesty's Ambassador to Turkey. To his surprise Abel found he'd been placed on the right of the Ambassador's wife, an honour he had never been granted in the past. When dinner was over he observed the quaint English tradition of the ladies leaving the room while the gentlemen chatted about more weighty matters over cigars and port or brandy.

Abel was invited to join Fletcher Warren, the American Ambassador, in the privacy of Sir Bernard's study. Sir Bernard took Warren to task for inviting the Chicago Baron to dinner before he'd dined at his own embassy.

'The British have always been a presumptuous race,' said Warren, lighting a large Cuban cigar.

'I'll say one thing for the Americans,' said Sir Bernard, 'they don't know when they're fairly beaten.'

Abel listened to the two diplomats' banter, wondering why he had been included in such a private gathering. Sir Bernard offered him a glass of vintage port, and Warren raised his glass.

'To Abel Rosnovski.'

Sir Bernard also raised his glass. 'I understand that congratulations are in order,' he said.

Abel reddened and looked hastily towards Warren, hoping he would help him out.

'Oh, have I let the cat out of the bag, Fletcher?' said Sir Bernard. 'You told me the appointment was common knowledge, old chap.'

'Fairly common,' said Warren. 'Not that the British can ever keep a secret for long.'

'Is that why your lot took such a devil of a time to discover we were at war with Germany?' said Sir Bernard.

'And then moved in to make sure of the victory?'

'And grab the glory,' said Sir Bernard.

The American Ambassador laughed. 'I'm told the official announcement will be made in the next few days.'

Both men looked at Abel, who remained silent.

'Well then, may I be the first to congratulate you, Your Excellency,' said Sir Bernard. 'I wish you every success in your new appointment.'

Abel flushed to hear aloud the appellation he had whispered so often to his shaving mirror during the past few months. 'You'll have to get used to being called Your Excellency, you know,' continued the British Ambassador. 'And a whole lot of worse things than that. Particularly all the damned functions you'll have to attend night and day. If you have a weight problem now, it will be nothing compared to the one you'll have when you finish your term of office. You may live to be grateful for the Cold War. The food in the Eastern Bloc is so awful you might even end up losing weight.'

The American Ambassador smiled. 'Well done, Abel, and may I add my best wishes for your continued success. When were you last in Poland?'

'I've only been back once, for a short visit a few years ago,' said Abel. 'I've wanted to return ever since.'

'Well, you'll be returning in triumph,' said Warren. 'Are you familiar with our embassy in Warsaw?'

'No, I'm not,' admitted Abel.

'Not a bad location,' said Sir Bernard, 'remembering you colonials couldn't get a foothold in Europe until after the Second World War. But the accommodation is appalling. I shall expect you to do something about that, Mr Rosnovski. The only thing for it is to build a Baron hotel in Warsaw. That's the least they'll expect from an expatriate.'

Abel sat in a state of euphoria, laughing and enjoying Sir Bernard's feeble jokes. He knew he had drunk a little too much port, which made him feel at ease with himself and the world. He couldn't wait to tell Florentyna the news, now that the appointment would soon be official. She would be so proud of him. He decided there and then, that the moment he touched down in New York he would fly on to San Francisco and make everything up with her. It was what he had wanted to do all along, and at last he had an excuse. Somehow he'd force himself to like the Kane boy. He must stop referring to him as the Kane boy. What was his name – Richard? Yes, Richard. Abel felt a rush of relief at having finally made the decision.

After the three men had joined the ladies in the main reception room, Abel said to his host, 'I should be getting back, Your Excellency.'

'Back to the Baron,' said Sir Bernard. 'Allow me to accompany you to your car, my dear fellow.'

As Abel said good night to the Ambassador's wife at the door she smiled and said, 'I realize I'm not supposed to know, Mr Rosnovski, but many congratulations on your appointment. You must be so proud to be returning to the land of your birth as your adopted country's senior representative.'

'I am,' Abel said simply.

Sir Bernard accompanied him down the marble steps to the waiting car. The chauffeur opened the door.

'Good night, Rosnovski. And good luck in Warsaw. By the way, I hope you enjoyed your first meal in the British Consulate.'

'I've dined here on many occasions, actually, Sir Bernard.'

'You've been here before, old boy? When we checked through the guest book we couldn't find your name.'

'No,' said Abel. 'Most of the time I ate in the kitchen with the cook. I don't think they keep a guest book down there.'

Abel smiled as he climbed into the back of the car. He could see that Sir Bernard wasn't sure whether to believe him or not.

As he was driven back to the Baron, his fingers tapped on the side window and he hummed to himself. He would have liked to return to America the next morning, but he couldn't cancel the invitation to dine with Fletcher Warren at the American Consulate the following evening. Hardly the sort of thing a future ambassador does, old fellow, he could hear Sir Bernard saying.

Dinner with the American Ambassador turned out to be another pleasant occasion. Abel was made to explain to the assembled guests how he had come to eat in the kitchen of the British Consulate, and they listened in surprised admiration. He wasn't sure if many of them believed the story of how he had nearly lost his hand, but they all admired the silver band, and that night everyone called him 'Your Excellency'.

54

THE NEXT DAY Abel was up early, impatient to return to America.

The DC-8 flew into Belgrade, where it was grounded for sixteen hours. Something wrong with the landing gear, they told him. He sat in the airport lounge, sipping undrinkable Yugoslavian coffee, searching for any journal that was in English. The contrast between the British Consulate in Istanbul and a snack bar in a Communist-controlled country was not lost on him. At last the DC-8 took off, only to be delayed again in Amsterdam. This time the passengers were made to change planes.

When he finally touched down at Idlewild, Abel had been travelling for nearly thirty-six hours. He was so tired he could hardly walk. As he left the customs area, he suddenly found himself surrounded by newsmen, cameras flashing and clicking. Immediately he smiled. The announcement must have been made, he thought; now it's official. He stood as straight as he could, and walked slowly and with dignity, disguising his limp. There was no sign of George as the cameramen jostled each other unceremoniously in their efforts to get a picture.

Then he saw George standing at the edge of the crowd, looking as if he were attending a funeral rather than greeting a friend who was returning in triumph. At the barrier a journalist, far from asking him what it felt like to be the first Polish-American to be appointed US Ambassador to Warsaw, shouted, 'Do you have any answers to the charges?'

The cameras went on flashing, and so did the questions.

'Are the accusations true, Mr Rosnovski?'

'How much did you actually pay Congressman Osborne?'

'Do you deny the charges?'

'Have you returned to America to face trial?'

He shouted above the crowd to George, 'Get me out of here!'

George squeezed forward and managed to reach him, then pushed his way back through the crowd and bundled him into the back of the waiting Cadillac. Abel bent down and hid his head in his hands as the cameras' flashbulbs kept popping. George shouted at the chauffeur to get moving.

'To the Baron, Mr Novak?'

'No, to Miss Rosnovski's apartment on East Fifty-Seventh Street.'

'Why?' said Abel.

'Because the press is crawling all over the Baron.'

'I don't understand,' said Abel. 'In Istanbul they treat me as if I were the ambassador-elect, and I return home to find I'm a criminal. What the hell's going on, George?'

'Do you want to hear it all from me, or to wait until you've seen your lawyer?'

'My lawyer? You've already got someone to represent me?'

'H. Trafford Jilks, the best.'

'And the most expensive.'

'I don't think you should be worrying about money at a time like this, Abel.'

'You're right. I'm sorry. Where is he now?'

'I left him at the courthouse, but he said he'd come to the apartment as soon as he was through.'

'I can't wait that long, George. For God's sake, tell me what's going on.'

George took a deep breath. 'There's a warrant out for your arrest.'

'On what charge?'

'Bribery of government officials.'

'I've never bribed a government official in my life,' protested Abel.

'I know, but Henry Osborne has, and whatever he did, he's now claiming it was in your name, or on your behalf.'

'Oh my God,' said Abel. 'I should never have employed the man. I let the fact that we both hated Kane cloud my judgement. But I find it hard to believe Henry's told them anything, because he'd be implicating himself.'

'Henry's disappeared,' said George. 'And the big surprise is that suddenly, mysteriously, all his debts have been cleared up.'

'William Kane,' said Abel, spitting out the words.

'We've found nothing that points to that conclusion,' said George.

'Then how did the authorities get hold of the details?'

'It seems an anonymous package containing a large file was sent direct to the Justice Department in Washington.'

'Postmarked New York, no doubt,' said Abel.

'No. Chicago.'

Abel was silent for a few moments. 'It couldn't have been Henry who sent the file,' he said finally. 'That doesn't make any sense.'

'How can you be so sure?' asked George.

'Because you said all his debts have been cleared up. The Justice Department wouldn't pay out that sort of money unless they thought they were going to catch Al Capone. Henry must have sold his file to someone else. But who? The one thing we can be certain of is that he would never have released any information directly to Kane.'

'Directly?' said George.

'Directly,' repeated Abel. 'Perhaps he didn't sell it directly. Kane could have arranged for an intermediary to deal with the whole matter, if he already knew Henry was heavily in debt and the bookmakers were threatening him.'

'That could be right, Abel, and it certainly wouldn't have taken an ace detective to discover the extent of Henry's financial problems. They were common knowledge to anyone sitting on a bar stool in Chicago. But don't jump to any conclusions before we hear what your lawyer has to say.'

The Cadillac came to a halt outside Florentyna's old apartment, which Abel had never sold, in the hope that his daughter would return one day. H. Trafford Jilks was waiting for them in the foyer. Once they had settled down in the apartment, George poured Abel a large whiskey. He drank it in one gulp and gave the empty glass back to George, who refilled it.

'Tell me the worst, Mr Jilks,' Abel said. 'And don't spare me.'

'I'm sorry, Mr Rosnovski,' he began. 'Mr Novak told me about Warsaw.'

'That's history,' said Abel, 'so we needn't bother with "Your Excellency" any longer. You can be sure if Frank Hogan were asked, he wouldn't even remember my name. Come on, Mr Jilks, what am I facing?'

'You've been indicted on seventeen charges of bribery and corruption of officials in fourteen different states. I've made provisional arrangements with the Justice Department for you to be arrested here at the apartment tomorrow morning, and they will make no objection to the granting of bail.'

'Very cosy,' said Abel. 'And what if they can prove the charges?'

'Oh, I think they'll be able to prove some of them,' said H. Trafford Jilks matter-of-factly. 'But as long as Henry Osborne can't be found, they're going to find it very difficult to nail you on most of them. But I'm afraid the real damage has already been done, Mr Rosnovski, whether you're convicted or not.'

'I can see that only too well,' said Abel, glancing at a picture of himself on the front page of the *Daily News*. 'I want you to find out, Mr Jilks, who the hell bought that file from Henry Osborne. Put as many people to work on it as you need. I don't care about the cost. But you find out, and find out quickly, because if it turns out to be William Kane, I'm going to finish him off once and for all.'

'Don't get yourself into any more trouble, Mr Rosnovski,' said H. Trafford Jilks firmly. 'You're knee deep in enough shit as it is.'

'Don't worry,' said Abel. 'When I finish Kane, it'll be legal and above-board.'

'Now listen carefully, Mr Rosnovski. Forget about William

Kane for the time being, and start worrying about your impending trial, unless you don't care about spending the next ten years in jail. There's not much more we can do tonight. I've already got several men looking for Osborne, and I'll be issuing a short press statement denying the charges and saying we have a full explanation that will exonerate you completely.'

'Do we?' George asked hopefully.

'No,' said Jilks, 'but it will give me some time to work on our defence. When Mr Rosnovski has had a chance to check through the list of officials he's supposed to have bribed, it wouldn't surprise me if he's never had direct contact with anyone on that list. It's possible that Osborne always acted as an intermediary without ever putting Mr Rosnovski fully in the picture. So my job will be to prove that Osborne exceeded his authority as a director of the Baron Group. Mind you, Mr Rosnovski, if you have ever met any of the people on the list, for God's sake tell me, because you can be sure the Justice Department will put every one of them on the witness stand. But for now, go to bed and try to get some sleep. You must be exhausted. I'll see you first thing in the morning.'

—◦—

Abel was arrested in his daughter's apartment at 8.30 the following morning, and driven by a US marshal to the Federal Court for the Southern District of New York. The brightly coloured St Valentine's Day decorations in the store windows heightened his sense of loneliness. Jilks had hoped that his arrangements had been so discreet the press would not have found out about them, but when Abel reached the courthouse he was once again surrounded by photographers and reporters. He ran the gauntlet into the courtroom with George in front of him and Jilks behind. They sat silently in the corridor waiting for their case to be called.

Although they waited for several hours, when they were finally called the indictment hearing lasted only a few minutes, and felt strangely anticlimactic. The clerk read out the seventeen charges, and H. Trafford Jilks answered 'Not Guilty' to every one of them on behalf of his client. He then requested bail. The Government, as agreed, made no objection. Jilks asked Judge Prescott for at least three months to prepare his defence. The judge set a trial date of May 17.

Abel was free again; free to face the press and more of their barbed questions and flashing bulbs. The chauffeur had the car waiting for him at the bottom of the courtroom steps, with the back door open and the engine running. He had to do some very skilful manoeuvring to escape the reporters who were still pursuing their story. When the car came to a halt on East Fifty-Seventh Street, Abel turned to George and put his arm around his shoulder.

'Now listen, George, you're going to have to run the group while I get my defence sorted out. Let's hope you don't have to go on running it after that,' he said, attempting a laugh.

'Of course I won't have to, Abel. Mr Jilks will get you off, you'll see. Keep smiling,' he said, and left the other two men as they entered the apartment building.

'I don't know what I'd do without George,' Abel told Jilks as they settled down in Florentyna's living room. 'We came over on the boat together forty years ago, and we've been through a hell of a lot since then. Now it looks as if there's a whole lot more ahead of us to worry about, so let's get on with it, Mr Jilks. Have you caught up with Osborne yet?'

'No, but I have six men working on it, and I understand the Justice Department has at least another six, so we can be fairly certain one of us will find him. Not that we want the other side to get to him first.'

'What about the man Osborne sold the file to?' asked Abel.

'I have some people I trust in Chicago detailed to run that down.'

'Good,' said Abel. 'Now the time has come to go over that file of names you left with me last night.'

Jilks began by reading the indictment, and then went over the charges one by one. Abel made notes.

◄○►

After nearly three weeks of back-to-back meetings, Jilks was finally convinced there was nothing more Abel could tell him. During those three weeks there had been no leads on the whereabouts of Henry Osborne, for either Jilks's men or the Justice Department. Nor was there any information on who Henry had sold his information to, and Jilks was beginning to wonder if Abel had guessed right. Not that they could find any direct connection to William Kane.

As the trial date drew nearer, Abel started to face the possibility that he might actually have to go to jail. He was fifty-four, and fearful of the prospect of spending the last years of his life the same way he had spent the first few. As H. Trafford Jilks pointed out, if the Government was able to prove its case, there was enough evidence in Osborne's file to send Abel to prison for a very long time. Abel doubted that any new business could make much progress without the kind of handouts and small bribes to various people documented with such sickening accuracy in Jilks's file. He thought bitterly about the smooth, impassive face of the young William Kane, sitting in his Boston office on a pile of inherited money whose doubtful origins were safely buried under generations of respectability.

In the midst of Abel's unhappiness came a ray of light. Florentyna wrote a touching letter enclosing some photographs of her son, and saying that she still loved and respected her father and believed in his innocence.

Three days before the trial was due to open, the Justice Department tracked Henry Osborne down in New Orleans. They would never have found him if he hadn't turned up in a local hospital with two broken legs, after welching on several gambling debts. They don't like that sort of thing in New Orleans. After the hospital had put plaster casts on Osborne's legs, the Justice Department assisted him onto an Eastern Airlines flight to New York.

Henry Osborne was charged the next day with conspiracy to defraud, and denied bail. H. Trafford Jilks asked the court's permission to be allowed to question him. The judge granted his request, but Jilks gained little satisfaction from the hour-long exchange. It was clear that Osborne had already made a deal with the Government, agreeing to testify against Abel in return for facing lesser charges.

'No doubt Mr Osborne will find the charges against him are surprisingly lenient,' the lawyer commented drily.

'So that's his game,' said Abel. 'I take the rap while he escapes. Now we'll never find out who he sold that goddamn file to.'

'No, that was the one thing he was willing to talk about. He assured me that it wasn't William Kane. He said he would never have sold the file to Kane, however much he offered. A man from Chicago called Harry Smith paid Osborne $25,000 for the file. Would you believe it, Harry Smith turns out to be an alias; there are dozens of Harry Smiths in the Chicago area and not one of them fits the description.'

'Find him,' said Abel. 'And find him before the trial opens.'

'We're working around the clock on that,' said Jilks. 'If he's still in Chicago, we'll track him down. Osborne said that this so-called Harry Smith told him he only wanted the information for private purposes, and had no intention of revealing its contents to anyone in authority.'

'Then why did he want the file in the first place?'

'The inference was blackmail. That's why Osborne disappeared: he wanted to avoid you. If you think about it, Mr Rosnovski, he could be telling the truth. After all, the contents of the file are extremely damaging to him, and he must have been as alarmed as you when he heard it was in the hands of the Justice Department. No wonder he tried to lie low, and then agreed to testify against you once they'd caught up with him.'

'Do you know,' said Abel, 'the only reason I ever employed Osborne was because he hated William Kane as much as I did, and now Kane has turned that to his advantage.'

'There's no proof that Mr Kane was involved in any way,' said Jilks.

'I don't need proof.'

—◇—

The trial was delayed at the request of the prosecution, who said they needed more time to question Henry Osborne, who was now their principal witness. Trafford Jilks objected strongly, and informed the court that the health of his client, who was no longer a young man, was failing under the strain of the false accusations against him. The plea did not move Judge Prescott, who agreed to the prosecution's request and postponed the trial for a further four weeks.

For Abel, those twenty-eight days could be measured in hours, and two days before the trial was due to open, he resigned himself to being found guilty and facing a long jail sentence. Then Jilks's investigator in Chicago found the man called Harry Smith. He turned out to be a local private detective who had used an alias under strict instructions from his client, a firm of lawyers in New York. It cost Jilks a thousand dollars and another twenty-four hours before 'Harry Smith' revealed that the firm concerned had been Cohen, Cohen and Yablons.

'Thaddeus Cohen is Kane's personal lawyer. They go back to Harvard days,' said Abel. 'And way back, when I bought the hotel group from Kane's bank, some of the paperwork was done by a man named Thomas Cohen. For some reason the bank used two lawyers for the transaction.'

'What do you want me to do about this?' George asked Abel.

'Nothing,' interrupted Trafford Jilks. 'We don't need any more trouble before the trial. Do you understand, Mr Rosnovski?'

'Yes,' said Abel. 'I'll deal with Kane once the trial is over. Now listen, Mr Jilks, and listen carefully. You must go back to Osborne immediately and tell him the file was passed on by "Harry Smith" directly to William Kane, and that Kane is using it to gain revenge on both of us, and stress "both of us". I promise you, when Osborne hears that, he won't open his mouth in the witness box, no matter what promises he's made to the Justice Department. Henry Osborne's the one man alive who may hate Kane more than I do.'

'If that is your instruction,' said Jilks, who clearly wasn't convinced, 'I will carry it out, but I must warn you, Mr Rosnovski, that Osborne's placing the blame firmly on your shoulders, and to date he's been no help to our side at all.'

'You can take my word on this, Mr Jilks. His attitude will change the moment you tell him about Kane's involvement.'

H. Trafford Jilks obtained permission to spend a further ten minutes with Henry Osborne in his cell. Osborne listened, but said nothing. It seemed to Jilks that his news had made no impression on him, but he decided he would wait until the next morning before he informed Abel. He wanted his client to get a good night's sleep before the trial opened the following day.

Four hours before the trial was due to start, Henry Osborne was found hanging in his cell by the guard bringing in his breakfast.

He had used a Harvard tie.

--<o>--

The trial opened for the Government without its star witness, and the prosecuting attorney appealed to the judge for a further extension. After hearing another impassioned plea by H. Trafford Jilks on the state of his client's health, Judge Prescott refused the request.

The public followed every word of the Chicago Baron Trial on television and in the newspapers – and to Abel's dismay, Zaphia sat in the front row of the public gallery, clearly enjoying every moment of his discomfort. After nine days in court, the prosecution knew that their case was not standing up, and offered to make a deal. During an adjournment, Jilks briefed Abel on their proposal.

'They'll drop all the main indictments of bribery if you plead guilty to misdemeanours on two of the minor counts of attempting to improperly influence a public official.'

'What do you estimate are my chances of getting off completely if I turn them down?'

'Fifty-fifty, I'd say,' said Jilks.

'And if I don't get off?'

'Prescott is tough. The sentence wouldn't be a day under six years.'

'And if I agree to the deal and plead guilty to the two minor charges, what then?'

'A heavy fine. I'd be surprised if it was anything more than that.'

Abel sat silently for a few moments, considering the alternatives.

'I'll plead guilty. Let's get the damn thing over with.'

◄○►

The State Attorney informed the judge they were dropping fifteen of the charges against Abel Rosnovski. H. Trafford Jilks rose from his place and told the court his client wished to change his plea to guilty to the two remaining misdemeanour charges. The jury was dismissed. Judge Prescott was uncompromising in his summing up, telling Abel in no uncertain terms that the right to do business did not include the right to suborn public officials. Bribery was a crime, and a worse crime when condoned by an intelligent and competent man who should not need to stoop to such levels. In other countries, he said pointedly, making Abel feel once again like a raw immigrant, bribery might be an accepted way of life, but that was not the case in the United States of America. He gave Abel a six-month suspended sentence and a $25,000 fine, plus costs.

George took Abel back to the Baron and they sat in the penthouse drinking whiskey for more than an hour before Abel said anything.

'George, I want you to contact Peter Parfitt and pay him the million dollars he wants for his two per cent of Lester's. Once I have my hands on eight per cent of the bank, I'll invoke Article Seven and bring William Kane to his knees in his own boardroom.'

George nodded sadly, aware that no sooner had one battle ended than another was about to begin.

◄○►

A few days later, the State Department announced that Poland had been granted most favoured nation status in foreign trade with the United States, and that the next American Ambassador to Warsaw would be John Moors Cabot.

55

ON A BITTER February evening, William Kane sat back in his armchair and reread Thaddeus Cohen's report.

Henry Osborne had handed over the file that contained all the information he needed to finish Abel Rosnovski, pocketed his $25,000 and disappeared. Very much in character, thought William, as he replaced the copy of the file in his safe. The original had been sent to the Justice Department in Washington, DC by Thaddeus Cohen.

Once Rosnovski had returned from Turkey and been arrested, William had waited for him to retaliate, expecting him to dump all his Interstate stock immediately. This time, he was prepared. He had warned his broker that Interstate might come onto the market in large amounts, and his instructions were clear. The stock was to be purchased immediately so the price would not drop. He was prepared to put up the money from his trust as a short-term measure, to avoid any unpleasantness at the bank. He had also circulated a memo to all the stockholders of Lester's asking them not to sell any Interstate shares without first consulting him.

As the weeks passed and Rosnovski made no move, William began to believe that Thaddeus Cohen had been correct in assessing that nothing was traceable back to him. Rosnovski must be placing all the blame on Osborne's shoulders.

Cohen had predicted that with Osborne as the prosecution's star witness, Rosnovski would end up behind bars for a long time, making it impossible for him to invoke Article Seven and ever be a threat to the bank or William again. William hoped a conviction might also make Richard come to his senses and return home. Surely these revelations about the Rosnovski girl's father could only make him embarrassed, and realize that his own father had been right all along. Divorce would be William's final vindication.

William would happily have welcomed Richard back. There were two vacant places on the board of Lester's, created by the retirement of Tony Simmons and the recent death of Ted Leach. Thaddeus Cohen had also reported that Richard had made a series of brilliant acquisitions on behalf of Florentyna, but surely the opportunity to become the next chairman of Lester's would mean more to him than working for a dress shop.

Something else that spurred William on was that he did not much care for the new breed of directors now working at the bank. Jake Thomas, the vice chairman, was still the favourite to succeed William as chairman. He might have been educated at Princeton and graduated summa cum laude, but he was flashy – too flashy – thought William, and far too ambitious, not at all the right sort to be the next chairman of Lester's. William would have to hang on until his sixty-fifth birthday in eleven years' time, hoping he would be able to convince Richard to return to New York and join him at the bank long before then. He knew that Kate would have had Richard back on any terms, but as the years passed he found it more difficult to give way to his better judgement. Thank heavens Virginia's marriage was prospering; and now she was pregnant. If Richard refused to give up the Rosnovski girl and come home, William would leave everything to Virginia – if she produced a grandson.

—◦—

William was at his desk at the bank when he had his first heart attack. It wasn't a serious one, and his doctor told him he could live another twenty years if he was willing to slow down.

William convalesced at home, reluctantly allowing Jake Thomas to take overall responsibility for the bank's decisions while he was away. But he soon became restless, disobeyed his doctor's orders and returned to his desk. He quickly re-established his position as chairman, for fear that Thomas had taken on too much authority in his absence.

From time to time Kate plucked up the courage to suggest that he should make a direct approach to Richard, but William remained adamant. 'He knows he can come home whenever he wants to. All he has to do is end his relationship with that woman.'

◄◌►

The day Henry Osborne committed suicide, William had a second heart attack. Kate sat by his bedside all through the night, and his obsession with Abel Rosnovski's forthcoming trial somehow kept him alive. He followed the proceedings in the columns of *The New York Times*, although he knew Osborne's death would put Rosnovski in a far stronger position.

When Rosnovski escaped with nothing more than a six-month suspended sentence and a $25,000 fine, William was so distressed that Kate feared he would have another heart attack. It wasn't hard to figure out that the Government must have made a deal with Rosnovski's lawyer. But within days William was surprised to find himself feeling slightly guilty, and somewhat relieved, that Rosnovski had not been sent to prison.

Once the trial was over, William didn't care if Rosnovski dumped his Interstate Airways stock or not. He was ready for him this time. But still nothing happened, and as the weeks passed, William began to lose interest in the Chicago Baron and to think only of Richard, who he now desperately wanted to see again. 'Old age and fear of death allows for sudden changes of the heart', he had once read.

One morning in September, he told Kate he'd changed his mind. She didn't question him; it was enough for her that William finally wanted to be reunited with his son.

'I'll call him immediately and invite them both to New York,' she said, and was pleasantly surprised that the words *them both* didn't cause her husband to fly into a temper.

'Fine,' said William quietly. 'Please tell Richard that I want to see him again before I die.'

'Don't be silly, darling. The doctor said if you slow down you'll live for another twenty years.'

'I only want to complete my term as chairman and see Richard take my place. That will be quite enough. Why don't you fly to the coast again and tell Richard how much I want to see –' he hesitated before adding, 'both of them.'

'What do you mean, again?' Kate asked nervously.

William smiled. 'I know you've been to San Francisco several times over the years, my darling. Whenever I've gone away on a business trip for more than a week, you've always used the excuse that you were visiting your mother. When she died last year, your excuses became increasingly improbable. You're still as lovely as the day we first met, but I do believe that at fifty-four you're unlikely to have taken a lover. So it wasn't all that hard to work out you had been visiting Richard.'

'Why didn't you mention that you knew before?'

'In my heart I was glad,' said William. 'I hated the thought of both of us losing contact with our only son. How is he?'

'Both of them are well and you have a granddaughter now as well as a grandson.'

'A granddaughter,' William repeated.

'Yes, she's called Annabel,' said Kate.

'And my grandson?' said William.

When Kate told him his name, he had to smile. It was only half a lie.

'Good,' said William. 'Well, let's hope Richard isn't as pig-headed as I am, and will agree to see me. Tell him I love him.' He had once heard another man say that when he'd been told he was going to lose his son.

Kate was happier than she had been in years. She called Richard later that evening to say she would be flying out to stay with them very soon, and that this time she would be the bearer of good news.

―◦―

When Kate flew back to New York three weeks later, she told William that Richard and Florentyna had agreed to visit them in the New Year. She was full of stories of how successful they were, how William's grandson was the image of his grandfather, how beautiful their new granddaughter, Annabel, was, and how Richard was looking forward to coming back to New York to see his father, and to introduce him to his wife. William liked everything he heard about Florentyna. He had begun to fear that if Richard did not return home soon, he never would, and then the chairmanship of the bank would fall into Jake Thomas's lap. William did not care to think about that. As William listened to her he found he was happy, and more at peace with himself than he had been for years.

--◦--

William returned to work the following Thursday, having made a good recovery from his second heart attack, now feeling he had something to live for.

On his arrival at the bank he was greeted by the doorman who told him Jake Thomas was waiting to see him. William thanked the senior employee of the bank – the only person who had served Lester's for more years than he had.

'Nothing's so important that it can't wait, Harry,' he replied.

'No, sir.'

William walked slowly along the corridor to the chairman's office. When he opened his door, he found Jake Thomas sitting in his chair.

'Have I been away that long?' said William, laughing. 'Am I no longer chairman of the board?'

'Of course you are,' said Thomas, rising from the chairman's seat. 'Welcome back, William.'

William had found it impossible to get used to the way the younger generation used first names so casually. He and Thomas had known each other only a few years, and the man couldn't be a day over forty.

'So what's the problem?' William asked.

'Abel Rosnovski,' said Thomas, without expression.

William felt sick in the pit of his stomach.

'What does he want this time?' he asked wearily. 'Won't he even allow me to finish my days in peace?'

'He intends to invoke Article Seven of the bank's bylaws, and hold a proxy meeting with the sole purpose of removing you as chairman of the board.'

'He can't. He doesn't have the necessary eight per cent, and the bank's bylaws clearly state that the chairman must be informed immediately if any outside person comes into possession of eight per cent of the bank's stock.'

'He says he'll have the other two per cent by close of business today.'

'That's impossible,' said William. 'I've kept a careful check on all the stock. No one would consider selling to Rosnovski. No one.'

'What about Peter Parfitt?'

William smiled triumphantly. 'I purchased his stock a year ago through a third party.'

Jake Thomas looked shocked, and neither of them spoke for some time.

William realized for the first time just how much Thomas wanted to be the next chairman of Lester's.

'Well,' said Thomas once he'd recovered, 'the fact is that Rosnovski claims he'll have eight per cent by close of business tonight, which would entitle him to elect three directors to the board and hold up any major policy decisions for at least three months – the very provisions you put into the articles of incorporation to protect your long-term position. He also intends to hold a press conference next Monday morning to outline his plans for the future of the bank. For good measure he's threatening to make a reverse takeover bid for the company if he meets with any opposition. He's made it clear there's only one thing that will make him change his mind.'

'What's that?' asked William.

'That you submit your resignation as chairman.'

'That's blackmail!' said William, nearly shouting.

'Possibly. But if you haven't resigned by noon next Monday, he intends to write to all shareholders demanding your resignation. And he's already reserved space in forty newspapers and magazines.'

'Has he gone mad?' said William, taking a handkerchief from his breast pocket and mopping his brow.

'That's not all,' Thomas continued. 'He's also demanding that no Kane replaces you on the board for the next ten years, and that your resignation should not give ill health or indeed any reason for your departure.'

Thomas handed William a lengthy document bearing the Baron Group's letterhead.

'Mad,' repeated William, once he had skimmed its contents.

'Nevertheless, I've called a board meeting for ten o'clock tomorrow morning,' said Thomas. 'We can't avoid discussing his demands any longer.' Without another word, he left the room, closing the door quietly behind him.

No one else interrupted William during the day. He sat alone at his desk trying to contact some of the non-executive directors, but he only managed to have a word with one or two of them, and quickly realized he could no longer be certain of their support, and that tomorrow's meeting was going to be a close-run thing. He checked the list of shareholders, and was still confident that none of them would release their stock. He laughed to himself. Rosnovski would fall at the first hurdle.

William went home early that afternoon and retired to his study to consider his tactics for defeating Abel Rosnovski for the last time. He didn't go to bed until 3 a.m., by which time he knew exactly what he intended to do.

56

WILLIAM ARRIVED well prepared for the board meeting, and sat in his office going over his notes. He was confident that his plan had considered every possible eventuality. At five to ten his secretary buzzed him. 'A Mr Rosnovski is on the phone for you, Mr Chairman.'

'What?'

'Mr Rosnovski.'

'Mr Rosnovski?' William repeated the name in disbelief. 'Put him through,' he said, his voice quivering slightly.

'Yes, sir.'

'Mr Kane?' The slight accent that William could never forget.

'Yes. What are you trying to achieve this time?' he asked wearily.

'Under the bylaws of the bank I have to inform you that I am in possession of eight per cent of Lester's shares, and I intend to invoke Article Seven of the bank's bylaws unless my demands are met by noon on Monday.'

'Who did you get the other two per cent from?' stammered William.

The phone clicked. William looked back over the list of shareholders, trying to work out who had betrayed him. He was still trembling when the phone rang again.

'The board members are waiting for you, sir.'

William entered the boardroom at three minutes past ten. As he looked around the table, he realized how few of the younger directors he knew well. But the last time he'd had to fight to be chairman, he'd known hardly any of them, and he'd still won. He smiled to himself, reasonably confident he could call Rosnovski's bluff. When he rose to address the board, his speech was well prepared.

'Gentlemen, this meeting has been called because the bank has received a demand from Mr Abel Rosnovski of the Baron Group, a convicted criminal, who has had the effrontery to issue a direct threat to me, namely, that he will use his eight per cent holding in my bank to embarrass us. Should this tactic fail he will attempt a reverse takeover bid, unless I resign as chairman of the board without explanation. I have only nine years left to serve as chairman and, if I were to leave before then, my resignation would be totally misinterpreted on Wall Street.'

He glanced down at his notes.

'I am willing, gentlemen, to place my entire shareholding in the bank, and a further ten million dollars from my private trust, at the board's disposal in order to counter any move Mr Rosnovski makes, thus insuring Lester's against any financial loss. I hope, gentlemen, that I can rely on your full support. I feel confident you won't give way to Rosnovski's crude attempt at blackmail.'

The room was silent. William felt sure he had won the day until Jake Thomas asked if the board might question him about his relationship with Rosnovski. The request took William by surprise, but he agreed without hesitation. Jake Thomas didn't frighten him.

'This vendetta between you and Mr Rosnovski,' said Thomas, 'has been going on for over thirty years. Do you believe that if we accepted your proposal, that would be the end of the matter?'

'What else can the man do? What else can he do?' stammered William, looking around the boardroom table for support.

'We can't predict what his next move will be,' said Thomas.

'And with an eight per cent holding in the bank, he can hold us all to ransom,' added Hamilton, the new company secretary – not William's choice, he talked too much. 'All we know is that neither of you seems willing to end this feud. Although you've offered ten million dollars of your own money to protect the bank's financial position, if Rosnovski were continually to hold up policy decisions, call proxy meetings and arrange takeover bids, while having absolutely no regard for the long-term interests of the bank, it could cause panic among our investors, and be taken advantage of by our rivals. The bank and its subsidiary companies, to which we have a fiduciary duty as directors, would at best be highly embarrassed, and at worst might eventually collapse.'

'No, no,' said William. 'With my personal backing we could meet him head on.'

'The decision we have to make today,' continued the company secretary, sounding as well prepared as William, 'is whether there are any circumstances in which this board wants to meet Mr Rosnovski head on, if it were to result in all of us being losers in the long run.'

'Not if I cover the cost from my private trust,' said William.

'It's not just a question of money,' said Thomas. 'Now that Rosnovski can invoke Article Seven, the bank could find itself spending its entire time trying to anticipate his next move.'

Thomas waited for the effect of what he had said to sink in before he continued: 'Now, I must ask you a very serious personal question, Mr Chairman, which concerns every one of us around this table. I hope you'll be nothing less than frank when you answer it, however unpleasant that may be.'

William looked up, wondering what the question could be. What had they been discussing behind his back? 'I will answer any question the board requires,' said William. 'I have nothing to hide and no one to fear.' He looked pointedly at Thomas.

'Thank you,' said Thomas, not flinching. 'Mr Chairman, were you in any way involved with sending a file to the Justice Department in Washington that caused Mr Rosnovski to be arrested and charged with fraud, when at the same time you knew he was a major stockholder of the bank?'

'Did he tell you that?' demanded William.

'Yes. He claims you were the sole reason for his arrest.'

William considered his reply for a few moments. He'd never lied to the board in over twenty-three years, and he didn't intend to start now.

'Yes, I did,' he said, breaking the silence. 'When the information came into my hands, I considered it was nothing less than my duty to pass it on to the Justice Department.'

'How did the information come into your hands?'

William did not reply.

'I think we all know the answer to that question, Mr Chairman,' said Thomas. 'Moreover, you decided on this action without briefing the board, putting all of us in jeopardy. Our reputations, our careers, everything this bank stands for – all because of a personal vendetta.'

'But Rosnovski was trying to ruin me!' said William, aware he was shouting.

'So in order to ruin him, you risked the bank's long-term stability and reputation.'

'It's my bank,' said William.

'It is not your bank,' said Thomas firmly. 'You own eight per cent of the stock, as does Mr Rosnovski. You may be chairman at this moment, but the bank is not yours to use at your personal whim without consulting the other directors.'

'Then I will have to ask the board for a vote of confidence,' said William. 'I'll ask you to support me against Abel Rosnovski.'

'That is not what a vote of confidence would be about,' said the company secretary. 'It would be about whether you are the right person to continue running this bank in the present circumstances. Can't you see that, Mr Chairman?'

'So be it,' said William. 'The board must decide whether it wishes to end my career in disgrace, after nearly a quarter of a century's service, or to yield to the threats of a convicted criminal.'

Jake Thomas nodded to the company secretary, and voting slips were passed to every board member. It was beginning to look to William as if everything had been planned long before the meeting took place. He glanced around the crowded table at the twenty-nine men. Many of them he had chosen himself. Some of them surely wouldn't allow Rosnovski to remove him from his own boardroom. Not now. Not this way.

He watched the members of the board as they passed their voting slips back to the secretary. Once they had all been handed in, Hamilton began opening them slowly, meticulously noting down each 'aye' and 'nay' in two columns on a piece of paper in front of him. William could see that one list was considerably longer than the other, but he could not decipher which was which.

Finally the secretary announced that all the votes had been counted. He then solemnly said that William Kane had lost the vote of confidence by seventeen votes to twelve.

William couldn't believe what he had heard. Abel Rosnovski had defeated him in his own boardroom. He managed to stand up with the use of his cane, but no one spoke as he left the boardroom. He went to his office and collected his coat, pausing only to glance at the portrait of Charles Lester for the last time, before walking slowly down the long corridor and towards the front entrance.

Harry opened the door for him and said, 'Nice to have you back again, Mr Chairman. See you tomorrow, sir.'

William realized he would never see Harry again. He turned and shook hands with the man who had directed him to the boardroom twenty-three years before.

Harry looked surprised. 'Good night, sir,' he said, and watched as William climbed into the back of his car and was driven home.

As William stepped out of the car on East Sixty-Eighth Street, he collapsed onto the pavement in front of his home. The chauffeur and Kate had to help him up the steps and into the house. Kate could see that he was crying as she put her arms around him.

'What is it, William? What's happened?'

'I've been thrown out of the bank,' he wept. 'My own board no longer has confidence in me. When it mattered, they supported Rosnovski.'

Kate managed to get him up to bed, and sat with him through the night. He did not say another word. Nor did he sleep.

—◇—

The announcement in *The Wall Street Journal* the following Monday morning was succinct: 'William Lowell Kane, the President and Chairman of Lester's Bank, resigned following last Friday's board meeting.' No explanation was given for his sudden departure, and there was no suggestion that his son would take his place on the board. William sat in his bed aware that rumours would be sweeping through Wall Street that morning, and that the worst would be assumed. He no longer cared for this world.

After Abel Rosnovski had read the same announcement he picked up the phone, dialled Lester's Bank and asked to be put through to the new chairman. A few moments later Jake Thomas came on the line.

'Good morning, Mr Rosnovski.'

'Good morning, Mr Thomas. I'm just phoning to confirm that I shall release all my Interstate Airways shares to the bank this morning at the market price, and my eight per cent holding in Lester's to you personally for two million dollars.'

'Thank you, Mr Rosnovski, that's most generous of you.'

'No need to thank me, Mr Chairman,' said Abel. 'It's no more than we agreed when you sold me your two per cent.'

PART EIGHT

1963–1967

57

ABEL WAS surprised to find how little satisfaction his final triumph gave him. A Pyrrhic victory.

George tried to persuade him to travel to Warsaw and look over possible sites for the new Baron, but he wasn't interested. As he grew older, he became fearful of dying abroad having never seen Florentyna again, and for months he showed scant interest in the group's activities.

When John F. Kennedy was assassinated on November 22, 1963, Abel became even more depressed, and began to fear for his adopted country. Eventually George managed to convince him that a trip abroad could do no harm, and that he might return invigorated.

Abel took George's advice and flew directly to Warsaw, something he never thought he'd do in his lifetime. His command of the language and long history of fighting for Polish recognition helped him to secure a confidential agreement from the Government to build the first Baron in a communist country. He was pleased to beat Conrad Hilton and Charles Forte to be the first international hotelier behind the Iron Curtain. But he couldn't help thinking . . . and it didn't help when Lyndon Johnson appointed John Gronowski to be the first Polish-American ambassador. But nothing seemed to give him any real satisfaction any more. He may have defeated William Kane, but he'd lost his daughter, and he suspected Kane was having the same problem with his son.

After the Warsaw deal was signed he roamed the world,

staying in his existing hotels, watching the construction of new ones and selecting sites for ones he may never live to see. In Cape Town he opened the first Baron in South Africa, then he flew to Germany to open another in Düsseldorf. He then lingered for six months in his favourite Baron, in Paris, roaming the streets by day and attending the opera and the theatre at night, hoping to revive happy memories of the days he spent there with Florentyna.

Finally he left Paris and returned to America. As he descended the metal steps of an Air France 707 at Kennedy International Airport, his back hunched and his bald head covered with a black hat, nobody recognized him. George, as always, was there to greet him; loyal, honest George, looking quite a bit older.

On the drive into Manhattan, George brought him up to date with the group news. The profits continued to grow as its keen young executives thrust forward in every major country in the world. Seventy-two hotels with a staff of over 22,000. Abel didn't seem to be listening. He only wanted news of Florentyna.

'She's well,' said George. 'She's coming to New York early next year.'

'Why?' asked Abel, suddenly excited.

'She's opening one of her shops on Fifth Avenue.'

'Fifth Avenue? Lucky you didn't take that bet, George.'

George smiled. 'The eleventh Florentyna's.'

'Have you seen her, George?'

'Yes,' he admitted.

'Is she well, is she happy?'

'Both of them are well and happy, and so successful. Abel, you should be very proud of them. Your grandson is quite a boy, and as for your granddaughter – she's the image of Florentyna when she was that age.'

'Will she see me?'

'Will you agree to meet her husband?'

'No, George. I can never meet that boy, not while his father's still alive.'

'What if you die first?'

'You mustn't believe everything you read in the Bible,' said Abel. They drove in silence back to the hotel, and Abel dined alone in his suite that night.

For the next six months, he rarely left the penthouse.

58

WHEN FLORENTYNA KANE opened her new boutique on Fifth Avenue in March 1967, everyone in New York seemed to be there to join in the celebration, except William Kane and Abel Rosnovski.

Kate tucked William up in bed and left him muttering to himself while she, Virginia and Lucy went off to attend the opening. George left Abel alone in his suite and set off for Fifth Avenue. He had tried to talk him into coming along with him. Abel grunted that his daughter had managed to open ten shops without him, and one more wouldn't make any difference. George told him he was a stubborn old fool and left for Fifth Avenue on his own. Abel knew he was right.

George arrived at the shop to find a magnificent modern boutique with thick carpets and the latest Swedish furniture – it reminded him of the way Abel used to do things. Florentyna was wearing a long green gown with the now famous double F on its high collar. She handed George a glass of champagne and introduced him to Kate and Lucy Kane, who were chatting with Zaphia. Kate and Lucy were clearly very happy, and Virginia surprised George by asking after Mr Rosnovski.

'I told him he was a stubborn old fool to miss such a good party. Is Mr Kane here?' he asked.

'No,' said Kate. 'I'm afraid he's another stubborn old fool.'

◄○►

William was still muttering angrily at *The New York Times*, something about Johnson pulling his punches in Vietnam, when he folded the newspaper and dragged himself out of bed. He dressed slowly, very slowly, before inspecting himself in the mirror. He looked like a banker. He scowled. How else should he look? He walked slowly down the stairs. He put on a heavy black overcoat and his old Homburg hat, picked up his black walking stick with the silver handle – the one Rupert Cork-Smith had left him – and somehow got himself out onto the street. It was the first time he had been out on his own for the best part of three years. The maid was surprised to see Mr Kane leaving the house unaccompanied.

It was an unusually warm spring evening, but William still felt the cold after being stuck in the house for so long. It took him a considerable time to walk to Fifth Avenue and Fifty-Sixth Street, each pace taking a little longer, and when he eventually made it he found the crowd inside Florentyna's was spilling out onto the sidewalk. He didn't feel he had the strength to fight his way through, so he stood on the sidewalk and watched. Young people, happy and excited, were thrusting their way into Florentyna Kane's fashionable boutique. Some of the girls were wearing the new mini skirts from London. What next, thought William. Then he spotted Richard talking to Kate. He'd grown into such a fine-looking man – tall, confident and relaxed; he had an air of authority about him that reminded William of his own father. But in all the bustle and movement inside the shop, he couldn't work out which one was Florentyna. He stood there for nearly an hour enjoying the comings and goings, regretting the stubborn years he had thrown away.

The March wind was beginning to race down Fifth Avenue. He'd forgotten how cold that wind could be. He turned his collar up. He must get home, because they were all coming to dinner that night, and he was going to meet Florentyna and the grand-children for the first time, and be reunited with his beloved son. He had told Kate what a fool he'd been, and begged her forgiveness. All she said was, 'I'll always love you.' Florentyna had written to him. Such a kind and generous letter. She had been so understanding about the past, and had ended with 'I can't wait to meet you'.

He must get home. Kate would be cross with him if she discovered he'd been out on his own in that cold wind. They could tell him all about the opening over dinner. He wouldn't let them know he'd been there – that would always be his secret.

As he turned to go home, he saw an old man standing a few yards away in a black overcoat, with his hat pulled down over his head and a scarf around his neck. Not a night for old men, thought William as he walked towards him. And then he saw the silver band on his wrist. In a flash it all came back to him, fitting into place for the first time. Tea at the Plaza, later at his office in Boston, then again on a battlefield in Germany, and now on Fifth Avenue. The man must have been standing there for some time, because his face was red and raw from the wind. He stared at William out of those unmistakable blue eyes. They were now only a few feet apart. As William passed him, he raised his hat to the old man. He returned the compliment, and they continued on their separate ways without a word.

—◁○▷—

I must get home before they do, thought William. The joy of seeing Richard and his grandchildren would make everything worthwhile. He must get to know Florentyna, ask for her forgiveness, and trust that she would understand something he could scarcely comprehend himself. Such a fine young woman, everybody told him.

When he reached East Sixty-Eighth Street, he fumbled for his key and opened the front door. 'Turn on all lights,' he told the maid, 'and build the fire up to make them feel welcome.' He felt very contented and very, very tired. 'Draw the curtains and light the candles on the dining-room table. There's so much to celebrate.'

He couldn't wait for them all to return. He sat down in the old maroon leather chair by the log fire and thought happily about the evening that lay ahead. Grandchildren surrounding him, the years he had missed. When had his little grandson learned to count? At last William felt he had a chance to bury the past and earn forgiveness in the future. The room was so nice and warm after that cold wind . . .

A few minutes later there was an excited bustle downstairs, and the maid came in to tell Mr Kane that his son had just arrived. He was in the hall with Mrs Kane and his wife and two of the loveliest children the maid had ever seen. Then she ran off to be sure that dinner would be ready on time. He would want everything to be perfect that night.

Richard entered the room, with Florentyna by his side. She looked quite radiant.

'Father,' he said. 'I would like you to meet my wife.'

William Lowell Kane would have stood to greet her, but he couldn't. He was dead.

59

ABEL PLACED the envelope on the table by his bed. He hadn't dressed yet. Nowadays he rarely rose before noon. He tried to put the breakfast tray on the floor, but the movement demanded too much dexterity for his stiff old body to accomplish. He inevitably ended by dropping the tray with a bang. It was no different today. He no longer cared. He picked up the envelope once more, and read the covering note for a second time.

'We were instructed by the late Mr Curtis Fenton, sometime manager of the Continental Trust Bank, LaSalle Street, Chicago, to send you the enclosed letter when certain circumstances had come about. Please acknowledge receipt of this letter by signing the enclosed copy and returning it to us in the stamped addressed envelope supplied herewith.'

'Goddamn lawyers,' said Abel, and tore open the envelope.

Dear Mr Rosnovski,

This letter has been in the keeping of my lawyers until today for reasons that will become apparent to you as you read it.

When in 1951 you closed your accounts at the Continental Trust after over twenty years with the bank, I was naturally very distressed and concerned. My concern was caused not by losing one of the bank's most valued customers, sad though that was, but because you felt I had acted in a dishonourable way. What you were not aware of at the time was that I had specific instructions from your backer not to reveal certain facts to you.

When you first visited me at the bank in 1929, you asked for financial help to clear the debt incurred by Mr Davis Leroy, in order that you might take possession of the hotels which then formed the Richmond Group. I took a personal interest in your case, as I believed that you had an exceptional flair for your chosen career. It has given me a great deal of satisfaction to observe in old age that my confidence was not misplaced. But in truth I was unable to find a backer, despite approaching several leading financiers. I might add that I also felt some responsibility for your predicament, having advised you to buy 25% of the Richmond Group from my client, Miss Amy Leroy, when I was unaware of the financial difficulties Mr Leroy was facing at that time. I digress.

I had given up all hope of finding a backer for you when you came to visit me on that Monday morning. I wonder if you remember that day as well as I do? Only thirty minutes before your appointment I had a call from a financier who was willing to put up the necessary money. Like me, he had great confidence in your ability. His only stipulation, as I advised you at the time, was that he insisted on remaining anonymous because of a potential conflict between his professional and private interests. The terms he offered, allowing you to gain eventual control of the Richmond Group, were in my opinion extremely generous, and you rightly took full advantage of them. Indeed, your backer was delighted when you were able, through your own diligence and hard work, to repay his original investment with interest.

I lost contact with you both after 1951, but soon after I retired from the bank I read a distressing story in the newspapers concerning your backer, which prompted me to write this letter, in case I died before either of you.

I write not to prove my good intentions in this affair, but so that you should not continue to live under the illusion that your benefactor was Mr David Maxton of the Stevens Hotel.

*Mr Maxton was a great admirer of yours, but he never
approached the bank in that capacity. The gentleman who
believed in you, and the future of the Baron Group, was
William Lowell Kane, the former Chairman of Lester's Bank,
New York.*

*I begged Mr Kane to inform you of his personal
involvement, but he refused to break the clause in his trust
deed that stipulated that no beneficiary should be privy to the
investments of his family trust, because of the conflict it might
cause at the bank. After you had paid off the loan and he
learned of Henry Osborne's association with the Baron
Group he became even more adamant that you should not be
informed.*

*I have left instructions that this letter is to be destroyed
if you should die before Mr Kane. In those circumstances,
he will receive a similar letter, explaining your total lack of
knowledge of his personal generosity.*

*Whichever one of you receives a letter from me, it was a
privilege to have served you both.*

I remain, your faithful servant,

Curtis Fenton

Abel picked up the phone by the side of his bed. 'Find George
for me,' he said. 'I need to get dressed.'

60

GRANDMOTHER KANE would have approved of the turnout at William Lowell Kane's funeral. Three senators, five congressmen, two bishops, most of the leading banks' chairmen and the publisher of *The Wall Street Journal* were all in attendance. Jake Thomas and every director of the Lester board were also present, their heads bowed in prayer to a God William had never believed in. Richard and Florentyna stood on one side of Kate, Virginia and Lucy on the other.

Few of the mourners noticed two old men standing at the back of the cathedral, their heads also bowed, looking as if they were not attached to the main party. They had arrived a few minutes late, and left quickly at the end of the service. Florentyna recognized the limp as the shorter man hurried away, and told Richard. But they didn't say anything to Kate.

Kate wrote and thanked the two men the following day. She hadn't needed to be told.

A few days later, the taller of the two men went to see Florentyna in her shop on Fifth Avenue. He had heard she was returning to San Francisco, and he needed to see her before she left. She listened carefully to what he had to say, and agreed to his request with joy.

Richard and Florentyna Kane arrived at the Baron hotel the next afternoon. George Novak was waiting in the lobby to escort them to the 42nd floor.

After ten years, Florentyna hardly recognized her father. He was sitting up in bed, half-moon spectacles propped on the end of his nose, still no pillows, but smiling defiantly. They talked of happier days, and both of them laughed a little and cried a lot.

'You must forgive us, Richard,' said Abel. 'We Polish are a sentimental race.'

'I know. My children are half Polish,' said Richard.

Later that evening they dined together – magnificent roast veal, appropriate for the return of the prodigal daughter, said Abel.

He talked of the present, avoided the past and told her how he saw the future of the group.

'We ought to have one of your shops in every hotel,' he told Florentyna.

She laughed and agreed.

He told Richard of his sadness about the long-running feud with his father, and that it had never crossed his mind even for a moment that William Kane could have been his benefactor, and how he would have liked one chance, just one, to thank him personally.

'He would have understood,' said Richard.

'Your father and I met, you know, the day he died,' said Abel.

Florentyna and Richard stared at him in surprise.

'Oh yes,' said Abel. 'We passed each other on Fifth Avenue – he had come to watch the opening of your new store. He raised his hat to me. It was enough, quite enough.'

Abel had only one request of Florentyna: that she and Richard accompany him on his journey to Warsaw in a few months' time for the opening of the latest Baron.

'Can you imagine,' he said, again excited, his fingers tapping the side table. 'The Warsaw Baron. Now there is a hotel that could only be opened by the president of the Baron Group.'

─◇─

During the following months the Kanes visited Abel regularly, and once again Florentyna grew very close to her father.

Abel came to admire Richard and the common sense which tempered his daughter's ambitions. He adored his grandson. And little Annabel was – what was that awful modern expression? –

she was something else. Abel had rarely been happier in his life, and he began to make elaborate plans for his triumphant return to Poland where he would open the Warsaw Baron.

—◦—

The president of the Baron Group opened the Warsaw Baron six months later than originally scheduled. Building contracts run just as late in Warsaw as they do in every other part of the world.

In her first speech as president of the group, Florentyna Kane told her guests that her pride in the magnificent hotel was mingled with sadness that her father could not have been present to open the Warsaw Baron himself.

In his will, Abel had left everything to Florentyna, with the single exception of a small bequest. The inventory described the gift as a heavy engraved silver bracelet, rare and of unknown value, bearing the legend 'Baron Abel Rosnovski'.

The beneficiary was his grandson, William Abel Kane.

Visit **www.panmacmillan.com** to read more about all our books and to buy them. You will also find features, author interviews and news of any author events, and you can sign up for e-newsletters so that you're always first to hear about our new releases.

www.panmacmillan.com

| GIFT SELECTOR |
| YOUR ACCOUNT |
| WISH LIST |
| WAITING LIST |

| HOME | ABOUT US | IMPRINTS | TRADE/MEDIA | CONTACT US | ADVANCED SEARCH | SEARCH | GO |

| BOOK CATEGORIES | WHAT'S NEW | AUTHORS/ILLUSTRATORS | BESTSELLERS | READING GROUPS |

Coming Soon...

Reading Groups

Competitions
Feeling Lucky?

Extracts
Sneak Previews

Interviews

Events
Meet Our Stars

Reviews
What The Critics Say

News & Awards

Editor's Choice
What We're Reading